Lambeth

KT-496-347

or before the last date stamped below, or over due charges will be made.

Renewals may be made by personal application, by post or by telephone.

SOUTH LAMBETH LIBRARY
180 SOUTH LAMBETH ROAD
SW8 1QP
TEL : 020 7926 0705

01/16

Items must be returned on or before the last date shown below, otherwise a fine will be charged.

Renewals may be made by personal application, by post or by telephone.

PENGUIN BOOKS

# The Immortal Crown

Richelle Mead, the *New York Times* bestselling author of *Vampire Academy*, lives in Seattle, Washington, with her husband and baby. *Gameboard of the Gods*, the first book in the *Age of X* series, is also published by Penguin.

Visit www.richellemead.com to find out more.

Withdrawn from
La...

LM 1544960  2

ALSO BY RICHELLE MEAD

AGE OF X SERIES

*Gameboard of the Gods*

BLOODLINE SERIES

*Bloodlines*
*The Golden Lily*
*The Indigo Spell*
*The Fiery Heart*

VAMPIRE ACADEMY SERIES

*Vampire Academy*
*Frostbite*
*Shadow Kiss*
*Blood Promise*
*Spirit Bound*
*Last Sacrifice*

DARK SWAN SERIES

*Storm Born*
*Thorn Queen*
*Iron Crowned*
*Shadow Heir*

GEORGINA KINCAID SERIES

*Succubus Blues*
*Succubus on Top*
*Succubus Dreams*
*Succubus Heat*
*Succubus Shadows*
*Succubus Revealed*

# The Immortal Crown

## RICHELLE MEAD

PENGUIN BOOKS

PENGUIN BOOKS

Published by the Penguin Group
Penguin Books Ltd, 80 Strand, London WC2R ORL, England
Penguin Group (USA) Inc., 375 Hudson Street, New York, New York 10014, USA
Penguin Group (Canada), 90 Eglinton Avenue East, Suite 700, Toronto, Ontario, Canada M4P 2Y3
(a division of Pearson Penguin Canada Inc.)
Penguin Ireland, 25 St Stephen's Green, Dublin 2, Ireland (a division of Penguin Books Ltd)
Penguin Group (Australia), 707 Collins Street, Melbourne, Victoria 3008, Australia
(a division of Pearson Australia Group Pty Ltd)
Penguin Books India Pvt Ltd, 11 Community Centre, Panchsheel Park, New Delhi – 110 017, India
Penguin Group (NZ), 67 Apollo Drive, Rosedale, Auckland 0632, New Zealand
(a division of Pearson New Zealand Ltd)
Penguin Books (South Africa) (Pty) Ltd, Block D, Rosebank Office Park,
181 Jan Smuts Avenue, Parktown North, Gauteng 2193, South Africa

Penguin Books Ltd, Registered Offices: 80 Strand, London WC2R ORL, England

www.penguin.com

First published in the United States of America by Dutton,
an imprint of Penguin Group (USA) LLC 2014
First published in Great Britain in Penguin Books 2014
002

Copyright © Richelle Mead, LLC, 2014
All rights reserved

The moral right of the author has been asserted

Printed in Great Britain by Clays Ltd, St Ives plc

Except in the United States of America, this book is sold subject
to the condition that it shall not, by way of trade or otherwise, be lent,
re-sold, hired out, or otherwise circulated without the publisher's
prior consent in any form of binding or cover other than that in
which it is published and without a similar condition including this
condition being imposed on the subsequent purchaser

PAPERBACK ISBN: 978-1-405-91358-4

www.greenpenguin.co.uk

MIX
Paper from
responsible sources
FSC
www.fsc.org        FSC™ C018179

Penguin Books is committed to a sustainable
future for our business, our readers and our planet.
This book is made from Forest Stewardship
Council™ certified paper.

For my newborn son,

who helped me write this and didn't even know it

*Brynhild said: "It is not fated that we should live together. I am a shield-maiden. I wear a helmet and ride with the warrior kings. I must support them, and I am not averse to fighting."*
  —From *The Saga of the Volsungs,* translated by Jesse L. Byock
    (Penguin Classics)

*Hugin and Munin fly every day*
*over the wide world;*
*I fear for Hugin that he will not come back,*
*yet I tremble more for Munin.*
  —From *The Poetic Edda,* translated by Carolyne Larrington
    (Oxford University Press)

# THE
# IMMORTAL
# CROWN

# CHAPTER 1

# ELECTI

Mae Koskinen was one of her country's most elite soldiers. She'd excelled enough in her early training to be hand-selected for the Praetorian Guard, a regiment of warriors whose lethal training was enhanced by small, high-tech arm implants that used natural endorphins to increase speed and strength. From that distinguished tier, she'd gone on to join a secret government mission involving the improbable—yet alarmingly real—return of supernatural forces to the world, putting her face-to-face with atrocities and wonders her fellow countrymen would never have believed. There was no one else in a position quite like Mae's, no one who'd seen the things she had. She was feared by ordinary people. She was feared by her own military.

"So why," she muttered to herself, "am I always breaking up bar fights?"

The well-dressed answer, she knew, stood a few steps behind her, staying out of the way as she swung a bar stool at a furious man who was charging her with more emotion than skill. The stool broke into pieces as it made contact, knocking him backward to land on the dirt-packed floor with a *thump*. He lay there, momentarily dazed, and Mae used the opportunity to quickly scan the rest of the room. Thankfully, none of his cronies seemed too eager to join the fray in their fallen comrade's place. The implant had Mae churning with fight-or-flight chemicals, and as much as she might have actually enjoyed a further altercation, she knew the smart thing to do was to get out of there while they still could. Their mission parameters always advised discretion, and they'd kind of blown it this time.

She tossed the splintered bar stool leg on the floor and turned to the man standing behind her. "Come on, let's go."

Dr. Justin March—her partner and the cause of this fight—hesitated. After a moment of deliberation, he pulled some local currency out of his pocket and set it on a nearby table. "Sorry," he called to the bartender, who was watching them in a stunned state of disbelief. Mae grabbed Justin's arm and led him out, moving at a brisk pace, before someone thought to come after them.

"Really?" she snapped, once they were outside. "Is it possible for you to go one day without hitting on someone?"

"That girl?" He sounded legitimately offended. "I wasn't hitting on her. I was just making conversation while I waited for my drink. How was I to know her boyfriend would flip out?"

Mae said nothing as they hurried through the busy, dusty streets. Part of her was too angry to respond to his excuses. The rest of her was too focused on their surroundings, as she scouted around them for any signs of danger. No matter how many times she left her homeland in the Republic of United North America, she never quite got used to the shocking and often primitive differences found in the provinces. Nassau was no exception. It was like something out of a movie, with dirt-filled streets crowded with pedestrians, horses, and bicycle taxis. Street vendors hawked their wares, and many sets of eyes followed Mae and Justin. She knew they stood out, not just because of their lighter complexions but also because of their clothing and general healthy appearance. The Bahamas had had a mostly African-descended population when religious extremists unleashed the Mephistopheles virus on the world a century ago. Countries with diverse genetic backgrounds had shown greater resistance to the virus, but being on an island had cut the Bahamians off from the chance of mixing with other gene pools. As a result, many had died from the virus, and those who'd survived had passed on Cain, Mephistopheles's hereditary parting gift, which marked its victims with hair and skin damage, infertility, and asthma.

The region was poor too, and Justin and Mae appeared wealthy to many of the locals. They'd already dodged two attempted robberies on this trip. Usually, the sight of her gun dissuaded would-be thieves, but many thought a foreign woman was an easy target. Mae was always quick to correct them.

"Come on, Mae," said Justin, when he realized she wasn't going to answer him. "I wasn't hitting on her. You know I have higher standards than that."

Mae wondered if she should feel flattered. Working with Justin these last couple of months had certainly given her a lot of insight into his preferences for flings—particularly since she'd been one of them. Things had ended abruptly when, after their one night together, he'd tersely informed her that a second time with her held no appeal. His subsequent cycling through other women had only driven home how meaningless she was in his list of conquests. What infuriated her the most was that she herself was no stranger to casting aside lovers. The problem was that, until Justin, she had never been the one cast aside. Her pride didn't handle injuries well, but she supposed she should be grateful Justin had walked away so easily, unlike her previous boyfriend—who'd wandered into dangerous obsession after their relationship had ended.

Justin sighed in frustration. "Fine. Be that way. We might as well head straight to Mama Orane's anyway. Maybe if we're there early, I can get a drink."

Mae certainly didn't mind staying away from their cramped hotel room, which had an unscreened window as air-conditioning and only one flyswatter as pest control. Justin's readiness to turn to drinking, though not unexpected, was more of a concern.

"Don't you think you should keep a clear head for this?" she asked. "You need to see what this woman's up to."

He seemed pleased to have drawn Mae out, and a little of his former professor mode took over. "I'd be very surprised if she turns out to be real. Fortune-tellers have been around since the dawn of time, no supernatural powers needed. It's easy to pick up on cues from people and make them believe what they want to hear."

Mae nearly said, "That sounds like what you do." She refused to be petty, though, and instead remarked, "Like Geraki?"

Justin grimaced at the reference to a would-be prophet back home. "Fortune-telling isn't the same as prophecy, and unfortunately for all of us, he's the real thing."

The weirdness of their conversation wasn't lost on Mae. Three months ago, she would've thought it was crazy. Their society denounced religion and the paranormal as blind superstition. The RUNA was so cautious of that kind of influence corrupting its citizens that it went to great pains to rein in those who worshipped higher powers. Anyone deemed dangerous was stamped out. The rest were cautiously allowed to continue but watched very closely. Justin, and the other servitors like him, were the ones who investigated and passed judgment.

That system had proved sound for most of the RUNA's history until their government—covertly—acknowledged that there actually were unexplained forces stirring in the world. Justin had the unique and rather obscure position of being both a star servitor and a believer, which had landed him—depending on one's view—the enviable or unenviable position of their lead investigator into such matters. And Mae, who had reluctantly seen enough to make her believe too, had been made his bodyguard. Most of their missions kept them safely within their comfortable and technologically advanced homeland . . . but every so often, they found themselves out in the wider world, in places like this.

After ten minutes of walking, the two of them reached their destination: the home of a woman whom the RUNA's intelligence had scouted as potentially being involved with supernatural forces. Mama Orane's bare-bones house was guarded by two hulking, armed men who looked Mae and Justin over with hard eyes. The small metal implant in her arm already had her on edge, and the sight of this new threat spun her up even more, triggering a greater flood of adrenaline and other neurotransmitters of battle. One wrong look from these guys, and she'd be on them instantly.

But once they saw the snake-engraved wooden charm Justin had bought that morning as a ticket to today's show, the guards waved them through, barely acknowledging the guns. Inside the house, a young woman collected the rest of the admission fee, which Justin paid in local currency. Mae didn't know the exact exchange rate but winced at what she saw as her tax dollars being handed over.

They were ushered through a beaded curtain, into a spacious living room filled with old velvet furniture and lit only by candles. At first, she thought that was simply for effect, until she realized there were no electric lights anywhere. For the price this place was charging, it seemed like they could've gotten on the island's grid, fledgling though it was. Everything in the room was cast in flickering shadows, and incense smoked in the air. Considering the lack of flies here, maybe the incense was as much repellent as ceremonial. Mae put a hand on Justin's arm to stop him from going farther as she scanned for hiding spots and points of entry. He leaned toward her and spoke softly.

"Look over there," he said. "We're not the only visitors from the RUNA."

He was right. Across the room, occupying two couches were five loud, laughing individuals—two women and three men. They were passing two bottles of wine between them. Their clothing and mostly healthy features marked them as fellow Gemmans, the term their country's citizens went by. This group's red hair and pale skin in particular identified them as patricians: Gemmans whose ancestors hadn't been part of the RUNA's early forced genetic mixing program. That program had resulted in a diverse ethnic population that had better resisted Mephistopheles until a vaccine was developed and had allowed the RUNA to become the dominant country it was today. Most Gemmans born of this mixed heritage—nicknamed "plebeians"—had tanned skin, with dark hair and eyes like Justin. Patricians, in not being part of that breeding, had kept their recessive traits but faced greater health issues. Many had either died out or passed on Cain. Mae herself was of Finnish ancestry and a rare patrician who was born in perfect health.

Her safety assessment complete, Mae waved Justin toward a love seat in the corner that afforded a full view of the room and its two doors. She sat down beside him, and they were immediately noticed by one of the Gemman men. He had shocking red hair and too-smooth skin that suggested cosmetic surgery to clear up Cain acne scars.

"Hey," he called, holding up his glass in a toast. "*Gemma Mundi!*"

Justin nodded back, instantly putting on that charm that never seemed to dim. "Hope you brought your own," he called. "That stuff they sell here's one step away from vinegar."

The redheads whooped. "We got it from a guy over on Augusta," said one of the women. "It's EA rice wine. Not bad. You can have some." She glanced around, apparently searching for a glass. Seeing none, she simply took the bottle in its entirety from the other woman and offered it toward him. "Come on, Roisin. We can share with our countrymen."

"Got my own." Justin pulled out a flask from his coat and held it up. "Rum—which they don't mess up."

After a little more friendly banter, the other Gemmans returned to their revelry. More guests began to trickle in, many of whom were from neighboring areas in Central and South America. A couple of businessmen entered together, greeting the Gemmans with Eastern Alliance accents.

Justin was smiling like he was at a high-class party as he watched everything, but as Mae studied the way the candlelight made shadows play over his face, with its chiseled profile and dark, thoughtful eyes, she knew there was more going on beneath the surface. His sharp and cunning mind was always in motion, something others rarely realized was beneath that friendly smile. Mae's upbringing in the Nordic patriarchy had taught her to conceal her feelings. Justin had simply picked the habit up along the way and used it to full advantage.

His words were quiet when he spoke to her. "About what I'd expect for tourists around here—except for those other Gemmans. Nassau's bargain beach resorts wouldn't be enough for them to leave the comforts of home, not when they could find safer escapes in Mazatlán."

"Dubiously safer," Mae corrected, recalling a trip they'd made there that had resulted in abduction and her fighting for her life. "Maybe they're here for the novelty. Maybe they want the risk."

"Maybe," agreed Justin. "Bored rich kids have certainly done stupider things. They'll be lucky if they make it back to their inn, though." His sharp eyes soon focused back on their surroundings, and she could see him taking in all the expressions and fragments of conversation that drifted their way. And more than that. Clothing, hair, posture, mannerisms . . . all of it was fodder for him. It was why, despite his many flaws, he excelled at a job that required him to use tiny clues to find dangerous influences.

"These latecomers are locals," he continued as a group of mixed ages and genders began filtering in. Most of the chairs and couches were gone now, but the newcomers happily took spots on the floor, laughing and chatting among themselves. "Friends or family. I'm guessing this is regular entertainment for them. And that must be the local beauty queen."

A young woman entered, maybe eighteen at most. Although her braided hair had the brittle quality often seen with Cain, her dark brown skin was lovely and smooth, free of any flaws. She raised her hands, and the room fell silent.

"Welcome, friends," she said. Although she spoke with an accent to Mae's ears, the girl's English was clear, her voice high and sweet. "Welcome to Mama Orane's house. She is honored to have such guests grace her home."

"Well-paying guests," muttered Mae.

"Mama Orane is special," the girl continued. As she spoke, two young boys brought in a small, low table. "Mama Orane has been chosen by the spirits and powerful ones who move unseen in the world to be their vessel, so that we may hear their wisdom."

A chill ran down Mae's back at those words. A sidelong look at Justin's face showed he'd had a similar reaction. Although the world of gods and the supernatural was still largely mysterious to her, one thing Mae had learned was that gods rarely spoke directly to humans. Usually they used dreams or intermediaries. Was Mama Orane possibly one of the latter? Life as they knew it would certainly be a lot easier if they had a direct line to the divine.

The girl tilted her head back. "Prepare yourselves. Prepare yourselves for wondrous, powerful things. Even Mama Orane never knows what to expect. She places herself in the hands of those forces beyond." The girl swept a flourish-filled bow toward one of the doorways, and a short, curvaceous middle-aged woman entered. Her skin was as dark as that of the girl who'd introduced her but showed many of the acne scars typical of Cain. Mae couldn't make out the woman's hair because it was concealed under a bright red head scarf embroidered with gold.

The locals on the floor showed their approval by rhythmically patting their legs and murmuring, "Ma-ma, ma-ma . . ."

Justin leaned forward, his elbows on his knees and his chin resting on clasped hands as he scrutinized her. The earlier banter was gone. This was serious, the reason they'd traveled out to the provinces.

Mama Orane stood in the middle of the room and hung her head so that she stared at the floor. Her assistant picked up a small drum from the table and began tapping out a steady beat as she murmured in what sounded like French. Although English was the island's main language, Haitian refugees had been coming to it both before and since the Decline.

The locals joined in with the girl, and Mama Orane began to shake. At first, she could have simply been dancing to the beat, but as her movements grew increasingly erratic, it was obvious she was having—or faking—some kind of fit. Despite all she'd witnessed in the past, Mae still entered these situations with a healthy dose of skepticism. She knew Justin, who was barely blinking, did too.

Mama Orane shook for several more moments and suddenly

froze. Everyone in the room fell silent, and there was a collective intake of breath. Slowly, she lifted her head, her dark eyes looking around the room. Then a sly smile crept across her face. *"Bonsoir, mes petits."*

The tension broke as the locals cheered. "Josephine! It's Josephine!"

Mama Orane, who'd entered in a slow and stately way, suddenly sauntered forward, swaying her hips with the sass of a girl half her age. She circled the room, still with that sly smile, taking the measure of her guests as her assistant trailed a respectful distance behind. At last, Mama Orane stopped in front of one of the EA men. Her expression went from sassy to outright flirtatious, and she completely caught him off guard when she sat down in his lap, much to the delight of the onlookers.

She spoke in French, but her hovering assistant quickly translated. "Why are you so sad, sweetie? You still miss her?" Mama Orane gently stroked his face. "Don't be sad. She's not the one for you."

Amazingly, the man's earlier amused expression immediately began to crumple. "No, she *is*."

The assistant performed two-way translation, and Mama Orane shook her head. "No. You were better off when she left. Just you wait—someone else will come along."

"Really?" he asked, a flicker of hope in his eyes.

"Really. And until then, I'll be happy to keep you company." She darted in with a quick kiss on his cheek that actually made him blush, and then she moved on with a wink.

"Well?" Mae whispered to Justin, who looked unimpressed.

"Easy to guess at a recent separation," he responded quietly. "You can tell from his finger he used to wear a wedding ring. And he tipped her off early that he was the rejected party."

Mama Orane—or Josephine—continued visiting with other members of the audience, all men. She flirted shamelessly and dispensed various tidbits of romantic advice and predictions. Justin didn't break down any more of them for her, but Mae could tell from his face that he wasn't buying in yet.

As it turned out, Mama Orane made him her last visit. She looked down upon him from her demure height, hands on her hips, as she tsked. "I won't even bother with you, love. Not many women can catch you."

He smiled back gallantly. "I've been waiting for you."

She laughed in delight and patted his shoulder before returning to her central position. Her assistant took up the drum again, and there was another bout of shaking and chanting. When she came out of this spell and looked up, she spoke in English, in a much flatter tone than Josephine had: "Where's my rum?"

Those on the floor were overjoyed. "Reynard!"

Mama Orane's Reynard guise moved with a stride that was simply laid-back, rather than attempting any sex appeal. He or she—Mae wasn't entirely sure which was accurate—told fortunes on a variety of topics. One of Reynard's targets included the Gemman woman who'd offered Justin the wine.

"What's your name?"

"Elspeth," she said meekly.

"You can't stay away, you know. You've eventually gotta go back home."

Elspeth stuck her chin out defiantly and tried to stare down the small woman standing before her. "I'm not! I'm done with them. No one can make me go."

"No," agreed Mama Orane–as–Reynard. "Only you can. You going to keep breaking your parents' hearts?"

Elspeth's lip quivered, and she looked away, refusing to make eye contact. Mama Orane left it at that and returned to the room's center, where another round of chanting and drumming began.

"What was that one?" Mae asked, her voice covered by the din.

Justin was silent as he studied the red-haired group. "Elspeth," he said after several moments. "She's a Scottish castal." He used the slang term for "patrician" without thought. "One of the others was named Roisin. Irish. She's fraternizing outside her caste. That's what she's dreading going home to."

"They could be from a meta-caste," Mae reminded him. "One with lots of Celtic varieties."

"The only two out there select for recessive-colored eyes. Hers are brown, which the Caledonians allow." Justin shook his head. "She's good. Really good."

Mama Orane's third transformation was into a man the others called El Diable.

"The Devil," said Justin. "Subtle."

This guise elicited none of the joy in the onlookers that Josephine and Reynard had. A hush fell over the room as those gathered sat tensely. Mama Orane's face was cold and devoid of emotion as she surveyed the room. Then astonishingly, she strode straight toward Mae and Justin. The woman herself posed no physical threat, but the look in her eyes made Mae's implant ramp up. There was something so eerie in that gaze, something inhuman that Mae couldn't quite put her finger on.

But even that was less shocking than what happened next. Mama Orane leaned forward so that she was at their eye level. When she spoke as El Diable, it was barely a whisper, like a snake's voice.

*"Electi..."*

# CHAPTER 2

# SOMETHING ELSE
# TO WORRY ABOUT

Justin's first reaction was panic. Then indignation.

*You told me it would work! You told me no one would be able to sense me if I made that charm!*

Magnus, one of the two unseen ravens that lived inside Justin's mind, was equally indignant. *It did work.*

His counterpart, Horatio, clarified: *As usual, you assume this is about you. You're not the one El Diable is talking to.*

A quick assessment showed Justin that the raven was correct. Mama Orane—or whoever the hell she was now—wasn't looking at him. That creepy gaze was fixed on Mae. Even more incredibly, Mama Orane then reached out and cupped Mae's cheek. Justin felt her go rigid beside him, and he instinctively reached over and squeezed her hand tightly, as both comfort and a means of restraint. Despite a history of casual liaisons, she did not react well to unsolicited contact, especially from a woman who looked like she feasted on souls. Justin wouldn't have put it past Mae to pull out her gun.

"*Cave bellum electi,*" whispered Mama Orane. Her assistant immediately appeared beside her, ready to translate.

"Beware the—"

"I know what it means," Justin interrupted. The assistant shot him a glare but said nothing as she waited for her mistress to continue.

Mama Orane was still touching Mae, who didn't even seem to be breathing as she locked eyes with the other woman. "*Cave bellum electi,*" she repeated. "*Inveni tuum deum.*"

Mama Orane and her assistant turned away, off to deliver cryptic wisdom to someone else. Beside Justin, Mae was breathing again, but they were rapid, shallow breaths. She was still wound up, and her eyes never left Mama Orane as the medium worked the rest of the crowd. As El Diable, she continued issuing ominous messages in Latin that her assistant translated to their bewildered recipients. Justin gave Mae's hand one last squeeze and then released it, trusting she'd stay put and not attack anyone.

Three was apparently Mama Orane's limit, because when she released El Diable, she returned to herself, sagging in exhaustion. The boys were there to catch her and lead her out of the room as the spectators clapped. Her pretty assistant gave a polite bow to the crowd and thanked everyone for coming.

Justin and Mae returned to their inn, speaking little until they entered the building. "So, what was that? Multiple personalities?" she asked. "Or the real deal?"

"The latter, I'm afraid." Mae had certainly seen stranger things in their missions together, but he was hesitant to elaborate this time. Fortunately, she didn't press him.

*Mama Orane wasn't a fraud,* he thought to himself. *She recognized Mae as one of the elect. But is she really? She broke free of the Morrigan.* The Morrigan was a Celtic goddess of death and battle, whose cult Mae had unknowingly been born into when her mother consecrated her to the goddess in exchange for healthy patrician genes. Mae had not only freed herself from the group, she'd also greatly reduced the Morrigan's power in the RUNA. Mae rarely spoke of those events now, and Justin knew that she believed she was free of any supernatural entanglements, aside from their investigations. He'd started to believe it as well.

*You don't need a patron god to be one of the elect,* said Magnus. *Being chosen doesn't make you one. You're chosen because you already are one.*

*Circular logic,* Justin pointed out.

*Not really,* countered Horatio. *And Mae is one. She has no ability to hide it. If you'd stop half-assing it and actually improve your skills, you'd sense it in her too.*

Justin wasn't so sure. *I didn't sense anything from Mama Orane. Does she have a charm?*

*She's skilled,* explained Magnus. *She's been doing this for a long time. She has no need for charms to hide what she is. Of course, it's not really a secret she's one of the elect when she flaunts and charges for her connection to higher powers.*

*Was she channeling gods?* asked Justin.

*Not exactly,* said Horatio. *There are other entities moving in this world.*

That certainly wasn't anything he'd heard much about. *Like what?*

*Like the ones you talk to every day,* said Horatio pointedly.

Justin took the hint and mulled this over. He did talk to the ravens every day—he'd done so every day for over four years, in fact. At times annoying, they had become a mainstay in Justin's life, and sometimes it worried him how much he relied on their input. They'd been gifted to him by Odin, the Norse god Justin had become inadvertently involved with. Whereas Mae had been tied to a deity at birth, Justin had become enmeshed relatively recently, when Odin had appeared in a dream and saved him from violent fanatics. Repaying that debt had put Justin on a path to learn some of Odin's craft and secrets, though Justin had thus far managed to dodge what Odin and the ravens wanted most: for Justin to swear complete loyalty and become Odin's priest. Getting out of that arrangement had proven especially difficult, particularly since keeping his freedom meant Justin had had to sacrifice something he wanted very, very much.

His rumination was paused as their seedy innkeeper up-sold them on dinner. They'd been stuck here a week, and although the food was passable, the prices were absurd. Considering some of the less savory options Justin had seen on the streets, however, he was willing to pay extra, particularly since it was Internal Security that was actually footing the bill.

They ate in relative silence, both because Justin was still mulling over the day's events and because Mae was on high alert, watching the room for potential threats. This was her normal mode, really: walled up and dangerous. Only rarely had he seen her vulnerable, one of those moments being their brief night together. Even then, he hadn't technically seen it, since the lights had been off. Nonetheless, Justin had sensed that shift in her . . . a softening. An acceptance. A yielding, even, that contrasted with the walled exterior she maintained in every other part of her life. It had proven to be an elusive, precious thing in her he often longed for again, though he knew expecting it was probably unreasonable, given their dangerous lifestyle and the fact that he'd pretty much screwed things up between them.

That, and she was the bargaining chip Odin held over him.

It had been part of the dream Justin had, when the god first appeared to him. Odin had marked Mae as special, calling her a woman crowned in stars and flowers. Justin had talked his way out of honoring his deal with Odin after their first liaison, but Odin had made it clear that if Justin succumbed again and "claimed" her, he would be bound to the god's service forever. Justin had fiercely vowed not to have any more romantic interactions with her and helped reinforce this by saying some pretty terrible things to her after their night together. It had successfully killed any interest she might have had in him, and if Justin at times regretted this turn of events and the hostile atmosphere it had generated, he tried to reassure himself that he at least still had his freedom.

When dinner was over, Mae found an urchin happy to carry a message (for a price) to an Eastern Alliance cargo plane that was currently docking at the local airstrip. The RUNA had almost no regular interaction with this region, so their travel was being conducted through their sister country's resources. The EA's trade planes weren't glamorous, but they did the job. Their mission accomplished, Justin was more than happy to endure an uncomfortable flight if it meant getting back to civilization.

Once they were back in Justin's room, Mae relaxed her guard—slightly—and finally launched into the questions that had apparently been burning within her since the ceremony.

"What did that mean?" she asked, as soon as the door closed behind them. She double-checked the lock and then sat in one of the chairs, crossing her arms over her chest. "What El Diable said? All I understood was *'electi.'* Which I'm guessing means 'elect.'"

Justin nodded and took his own chair, promptly pouring rum. He'd had enough time of his own to process the weird goings-on and also welcomed a moment with her that wasn't antagonistic. *"Cave bellum electi.* 'Beware the war of the elect.'"

"Which is?"

He downed the shot. No need to hold back now that he was off duty. "I'm not really sure."

"Geraki said the gods are playing a game," she reminded him. "A war is kind of an upgrade."

It was the second time Geraki had been brought up today, and Justin didn't want to expound on him. Mae knew Geraki was a prophet deeply involved with a religious group that had eluded the Gemman government's attempts to uncover it. What she didn't realize was that Odin was the god Geraki served, nor did she have any idea just how much time Justin had—reluctantly—begun spending with him, as part of the deal to learn Odin's ways. Mae thought Geraki was just a contact for clandestine information, and Justin preferred she keep believing that.

"Maybe it's all perception," he suggested. "Maybe they're playing a game with us—and waging a war with each other."

Mae pondered this a few moments. "Why did she—or he—tell me that then? I'm not involved in any of this."

Justin couldn't help a smile at that. "Aren't you, Mae? Look where you are."

"That's not what I mean. I'm not tied to anything specifically—no god. No ravens."

*I wouldn't mind being tied to her,* said Horatio.

"Perhaps. But you *were* conceived as part of a sacrifice to a Celtic death goddess," he reminded her.

Her face showed that wasn't something she liked having brought up. "I broke free of her."

"You're still one of the elect, whether you want to be or not. And gods are interested in you." He hesitated a moment. "That was the other thing El Diable said. *Inveni tuum deum.* 'Find your god.'"

"I don't want a god," she said, in an uncharacteristic moment of petulance. "I don't want to be one of the elect."

The elect. Those humans marked as special who had the potential to be strong servants for the gods who were scrambling to regain power and footing in the world. Justin hadn't wanted to be one either, but there was no point in crying over what had already happened. The only thing to do was move forward and find a way to survive. He knew Mae well enough to understand she realized this too. She was pragmatic. She was used to being proactive. The problem was, theirs was a situation that didn't lend itself well to decisive options.

As the night wore on, they settled in for what was a typical routine for them: both reading, he in bed and she at rigid attention in a chair. Praetorians never slept, thanks to their implants, and she'd spend the night ever watchful. Justin didn't sleep simply because his mind had trouble spinning down, so he popped one of his favorite sedatives and made himself comfortable reading reports on the upcoming cases Internal Security's subdepartment Sect and Cult Investigation, or SCI, had dredged up for him. The day's heat had settled down but still required the window be left open, which now welcomed mosquitoes instead of flies. This, at least, was something they could combat, having preemptively brought small repellent devices from the RUNA that did an effective job of keeping the mosquitoes out.

Justin read his caseload with bleary eyes, occasionally daring glances at Mae. Although the tension in her body promised readiness for any threat, her focus was on her ego as she read what Justin suspected was a novel. The heat and sweat had made escaping tendrils of her blond hair curl up along her cheek and neck. His fingers itched with the need to brush them back from her face and touch that flawless skin . . . then he remembered that any further romantic dealings with her would inextricably bind him to Odin forever. It was kind of a buzzkill.

"Goddamn!" he exclaimed, sitting upright. Mae nearly jumped three feet in the air at his outburst. He'd seen something move out of the corner of his eye and at first wrote it off as one of the daring moths that would occasionally fly in. But no, the ugly little beast crawling in underneath their door was a large black beetle. A very large black beetle. Wordlessly, he pointed.

Mae, gun drawn and aimed, scoffed. "That?" she demanded.

"Hey, that's a big-ass bug," he said, feeling slightly sheepish. "Surprised me, that's all."

"Well, rest easy, your lordship. I'll take care of it." She strode over and smashed the beetle with a booted foot. When she removed it, they were treated to the sight of a mushy black mess . . . which then suddenly reassembled itself and continued crawling forward. Mae's smugness faded. "What the hell?"

Before she could do anything else, the beetle suddenly spit a small dab of green ooze onto the wooden floor—ooze that briefly smoked, seeped into the wood, and left a scorch mark behind. Mae quickly stepped on the bug again, only to have the resurrection repeated.

"Mae, look!"

Two more beetles were coming in under the door. Then three. Mae, in a way that would have been comical were the situation not so freakish, rapidly kept stepping on them over and over, with no effect. They continued to advance, spitting the acidic goo. When two more came in, Justin donned his shoes and joined her.

"What are they?" she demanded, going so far as to grind one into the floor with her toe. It was as ineffectual as everything else.

"Do you seriously think I know?"

"You're the expert in all things that aren't from this world!"

"Well, then, you know as much as I do. They aren't from this world. Shit!"

There were about a dozen in the room now, with more coming. In the onslaught, some of the ooze got on Justin's shoes. Although the slime didn't penetrate to the foot, the leather definitely took damage. A sickening image of the beetles crawling up his body seized him. He and Mae, now having difficulty keeping up with the bugs, backed up and both jumped on the bed. Like a dutiful army, the little black soldiers began marching up the post.

*Your wisdom would be appreciated now,* Justin informed the ravens.

*Use the knife,* said Horatio.

*What knife?*

*The only one you guys have.*

Justin glanced around as he helped Mae kick off members of the black tide. "Knife," he said aloud. "What knife?"

"My knife?" she asked.

His eyes lit on her boot, where he could barely make out a gleam of metal from within. "Yes! Use the knife on them."

She frowned but didn't argue as she withdrew it from its hidden sheath. The knife was as much art as it was weapon, a beautiful piece of craftsmanship whose handle was wrapped in amber. Mae traded it for the gun in her right hand and, after a brief assessment, jumped off the bed. Since the beetles were swarming it now, there was a fair expanse of open floor available. Justin wasn't thrilled at being on lone duty but continued trying to play keep-away, even managing to expel a fair number of them by lifting and shaking the covers. He didn't have to defend himself long, though, because the bugs soon turned in the opposite direction and advanced on Mae.

*She's the one they're here for,* he realized.

*Well spotted,* responded Horatio dryly.

But Mae was ready, plunging the knife down with the remarkable speed and accuracy born of her implant, excessive training, and natural talent. The dagger's blade struck a beetle right in the middle of its carapace. The small creature shattered into black fragments . . . which stayed where they were. Driven by her success, Mae went after the others, her blade making contact each time it struck. No misses. Keeping ahead of them was difficult, and Justin leapt off to help her, kicking them back as best as he could so that she had a chance to take out new targets. He lost track of time as they played their game of keep-away until, at last, they both paused and saw that nothing else was moving. Mae still held her knife poised, eyes sweeping the room for several more seconds until she finally returned the knife to its boot.

Justin kicked at piles of black debris covering the floor. "You don't think they'd give us a broom, do you?"

She shook her head in exasperation. "Around here, that might be—look!"

Mae pointed toward the door, and Justin was just in time to catch a blur of black movement disappearing underneath. With that remarkable speed, Mae sprinted over and flung the door to the hall open. Justin joined her and watched as one lone beetle made its retreat from them. The knife was in Mae's hand again, but he caught hold of her arm before she could act.

"Wait," he said. "Don't you want to know where it's going?"

Their eyes met as the suggestion hung in the air. They were few and far between, but in moments like these, there was no animosity. A fierce solidarity burned between them, one that united them in a single purpose and understanding. No matter what other drama existed around them, Mae was the only person who really "got" what was going on, and ultimately, that meant far more to Justin than the inconvenience of enduring all the slings and arrows of working together.

Without another word, they set off down the hall, following their insect guide. It moved at a pretty good clip, but they still had to pace themselves to let it stay ahead of them. There were a few more people in the inn's common area, but no one who gave them much notice. Justin supposed around here, one more bug wasn't worth paying attention to.

*And sadly*, he thought, *this isn't even the weirdest thing I've ever done.*

*Not by a long shot,* agreed Horatio.

Darkness had fallen on the streets outside, though there was still enough light from the hodgepodge mix of electric and gas sources to illuminate the road and the beetle's path.

Justin found himself thinking of Panama as they walked. He'd grown to despise that province in the almost four years of exile he'd spent there after filing a report claiming the existence of supernatural forces, but the more he traveled in other provincial areas, the more he began to appreciate it. Panama's streets would've been full of revelers this time of night, along with the ubiquitous gangs that strutted around and vied for dominance. If you had no conflict with them, you could actually move about fairly safely after dark, since they were far more interested in each other. Here, the quiet streets had a more sinister edge. Regular citizens were inside and getting ready for sleep. Many of those who were out had more nefarious goals and were searching for easy prey.

Maybe it was because they seemed to have purpose that Justin and Mae were left alone. It wasn't until they'd walked almost ten minutes that a shout up ahead made Mae stop in her tracks, grab Justin, and pull him over to a building's side. She put herself between him and the movement ahead, her gun out without his having seen her draw it. The scent of her apple blossom perfume drifted over him, a bizarre contrast to the scene at hand.

The conflict on the streets had nothing to do with them, however, or any other unsuspecting tourist. It was between two local men, shouting and pacing around each other as each dared the other to make a move. Friends and curious spectators hovered nearby, eager for a fight. From what Justin could make out, the dispute seemed to be over a woman.

One man finally landed a punch on the other, igniting the tinderbox. The two went at each other, even dropping and rolling to the ground. Bystanders cheered, while wiser ones tried to pull the two men apart. The whole altercation lasted barely a minute, but

Mae wouldn't budge until the kicking and screaming combatants and most of the audience had left the scene.

Unfortunately, the beetle had also left the scene.

Mae swore in Finnish, but Justin had already realized they were in familiar territory. "I think I know where it went," he said, pointing.

She lifted her eyes to follow the gesture, and he heard her catch her breath when she saw Mama Orane's house.

"Well, why not?" Justin asked. "Makes sense that a supernatural attack would come from our known supernatural source around here."

They walked a little farther down the block and then came to a halt directly across from the house. Mae narrowed her eyes as she studied it, her hand still tense on the gun. Lights burned inside the windows, and a bodyguard paced outside.

"But why?" she asked. "If they'd wanted us dead, why not try it while we were there? They certainly had the manpower."

"You," Justin corrected. "You're the one those things were after. She couldn't tell what I was. As for why—"

"You!"

The bodyguard had noticed them and came jogging across the street, his automatic weapon bouncing almost comically at his side. Mae took up a protective stance in front of Justin and pointed her gun at the man's chest. It took him several moments to notice, and he came to a slow halt.

"Don't come any farther," she warned.

"You," he repeated. "You're *electi*. Come. You can help. You can help her."

"Help who?" asked Justin.

"Mama Orane. Please. She's in bad shape." Grief and worry lined the man's face as he looked pleadingly between Justin and Mae.

"I don't think he's a threat," Justin said.

Mae decided to agree and slowly followed when the bodyguard returned to the house, though she kept her gun out the whole time.

Inside, they found a flurry of drumming, chanting, and

incense—much like they had at the ceremony. Only, whereas that had been celebratory, the main room was now thick with tension and grief. The bodyguard led them through the crowd, one composed not of tourists but of worried friends and neighbors. He spoke rapidly in French, clearing a path to a staircase on the far side of the room. After a quick glance to make sure Justin and Mae still followed, he hurried up to a second floor that showed where the tourist money had been going. Modern furniture, electricity, and tech pieces that were antiquated by Gemman standards but state-of-the-art around here. Justin would've liked to study it all more closely, but his attention soon snapped to a bedroom they were ushered into, the center of which held a flower-strewn bed.

And Mama Orane.

Justin felt a lurch in his stomach as he took in the woman's bloodstained clothes. Violence might have been Mae's thing, but it was nothing he would ever be comfortable around. Someone had done a neat job of wrapping Mama Orane's stomach with bandages, but they were already wet and slick with blood seeping out from beneath. Her skin was ashen and sweaty, her eyes unfocused.

"Help her," begged the man who'd led them in.

"She needs a doctor," said Justin.

"We sent for him," said a young woman sitting by the bed. It was the pretty assistant from earlier. "I took care of her in the meantime. I wrapped her wounds and said all the prayers and songs."

Mae grimaced. "Prayers and—never mind. What happened? Was she shot?"

"Stabbed," said the assistant. "By a red-haired woman—one of the ones who was here earlier."

*Ask what she was stabbed with,* ordered Magnus.

"What kind of blade?" Justin asked.

The assistant held her hands about a foot and a half apart. "A dagger. It happened so fast—I could barely see it. It looked like there were bugs on it. We were sitting down for dinner, and she was gone before—"

"Bugs?" interrupted Mae.

The girl nodded. "Like golden beetles."

Justin and Mae exchanged a brief glance. Before either could speak, Mama Orane stirred, causing the girl and the bodyguard to go rigid. Mama Orane blinked a few times and managed to focus on him and Mae.

"H-hello, *electi*," she said. A trickle of blood appeared at her lips.

*That was to both of us. She knows me this time,* Justin told the ravens.

*She's dying,* said Magnus. *Those leaving this world have greater senses. She can see through the powers hiding you now.*

Mama Orane's assistant seemed to have the same idea the bodyguard had. "You can heal her?" she asked hopefully.

Mama Orane tsked. "That is not their province. And it's too late anyway." She tried to speak again but had difficulty forming the words. Her assistant offered her a small sip of water. "They didn't come for you?"

"They did." Mae's eyes flicked to the blood. "But not in the same way."

"I'm sorry." Mama Orane swallowed and closed her eyes. "They came to find me, and I called you out. I identified you to them. It was careless, though not as careless as parading myself around. El Diable always warned me, and I wouldn't listen. This is no more than I deserve."

The big, hulking bodyguard stifled a sob.

"Who are they?" asked Justin. "Who do they serve?"

Mama Orane opened her eyes again. "I don't know. It doesn't matter. They are other *electi*, and they are about their master's business."

"Gods want to convert the elect and get them on their side," said Justin. "Why would they try to kill them—us?"

"Because not every *electi* can be c—c—" Coughing broke her up until more water was offered. "Converted. Better then for a god to eliminate his rival's servants. Better for other *electi* to eliminate their own competition."

"The War of the Elect," said Mae in sudden understanding.

"Because we totally need something else to worry about," muttered Justin.

"Serve your gods well," said Mama Orane, her voice raspy now. "For others will be serving theirs."

Mae opened her mouth to speak, and Justin was almost certain she was going to issue her usual line about how she had no god. She seemed to think better of it and paused, saying instead, "You need to rest until the doctor gets here."

"No doctor can help me now." Mama Orane's eyes closed, and she went so still that Justin thought she'd already died. They suddenly fluttered open as she focused on him. "But perhaps you will lend me a guide to take me to my gods."

Justin didn't know what she meant, and then Magnus said, *I will go.* The raven paused and then added reluctantly, *If you will let me.*

*Yes,* said Justin. Before he could even really wonder what he'd agreed to, he felt the searing pain in his skull that happened whenever one of the ravens left him. Mama Orane's eyes opened wide, and a light filled her face. It was almost enough to make one think she might make a miraculous recovery. Then—she exhaled and grew still again. Everything about her seemed to diminish as she sank into the bed. Her assistant choked and buried her face in the shoulder of the bodyguard, who was openly weeping.

Justin felt Magnus return to him. *It is done,* said the raven.

Mae's greenish-blue eyes studied Mama Orane with a mix of sorrow and disdain. "This wouldn't have happened in the RUNA."

Justin knew she meant dying without medical care, but his mind was still on what had actually precipitated this: the elect preying on each other to further their gods' causes. "I have a feeling it's going to happen a lot more than we'd like in the RUNA." He touched Mae's arm. "Come on. It's time to go home."

# CHAPTER 3

# SECURITY-TYPE STUFF

The Institute for Creative Minds and Experiential Thinking was the third private school that Tessa Cruz had attended. Counting her brief stint in one of the public schools, it was her fourth school overall since arriving in the RUNA a few months ago. This was the first one she'd picked out herself, and Justin hadn't been thrilled about it. "It sounds like the kind of place that breeds political dissidents," he'd told her. He'd been even more dismayed when he learned what a loose teaching style it had, and his sister, Cynthia, had laughed this off as the real reason he was upset. "He used to teach," she'd reminded Tessa with an eye roll. "So he expects everyone to be able to sit in orderly rows and dote on their teacher's every word, just as I'm sure his adoring students did."

Tessa believed that but also suspected there was more to Justin's dislike of the school. He'd always felt he owed a debt to Tessa's father for her father's help during Justin's four-year Panamanian exile. Justin had decided the best way to repay this debt was to take Tessa—whom he believed to be too smart and talented for her provincial background—and bring her back with him for a dose of Gemman education and culture. The terms of her student visa required her to attend school, and she knew Justin felt a "normal" Gemman education was the best way to prepare her for the civilized world. She would've liked to please him in that, but there was no denying she just hadn't fit into more traditional programs.

Tessa liked this new school, mostly because it left her alone to do what she wanted. The institute's philosophy was simple. "Creative minds" could be trusted to pursue their own interests. They could also be trusted to pass the country's standardized tests that were required in all schools, public or private, with high scores that maintained the institute's reputation. Students who could not do this were politely told to leave.

And so, Tessa found her days split. Half the periods were free time devoted to self-chosen projects in humanities, social issues, and science. The rest of the school day was set aside to prepare for the tests, which involved endlessly going over sample questions and utilizing tutors if needed.

Perhaps most importantly, Tessa found she was treated with civility. The faculty was paid very well for that. Some occasionally eyed her curiously, but most of the teachers were pragmatic about the matter. Being provincial meant less than the money and influence it took to get you into the school in the first place. If you were in, you were in. Her fellow students, though not paid to accept her, nonetheless operated on that same principle: If she was there, she deserved it. Most left her alone. The popular belief was that she was the daughter of some important ambassador from Panama and could eventually be a useful contact.

"You should get an expert, dear."

Tessa looked up. She was curled up on a giant puffed cushion on the floor (creative minds didn't need ordinary desks), scanning headlines on a reader. The speaker was a woman named Clarissa (creative minds also could treat their instructors as equals, on a first-name basis), one of those who supervised the free project time.

"You're still working on a media analysis?" prompted Clarissa.

"Yes."

The RUNA's flood of media had perhaps been the biggest bit of culture shock when Tessa had arrived from Panama. From an infrastructure point of view, there was simply no equivalent to the telecommunications, entertainment, and data that flooded the Gemman airwaves and were accessible to all citizens. It also tied together their daily activities. There was more to it than that, though. Exposing every aspect of life was completely unheard-of where she'd come from, especially after having been raised in one of the more cloistered tiers of Panamanian society. Gemmans seemed to want to share every bit of their lives and opinions, as well as delve into those of celebrities and other public figures. At the same time, there was always a vibe to everything that made Tessa wonder just how free this flow of information was. Everything around her always seemed to hum with adoration and fealty for the RUNA and its way of life.

It was this fascination that had spurred her to examine the country's preoccupation with itself and how the media defined its image. Tessa had chosen this for her project in social issues, and this wasn't the first time Clarissa had been on her to find someone in that field to advise her.

"I know you glean a lot from your research with the stream." Clarissa's voice was gentle. "But if you want to truly understand how what's out there"—Clarissa pointed out the window—"ends up here"—she pointed at the screen—"then you need to talk to someone who plays a role in that."

"Like who?"

Clarissa shrugged. "Any number of people. An editor. A reporter. A director. We fully endorse and support real-world experience. You could shadow a mentor and learn firsthand how the process works."

"Would anyone want me?" asked Tessa reluctantly.

Clarissa looked indignant. "My dear, we are the Institute for Creative Minds and Experiential Thinking. Some of the most important and influential people in this country send their children here. When we offer our students for internships and mentorships, people take notice. The field experience office is downstairs. It's mostly used by the tertiary students, but certainly exceptional secondaries like you can also receive placement. Why don't you go, now that the day's almost done? Start an application and see what happens."

Tessa had no good reason to refuse and easily found the office.

It was a tiny room adjacent to the much larger administrative office that governed most of the school's day-to-day activities. When she arrived, she discovered a line of two others ahead of her. The young man in front of her was tall and lanky, with bright blond hair. When he glanced back at her, his fair skin and blue eyes confirmed him as a castal. That wasn't surprising since castals—or patricians, as they liked to call themselves—were often among the RUNA's elite, and this school certainly claimed many. A moment later, she realized with a start that she knew him. His double take told her he'd recognized her as well.

"Tessa?" he asked.

She groped for the name. "Darius. What are you doing here?"

She'd met Darius a few months ago, during a visit to the Nordic caste's land grant. His family had played a surprising role in one of Justin's investigations, and Darius had used Tessa's connection to get help from Internal Security. Darius hadn't threatened her or anything, but he'd certainly been forceful in soliciting her help, making the whole experience a bit overwhelming. His face brightened as he looked down at her.

"I go here," he explained. "I transferred from the Nordic Tertiary Academy after . . ." A little of that enthusiasm dimmed. "Well, after things wrapped up in the spring. Dad hardly knows me these days, and everyone else is gone. It was time to move on."

Tessa felt a pang of sympathy for this odd and often frenetic young man. He'd lost his mother and older brother to the actions of a demented cult, the aftermath of which had landed his father in a convalescent home. Darius had sought justice for them for a long time, and Tessa supposed that resolving something as big as that might very well spur the need for a fresh start.

He looked as though he wanted to say more, but the receptionist called him up next. Tessa busied herself checking messages on her ego, the small device that handled both telecommunications and daily activities for Gemmians. She only half-listened as Darius put in a request for an internship in one of the many government agencies based in Vancouver. When it was her turn, he caught her arm.

"Is it okay—that is—do you mind if I stick around and walk out with you? There's something I need to ask you."

"I'm only going to the subway stop a block away," she said, having uneasy memories of the last time he'd asked her for help.

"It won't take long, I promise."

The earnestness in his eyes melted Tessa's worries. Besides, it seemed unlikely he could be caught up in *two* death cults. She agreed to talk to him and then stepped up to make her application. Darius had been seeking a full internship, but Tessa didn't need anything that extensive. She put in a request to interview a member of one of the professions Clarissa had suggested, along with the chance to shadow said person a few days and get a sense of the job's scope. The process was relatively painless, and once Tessa's information was in, the receptionist told her they'd submit it to the agencies they worked with and follow up once there were some hits.

Darius was waiting outside for her, as promised, leaning against the side of the institute's brick wall. The school was on the east side of downtown Vancouver, far from the larger businesses and government buildings, but still abuzz with commerce and activity. It was July, high summer, and what passed as the city's hottest time of year still felt mild compared to the heat and humidity Tessa had grown up with. She didn't mind the difference, though. There weren't as many mosquitoes, and she didn't sweat as much, even in the full force of today's sun.

"I'm not just here for a change for myself," Darius told her as they walked toward the subway. "I'm here for real change. Change for everyone."

The rush of the light rail roared overhead, and Tessa waited for it to pass before speaking. "What do you mean?"

"I want to serve our country," he explained. His long legs moved him farther than hers, and he forcibly paused and slowed. "After I saw what your friends in Internal Security did—the way they took down that group—I realized I have to be a part of it. I have to fight the good fight too."

"You want to work for Internal Security?" she asked, startled.

"Maybe. If not them, something like them. I'm not sure what area I'll specifically get into. Law. Politics. I just know I have to start by getting my foot in the door. That's why I was at the internship office—I'm trying to get a position somewhere, anywhere. It's not easy, though. Those spots are in demand."

"According to Clarissa—one of my instructors—businesses want students from Creative Minds."

Darius grinned. "Us and every other tertiary student from the elite schools in the area. The competition's stiff."

They reached the subway stop just as the purple train pulled up. "That's mine," she said.

His smile faded. Apparently his question hadn't been as quick as he'd expected. After a moment's thought, he shrugged and gestured her forward. "I'll ride with you."

"I'm going to the suburbs," she warned. She had to assume he lived in some block of student housing in the city.

"It's okay. I'll just catch it back." Early commuters were beginning to go home, and she and Darius had to jockey for a spot against a window. "So," he continued. "Here's where I was wondering if you could help me. You've got connections to Internal Security. Maybe you could help me get an internship."

That was his question? She shook her head. "I wouldn't say I have 'connections.' The guy I live with just works for them." Defining her relationship with Justin was always a little weird. It was hard to explain to people how he'd obtained a student visa for her as part of payback to her father for help during Justin's exile in Panama—the reasons for which even she still didn't know.

"Yeah, but he must know people, right?" Darius had that eager gleam in his eye as he leaned toward her. "One good word is all I need. It can be in IS. It can be anywhere. Anywhere I can make a difference. Haven't you wanted to do that? Help your country—er, province?"

Not so much. Panama's ever-shifting government didn't exactly inspire confidence and devotion. Sure, like many, Tessa had wished for stabilization and enjoyment of privileges like the RUNA and EA possessed. It had never occurred to her while living there that a young woman like herself might have any role in something like that. Even here, she was still content to be an observer of the world around her, rather than an active participant.

But yet again, something endearing in Darius broke through to Tessa. Maybe it was because he actually made her feel like he wanted to improve his country for the sake of doing good, rather than out of the unquestioning devotion she so often saw in others.

"I can ask," she said at last. "But I can't promise anything."

He gave her that big grin again, and she found herself smiling back.

His favor in place, Darius shifted the attention from himself and engaged Tessa in conversation. To her surprise, he asked her very little about Panama. Most people who made attempts to get to know her started with differences between the regions, and she couldn't blame them. It was an easy opening. Darius seemed to care less about where she was from than who she was and where she was going. He was especially interested in why she'd been in the field experience office and grew absolutely delighted when she explained her media project.

They grew so engrossed that he even went so far as to ask if he could walk her home when they got off the train in Cherrywood. Tessa had a weird moment of anxiety, the kind that often came when she was faced with something so different from her upbringing that she couldn't quite adapt. Although she'd accepted that gender relations were more liberal here, the exclusive attention of a guy always gave her pause. Not that it happened all that much to her. But in these moments, an image of her horrified mother promptly came to mind.

It then occurred to Tessa that Darius, zealous and ambitious, was probably making the offer in the hopes of running into Justin at her house. She relaxed a little at that, both because that kind of pragmatism was something she could handle and because Justin was still traveling for work.

Darius walked her right up to the front door, but, to her surprise, made no attempts to invite himself in.

"Thanks again," he said. "Seriously—anything you can do means a lot. And this was actually really fun." He spread his hands out and looked around. "It'd be weird doing this back home. Hanging out a lot with a plebeian. Even if it's business, people still don't always—"

His rambling was interrupted when a large, hulking body slammed into Tessa, pushing her up against the side of the house. Her impulse was to scream, but the abrupt impact had knocked the wind out of her and momentarily cost her her voice. A hand clamped over her mouth, and she felt the point of something against the side of her neck.

"Don't move," growled an unfamiliar voice. "Don't fucking move. You either, boy. One twitch or squeak, and this goes through her neck."

There was no danger of Tessa moving. She was paralyzed with fear. From Darius's dumbstruck expression, he wasn't going anywhere either.

"Get out your ego," her captor said. "Slowly."

Tessa obediently did as she was told, lifting the device from her purse and holding it in the palm of her hand.

"Unlock the door."

She held the ego up to the door's panel, pushing the combination of keys that let the ego identify her and deactivate the lock. As she did, her fingers faltered. How hard would it be to enter an emergency code?

The sharp point pressed harder against her neck. "Just unlock it," he said, guessing her thoughts.

She obliged, and the man ordered Darius in first before entering with Tessa. The door slammed behind her, and she again wrestled for options. The home's system had voice commands built in. She could call for the police. But would it do any good if her jugular was pierced immediately afterward? With great effort, she made her racing thoughts slow down. There was a way out of this. There had to be. For all she knew, a neighbor had witnessed the brief altercation outside, and the authorities were already on their way.

"Where is he?" demanded Tessa's captor. "Where is that bastard servitor?" He lifted his hand from her mouth, but the pointed weapon—which seemed to be some sort of stiletto—remained pressed to her skin.

"I-I don't know," she stammered. "He's traveling."

"When does he get back?"

"I don't know," she repeated. Her eyes lifted to Darius, who looked as dumbstruck and terrified as she felt.

"Of course you do! Why wouldn't he tell you?" The man's voice was frantic, and he was no one she knew. He also reeked of desperation. Despite the compromised position she was in at the moment, his approach seemed haphazard and unplanned. Whatever his intentions, they couldn't work out.

She gulped. "He's out of the country. We never know how long he's going to be gone."

That seemed to give the man pause. And although he still kept the weapon to her neck, his grip eased a little. "That doesn't make any sense! Why the hell would a servitor be outside the country?"

It was an excellent question, one Tessa and Cynthia often speculated about. Justin always rebuffed their attempts at interrogation, saying things like, "Remember the part where I work on this country's security? That's all you need to know."

"We don't know," Tessa said. "We just know—"

*Whack.*

Tessa had been so paralyzed by her own fear that she didn't even realize Darius was moving. Her captor had been preoccupied too, because he wasn't able to make any attempt at defense when Darius slammed a coatrack into the man. The coatrack was a new addition to the foyer, one that had caused a fair amount of contention between the March siblings. It was shaped like a tree, and Cynthia thought it was "quaint." Justin thought it looked like someone's bad arts and crafts project and was useless since they already had a coat closet.

Whatever the coatrack's true nature, it proved an effective weapon, and Darius had actually managed to strike in a way that made the man lose his grip on the stiletto. Tessa sprang away and shouted for the house's security system to call the police. Although the attack had knocked her captor back against the wall and clearly caused discomfort, it still wasn't enough to keep him down. Darius's second strike, however, did. He swung out as hard as he could when the man advanced, landing what looked like a pretty painful blow to the head. The assailant slumped to the ground and didn't move.

"Holy shit," exclaimed Darius, eyes wide. "Did I kill him? I've never done anything like that! I've never even thrown a punch!"

Gingerly, Tessa knelt down and touched the man's neck, feeling a pulse that seemed strong and steady. "I think he's okay. You just knocked him out."

Things moved rapidly after that. The police arrived just before Cynthia, who was understandably dumbfounded at what had taken place in her home. A medic confirmed the man would be all right, and a preliminary ID check from the police revealed that he was a member of a cult that had recently been denied a license from SCI. Tessa had a pretty good idea who had done the inspection.

The man was carted off long before Justin came home early in the evening. The police, having finished up their reports from Tessa and Darius, were about to leave but were more than eager to get a statement from Justin. He identified the man as one he'd met on a recent case and said that the man hadn't taken kindly to having his faith ripped out from underneath him.

When the household was finally left alone, Justin took a seat at the kitchen table and wore an uncharacteristically stunned expression. He was usually so quick on the uptake, so ready with a plan, that Tessa was more than a little unnerved by seeing him so at a loss. It was Cynthia who finally snapped him out of it.

"And you said that coatrack was a blight on humanity." Her tone was snide, but she too radiated tension as she drew her eight-year-old son, Quentin, to her and absentmindedly patted his back.

Justin shot her a wry look. "It is. I hope it was irrevocably damaged." He focused on Tessa, growing more serious. "Are you okay?"

She gave a weak nod. "It was all so fast . . . it doesn't even seem real. Why did he come here? Was he really that upset at being shut down?"

"They're always upset." Justin leaned back into his chair. "And there was no reason to think he'd retaliate. I mean, they do sometimes. It's not easy to hunt a servitor down, but of course, some do it. He was just some random guy. Out of all the things that'd actually be a threat, it was something like this. . . ." He stared off, his thoughts far away. "It was just a routine case, of all things. Totally unrelated." That last part was muttered more to himself than the rest of them.

Tessa realized then that while Justin was certainly upset about the threat to her, he was just as bothered by the fact that he hadn't noticed anything at the time of his visit to suggest this man presented any special danger. *And that drives him crazy,* she thought. *He's so good at reading people, but he missed this. Anyone probably would have, but he holds himself to a different standard.*

His eyes focused back on the scene at hand, and he seemed to notice Darius for the first time. "Who are you?"

Darius flinched and then straightened up, doing so in a way that made his long limbs seem unwieldy and in the way. "Darius Sandberg." After a moment's hesitation, he extended his hand. "It's an honor to officially meet you."

Justin shook it automatically, recognition lighting his features. "Sandberg. From New Stockholm."

Darius's head bobbed up and down. "I can't thank you enough for what you did, Dr. March. For my family."

"I think you helped me as much as I did you." As the memories of that grave case returned, Justin added, "I'm sorry for your loss."

"Thank you."

Justin's brows knit in a frown. "You aren't here to thank me in person, are you? Long trip."

When Darius faltered, Tessa jumped forward. "He goes to my school. For tertiaries."

"Ah." Justin relaxed. "Another freethinker, huh?"

"Creative thinker. He was hoping you could help him get an internship," explained Tessa, now feeling obligated to Darius. "You know, with your Internal Security connections."

That brought about Justin's first smile since returning home. He shook his head. "You don't want to work for Internal Security. Especially SCI."

Darius's earlier zeal returned. "I want to work for any place I can be useful! Any government branch that'll let me get a start."

Justin shook his head again, and Tessa could tell he was on the verge of politely refusing. After a few seconds, though, Justin glanced at Tessa, and his expression softened a little.

"He saved my life," she said, guessing what Justin was thinking.

"I don't suppose you broke that coatrack, did you?" he asked at last.

"Justin," growled Cynthia.

Darius, not knowing the coatrack's history, looked startled. "I . . . I don't know. I'm very sorry if I did. I can replace it."

Justin waved off the comment. "Forget it. I'll see what I can do for you."

The euphoria filling Darius's features was so cute that Tessa couldn't help but smile over it—and at the subsequent outpouring of gratitude that obviously discomfited Justin.

"Thank you, thank you, Dr. March! This means so much! I mean it. You have no idea. Wow. Thank you. And if there's anything I can do for you . . . wow . . . thank you and—"

"It's fine, it's fine," interrupted Justin. "If you want to help, stay for dinner, and keep your coatrack handy until I get real security around here."

That brought Cynthia back in. "What are you talking about?" she asked warily.

"Some guy showed up here brandishing a weapon. You think I'm going to leave you guys exposed after that?" Justin demanded.

His sister put her hands on her hips and tossed her dark hair back. "You just said it was a random attack—and a rarity. You think we'll be 'lucky' enough to get another any time soon?"

Justin took his time to phrase a response, and Tessa watched him very closely. He'd once told her that she had observation skills to match his own. She wasn't always so sure of that, but just then, she was almost certain that Justin had more on his mind than a random dissident. *There are other threats worrying him,* she realized.

"Probably not," he said, almost smoothly enough to convince Tessa. "But do you want to take the chance? You want to take the chance with him?" He nodded toward Quentin, and Cynthia faltered, as Justin had no doubt known she would.

"What do you have in mind?" she asked.

"We'll hire personal security. Bodyguards."

Cynthia's eyebrows rose. "Did you just use a plural?"

"You don't all travel together," pointed out Justin. "You're each going to need someone with you."

Even Tessa was surprised at that. "Like, all the time?" she asked. "A shadow?"

Justin stood up. "You'd be surprised how used to it you get. Don't look at me like that, Cyn," he warned. "You can make the calls around here on decorating, food, and what, uh, lifestyle choices are allowed in the house, but this one's all me. None of you are going around unprotected."

Tessa had a feeling Cynthia wanted to protest, simply because she was used to contradicting Justin, but she finally gave a nod of acquiescence. It was hard to fight the logic. "Where are you going?" she asked, seeing him move toward the door. "You just got back!"

Justin held up his hand in farewell and then turned toward the front door. "Off to find someone who's an expert on security-type stuff," he called.

# CHAPTER 4

# MOONLIGHTING

I t wasn't difficult finding Mae. Many facets of her were still a mystery to Justin, but some things were pretty predictable. After leaving his house, he immediately got on a train for downtown, knowing she'd be at either her place or a bar. When he called her, and she answered with voice only, he had his answer.

"Where are you drinking?" he asked promptly.

"How do you know I'm drinking?"

"Because you were instantly sending messages the moment our plane had stream access. You only do that on our trips if you plan on going out afterward."

"Well, congratulations on another brilliant deduction. Are you trying to find out where I'm at so you can verify some other amazing guess?"

"It wasn't a guess," he retorted. "And I need to find you so we can talk."

There was a moment of heavy silence. Then: "We were stuck on a plane for ten hours. Couldn't we have talked then? There's such a thing as personal space, you know."

He sighed, mentally and physically exhausted after the long day of travel. "Something's happened. Something involving danger and death and all that other stuff you like."

She fell into thought again and then yielded. "I'm at Brownstone."

"Where is it?"

"Really? There's a bar in the greater Vancouver area you don't personally know every inch of?"

"Man, you're in a bad mood," he grumbled. "I'll look it up. See you soon."

A quick check on his ego told him Brownstone was a bar frequented by military personnel, due to its proximity to a train stop used exclusively for traveling to the base just outside the city limits. Justin uneasily wondered if he might be walking into a praetorian drinking party. Mae's two regular sidekicks, as Justin thought of them, could be trying enough on their own, let alone when they were en masse with others. No use worrying about it now, he supposed. And, for all he knew, maybe they'd have recommendations on this latest complication in his life.

He was still blown away that Antonio Song, the devotee of Mithras who'd attacked Tessa, had proven that unstable and vindictive. Justin had meant what he said about these sorts of retaliations being rare. Most shut-down churches blamed the government as a whole, not its individual servants. And Justin had also meant it when he said this was just a random, routine zealot. He didn't believe Song was part of some larger conspiracy or one of the dangerous elect Mama Orane had warned about. Song was a fluke, but he was a fluke who had driven home to Justin just how great a potential for harm this job presented. Enough supernatural sightings and trips to the provinces had reinforced the dangers of his work. He'd accepted it, just as he'd accepted Mae as his shield from those threats.

But having his family targeted? It was a startling and disturbing revelation, especially in light of this "war of the elect." And from what he knew, there were just as many elect and godly devotees walking the RUNA as the provinces—maybe more, considering Geraki had told him the religious vacuum the RUNA had maintained for so long was opening itself up to divine influences. If elect were willing to attack other elect they considered threats, then the loved ones of the enemy could be a starting tactic. Song might have been a nobody in the grand scheme of things, but he was a warning of what could be much more dire things to come.

Mae was easy to spot when Justin got to Brownstone. There weren't a lot of castals in the military, and her light features stood out among the predominantly plebeian soldiers. More than half of the bar's patrons were in uniform, mostly the gray and maroon of the regular military. There were a few black-clad praetorians among them though, creating spots of shadow in the cheery environment. Even off duty, the regular military moved deferentially around them.

Two such praetorians were sitting with Mae: Valeria Jardin and Linus Dagsson. Justin paused near the bar's doorway as he studied the threesome. Just as he'd known he'd find Mae in a bar, he knew she wasn't actually here to drink. Praetorians couldn't get drunk, at least not on the stuff a place like this served. Their implants metabolized regular alcohol too quickly. Mae wasn't here for the drinks or the establishment. She was here for her friends. She always returned to them after a case, taking therapeutic comfort in them, even if she didn't ever discuss many of her cases' details. The dynamic she had with them fascinated Justin, both because solitary Mae wasn't nearly as close to her biological family and because Val and Dag seemed like such opposites for a highborn Nordic girl.

*And because you're jealous,* said Horatio. *She bares her heart to them but not to you.*

*Neither of those things is true,* Justin retorted. *She has walls within walls that not even those two have seen through. And I'm not jealous.*

*You could've had a more exalted place in her heart,* said Magnus. *And at our master's knee.*

*I don't need either of those things,* Justin said. But he couldn't help but feel a little wistful as he noticed the rare ease with which Mae sat in her chair, elbow propped on the table and chin resting in her hand as she smiled at some wild story Dag was telling her. There was still tension in her, of course. There was *always* tension in her. Just now, though, it was about as low as he'd ever seen, excepting their ill-fated one-night stand. And as he approached the table, Justin watched her normal tension return as her blue-green gaze settled on him. Her companions, sensing the change in her, immediately turned to him as well.

A grin lit Val's face. "Dr. March," she said, going so far as to stand up and kiss him on the cheek. "And here I thought suits like you didn't go slumming with the likes of us."

"Suits don't usually get invited," he explained. Although she'd been joking, Justin noticed that he was, in fact, the only person literally wearing a suit in there, earning a few curious glances. He might as well have stamped BUREAUCRAT on his forehead.

"Well, then, consider yourself to have a standing invite," declared Dag, spreading his hands grandly. "Especially if you can get IS to pick up our tab." Whereas Val was small and—deceptively—fragile looking, Dag was a schoolgirl's dream of muscles and rugged looks.

"I don't see why not," said Justin, bringing up the table's ordering panel. "I can get them to pick up everything else."

"So where's all the death and danger that you mentioned?" asked Mae pointedly.

Justin finished his order and turned off the panel. "At a police station, vanquished by a coatrack. For now."

He told them the story as it had been told to him and watched as another transformation took place in the praetorians. The jovial, laid-back expressions vanished, as did the smiles. Calling Mae tense earlier had been a mistake, because that was nothing compared to the rigid posture that now seized her. Even for a fight long since passed and far away from them, the praetorians' implants sprang to life, filling their bodies with adrenaline and other fight-or-flight chemicals.

"She's okay?" demanded Dag, when Justin finished. "Our girl's okay?"

Justin wondered when Tessa had become "our girl." By Justin's count, she and Dag had met twice, the first being a particularly traumatic time when she'd been dragged home after she and drunken friends had trespassed on federal property. Dag had led her to believe she was in more trouble than she was, going so far as to suggest she'd be sent to a girls' reform camp. Their second meeting, a chance run-in downtown while Justin's family was out to dinner, had mostly consisted of Dag asking her how her camp application was coming.

But he and even Val looked fiercely protective as Justin assured them Tessa had survived the incident unscathed. Mae didn't ask about Tessa, not because she didn't care, but because she knew Justin wouldn't be here if anything was wrong with Tessa.

"And he was just some random zealot?" Mae asked. Justin met her eyes, knowing what she was really asking: Did the attack have anything to do with the elect and the divine "game" being waged?

"Random," he confirmed. "Just some upset guy who got it into his head to come after the servitor who shut him down. But next time—well. Who knows?"

He left it at that and could tell from her face that she understood.

"So what now?" asked Dag. His face brightened. "You want us to go rough him up a little?"

Val nodded in agreement. "We can scare the shit out of him if you want. Make sure he never messes with you again."

"I don't think he will anyway, but thanks for the offer." Justin paused to accept a glass of bourbon from their waitress. "I am, however, concerned about other malcontents coming and calling on my family. I think I'm overdue for looking into security for them and figured I should ask the person—well, people—who know it best. I mean, I'm sure IS has people—"

"Screw that," said Dag. "You don't want government contractors involved. They're just watching the clock. I mean, they're fine if you're just some rich person worried about your house, but with your job? You're dealing with some serious shit."

*He doesn't know the half of it,* said Horatio.

"So your suggestion is?" asked Justin.

Dag held up his hands. "Us."

The amazing part was that he looked perfectly serious. Justin shook his head. "Right. Because you don't have any other job to do."

"We're on capital duty," said Val. "We have nine-hour workdays. We need to do something else with the other fifteen. Moonlighting's as good a thing as any."

With the way Mae tended to keep her friends close to her, Justin would've expected some protest. Amazingly, she looked as though she thought this was perfectly reasonable. "I have to stay with him." She nodded her head at Justin. "And there's only two of you and three of them."

"You know we can get another Scarlet to help." Val looked truly inspired. "Hell, we could get a bunch of them. Do kind of a rotation for when our shifts don't line up."

"Whoa, hang on," said Justin, unable to believe this was still going on. "I don't think I can afford a whole 'bunch' of moonlighting praetorians."

"Oh, we'd do it for Finn," said Dag. For a moment, Justin thought he'd actually said "fun" instead of the praetorians' pet name for Mae. "We take care of our own."

It was a weird bit of logic—that Justin had somehow become part of that inner circle. If, say, they'd been talking about protection for Mae's sister and nephew, Justin didn't doubt they'd have the Scarlets and every other praetorian cohort ready to help. It was hard to believe they'd go out of their way for someone like him.

"We can't base their protection solely on when capital praetorians are between shifts," said Mae. "He's going to have to hire out someone—just to have a regular person on hand. The Scarlets could be pulled out without notice."

"There are agencies for that," said Justin.

"No agencies," she said. "Unless you can find someone who's ex-military looking for security work. They're out there. Probably a number of them in this bar, even." She glanced around as though the lucky candidate might come strolling right up to them. "But you'll have to advertise and do interviews. Well, *I'll* advertise and do interviews." The look on Mae's face said that she expected, if left to his own devices, that he'd end up hiring call girls.

The three praetorians soon seemed to forget about him as they threw themselves into making plans. They compared Dag and Val's schedules to Justin's family's and began working out a system where there'd always be one person on duty in the house at night, and then individuals to escort various family members to their respective schools throughout the day. Mae even worked herself into the rotation, volunteering to come over tonight and do the all-night watch. Justin nearly protested that, seeing as she'd barely gotten back into town, but he thought it might help his family adjust to this new system a little easier if they dealt with Mae before the others. As it was, Tessa would probably have a panic attack being under the same roof as Val or Dag.

"If I can get an ad up tonight, maybe I can do interviews tomorrow or the next day," said Mae, letting Justin back into the conversation. "We're good for that long, right?"

"Should be," he said. "Nassau ran longer than they expected. We should have at least the next two days off and then stay domestic for a while." It was one nice side to their job, at least. When they went away for a long provincial trip, they could usually count on local assignments upon returning.

"Listen to you guys," said Dag, eyes shining. "Tossing around Nassau like it's no big deal. You've been to more provinces with March these last few months than I've been to in my whole military career. I wouldn't mind dropping in on one of your trips if you ever need help."

*That's it,* Justin realized. *That's why they're helping. They're bored. Praetorians are proud to serve in their capital, but it's a lot of show, and they'd rather be fighting. They're hoping helping me will send a little more action their way.*

*They're doing it for her too,* Horatio said. *She doesn't always like you, but she does care about you and the others. Her friends can tell, and that carries a lot of weight with them.*

And *they want to defend my house from raging religious zealots,* Justin insisted.

*Well, yes, obviously.*

Even though Val and Dag seemed excited about this new enterprise he'd brought them, Justin couldn't shake the feeling of overstaying his welcome. He finished and paid for his drink—and theirs—and then made motions to leave. Mae quickly downed her own drink and stood up as if to follow.

"No, no, you can stay," he said. "Enjoy your break."

"I don't need a break. Besides, I'm working the first house shift tonight. I have to go with you anyway."

"I'm not going home."

Mae's disapproving look spoke legions, and he knew he could have easily kept her away if he made up some story about a liaison. As it was, the truth was nearly as effective.

"I'm going to see Lucian."

"Really?" she asked, after several moments of scrutiny.

"I need to ask a favor."

"Lucian Darling? Our security's not good enough?" asked Dag with a wounded look.

Justin gave him a small smile. "Different favor." To Mae, he said, "You're welcome to come, if you want."

That unreadable mask of hers slipped into place. Mae's relationship with Lucian Darling—Justin's old friend and one of the country's most powerful senators—was an enigmatic thing. He was infatuated with her. She seemed to neither like nor dislike him. A plebeian senator, even a liberal one, couldn't be seen publicly dating a castal woman, so he'd contrived a number of events in the past for her to attend, like dinners and other fund-raisers. She'd gone to a couple, always polite and always showing as much emotion as any good Nordic debutante would when out in society—meaning, no emotion at all.

"I'll walk you to the subway," she said. "Tell Lucian you're coming, and he'll have his car sent to his station for you. The timing should work out well."

So. She didn't want to go. That was telling—as was the familiar way in which she spoke about getting to his home.

Val leaned toward Justin. "You're going to tell us all about how our Finn knows the good senator, right? I mean, we'll have all sorts of time to kill when we're protecting you and your loved ones out of the goodness of our hearts. Surely the least you can do in return is tell us what *some people* have been unfairly tight-lipped about."

Mae rolled her eyes. "Because there's nothing to tell."

Her friends looked skeptical, and Justin suspected he had more badgering in his future. For now, he was able to slip off relatively unbothered, after offering more sincere thanks to the praetorians. He was equally gracious to Mae as they walked out into the busy summer night toward the subway stop across the street, thanking her for her role in everything.

"I get that they're doing it for you," he added when they reached the stairs leading underground. "But I'm not sure why you're doing it."

"Because I like your family," she said, confirming what the ravens had said. They reached the platform, and a monitor informed them that the gray-line train—which led out to Lucian's suburb—was seconds away. "And I know better than anyone else what kind of stuff is coming after you—and could come after them. You need extra help."

The train pulled up and opened its doors, letting crowds of people move in and out. Justin paused before boarding to give Mae one last glance. "You think praetorians will be enough?"

She had that unreadable expression back on. "They'll have to be."


Justin had given Lucian plenty of notice that he was coming by that night. He'd also told Lucian he was bringing Mae.

"Really?" Lucian asked, upon realizing he'd been tricked. "You don't think I would've let just *you* come over?"

Justin peered around the expansive living room, which a bodyguard had just escorted him into. The house and upper-class suburban neighborhood weren't unlike his own, though there was a sterile, too-neat feel to everything. No surprise, he thought, since Lucian probably spent more time on the road these days than around the house.

"Hedging my bets," Justin said. "I had no idea what kind of long day you might have had. You might not want any guests at all. But you'd still probably want her."

"Probably." Lucian, upon closer examination, actually *did* appear as though he might have had a long day. He was settled into the corner of a leather sofa, with his arm stretched along its back and his feet resting on a coffee table. The top buttons of his dress shirt were undone, its sleeves rolled up. If he'd had a tie on at some point today, it'd been discarded. There was an easy smile on his face—it was hard to find Lucian without one—but it was underscored with fatigue. "Though believe it or not, there actually has been something I've wanted to see you about. So this works out happily for everyone. Make yourself a drink, and we'll talk." He held up an empty glass. "Make me one too."

Justin took the glass over to a bar between the kitchen and living room. It too was beautifully laid out and well stocked, straight from an entertaining magazine but not seeing much use. "Why don't you give up on your unattainable Nordic obsession and find some well-bred plebeian wife to smile in your campaign ads and throw dinner parties for you?"

Lucian's grin broadened. "No time. Maybe after I win. Right now, that's where all my real energy's going."

Justin sat down in an armchair near the sofa, handing over Lucian's drink as he did. "Does it take that much energy? Don't you have this sealed up?"

"Never assume anything in politics. We're still in the lead, but Chu from the New People's Party has been going up in the polls. Very quickly." Lucian's dark eyes stared off into space as he sipped the drink, his mind spinning with numbers and points. "We need something big. No more well-written speeches and school visits. Something that'll stick in the hearts and minds of people and make them see me as a leader, not just someone trying to win a contest."

Justin nearly made a joke, but the intensity in his old friend's gaze made him reconsider. *He's into this. He's really into this. In any other politician, I'd say that makes him more dangerous than someone who's just trying to reap the fame.*

*Any other politician? Are you saying he's not dangerous?* asked Horatio.

*That remains to be seen.*

To Lucian, Justin said, "Do you have something in mind? A great hearts-and-minds-winning stunt?"

"Not a stunt." Lucian's eyes focused back on Justin. "But it can wait. Tell me what you need."

"What, after a buildup like that? I can't compete. You go first."

Lucian hesitated only briefly, took another sip, and then leaned eagerly toward Justin. "Arcadia."

The name of the RUNA's volatile neighbor was not what Justin had expected to hear. Composed of the southeastern part of the former United States, Arcadia had formed after the Decline when the rest of its American countrymen had banded together with Canada. Relations between the RUNA and Arcadia weren't friendly, a situation made more difficult by the fact that Arcadia was neither advanced enough to be treated as an equal nor backward enough to be casually dismissed like other provinces. Frequent border disputes in recent years had only worsened political tensions.

"You want to take it over? Annex it?" Justin asked. "That would certainly get people's attention." He was mostly joking, but from the fervent look in Lucian's eyes, Justin wondered just how extreme the senator might be willing to get.

Lucian clasped his hands together. "No. Not yet. Just go there. There's been talk for a while between both countries about a diplomatic visit—some sort of friendly delegation going in to try to better understand our neighbors and their ways." A bitter smile played at the edges of Lucian's lips. "There's been particular interest in this after rumors of the Arcadians amassing new weapons—not that I expect them to tour us around that."

Justin parsed his words. "Us. As in *you*—you'd be a part of this delegation?"

"Exactly."

Lucian settled back into the couch, face triumphant as he gauged Justin's reaction—which was one of astonishment. "That's crazy! People like you don't go to Arcadia . . . or any province. You're supposed to stay on the campaign trail, in posh hotels surrounded by bodyguards."

"And that's what makes this so big. There are no heroes anymore, Justin. Leaders get elected with words, not actions, and when people go to the polls, they're usually just voting for the lesser of evils because there's nothing better. But *I* intend to be better. I can't be Mae, fighting gloriously out there on the battlefield, but I can be the first leader in the RUNA's history to ever set foot in semi-hostile territory, unafraid to further this country's interest. People will respect that. That'll mean something, whereas my rivals' words will just be . . . words."

"See, that's your problem right there," said Justin, unable to believe what he was hearing. "You can put 'semi' in front of it, but 'hostile' will still get you killed."

Lucian looked more confident than he had any right to be. "You visit plenty of hostile places. You're still alive."

Justin downed his drink. "I don't go there as a public official, decked out in fanfare. I go in covertly—well protected—and don't always get out so smoothly."

"Well, I'll be well protected too. Even the Arcadians aren't foolish enough to think our party'd go in without our own soldiers."

"A dozen Gemman soldiers won't mean much if you're surrounded by the entire Arcadian military," Justin pointed out.

"The Arcadians won't touch me or the people with me. They don't trust us, sure, but they don't want an incident. Some of them really even *do* want to stabilize relations between us." Lucian stood up and began to pace. "In this case, the fanfare pays off. They can't do anything when this is all so public. I'll be fine. *You* would be fine."

Justin had been about to stand and make another drink but now found himself momentarily frozen in place. "Me? I assume you're speaking hypothetically."

"It's only hypothetical if you don't go."

The smug grin on Lucian's face was maddening. Justin was used to reading the truth in people's expressions, but he couldn't read Lucian just then. Was this some kind of joke? No . . . the more Justin studied the other man, the more it seemed Lucian was in earnest. The question was, *why*?

"Give me one good reason I'd want to go with you on a suicidal trip to Arcadia," said Justin at last.

Lucian chuckled. "Well, as I already told you, it's *not* suicidal. As for a reason . . . don't you study religion? That place is a hotbed of it—getting hotter from what I hear."

"I study religion to protect my own country. What others do to destroy theirs is up to them."

But as Justin spoke, a chill ran down his spine. Whereas the RUNA had renounced religion after the Decline, Arcadia had clung to it—so fiercely, in fact, that it had become intertwined with the government. The Arcadian faith was rigid and authoritarian, and the idea of its "getting hotter" was slightly terrifying. And yet, there was no question religion really was heating up in the RUNA and other parts of the world. Was the divine game—or maybe even war, at this point—active in Arcadia as well?

*It would certainly be something worth looking into*, said Magnus. *And our master would especially be interested in knowing the state of godly affairs there.*

*I don't owe him that*, Justin reminded the ravens. *I only answer to Internal Security, and they haven't asked this of me. I'm not going to volunteer because Lucian wants company.*

"You can bring Mae," added Lucian unexpectedly. "Most of our security detail will be praetorians, actually."

Justin suppressed a groan. "Is that what this is about? Unbelievable. You'd seriously go this far to get some alone time with her?"

Lucian held out his hands in an appeasing gesture. "No. Believe it or not, you're actually the one I want more on this trip. We'll have other cultural experts with us to help us 'learn' about the country. A religion expert is vital with these people—as are your observations on human nature. I don't just want election results from this trip, Justin. I want long-term results. I want to know how these people breathing down our necks think, and understanding how their superstition affects them is the key to it. There's no one else I trust more than you to get inside their heads."

*He's actually complimenting you,* observed Horatio.

*First time for everything,* said Justin.

"I already have a job," he told Lucian. "IS has assignments for me. I can't just drop them for a field trip."

"I think they'd spare you if I asked."

Yes, Justin was sure they would. Especially if they sensed a supernatural threat lurking within Arcadia's borders. But Justin still wanted no part of it. Arcadia was its own unique brand of dangerous, and Justin especially didn't want to be tied to some much-hyped, very public trip.

"Sorry," said Justin firmly. "I pass."

Lucian weighed him heavily for several moments and then gave a nod, his customary smile returning. "Okay. But think on it. And if you change your mind, you've got a week to get in on one of the biggest international moves in this country. Now. What did *you* want to talk about?"

*He dropped that awfully fast,* thought Justin warily as he began explaining about Darius's internship. *Too fast.*

*Yes,* agreed Horatio. *He certainly did. Be careful.*

# CHAPTER 5

# THE RED VELVET CLOAK

Y ou've been with Lucian the whole time?"

Justin seemed startled by Mae's voice as he trudged past the living room at three in the morning. He came to a halt and squinted at where she was curled up on the couch with a reader she hadn't really been paying attention to, save to occasionally check the house's exterior security settings. Her mind was too full of the latest developments, both domestic and abroad, to focus on books or movies.

"Yup," said Justin. "Don't worry, just us boys. No side trips."

"I'm more worried about you staggering home drunk in the middle of the night when there are people out there who want you dead. You're going to a lot of pains for everyone else but not taking much care with yourself. I thought this was going to be a quick trip."

Justin rubbed his eyes before answering. "Me too. But Lucian kind of dropped a bombshell on me." Mae was too self-controlled to ask, but he read the interest on her face. "You wouldn't believe me if I told you."

"Wouldn't I?" she asked archly.

He reconsidered. "Yes, you probably would. I'll tell you tomorrow. I need sleep now."

"Did you at least get what you initially went there for?" she called, as he started to turn.

"I did actually. Young Master Sandberg is going to be serving our fine country as a senatorial intern. We'll see how long he enjoys his 'reward.'"

Mae felt a smile spread over her face. "That's what you went to Lucian for?"

"It's what the kid wanted." Justin suddenly seemed uncomfortable at having been caught doing a good deed. "What's wrong with that? He defended my home."

"There's nothing wrong with it," she said, trying to look serious. "I just think it's sweet you went out of your way for him, especially when you could've just called Lucian."

"Did you just say—" He shook his head and stifled a yawn. "Never mind. I pay my debts, that's all. See you in the morning."

Mae watched him go, biting back any further remarks she might have made about his disregarding his own safety. He deserved chastisement, of course. He had no business being out there alone and intoxicated, especially after what they'd seen in Nassau. An image of a bloodied Mama Orane flared in Mae's mind, reminding her of the severity of the forces they were dealing with. Justin had been insistent, however, that his family get Mae's protection tonight, not him. His safety was also apparently secondary to his repaying an imagined debt to a boy he barely knew.

Mae sighed and leaned back, frustrated—as she often was—at these surprising streaks of nobility in Justin that popped up in what was otherwise a sea of selfishness. Apparently not even a mob of rampaging, deadly insects capable of regeneration was enough to deter him when he decided he had to do the right thing. Remembering the beetles made her sit up again and reach for her boot, where the amber knife was safely sheathed once more. She took it out and studied it in the light of a small table lamp.

Even in the dimness, golden fire played in the dagger's handle, providing an almost fanciful contrast to the efficient, no-nonsense blade. A blade that had been capable of killing supernatural creatures when nothing else could. *I should get rid of it,* she thought. She'd meant what she told Justin: She didn't want anything to do with the powers surrounding them. Investigating them as part of her job might have been inevitable, but personal involvement was not—and this knife was personal. It had been sent to her anonymously in the spring, and that alone should've been reason for mistrust. Her initial thought had been that it was an unwelcome gift from Callista Xie, a religious leader and former lover of Justin's. When asked, Callista had insisted she had nothing to do with it, increasing the knife's mystery.

Mae still wasn't sure if Callista was lying—or why she would. Regardless, the knife was Mae's now unless she did something about it. It wouldn't be hard. There were plenty of other daggers she could afford of comparable quality, if not style. Gingerly, she reached out and touched the blade, admiring the precision and workmanship. The gleaming edge was lethally sharp, showing no wear from the beetle attacks or the time she had killed the servant of a death goddess intent on—

"Damn!"

Mae jerked her hand back as she felt a sting in her fingertip. She looked down in surprise and saw blood beading on her skin. It was only one drop, and she started to wipe it on her jeans—but then paused. In the poor lighting, the blood had looked almost black when she'd first cut herself, but suddenly, it began turning a brighter red. She blinked, certain her eyes were playing tricks on her. But no, there it was. A rich scarlet, like the pip on her uniform's collar. That didn't last, though, and moments later, the blood covering her hand brightened into crimson.

Covering her hand?

What had started as a bead was expanding rapidly. Mae stared in mingled fascination and horror as that swathe of red enveloped her hand and then her arm. From there it spread to the rest of her body, wrapping around her like a cloak. No, it *was* a cloak, made of a heavy velvet that felt oppressive in the sun. There was sun everywhere, golden and glorious as it shone down from a clear blue sky. Mae felt that warmth enter her body, felt it connect her to every green and growing thing on the planet, to all that was alive and thriving. She threw the smothering cloak off and saw that she was naked underneath. It felt right somehow, that there was nothing between her body and the world around her.

A fragrance so intense it made her dizzy filled her nostrils, and Mae reached up to discover a wreath of flowers on her head. They were apple blossoms, just like the perfume she normally wore. The air around them shimmered, and suddenly, they were small, white stephanotis flowers. Then they were peonies. Then roses. The wreath fell apart in her hands, and a sudden wind picked up, scattering the petals away like shooting stars. They brushed delicately against Mae's skin as they went, before disappearing altogether.

*Do not be deceived by the crown. It may look fragile, but there is power in it. There is power in love and beauty and desire. There is more power in creating life than taking it.*

Mae looked around for the speaker but could find no source for the woman's voice, only the sun above. Or was it truly the sun? As she squinted, trying to make out that brilliance, she couldn't be sure if it was actually a woman's face, too dazzling for mortal eyes to behold. A small laugh made Mae look down, to where the red velvet cloak rested at her feet. Something under it stirred, and she flinched as a small face suddenly peered up at her. It was a girl's face, a familiar face: the face of Mae's niece, sent away when she was born for not possessing a pure Nordic gene set.

Mae had spent years trying to find her, her closest lead being a servant of the Morrigan named Emil—a servant Mae had killed with the amber dagger. Emil had promised Mae a lead to the girl in Arcadia, as part of his attempts to get Mae to join their cult and fulfill the pact her mother had made at Mae's conception. Mae had refused and thought she'd lost her chance at finding her niece forever. And yet, here, right in front of her, was the girl, looking up with hazel eyes that showed glints of green in the sunlight. She grinned, but when Mae reached for her, the wind stirred again, picking up the red velvet. It was no longer a cloak but a flag, rippling in the air, blocking Mae from her niece. Angrily, she tried to catch hold of the waving fabric, but when she finally did and jerked it aside, the girl was gone.

So was the sun. So was everything.

Mae was sitting in the March living room, dressed, with no blood on her hands. There wasn't even a cut. Glancing around, she saw the amber dagger lying on the floor but had no memory of dropping it. In fact, as her eyes passed over a clock, she was startled to realize she was apparently missing a few memories. To Mae's perception, barely five minutes had passed, but the time—and other signs—said nearly three hours had gone by. The faint light of sunrise was seeping through the windows, and the coffeemaker in the kitchen had turned itself on. Weirdest of all, she felt exhausted, as though she'd been through some great physical activity—not a sensation she felt often these days.

Chills ran through her, and she fixed her gaze back on the knife. *I have to get rid of it.* But how? And where? A sound from the other end of the house startled her out of her fear. Someone was stirring, probably Cynthia. Without further thought, only knowing that she had to get the knife away from her and not have to explain how she'd just spaced out on guard duty, Mae grabbed the blade and dropped it inside an ornamental basket on a high shelf near the media screen. Several other artistic oddities were on the shelf, and in all the time she'd spent here, Mae had never seen anyone disturb them. She would come back for the knife later and find a proper way to dispose of it—if such a thing even existed.

"Quiet night?"

Mae spun around as a yawning Cynthia entered the kitchen and checked the coffeemaker. Forcing calm, Mae strolled into the kitchen and put on a smile.

"Sure was. Not that I'd expect different, if word of your deadly coatrack's gotten around."

Cynthia scowled as she poured two cups. "That kid's lucky he didn't break it."

Mae accepted the offered coffee and tried to ignore the fact that she'd just lied. Technically, she didn't know if it had been a quiet night or not. Anything could've happened in those three hours. There could've been another attack, one she would've just let happen while hallucinating with a cursed knife. Fortunately, Cynthia was too preoccupied with breakfast plans to notice Mae's unease. Or maybe Mae was just that good at covering it up.

The rest of the household began to wake up shortly after that—aside from Justin. Tessa and Quentin got ready for school as Cynthia cooked, and Mae checked her messages, discovering she'd received a few responses to her security ad. A couple looked promising, and she set up interviews for that afternoon. She'd just finished responding to the last applicant when Val and Dag showed up at the door, more excited than she'd seen them in a while. Capital duty really was starting to wear on them.

"Anything exciting happen overnight?" asked Dag. Like Cynthia, he assumed the answer was a given, and it bothered Mae that the night hadn't been nearly as tame as she would've liked.

"Not around here," she said easily, showing them into the kitchen.

Cynthia had resigned herself to having household security as a necessary evil and considered feeding them part of her responsibility, especially upon learning they were doing it for free. Val and Dag—driven by the same supercharged metabolism as Mae—had no problem with this. They set into their food with gusto, much to the delight of a wide-eyed Quentin. He was so used to Mae now that she was old hat, but having "real" praetorians in the house was as new and exciting as movie heroes come to life. He peppered them with questions while Tessa watched in wary silence.

A little of the previous night's weirdness faded as breakfast wound down. Val and Dag always had a calming effect on Mae. She was closer to them than her blood family and trusted them implicitly . . . almost. As the Marches dispersed for the day, a pang of guilt shot through Mae that her friends were blindly taking on this bodyguard job as a friendly favor, little knowing the truth of what they were facing. Would they be strong enough to take on what was to come? The answer, Mae decided, hadn't changed from what she'd told Justin last night: They would have to be.

Justin himself didn't surface, which wasn't surprising after his late night. Mae, who was escorting Tessa and then going on to the Internal Security building, had simply hoped he'd come along with her. For all she knew, he wouldn't get out of bed until that evening, so she and the others finally set off for the day's tasks, with Val and Dag escorting Cynthia and Quentin respectively.

"How long are we going to be doing this?" Tessa asked Mae, as they rode the subway into the city. "The bodyguards?"

*Excellent question,* Mae thought. "Until Justin thinks it's safe, I guess."

Tessa frowned. "That's vague."

"It's kind of a vague situation." Hoping to deflect further questioning, Mae added, "It should be like the old days for you. Didn't you always leave the house in Panama with an entourage?"

Tessa gave her a faint smile and glanced out the window. "Yeah . . . but I've sort of gotten used to coming and going on my own. I like it."

Mae smiled back. Her upbringing hadn't been quite as cloistered as Tessa's, but it had had its share of restrictions. Mae could certainly appreciate wanting to come and go on one's own and hated to put these fetters on Tessa . . . but at the same time, it sickened Mae to think of this girl she'd come to love facing the same kinds of threats she and Justin found themselves continually surrounded in.

"Soon," said Mae, gently patting Tessa's arm. "Soon."

After seeing Tessa safely to school, Mae headed over to the Internal Security building. She had no official position there since her work with Justin was done through an arrangement between IS and the military. Still, enough people knew her that no one questioned her presence, even without Justin. She figured she wouldn't have any trouble talking her way into a conference room to conduct her interviews, but as bureaucratic luck would have it, all of those controlled by the Division of Sect and Cult Investigation were booked that morning.

"Sorry, praetorian," said the department's receptionist, seeming genuinely apologetic—and terrified.

Mae weighed her options, wondering if she should contact the interviewees and relocate elsewhere. She'd really wanted to have the full power of IS behind her to impart gravity on the situation, and a coffee shop or even Justin's house just didn't have that same effect.

"There's nothing we could use in another department?" Mae asked.

The receptionist shook his head. "Not that I have access to. Why don't you just use Dr. March's office? I'm sure he wouldn't mind."

Mae hesitated and then agreed. She'd wanted gravity, and Justin's official office certainly conveyed it. He'd received a significant upgrade upon becoming SCI's covert investigator of actual paranormal phenomena, earning a corner spot with wide glass windows that looked down upon the bustling streets of Vancouver below. As Mae walked around the office after the aide had left, she was surprised at how little of himself Justin had put into it—and that she was even aware of that fact. Most of his work was done on the road in their missions or in his home office. This place, with its expensive glass desk and grand view, was just a formality. There were no personal effects. Even the art on the walls was just part of the set that SCI's interior designer had obtained to match the rest on the department's floor.

Only the leather chair, which had managed to retain the scent of his cologne, indicated he spent any time here at all. Mae sank down in it and closed her eyes, allowing herself to be momentarily lost in the thought of him. She soon snapped herself back to attention and readied herself for the task at hand. She wished she'd had the foresight to stop at her apartment and change clothes—if not into her uniform, then something more formal than the linen pants and sleeveless blouse combo that tended to make up most of her summer wardrobe. Hopefully her personality and presence would carry through. She had very little experience with interviews. She'd never had any other job outside of the military and expected to base most of her decisions today on gut instinct . . .

. . . which, as it turned out, didn't have much good to say.

Sure, there was nothing wrong with the two men and one woman who came in for their respective interviews. They were all ex-military and treated her respectfully when they learned her rank, even if one of the men looked a little dubious at first. They all possessed suitable track records, but as she spoke to them about their duties and the kind of schedule they'd be on, she kept thinking about Dag's offhand comment about hiring security to watch one's property. She could tell that was all these candidates really thought of themselves as, and although they seemed experienced and steady, she kept wondering what they would do if an army of supernatural beetles came after them. Would they be able to handle it?

Would anyone?

After she'd escorted the last candidate out, Mae returned to the chair and put her feet up on the desk with a sigh. A scan of her messages showed a few more applicants with similar military backgrounds, and she wrestled with the decision to invite any others in, wondering if she'd get any truly different results. She'd nearly talked herself into putting it off for another day—surely she and Justin had at least that much time before their next mission—when one person's résumé caught her eye. He was the only one who'd ever served actively in the provinces. There was still no comparison to the kind of things Justin and Mae faced, but it meant he'd had experience with the unpredictability of a setting outside the normal Gemman experience. Surely that was worth something.

She responded, asking him when he'd be able to meet at Internal Security, and was surprised to receive a reply almost instantly, saying he was in the area now and could meet her whenever she wished. With nothing else to do, Mae accepted and invited him by.

His name was Rufus Callaway, and he showed up an hour later, bearing a bag of donuts. Mae accepted them in astonishment.

"Are you trying to bribe your way into this job?" she asked. She actually had to fight the urge to tear into them then and there. They were from one of her favorite bakeries, and she was almost certain she could smell the kind she liked best, the store's signature hazelnut and chocolate blend.

"No, ma'am," he said gruffly, taking the seat she pointed to. He was short but solidly built, still obviously strong and muscled despite his graying hair. "But I served with praetorians during my tour in Belgium. I learned two things. One, they like to eat. Two, they don't like to sit still. Puts 'em in a bad mood, especially if they're hungry. You said in your message you were conducting interviews all day, so I figured some deep-fried sugar might improve things. Don't want to be at a disadvantage just because I've caught you after a long day when you haven't had time to eat."

"It hasn't been that long," said Mae, but she dared a peek and saw that he had indeed gotten the hazelnut-chocolate kind. "You got my favorite."

"They're everyone's favorite, ma'am."

She smiled. "Tell me about Belgium."

He talked about his time in the military, and Mae found herself caught up in it. The volatile European provinces were an area even she hadn't been to. SCI usually just sent her and Justin around the Americas. Rufus described his experiences in a brisk, no-nonsense way and then listened with intent, narrowed eyes as she described the job's specifics.

"I don't know much about religion," he told her. "Don't really want to. But I know most of the people who practice it are nuts. I think you're being too lax here."

Mae felt her eyebrows rise. "Praetorians and a regular night guard are lax?"

He shrugged. "You say you leave once the kids are at school."

"The schools have security. And we don't have the manpower to keep someone there all the time."

"You don't need to. Just make things unpredictable. I'll show up unexpectedly sometimes, patrol the school grounds. Just so no zealots get complacent. These people don't think in ordinary ways. Neither can we."

He was right about that, and even if he didn't realize just how right he was, Mae appreciated that he was thinking creatively. "You'll already be staying at the house for night shifts—and filling in the gaps for when I don't have praetorian coverage," she warned. "That's a lot of hours."

"What else do I have to do?" he asked dismissively. "Retired, no family. I can't serve my country as a soldier anymore, but I can serve this way. I'm licensed to carry arms, a good shot, and don't mind catching sleep on the run. If I'm fighting to keep religious nutjobs at bay, then I don't mind putting in the hours." He hesitated. "If you can pay me for them."

"Well, I'm not actually the—"

The door opened, and Justin walked in. If he was surprised at all by what he found, he didn't show it. "Oh. Should I have scheduled an appointment?"

"He's the one who'd be paying you," said Mae. Rufus jumped up, and she made introductions. To her surprise, he began peppering Justin with questions about his family and his family's habits. The more she heard, the more she felt Rufus was the right choice. Something about him and the way he thought felt reassuring to her. He was about as close as they'd get to someone qualified to take on the supernatural.

"How big's your budget?" she asked.

Justin sat on the edge of the desk, glancing at Rufus, then back at Mae. "Is he our guy?"

"He's our guy."

The three of them haggled out an hourly rate, one that made Justin wince when he realized just how many hours this could entail. But she knew he could afford it, and she also knew he trusted her. As Mae hashed out some final details with Rufus, Justin took hold of the bakery bag and looked inside.

"Stocked up on your favorite, huh?"

She glanced up in surprise. "How do you know they're my favorite?"

"Anyone who's spent any appreciable time with you knows they're your favorite."

Mae returned her attention to Rufus, who was watching the two of them quizzically. Justin's whole life was about noticing small details, so she supposed it shouldn't surprise her he'd pick up on something like this. It was just that usually, he used his observations to gain some advantage over others.

"So," said Justin, after Rufus left. "That's all that stands between my family and the forces of the unknown?"

Mae immediately dug into the donuts. "Him, some freelancing praetorians, and whatever tricks you've got up your sleeve." She hesitated. "Want one?"

"No thanks. Had a hard enough time getting my stomach to accept coffee this morning."

"It's two o'clock." She stretched out and put her feet back on the desk, figuring he'd be more than forthcoming in telling her to move if he wanted the seat back. For now, he seemed comfortable perched on the desk's corner. "Not really morning. But you look pretty recovered. Hope Lucian is. I'm sure he's got a day of photo ops ahead."

Justin chuckled. "Well, I'm also sure he's got a team of makeup artists who can make him look bright-eyed and bushy-tailed through the worst hangovers." Although his gaze was fixed on the window, Justin seemed to be looking at something much farther away. "Just hope he remembers his promise to get that Darius kid an internship. I honestly thought I wasn't going to get that—or even get out of there last night—if I didn't agree to his scheme."

"Darius's scheme?" asked Mae, puzzled.

"Lucian's. He has this crazy idea that he can sway the polls by going off on some great ambassadorial trip to Arcadia to foster friendship between our countries."

It was enough to make her set the donut down. "I know

praetorians fighting down on the borders in the south. I think we're a long ways from true friendship. That could be a dangerous trip."

"Well, he won't be in the border areas," admitted Justin, "but I agree, it's a risky thing for him to do. He thinks it's worth it, though. Was going on about how there are no heroes anymore and politicians need to act, not just talk."

Mae resumed eating and kept her expression neutral because Justin was probably scrutinizing her reaction to those words. There *was* something particularly inspiring about them, and from what she'd learned about Lucian, he probably meant them. She'd grown to like him in their brief acquaintance, enough that she enjoyed spending time with him but not enough to want to pursue anything particularly intimate. No matter how sincere and passionate he was at times, it was hard to shake that "politician-y" air around him. That wasn't Mae's style, but she certainly wasn't going to let Justin know, both because it was good for him to be in the dark about some things and because he occasionally encouraged her to spend time with Lucian—only to then seem annoyed if she did. She was still trying to figure that out.

"What's crazier still is that he wants us to come with him," continued Justin. "He's got all sorts of cultural experts—and praetorians—going along and thought we'd fit right in."

"Judging from your tone, you refused the invite."

He snorted. "Of course. We've already got plenty of religion to wade through for SCI without getting wrapped up in that autocratic one. Besides, I really have no desire to spend any appreciable time in that backward place. No red velvet flags or wide-brimmed hats for me."

Mae stopped midbite. "Red velvet flags?"

"The Girls' Salons. You know they traffic in women, right?" Mae did. After being ravaged by Mephistopheles, Arcadia had suffered severely from fertility problems, a situation made worse by polygamy. Men desperate for wives went to extreme measures, often stealing children and women from other provinces. "The salons are the places that raise orphan girls. When they've got some girls 'for sale' who have reached puberty, they hang a red velvet flag outside their door." Justin shook his head in disgust. "Fucking barbarians. Makes Panama look like the height of civilization. Oh, plenty of shady stuff went on there with women too, but at least it wasn't a sanctioned part of mainstream society."

Mae, although no longer hungry, bit into another donut to hide her expression. *Red velvet flag.* The vision from last night came back to her, the cloak that had turned into a flag waving in the wind—and the young girl hidden underneath it. A sick feeling welled in Mae's stomach. Was that what had become of her niece? She would only be eight by now, but did she have a future of being sold off as some Arcadian's third wife? Emil, the Morrigan's servant, had hinted about Arcadia, but Mae hadn't truly focused on the reality of her niece being there. And Mae had certainly never thought she herself might have an opportunity to go there.

"Maybe we should join him," she said at last.

Justin's eyebrows rose, but she took no satisfaction in surprising him. "Looking for some extra time with Lucian?"

"No," she scoffed. "But our whole purpose is to seek out divine activity in the world. Arcadia's got a strong religious presence. When are we ever going to get a chance to get in? And be so well guarded?"

"Ah, that's it, isn't it? You're looking for a praetorian getaway, huh? Hoping to sneak some ree in for you and your buddies?"

She held back from rolling her eyes. "Why do you assume there has to be a selfish motive?" she asked. "I'm just saying, if it's something we should eventually look into, maybe we should take this opportunity."

Justin stood up and stifled a yawn. "You say that, but believe me, you wouldn't like Arcadia. Independent, progressive women like you wouldn't really fit in there."

"I think I know something about girls being forced into conservative roles," she reminded him.

"You know something about Gemman girls being forced into

conservative roles. Maybe you had to wear a pink dress and study 'ladies' subjects,' but no one could ever publicly—or privately—beat you with the government's sanction. You can go to school. You can own property. You can vote. Believe me, Mae, we're much better off not going there. Let Lucian make his daring stand. We'll stick to our wild provinces." He moved to the door and rested his hand on its knob. "I'm going to go check in with the illustrious Cornelia. You and your donuts going to stay here?"

Mae nodded wordlessly, too stunned to think of any other response. As Justin shut the door behind him, the image of that red velvet flashed through her mind, and she wondered if she may have just let the door shut on any chance of finding her niece.

## CHAPTER 6

# NO LIVING WITH THEM

Justin left Mae to her donuts and mulled over their conversation as he headed down the hall to Cornelia's office.

*If I didn't know any better, I'd think she wanted to go to Arcadia,* he mused.

*Worried she wants to spend time with Lucian?* asked Horatio.

Justin considered this a moment, analyzing both Mae's reaction and his own insecurities. *No. I don't think so. There's something else.*

*Maybe she needs more danger and excitement,* suggested Horatio.

Justin was skeptical. *We were attacked by a horde of beetles and witnessed a woman being possessed by supernatural forces. How could Mae possibly need more danger and excitement?*

*She's a Valkyrie,* countered Magnus. *She'll always need more danger and excitement.*

*Well, she'll have to find it somewhere else,* Justin told them. *Because we aren't going to Arcadia.*

"Justin." Cornelia Kimora, head of SCI, opened the door to her office just as he was about to knock on it. "Excellent timing. Let's talk about you going to Arcadia."

Justin froze, momentarily disoriented at the lack of transition between internal and external conversations. "I'm sorry, what did you say?"

Cornelia stepped to the side and gestured him in. "Senator Darling's office has been in touch with us this morning about the trip. I initially declined, but they were very insistent. And once Director Kyle heard you were on board—"

"I'm not," exclaimed Justin. "I told Lucian no!"

"Did you?" Cornelia arched an eyebrow. "I admit, I thought it odd that you were so supportive, but then one never can presume what you'll—"

"I'm not supportive! I'm not going."

She pursed her lips in thought, damnably calm, considering the outrageous nature of what they were discussing. "Well, there may be a problem, then, because arrangements have already been made for you and Praetorian Koskinen to accompany the delegation. There's actually a briefing scheduled later today, and they'll be announcing it all to the press this week."

Justin was unmoved. "Well, none of that's happened yet, so there's still time to fix this."

Cornelia fell into thought and absentmindedly tucked her orangey-red hair behind her ears. "Are you so sure this isn't something you should do? We don't know if . . . what's happening here is happening in Arcadia as well. This might be our only chance to find out." Even though she was the head of the department and oversaw Justin's project, she still had difficulty giving voice to anything that lent credence to the supernatural.

"I can respect that," he said, through gritted teeth. Calm was key. This was Lucian's fault, not Cornelia's. "But I'd rather not do it when every single move is being scrutinized as part of some bigger political game I never asked to be a part of. How do you really expect me to get any efficient work done?"

That, an appeal to Cornelia's work ethic and pragmatism, got through. "Well, then, you'd best talk to Director Kyle immediately. He's probably the only one who can stop this."

Justin was already moving toward the door. "Thanks. I'll go upstairs now."

"He's not there today," she called after him. "He's in his other office, in the Citizens' building."

Justin stopped by his own office first, where he found Mae checking messages on her ego, with no donuts left. "I'm going across the square to find Francis Kyle. You won't believe what's fucking happened."

He gave her a brief recap. She listened to it all calmly, not appearing nearly as outraged as she should have—but then, she allegedly wanted danger and excitement. In fact, when he moved to leave, she sprang up after him.

"Justin, wait." She came to stand by him at the door. "Think about this. It's already in motion. There won't be another chance to find out if the game has spread to Arcadia."

"We don't know that it's our only chance," he said. "Maybe Lucian will wow them with his wit and charm so much that we'll open all borders, and then you and I can go investigate with a lot less pressure riding on us."

"Is that what bothers you?" Mae asked, peering up into his eyes. "That Lucian got the better of you here?"

"Lucian's never gotten the better of me in his life. But yes, if you must know, I don't like that he manipulated me and went behind my back. So now I'm going to undo it. Francis Kyle loves me. He'll do whatever I want."

"Wait—" She caught Justin's hand, and he halted more from surprise than any force of hers. "Justin—I . . ." Her remarkable blue-green eyes looked away for several moments and then met his with resolve. "I want to do this. I can't explain it, but I want to. I need to. Please, let this go through. If not for our country—then, I don't know. Do it as . . . as a personal favor to me."

Justin was dumbstruck. In their time together, many things had happened, but he couldn't ever recall her asking for something for herself. As it was, she sometimes grew uncomfortable when he bought her coffee.

"Why?" he demanded. "Why is this so important to you?"

"It just is," she said lamely. "I told you, I can't explain it. Please. *Please.* Do this for me, and I'll try to tell you one day."

While a number of memories from their night together still remained with him, one of the most powerful was a rare show of openness in Mae. Even then, when he'd barely known her, he'd gotten the sense that he was seeing something elusive, that this was a woman who kept herself well guarded and rarely let down those walls to show others what was within. Now, unexpectedly, he was seeing it again, and it unnerved him. Sure, it was very different in feel from what he'd witnessed in the act of passion, but the power of it was still there. What surprised him the most was that it triggered a sense of unworthiness in him. Normally, he thrived on having power over others, on being able to hold knowledge or favors over them. Yet, now all he could wonder about was how a man like him deserved to have a woman like her open up to him.

*Why does she have this effect on me?* he asked the ravens. *Why am I even hesitating? This isn't a small thing, like asking me to pick up dinner tonight.*

*Maybe it's more like organizing massive security for you and your family,* suggested Horatio slyly.

Justin considered. *No. That's big, yes, but getting her friends to pull shifts at my house still isn't on the same level as being part of a highly public entourage that's traipsing into a hostile country.*

*You thrive on attention,* argued Horatio. *Why is the public spotlight a problem? And you're probably safer with all that security there than you are here and on your regular assignments.*

*Why are you so in favor of me going?* Justin asked suspiciously. *Is it because of your obsession with her? Or is this really that relevant to Odin's interests?*

It was Magnus who answered. *You make it sound as though there can only be one reason.*

Before Justin could ponder this further, Mae asked softly, "What are they saying?"

He tuned back in to her. That earlier anxiety was still written on her face, but there was also a small smile as she regarded him. "Hmm?"

"The ravens," she said. "I know that look you get when you're talking to them."

"They . . . they want to go to Arcadia."

"Yeah?" She tilted her head, and though the smile broadened a little, her tension remained. "So are you going to be contrary just to spite them?"

*Good question,* remarked Horatio.

"I—"

Justin was interrupted by a knock at the door. He opened it and found Cornelia, looking understandably surprised to find him and Mae both standing right there. "Director Kyle just came back to the building. If you hurry up to his office, you can catch him."

It was perhaps one of the more considerate things Cornelia had ever done for him, but Justin had no time to expound on her kindness. "I . . ." He glanced back at Mae, and although she'd switched to tough praetorian mode for Cornelia's benefit, he still thought he could see a glimpse of that lingering vulnerability. Filled with resolve, hoping he wasn't being an idiot, he turned back to Cornelia.

"We're going to go. To Arcadia, that is."

Cornelia's only visible sign of surprise was an arching of one orange eyebrow. "Well, then," she said. "That will certainly save a lot of hassle."

"Or create some," he muttered. "What time was that briefing?"

"Six," she said. "In the senate—if you don't change your mind again."

Justin ignored the snide tone and watched her walk away. A light touch on his shoulder made him look back at Mae. There was wonder in her face, wonder and disbelief and a gentleness that was almost as uncharacteristic as the earlier vulnerability—and even more disconcerting.

*Life is easier when she's mad at me,* he suddenly realized.

"Justin," she breathed. "Thank you. I—"

He held up a hand and backed away from her. "Forget it. There'd be no living with you or the ravens. That, and I wouldn't be surprised if SCI did eventually find a need to send us there someday. Better do it now under the comfort of Lucian's banner."

Mae looked dumbfounded. "Then where . . . where are you going now?"

"Gotta check on something. I'll meet you back here in time for the briefing."

He ignored her protests about her coming with him for safety, assuring her that he wasn't going far from Hale Square, which was swarming with federal security. It wasn't his sense of safety that made him urge her to stay behind, however. The truth was, Justin wasn't sure he could handle the face of her gratitude. He'd meant it: Her anger was easier to deal with. He could stay strong against that. But a kinder, gentler Mae . . . one who was looking at him like *that* . . . well, that was too much. It was too great a reminder of what hung over him, that she was the woman Odin had picked out for him, one who held the key to his undoing.

And Justin was honest enough with himself to know why he'd given in to her Arcadia request: because despite all that had fallen out between them, there was still something about her that left him breathless and weak in the knees. He might run away from her regard . . . yet he hypocritically longed for it too. And that longing was strong enough that he'd agreed to the trip without extracting any other promises or badgering her about her reasons.

The ravens' reasons . . . well, that was something he needed to investigate.

He had his ego out before he even reached the elevators. "Call Demetrius Devereaux."

Fifteen minutes later, Justin was in a café two blocks away, finishing a cup of coffee, when his contact arrived. Demetrius Devereaux might have been his legal name, but he called himself Geraki, a name that meant "Hawk," and asked that others did as well. Justin had known him for years because the servitor's office had been trying to implicate him as the leader of an illicit religious group. It was only in the last few months that Justin had finally gotten proof of Geraki's allegiance and the god he served. The problem was that Justin could hardly tell the authorities, seeing as Justin occasionally served the same god now and obtained guidance—often in the form of cryptic messages—from Geraki.

"Justin," said Geraki cheerfully. "So glad you're back. I always worry when you're away, not that I should when you travel in such excellent company." He pulled a bottle of water out of his backpack, some elitist brand with a label declaring it "all-natural," not that water could be much else. Geraki maintained what he said was a pure state of living in order to hear the voice of Odin, abstaining from caffeine, alcohol, women, and pretty much anything else fun. "I knew you'd be back this time, though. I have a message for you. From our master."

Justin sighed and slouched into his chair. "I had a feeling you might. That's why I called you."

Geraki tsked. "If you would just fully commit to our god, he would speak to you himself. You wouldn't have to wait for me or your feathered intermediaries."

Justin glanced around the crowded coffee shop uneasily. "Don't say that word."

" 'Feathered'?"

"You know which word. And I don't want him talking to me directly. I have no desire to go through the rigors you do."

Geraki straightened up in his chair. "I'm a prophet. I not only hear his voice, I may call upon it—a privilege which is not given lightly. You, as a priest, don't have such easy access, but he would speak to you in dreams if you'd only be more cooperative. Or you could be gifted with some relic to facilitate communication."

"Well, we can have that discussion for the hundredth time some other day. Tell me what the message about Arcadia is."

Geraki raised his eyebrows. "Arcadia? Ah, that makes sense. The vision that came to me last night was that you'd be going into a hostile land and that you would not be going alone."

"I know that," snapped Justin, irritated as always at the asinine nature of prophecies. "What I want to know is what *he* finds so interesting there. The ravens support the trip, so I assume *he* has an ulterior motive."

"It's Thought and Memory that have driven you to me, hmm? Well, they do know our master's mind."

*Flattering,* said Magnus. *But no one can truly know it. We are simply more privileged with insight than you two.*

Justin didn't bother correcting Geraki. "Was there anything else? Basically what you described could be any of my other jobs. What's so special about this one, aside from the magnitude?"

Geraki shook his head. "That's not for me to know—or even deal with. Our master has left it to you. He says there is a force there that threatens his plans and that you must eliminate it."

"Eliminate it?" Justin nearly dropped his cup. "I accept that I might be able to sneak in some investigations to check out the religious scene there, but I'm certainly not there to make some decisive strike."

Geraki met his gaze levelly. "He says it affects our country as well. If you feel no loyalty to him yet, surely that will persuade you."

"Those types of threats are for people like Mae and the other military to deal with. I'm there to observe—nothing more. Unless, by chance, you have any specific details about this threat?"

Geraki shook his head, which didn't surprise Justin in the least, and then said almost hesitantly, "In my vision, I saw a golden eagle."

Justin waited expectantly, but nothing else came. "That's not particularly helpful."

*I don't suppose that means anything to you guys?* he asked the ravens.

*No,* admitted Horatio. *Except that eagles are arrogant.*

*And,* added Magnus, *that if Odin sent his prophet a vision about it, it is a dire matter, one you should be taking seriously.*

*Give me more details, and we'll talk.*

But the ravens had none to give, and Justin could only write it all off as another part of the frustration of working with gods.

"At least go in prepared," Geraki told him. "Have your weapons ready."

"I don't use weapons either," said Justin.

"You know what I mean," Geraki told him. "You've learned many of Odin's secrets from me, from the ravens."

It was true to a certain extent. In the last couple of months, Justin had unwillingly received a crash course in Odin's lore and the Nordic runes: the mystical symbols his followers used for both guidance and spell casting. It was part of the oath Justin had taken to learn such things, and his quick mind couldn't help but take it in. But he'd gone out of his way not to put what he'd learned into any sort of practical application, aside from the charm that had hidden him as one of the elect in Nassau.

"Learning isn't the same as practicing," said Justin. "And I'm doing just fine with the former."

Geraki sighed and crossed his muscled arms over his equally bulky chest. "Then you're a fool. If a god told me I was walking into danger, I'd take every precaution necessary."

"I don't need him to tell me. And I've got more faith in our military than him, I'm afraid."

"You're a fool," Geraki repeated.

The words had little effect on Justin, seeing as he heard them pretty regularly during their meetings. Geraki always spoke them with a kind of grudging fondness, though, as if Justin were simply an unruly child. After a few more ominous words from Geraki, Justin was able to ascertain that the other man truly knew nothing more about Arcadia. The ravens didn't either, save that Odin had a task in mind. Satisfied he'd get nothing else, Justin took another cup of coffee to go and then headed back to his office to meet up with Mae for the briefing.

Fortunately, she was back in business mode and made no mention of her earlier pleadings or subsequent gratitude. Over in the senate, they were led to a conference room filled with a dozen men and women in suits and several black-uniformed praetorians. Mae didn't let down her guard as she and Justin took seats near the end of a long table, but he saw her flash a smile to many of the praetorians, who smiled in return. Conversation buzzed around them in small clusters, with no one really taking charge of the meeting. It wasn't until ten minutes after the start time that Lucian burst in with aides and security trailing in his wake. He beamed at the room with his trademark smile.

"Sorry I'm late," he said. "Got waylaid by some lobbyists who just couldn't seem to understand that our country's security was more important than setting up a golf date."

There were polite chuckles around the room, and from the shining eyes of some of them, Justin found it hard to believe Lucian had anything to worry about in the polls. These people were eating out of his hand.

A man named Atticus Marley soon took charge—after making sure Lucian was comfortable, of course—and Justin learned he was the closest the RUNA had to an ambassador in Arcadia. He'd been instrumental in many negotiations and was an expert in the country's culture and social systems. Lucian might have been the mascot in their party, but Atticus was the unofficial leader and guide. Most of the suits in the room were advisers staying in the RUNA, and he introduced them to the other key personnel who'd actually be traveling to Arcadia. One was a man named Phil Ramirez, who would be working on some technology and trade issues as a sign of goodwill toward the Arcadians. The other man, named George Yi, was posing as a professor of comparative cultural arts but was, in reality, a military analyst hoping to spy out any illicit doings on the Arcadian side. He seemed pleasantly surprised that Justin was, in fact, a real religion expert.

"Here," said Atticus, turning on a screen at the front of the room, "is where we'll be staying. Although there are inns and hotels in Arcadia, it's considered bad form to put high-profile guests there." A satellite image appeared, showing a top-down view of a cluster of buildings around some land covered in yellowing grass. He chuckled as he glanced back at the group. "So you can take pride in being shown this regard."

Phil Ramirez looked dubious. "I'd rather have a high-rise with room service."

Justin silently concurred. The compound looked like a glorified farm to him, and he listened as Atticus explained that their host was a high-ranking government official who'd go to the trouble of displacing his wives and children in order to accommodate them.

"Wives?" asked George Yi. "And here I thought that was just something out of the movies."

"Not among the more powerful members of Arcadian society," said Atticus. "They can afford multiple wives and concubines. Some among the lower classes have the brute force to kidnap them."

One of the praetorians crossed her arms. "What's the difference between a wife and a concubine?"

"Alimony?" suggested Phil.

"Not far off," said Atticus. "A wife is forever in Arcadia—barring rare examples of divorce. A man has certain obligations to provide for her and her children, though you'll find some fulfill those responsibilities questionably. Wives are also afforded a certain status and protection. Concubines are more transient. Sex and other labor only. A man can share or sell his concubine. He can sell her children. And although an Arcadian wife has few rights, as we view them, a concubine has even less." His eyes fell on Mae and the other three praetorian women in turn. "And you, I'm afraid, are going to be fulfilling the roles of concubines."

"I beg your pardon?" demanded another praetorian woman.

Atticus actually flushed. "I should be clearer. You'll be, uh, playacting. Not actually performing any duties. The gender disparity you're seeing here isn't an accident." He nodded to Lucian, Phil, George, and Justin. "They—and myself—are the principal players on this trip. This is what the Arcadians will expect. It wouldn't even occur to them that important, powerful diplomats would be anything but men. And, although their military will certainly outnumber ours, they also would expect us to show up with our own protection—which is what you gentlemen and a number of regulars will be doing." That was to a group of praetorian men.

"Where do we fit in with our 'playacting' then?" asked the first praetorian woman.

"Arcadians would consider it perfectly normal for high-powered men to travel with concubines. Not wives—at least not into dangerous territories. But they figure men have needs, and if a man can bring his concubine along, then why not?" Atticus let his rhetorical question hang for a few moments. "Having the praetorians pose as concubines will provide an extra level of security behind closed doors when we aren't out on official business. You can stay in our bedrooms all night, awake, on guard."

Mae leaned forward. "Two questions. First: They must know we don't have the same social order as they do with these wives and concubines. Won't they think it's suspicious if we show up matching their customs?"

Atticus smiled. "Yes, they know we don't have that same formal structure, but they also know we have much looser mores when it comes to sex outside of marriage. Honestly, they all think we're sinners and whores, and if we're traveling with women for sex, then the Arcadians have an easier time accepting those women as part of the concubine system. That makes them controllable property."

"I see," said Mae, hiding any distaste she might have felt. "But even if the Arcadians don't have women in their military, they must know we do in ours. Don't you think it might occur to them that maybe we're playing them and sending trained soldiers undercover?"

"Some might," he agreed. "But they won't take you seriously. No offense." He narrowed his eyes as he regarded Mae, seeming to truly notice her. "You're a patrician, praetorian? Some northern European group?"

"Nordic," she said warily. "Why?"

"The group makes no difference. It's more your recessive genes I'm noticing—and the Arcadians will as well. They had no pre-vaccine defense against Mephistopheles, and Cain runs rampant among them. A woman with your coloring who's also so—pardon me—attractive will draw attention." He glanced at the other praetorian women and frowned. "Honestly, in my opinion, you're all too attractive for this mission, plebeian or patrician. A healthy brunette might not be as rare as a healthy blonde, but you're all going to be head and shoulders above many Arcadian women."

"Worried the Arcadians will steal our women?" asked Justin.

Atticus didn't laugh at the joke. "This group of women? Not without a fight. But I'd rather you four didn't attract any unnecessary attention. I don't suppose we could find any praetorians marked with Cain? No, I don't suppose such a thing even exists." He sighed and focused back on Mae. "At the very least, it might be worth swapping you out for a plebeian. We're waiting to get another woman assigned to us as it is. I could ask for two."

Justin stiffened in his chair and sensed a similar reaction in Mae as well. This whole ordeal he'd gone through for her would be worthless if she got cut from the mission. "No. Praetorian Koskinen has to go. I need her. That is, she's not just here for security. She's also essential to my work specifically."

Phil frowned. "What exactly *is* your work? Are you seriously here just to learn about religion?"

"It's classified," said Justin. "Internal Security stuff."

*It sounds so official when you put it like that,* said Horatio.

That pleased Phil, who seemed to read it as a subtle way of saying Justin was some sort of ballistics expert planning strikes against Arcadia. That seemed to be much more reasonable than anyone being truly interested in local culture. Atticus looked unconvinced, but Lucian preempted whatever protests he might have made.

"Best not to interfere with Internal Security's plans," he said. "And I've seen Praetorian Koskinen's work in the past. I don't think we need to worry about some ill-behaved man doing something she doesn't want."

Justin wondered if that was a subtle reference to Lucian's own lack of success with Mae. If so, he seemed to be taking it with good humor. Mae had on her usual poker face, and Justin couldn't help but think that whatever reason Odin had had for having Justin encourage the two to go out, it apparently wasn't strong enough to have an effect on her.

*Maybe she's not the one who matters,* suggested Horatio.

*You're saying Odin just wants Lucian hooked on her? Why?*

*Might be a handy thing having a politician dancing at your every command,* said the raven.

*I wouldn't say it's gone that far or that Mae's encouraging it,* said Justin. *And she doesn't serve Odin, so how can he reap the benefit?*

The birds had no answer, and Justin focused back on Atticus, who'd given up his protests about Mae and was finishing off his outline of the mission specifics. Since it was supposed to be a friendly diplomatic mission, the majority of the time would be spent with Justin and the other key men being shown around relevant sites—together or separately—in Arcadia while they tried to gather as much intel as possible. Justin thought that would wrap up the briefing, but then another touch of the screen initiated a presentation titled "Arcadian Culture and Customs."

"The mission details are easy," Atticus told them grimly. "Now comes the hard part. Sit back, get comfortable, and forget everything you know about civility."

# CHAPTER 7

# HARD-LUCK CASES

D arius was only the first surprising person Tessa found waiting for her after school the next day. He was standing outside the cushioned room that creative thinkers used to brainstorm their independent projects. Actually, it was more like he was slouching outside of it. Each time she saw him, Tessa was kind of amazed that he managed to get around as well as he did. He seemed to be all arms and legs sometimes, and no encounter went by without his stumbling at least once. But he straightened up effortlessly now, a smile lighting his face.

"Hey," he said.

"Hey," she said.

They stood there in a moment of awkward silence as her classmates moved around them. Darius cleared his throat. "Are you doing anything right now? Do you want to go get coffee?"

Tessa had two immediate reactions. The first was relief that he was asking for coffee. That was something she understood. On the rare occasions she did get asked out socially by classmates, it was usually to eat Asian food, something she was still coming to terms with. The RUNA's culture was so inextricably tied to that of its sister country, the EA, that Asian cuisine was pretty ubiquitous. Although she'd made great strides in differentiating Chinese, Japanese, and Thai cuisine, chopsticks still remained an embarrassing social experience for her. But coffee? Coffee she could handle.

Once she'd accepted that, her next reaction was wariness. Every time Darius wanted to talk to her, it was to ask for something. What could he possibly want from her now? She was pretty sure she couldn't get any more favors out of Justin. Darius didn't seem like the type who wanted to hang out with her just for the novelty of gawking at a provincial, but maybe she was mistaken. Whatever his reasons were, she couldn't guess them and was too polite to make up a lie to decline. That, and her curiosity got the better of her yet again.

"Okay," she said. The two of them began walking toward the stairs. "But someone'll have to come with us."

"Who?" asked Darius, looking understandably perplexed.

"Ah, well . . . um, after what happened last time you were over . . ." Tessa paused, not that there could be any question of which incident she was referring to. "Well, after that, Justin got security for us. I'm not really supposed to go out without a body-guard, so he should be waiting for me downstairs."

Darius looked impressed. "You have your own bodyguard?"

"We kind of share a group of them," she explained, blushing. "Today I'm with a guy named Rufus. He seems okay."

Tessa had only met him this morning. He'd said very little on the ride to school, which she'd liked. It was a nice change from Mae's praetorian friends. Rufus might not have had a reflex-enhancing implant in him, but she would gladly go without that extra protection in order not to be constantly reminded of the Miscreant Terrorist Girls' Reform Camp.

Only, it wasn't Rufus who greeted Tessa when she reached the bottom of the stairs. A woman she didn't know was standing there, one whom Tessa's eyes initially passed over until she did a double take and saw the stranger staring pointedly at her.

She strode up to Tessa on five-inch heels that were a perfect match for the tight red blazer and skirt she wore. A plunging neck-line showed ample cleavage and left one to wonder if there was anything on underneath it. The woman's lacquer lipstick was the same shade of red, providing a bright contrast to her dark eyes and wavy hair. She held out a hand to Tessa and smiled with gleaming white teeth.

"You must be Teresa," she said. "You look just like your picture, except dressed better. You ready to go?"

Tessa came to a halt. "Go where? Who are you?"

The woman's eyebrows rose. "I figured they would've told you. Or that you would've recognized me." She waited for a response from Tessa and then glanced at Darius. Both shook their heads. "I'm Daphne Lang." There was an expectant tone in her voice, like her name should've meant something. After a few more moments, the woman threw up her hands in frustration. "Really? Nothing?"

Tessa shook her head again. "I'm sorry."

"Everything okay here?"

Rufus came strolling up to them, hands in his pockets and body language casual. But his eyes were fixed sharply on Daphne, and Tessa realized he'd probably been waiting down here and watching the whole time.

"Who are you?" Daphne asked.

"He's with me," said Tessa. "My, uh, bodyguard. Rufus."

Daphne looked more impatient than anything else. "Fine. The more the merrier. Let's go."

"But I don't know who you are!" exclaimed Tessa.

"I told you, I'm Daphne Lang." Daphne darted a quick glance at a still-wary Rufus, but if her name sparked any recognition with him, he didn't show it. She sighed. "Look, do you want an internship or not? I didn't come all the way down here for the hell of it. I figured a kid like you at a school like this was serious."

"I . . ." Tessa faltered. "I am, but I never asked for an internship. I was just supposed to shadow someone."

Daphne shook her head. "No half-ass shadowing with me. You want to learn the reporter business? You're doing the full deal. You come down to my office, you go out on assignments with me, run errands, help do research. All of it. *If* I approve you, that is. That's what today is about. I need to get to know you, figure out what you're like and where you come from. Not just anyone can work for North Prime."

North Prime? Actually, from what Tessa had learned in her inundation of Gemman media, anyone could work for North Prime. The entertainment portion of the RUNA's media stream contained a vast selection of channels with both on-demand and live programming. Mixed in with that were myriad news options, some more reputable than others. The more prestigious ones had regular journalists who were celebrities in their own right. Other media news channels—like North Prime—were built on sensationalism and allowed freelance journalists to file stories with them on a first-come, first-served basis. Tessa had only watched a little of their programming but suspected she could upload a video to them herself and probably have it accepted.

Darius clutched Tessa's arm, earning a warning look from Rufus. "Tessa, this is amazing! It's even more than you asked for. You should totally do it." She wondered if he simply appreciated any educational opportunity or just had poor taste in news. Before she could respond, he added, "You'll get a pass now to be out of school."

She slowly turned to him. "What?"

"Didn't they explain it?" he asked. "If you've got a full internship, you don't have to be here during prescribed hours. You've still got to show proof you're up on your independent projects—this'll sub in for one—and your tests, but they figure the real-world experience trumps their schedule."

Tessa regarded Daphne with new appreciation. Was it possible that this garishly dressed woman might offer even more freedom than the institute's free-form policies already did? Rufus cleared his throat loudly, interrupting her thoughts.

"I don't want to trample anyone's dreams here, but do we have any proof of who you are?" he asked. "And I don't mean just looking up whatever fluff you've been working on." Rufus, apparently, *was* up to speed on his news channels. "I mean, do we have any evidence that you've actually been authorized by the school to approach her?"

"Approach her?" asked Daphne with a chuckle. "Is she provincial royalty?"

But he was right, Tessa realized. The attack at the house should have had her on high alert around every new person she met. If someone had been enraged enough at Justin to go to his house and threaten her, wasn't it just as likely someone might go and stage a scam internship to lure her into danger?

A check with the school's field experience office verified that Daphne's offer was legitimate. She'd been vetted and passed a background check. The only irregularity was that she was offering a much larger opportunity than the one the school had advertised for on Tessa's behalf. When Rufus grilled Daphne on this, she simply shrugged and reiterated, "I don't half-ass things."

And so, Tessa found herself agreeing to the opportunity, though Daphne was quick to emphasize that *she* still had to accept Tessa. "It's not so much an interview as it is the chance to see if we can work together," she explained. "You hungry? I'm hungry. Why don't we go talk over sushi?"

Tessa winced. "Do you have a second choice?"

"You don't like sushi?" asked Daphne. The tone of her voice made Tessa wonder if this could make or break the internship.

"I just had it yesterday, that's all," she lied.

"We'll do Greek then." Daphne's voice offered no argument, and she gave Rufus and Darius a once-over. "Does your entourage have to come?"

"Rufus does," said Tessa firmly. "Darius . . ." Looking at him, she faltered and suddenly felt like an idiot. He'd asked her out first today, and she'd completely rolled over his invitation and taken on a new one. Admittedly, he *had* been instrumental in urging her to do so.

Daphne, either impatient or hungry or both, shrugged and turned abruptly on her high heels. "Makes no difference to me. Let's go." Tessa meekly followed, and after a few moments, so did the men.

Daphne claimed it wasn't an interview, but it certainly felt like one as their afternoon meal proceeded. Actually, "interrogation" might have been a more accurate term. Daphne managed to quiz Tessa about every part of her childhood and subsequent arrival in the RUNA while effortlessly going through a plate of souvlaki. Tessa had found a lot of Gemmans displayed mixed feelings about her provincial history, but Daphne took it in stride. "Well, I'm willing to give this a shot if you are," she told Tessa.

"Don't you need a parent or guardian's signature before starting work?" asked Rufus.

Tessa nodded, recalling the forms she'd filled out. "We can do it remotely."

"Too impersonal," declared Daphne. "Let's go over to your place and meet this servitor who took you under his wing. We'll make sure he's doubly okay with you working for me, and I'll make sure I'm not indirectly getting involved with some political dissident."

"Why in the world would you think that?" exclaimed Tessa.

"He was kicked out of the country," said Daphne.

"We don't know that for sure." The mystery of Justin's exile in Panama was still exactly that: a mystery. "Besides, if he's back, he can't be in that much trouble."

"Maybe he just has powerful friends." Daphne waited for confirmation, but Tessa refused to play along. "Well, whatever the reasons, we need his signature, so let's head out and find him."

Tessa glanced at the time. "I don't know if he's home. But his sister can sign anything from the school too."

"That'll work." Daphne brought up the table's panel and requested a split bill. "Just so you know, even when you're officially working for me, you cover your own expenses."

And so, the bewildering day proceeded with Tessa taking Daphne (and the others) back to the suburbs to meet the March family. The train was crowded with commuters, leaving standing room only. Tessa made herself small near a window, casting occasional nervous looks at both Darius and Daphne—who unnerved her for completely different reasons.

"Be careful," a voice murmured in Tessa's ear.

She flinched, startled to find Rufus right beside her. "With what?"

"Her." Rufus's eyes stared at the window as he kept his voice low. "She hasn't written a single word down, no notes. Even for an intern's interview, that's weird for someone who works in the information business. That means she's probably recording everything."

The idea had never occurred to Tessa. She gulped. "I didn't say anything incriminating . . . did I?"

"No, but you're bringing her into the house of someone who works for Internal Security. We'll have to make sure she doesn't leave with any info she shouldn't."

"I . . . I'll see what I can do," stammered Tessa.

Rufus glanced down at her and winked. "Don't worry. I'll take care of it."

He made good on his point by checking Daphne over for surveillance equipment before they crossed the threshold into the March house. Along with a physical check, he also had a device he could scan her with. Daphne acted affronted but, to Tessa's surprise, did actually turn out to be wearing a microphone.

"Standard journalistic practice," she insisted.

"And removing it is standard practice before entering the home of a government official," Rufus told her sweetly.

It was actually a relief to Tessa to find that only Cynthia and Quentin were home. Daphne still peppered Cynthia with questions, including specifics about Justin and any "powerful friends."

"I have no idea what my brother does all day," Cynthia snapped. "It's a boring government job. And Tessa has nothing to do with any of that anyway—not that it should matter if you just need an intern to get you coffee or whatever. Explain again all she'll be doing. I want to understand it before I sign anything."

This put Daphne on the defensive, quick to protect herself and the golden opportunity she presented. Tessa, watching the two women go back and forth at the kitchen table, was simply glad to have the pressure taken off her. Rufus relieved a praetorian who'd been hanging around the house and then joined Quentin in front of the living room screen, ostensibly out of the way but still easily accessible. That left Tessa standing alone with Darius.

"This is so weird," she said. "Did you have to go through all of this for an internship?"

He shook his head. "No. At least not yet. The senate's human resources department sent me a questionnaire and then wants me to come in to talk about finding the best placement. I never would've gotten fast-tracked like that without your help."

"I didn't do anything," said Tessa, feeling shy. "And you were the one who did all the work with that guy."

Darius grinned. "I don't want to do it again, though. I'll leave the heroics to Rufus and your praetorians."

Daphne almost had Cynthia on the verge of signing the permission document when Justin came home with Mae. He raised an eyebrow at Darius and came to a complete standstill over Daphne. She leapt to her high-heeled feet and glided over to him, extending a hand.

"You must be Dr. March. It's a pleasure to meet you," she oozed.

Justin gave her a quick head-to-toe assessment that lingered on her short skirt and then put on the smile he usually reserved for pretty women. "Likewise, Miss . . . ?"

"Lang. Daphne Lang."

Again, Tessa heard that expectant tone in her voice, like she was hoping to be recognized. Cynthia saved him the trouble of further fact-finding.

"She's a North Prime reporter who wants to adopt Tessa," said Cynthia. In her periphery, Tessa saw Rufus sidle up to Mae and whisper in her ear.

Justin's hand dropped, as did his smile. "No. Tessa is not going to be the subject of some poor-provincial-girl-in-the-big-city piece for that crap news channel."

A slight pursing of the lips was Daphne's only sign of irritation at all about her employer's being called a "crap news channel."

"That's not why I'm here at all. She sought me out, through her school's internship program."

Justin shot Tessa a surprised look. "You applied for an internship? You . . . want to be a reporter?"

"Not exactly," she said. "I mean, I don't know. It just kind of happened."

The story tumbled out in bits and pieces, put together by both Daphne and Tessa. Justin shook his head in exasperation when they finished. "Maybe you should see if another news channel bites," he said.

"North Prime puts out some very excellent pieces," Daphne said stiffly. "This is a big opportunity for her."

"I'd rather she just sat at a desk for a whole class period and actually listened to a lecture or something," said Justin. "I don't like all this experiential stuff."

"It's not a bad idea," said Cynthia. "The internship, I mean. I've always thought real-world experience can carry more weight than classroom learning."

"That's because you—" Justin wisely bit off his words and turned back to Daphne. "Look, if you want Tessa to be your errand girl, I want a different document that *you'll* sign saying you won't turn her story into trashy entertainment."

Daphne pouted, but Tessa could tell she wasn't truly offended. "You really think that's why I'm here? Fine, I'll sign whatever you like."

Mae strode forward and stood at his side, fixing Daphne with a stare that chilled the room. "I'm sure it'll take time for their lawyer to draw that up. The family will be in touch when everything's ready for signing, so that should wrap things up for now." There was no need to voice the unspoken *Now get out* at the end of her words.

The come-hither look Daphne had used on Justin turned into something much harder as she sized up Mae. "I don't believe we've met. You are . . . ?"

"Praetorian Mae Koskinen. Dr. March's bodyguard."

Daphne arched an eyebrow and then glanced at Justin. "Everyone's got a bodyguard around here. And you have a formidable one . . . for a boring government job."

Justin looked a little surprised to hear her using Cynthia's earlier wording but didn't comment on it. "Just precautionary diligence on the government's part."

Quentin's voice suddenly piped up from the living room. "Uncle Justin? You're on the news!"

Everyone's head swiveled toward the screen. There, one of the RUNA's most famous journalists—who worked for a far more prestigious network than North Prime—was reporting on Senator Lucian Darling's just-announced trip to Arcadia.

"The senator, as part of a gesture of goodwill and desire to exchange ideas with the Arcadians, will be accompanied by a number of cultural experts," the reporter was saying as several headshots—including Justin's—were displayed on the screen. "Atticus Marley, special diplomatic envoy to Arcadia. Professor George Yi of the comparative culture department at Vancouver University. Dr. Justin March, IS servitor and former instructor of religious studies. Phil Ramirez, international trade expert and analyst."

The scene cut to live footage of Lucian Darling standing gallantly on the senate steps, holding a press conference. "It is our hope," he was saying, "that by showing our willingness to learn about their culture, the Arcadians will in turn be more open to learning about ours, thus helping forge new connections and ease hostilities between our nations." When one of the attending journalists asked about the danger the trip involved for him, especially during election season, Lucian simply smiled and shook his head. He launched into what Tessa could tell was a well-prepared statement on how it was more important to take a risk for his country's well-being than stay safe on the campaign trail.

"He's so, so good," murmured Daphne.

The reporters at the senate erupted in questions. Back in the March house, Justin muttered something uncomplimentary, and

Cynthia shot him an outraged look. "When the hell were you going to tell me?"

He sighed. "In a quiet moment, without reporters. Anywhere."

Cynthia, eyes wide, turned back to the screen as Lucian fielded another question about the risks of traveling into Arcadia. "It's crazy! It doesn't matter what nonsense he's touting about bravery to the country!"

"It's a very public expedition," said Justin calmly. "It wouldn't be worth the fallout for them or us to screw it up. Besides, with Lucian around, I'll even have more protection than I do on my regular trips. Nothing can happen."

"You don't go to places as bad as Arcadia on your regular trips!" Cynthia exclaimed. When Justin didn't respond, she turned even more incredulous. "Do you? Where the hell do you go?"

"Where do you think I go when I say I'm leaving the country?"

"I don't know!" She threw up her hands. "The EA. Panama. It's state business. I didn't think I should ask too many questions. Maybe I should have."

"When are you—and Lucian—coming back?" asked Daphne.

Mae, clearly not liking what she saw as an outsider poking into family business, swiftly moved to the reporter's side. "Miss Lang, I think it's time you go. As I said, someone will be in touch with you about the paperwork. I'll walk you to the door now." Mae's voice was perfectly polite, but Tessa could sense the praetorian steel within. Daphne apparently could as well.

"I'll find my own way out," said Daphne stiffly. "But thank you, praetorian."

"I insist," said Mae.

She and Daphne locked eyes, igniting a battle of wills that left everyone uneasy. Tessa admired that Daphne even managed a fighting chance, but ultimately, it seemed Mae would win since she could literally throw the other woman out of the house. Tessa took a tentative step forward.

"I'll walk Daphne out. I brought her here. It's only polite."

Mae's sharp gaze turned on Tessa, apparently to ponder whether or not Tessa could be trusted to make sure Daphne actually left. After several long moments, Mae gave a nod. Daphne made simpering farewells to Justin and Cynthia—though both were too preoccupied to really hear them—and then let Tessa lead her to the door.

"Well," she told Tessa when they were alone. "I guess that answers my question about Dr. March having 'powerful friends.'" She paused eloquently. "And just between you and me, I think there's some serious family dysfunction going on around here."

"That's an understatement," said Tessa wearily, opening the door. "But thank you for your time."

Daphne crooked her a grin and leaned against the side of the doorway. "Such finality. I really hope you'll get your paperwork in order and come work with me, because you can have the position if you want it. Your benefactor may roll his eyes at North Prime, and that castal praetorian can glare all she wants, but here's the truth. You aren't going to get a lot of people answering Creative Minds' ad for you. They spell out that you're provincial, and not many people are going to go for that. They won't even think you can speak English."

Tessa flinched. She'd gotten so used to the acceptance at Creative Minds that she'd nearly forgotten the prejudice toward provincials that she'd experienced in other schools. She'd run into enough of it in the RUNA, however, to know that Daphne's words weren't entirely made up as part of some sales pitch.

"Why don't you have a problem with provincials then?" Tessa asked. "Do you really want to do a story on me and my great transition?"

"Nope. And I'll sign what you need to prove it." Daphne leaned forward. "You want to know why I answered your ad? It's because I grew up in an annexed region, and even after those places become Gemman, it's only marginally less difficult to make something of yourself in the 'real' RUNA than it is coming from the provinces." She chucked Tessa's chin. "That, and I like hard-luck cases."

"You sound like Justin," muttered Tessa.

"How so?"

"Half the reason he brought me here is because he felt like he owed my father. The other half is because Justin said I reminded him of him. He grew up in a bad-off area and got some sort of lucky break."

Daphne grinned. "See? We're meant to work together. I'll be in touch."

And with that, she headed out the door, off down the suburban sidewalk in those red heels. Tessa watched her go until she was out of sight, taking it on faith that Daphne would go toward the transit station and not double back around and spy on the house, like Mae and Rufus seemed to think she would. Of course, Mae had also made sure all the peripheral security sensors and cameras were working and updated, so there probably wasn't any way Daphne could've staged espionage—if that truly was her goal.

When Tessa returned to the kitchen, she found Justin and Cynthia wrapping up an argument about his trip that neither seemed satisfied with. In just a few seconds, Tessa picked up that Cynthia had asked him to drop out, and he'd refused. She pressed her hands to the sides of her head and groaned.

"I don't want to talk about this anymore. I'm so upset, I can't even cook." With that unprecedented statement, she stormed off to her room.

"Looks like delivery," said Justin, watching her go. When he noticed Tessa, his expression turned wry. "And you. You brought a reporter under my roof."

"I didn't really expect a family argument," said Tessa. "Besides, it's not like that Arcadian news was top secret."

He exchanged a pained look with Mae. "True. I thought they were going to wait a couple of days before releasing it," he said. "But look, if you really are crazy enough to want to work with a reporter, wait for someone else from a better channel."

"Daphne doesn't think there'll be anyone else," said Tessa. She told them what Daphne had said about Tessa's being provincial, both how Daphne found it endearing and how others wouldn't. Justin and Mae exchanged looks again, this time of a different nature that Tessa couldn't interpret.

"She's not wrong," said Rufus, from the living room.

Justin was silent for several moments, then he sighed again and began rummaging through the wine cabinet. "Fine. You can work with her if you want, but not before she signs a nondisclosure agreement about your life story. And for God's sake, don't bring her back in this house again."

Tessa nodded and turned around, noticing then that Darius was still there, leaning against the wall. She groaned. "I'm so sorry about all of this. About blowing off coffee and everything else. Come on—I'll walk you out too, and maybe we can reschedule. Again—I'm really sorry."

"Don't be," he said, as she led him to the door. "One thing I'll say for sure: It's never boring when I come over here."

# CHAPTER 8

# A WARM WELCOME

M ae didn't retrieve the amber knife until the morning of their flight to Arcadia. She'd wavered on whether she wanted it back at all. In the past week, she'd replayed every detail of the vision she'd had in the living room, trying to make sense of it. She couldn't write it off as a dream because praetorians didn't sleep. They could, apparently, be overpowered by divine forces and made to "see" things they didn't want to. And no matter how much Mae wished that wasn't true, there was no denying it had happened . . . and that she had let that cryptic vision drive her to coerce Justin into a trip he hadn't wanted.

His agreeing to it was almost as unbelievable as the vision itself. She'd seen his face and knew him well enough to recognize that he truly hadn't wanted any part of the diplomatic mission. Whether that was because of Lucian or Arcadia or some other factor, she couldn't say. All she knew was that he'd agreed—for her—and that made her feel a mix of guilt . . . and unwelcome affection. Whenever she tried to bring up the favor, even to express small thanks, he gruffly made it clear that it wasn't anything he wanted to discuss further.

And it was that frustration—that she couldn't properly repay him or even convey her gratitude—that drove Mae to bring the dagger to Arcadia. Part of her wanted to believe she needed no more divine assistance. She had the information she'd received from Emil and the vision . . . would that be enough? Mae couldn't say for sure, and if it were only herself she was inconveniencing, maybe she'd have taken the risk. But after forcing Justin to so radically alter his plans, she felt obligated to do everything she could to follow through on the sketchy leads to her niece—even if he knew nothing about it.

"Did you just get that from the basket?"

Mae turned in surprise from where she'd just replaced the knife's basket back on its shelf. Justin had just entered the living room, coffee cup in hand. It was early, and the rest of the family was still waking up, but the two of them were dressed and ready to rendezvous with Lucian's party soon.

She slipped the blade back into its usual place in her boot. "I took it out overnight and wanted it somewhere Quentin wouldn't find it," she lied. "Do you think they'll let me bring it into Arcadia?"

"I'd say so. They're letting the uniformed military bring in guns—with restrictions. Probably figure a sweet, innocent woman like you couldn't possibly cause any damage with a knife."

Mae grinned at that and briefly toyed with trying to thank him again for his part in their upcoming trip. After a moment, she decided against it. He was in as good a mood as she was going to get, and there was no point in spoiling that. Besides, as the rest of the family trickled into the kitchen, there was no time for the two of them anymore. After a week of battling her brother, Cynthia had finally resigned herself to his going.

"Make sure you come back this time," she grumbled, resting her head on his chest when they hugged good-bye. "No more four-year sabbaticals."

"Stop being melodramatic," he told her. "Nothing's going to happen. Besides, I'm sure Lucian can talk us out of any trouble. And if anything *does* happen, you won't have to worry about finances."

Cynthia groaned. "I knew it. I knew you were preparing for the worst."

Mae, feeling as though she were intruding, turned from them and pretended to be interested in checking security features on the house's windows. Little did Cynthia know that Justin had made arrangements for her and Quentin a while ago. When he'd first returned from Panama, he hadn't known if he'd be exiled again and had made sure his assets would be accessible to her in the event of a temporary or permanent disappearance. He'd made further arrangements once he'd accepted the responsibilities of his new job and its frequent provincial travel. Cynthia really had no idea that Arcadia wasn't the first dangerous place he'd frequented these last few months.

Hearing Tessa's voice, Mae dared a glance back and saw the girl hugging Justin for her own good-bye. *How is he like that?* Mae wondered, watching him wrap up Tessa in his arms. *So selfish and pleasure-driven most of the time, yet completely devoted to them.* Because no matter how much he tried to hide it, she knew he was feeling emotional at the good-byes as well. And although Mae didn't know the exact details, she was willing to bet anything that Justin had set aside some pretty generous resources for Tessa too, in the event something happened to him.

"Everyone's so grim for an adventure that's supposed to usher in an era of peace between us and Arcadia," Mae heard Rufus say.

She smiled as she found him standing behind her. He had an uncanny, stealthy way of moving that rivaled a praetorian's. In the week he'd spent as the family's regular bodyguard, she'd grown to like him more and more and was pleased with her decision.

"Hopefully it will," she told Rufus. "I'm not sure I'd give the average Gemman good odds wandering around alone in Arcadia, but our group? No one on any side wants this to go badly. So long as we survive their customs, nothing's going to happen to us. And I'm hoping that if it's widely known that Justin's out of the country, no one will come after these guys while we're gone. No point in punishing the servitor if he's not around to see it."

Rufus nodded. "True, but I don't plan on changing anything. I'll keep up with the usual procedures and coordinate with your praetorian friend and his people."

Something in the way he said "praetorian friend" amused her. "You aren't a fan of Dag?"

"Oh, I'm sure he's a fine soldier. I just don't really bond with that showy, alpha-male type. As long as he does his job and keeps us supplied with backup, I've got no problem with him."

Mae laughed. "I don't know, Rufus. There's something about you that makes me think *you* might have been one of those showy alpha-male types back in the day. Maybe you're feeling competition from your youth."

"Hmphf," said Rufus, hiding a smile of his own. "That guy's no competition at all. And who says I'm out of my youth?"

Despite his joking, he was right about one thing: The mood was certainly somber when the hired car came to pick up Justin and Mae. Both Cynthia and Tessa had tears in their eyes, and Mae couldn't help but feel a little guilty for her role in the emotional farewell. *It's no more dangerous than anything else we do,* she reminded herself. *Probably less so. It's just that none of them know what we do regularly. They'd probably cry every time if they knew we were facing supernatural hordes of beetles and other monstrosities.*

The car took her and Justin to the senate, where they were led in through a back entrance. Here, they went separate ways. Because the Arcadian government could access the RUNA's media on occasion, the female praetorians weren't being publicized on the trip, lest the Gemman press pull up the military's bios and report on their true identities.

"Good luck," Mae told Justin. He and the other men were due at another press conference before going to the airport.

"Nothing to it," he said. "I'm sure Lucian'll do all the talking anyway."

One aide led him away to a press room, while another took Mae to a private suite used by senators for breaks between sessions.

There, she found the other praetorian women from their initial meeting, plus an assistant from Arcadian expert Atticus Marley's office. The woman introduced herself as Olivia and led Mae to a curtained-off area with a hanging dress.

"You're not expected to wear Arcadian fashion, thankfully," Olivia explained. "But you will need to conform to all of their rules. We got you the least horrendous clothes we could find."

But she didn't really sound that convinced, and Mae could understand why. The dress, though cut to Mae's measurements, didn't offer much in the way of shape. It was made of a light, tan material that touched her feet. The neckline went as high as the top of her collarbone, and the sleeves were elbow length.

Olivia offered her a jacket and hat in the same color. "You don't have to put these on until you leave the plane. And then make sure you aren't ever seen in public without them. Short sleeves and uncovered hair are big taboos."

"It's midsummer," said Mae, holding up the jacket. It had long sleeves and looked like it would land just past her hip.

"We got the lightest, most 'modest' material we could," said Olivia sympathetically. "If it helps, you probably won't be outside very often. But you should leave the hat on even when you're inside, and always keep your hair pulled up."

"Right," said Mae, remembering Atticus's warnings. "My problematic blond hair. I don't get it. Arcadia's more advanced than other provinces, and all of them have hair dye. They should be able to fake recessive genes just like our plebeians do."

"It's not about the ability. It's about custom." Olivia settled the hat—a bell-shaped cloche that actually would've been pretty stylish in autumn—on Mae's head to test the fit. "No hair dye. No makeup. There are even color restrictions. Something to do with that god of theirs and his rules on vanity. Your friend Dr. March could probably explain it better."

"In fact," a new voice said, "he's on the stream right now."

Mae turned in amazement. "Val?"

Her friend, wearing a dress of similar cut but in dark brown, grinned at her. "Surprise."

Olivia gave a nod of dismissal, and Mae hurried over to Val for a quick hug. "What are you doing here?"

"I got assigned to this a couple of days ago." Val's eyes narrowed thoughtfully. "The request came specifically from Senator Darling's office, so I figured you were behind it."

Mae shook her head wonderingly. "I had nothing to do with it. Lucian must've done it on his own." *For me*, she realized. They'd needed a fifth female praetorian, and it wouldn't have been that hard for Lucian to ask a few questions and find out who Mae was particularly close to. Of course, as much as Mae loved her friend's company, she almost would've preferred Val was safely on bodyguard duty for the March family and not tied into this strange vision-driven mission that Mae had let herself get involved in.

"There you go again with his first name. I think it broke Dag's heart that we get to go off adventuring without him, but hell, I'll take undercover work in some backwoods country any day over monument duty. I thought we would've been pulled by now, but for all I know, the Scarlets'll be in the capital through the election." Val linked her arm through Mae's and tugged her away. "Come on, let's go watch the guys be manly and heroic for the cameras."

They found the other praetorians watching the screen in the lounge part of the suite, where press coverage of the delegation's send-off was already in full swing. As Justin had predicted, most questions went to Lucian, many of them being variations of what she'd heard all week about the dangers of going into enemy territory. Lucian likewise reiterated what he'd said before about duty and how he didn't care if it cost him in the election, so long as he aided his country. Whenever a question occasionally got tossed Justin's way, he answered with equal finesse.

Val chuckled. "He could be a politician himself."

"They've all been coached," said Mae. "Everyone's on their best diplomatic behavior, both for our people and for the Arcadians."

"No one had to coach him on that," scoffed Val. "That's the kind of stuff he's born with."

Mae's eyes lingered on Justin a few moments more until the camera cut away. She had to agree with Val's assessment.

Once the praetorians were outfitted and given their final instructions, they were taken out to Vancouver's military base to rendezvous with the rest of the party, who were still with the press and would be filmed and photographed leaving the senate in their cars as part of the media spectacular surrounding the trip. Mae hadn't been out at the base since she began working with Justin, and as their car cleared the security checkpoints, it felt strange that her return would be in this drab dress and not the black uniform she'd missed.

The men joined them about an hour later, and when they were all aboard the jet flying them to the Arcadian border, the atmosphere took on an almost festive attitude. The press conference had been a dazzling success, and Lucian's enthusiasm over their impending trip was infectious. If the others hadn't been voters of his before, they were now, Mae thought. Even stern-faced George Yi looked caught up in Lucian's visions of a brighter RUNA and accepted a glass of champagne as everyone settled in for the long flight.

"Cheer up," said Justin, coming to sit beside Mae. She was scanning through images and charts of Arcadian data on her ego. He handed her a glass of champagne that she took but didn't drink. "We're embarking into the great unknown."

Her own preoccupation with what she'd find in Arcadia was interfering with her ability to fully give in to the party vibe. "Not that unknown. Our spies and satellites have made sure of that."

"See, now, that's the spirit I'm looking for." Justin settled back into his seat, and Mae suspected there may have been champagne on his car ride from the senate as well. "You should drink that, you know. Won't be much on the other side. They don't like their women to drink."

She sipped the champagne, mostly out of habit. "They don't like their women to do a lot of things, it seems. Wearing too much color being among them. How does that happen? Arcadia and the RUNA have the same roots. How could we have gone in such wildly different directions?"

Justin knocked back the rest of his drink. This was the kind of philosophical question he lived for. "Well, there were already a lot of regional differences in the former United States before the Decline. This extreme? No, certainly not. It's a common misunderstanding that people think pre-Arcadia was already way off the mainstream. That was true for some, but not all. Some of the greatest works of American music and literature came out of this region. There was a lot of thinking, a lot of culture." He paused to eye his empty glass, and Mae helpfully poured her champagne into it. Giving her a mock toast, he continued, "But per what usually happens in catastrophic situations, people panic and open the door for the loudest voices to seize control. And once they get power in a world where everything's been destabilized, they can then rebuild that world in their own image."

"*Is* that what usually happens?" Mae asked skeptically. "The loudest voices seize control? Not the reasonable ones?"

"Loudest," affirmed Justin. "At least in times of disaster. You see, you're not aware of it because you're part of the military—which often is the loudest voice and, hopefully, the reasonable one. But back in the fallout from the Decline? The military was fragmented. Hell, half of it wasn't even in the country. You and I are lucky that our ancestors listened to the loud voices that joined up with Asian countries against Mephistopheles." He paused to rethink his words. "Well, perhaps 'listened' isn't the right word. I'd say some of them were forced to hear."

"Not many."

"More than you'd think. Your pretty blond ancestors bought their way out, but plenty of people opposed to 'optimal genetic reproduction' didn't have that luxury. It was an ugly time—uglier than most people realize. But look at us now." He spread out his hands. "The height of civilization. The Jewel of the World. Meanwhile, the Arcadians listened to voices that said they didn't have to swap out their population and mix ethnicities . . . and they let a theocratic government take over and push a new religion that keeps its citizens ignorant and is afraid to let their women show their necks." Mae flinched in surprise as he gently trailed his finger along her dress's collar. "So, you tell me, did our ancestors make the right call?"

She shook her head and noticed Lucian watching them across the jet's cabin. "I don't know," she said. "I don't know enough about the intricacies of the Decline. My guess is they made the best decision they could at the time with the information they had."

"As do we all." Justin dropped his hand and reached into his pocket. Moments later, he pressed something into Mae's palm. "Here. Put this on before we land. Not now, not while Lucian's watching us."

"How do you know that?" she asked. "I mean, you're right, but your back's to him."

"I can feel it. That, and it's no coincidence he picked a seat with a clear line of sight on you. Why sit there if he's not going to use it to its full advantage?"

Mae looked at what he'd given her. It was a small wooden rectangle attached to a cord that was about the right length to wear as a necklace. Etched on the wood was a symbol that looked like a cross between an *N* and an *H*.

"What is this?" she asked.

"*Hagalaz,*" he told her. "The ravens told me I could put it on a silver or gold chain, but that would violate Arcadian vanity rules, so I went old-school. You should keep it under your clothes, but if anyone does see it, hopefully it's crude enough to be ignored."

"You made it?"

"Yeah." He sounded more amused than proud. "You had no idea I was so crafty, did you?"

A few moments later, the full implications hit her. "Wait . . . is this something magical? Or supernatural?" She started to hand it back, and he pushed her hand away.

"It'll obscure you as one of the elect. Unless you want the Arcadian equivalent of a beetle mob coming after you."

She still couldn't help but regard the necklace with suspicion—though she didn't give it back. "I didn't know you were involved with stuff like this."

"Not happily," he assured her. "But I keep my promises and look out for my own."

Mae looked up to meet his eyes. "Are you claiming me as your own?"

He winked and stood up. "Wouldn't dream of it. But humor me and keep it on for this trip. Actually, wear it when we're back too. Now." He glanced around. "Where's the rest of the cham—"

He froze as his gaze fell on Mae's ego. "What's that?"

"Just refreshing myself on mission details." The image currently shown was one of the high priest of the Arcadian religion. His title was "the Grand Disciple," and he wore robes and a headdress that were almost comically heavy with jewels. In one hand he clutched a golden cup, and in the other, he held a short golden staff with an eagle on top. "I figured you'd know who this is," she added.

"Of course I do." Justin stared for several more moments. "Does that particular document say anything about the staff he's holding?"

"Not specifically. It just says this is the Grand Disciple's most formal regalia, worn for important services and holidays."

With a sigh, Justin dragged his eyes away and stood up. "Wonderful," he muttered. "I guess Geraki didn't imagine it."

He wandered off, leaving Mae puzzled as she clutched the necklace he'd given her. Putting it on seemed like an active admission that she was getting personally involved with the supernatural. But, as Justin had aptly pointed out, did she really want to advertise that she was one of the elect? When she'd asked him how Mama Orane hadn't initially known he was an elect, he'd simply said that he had "ways to keep that under wraps." Presumably, this was what he'd meant, and it had worked. Resolved, Mae waited until no one was watching and then slipped the necklace over her head and tucked the charm under her dress.

It wasn't lost on her just how significant it was that Justin had actually made the charm himself. He'd told her the story of how, a long time ago, he'd been approached by a god who'd saved Justin's life in the hopes of procuring his services and devotion. When Justin had related the tale, he'd made it sound as though he'd dodged any need to pay back the god . . . and yet, somewhere in the last few months, Mae had gotten the impression that something had changed. Justin wouldn't talk about it when pressed, but this charm was a strong indication that—willingly or not—Justin was more involved with this god than he'd initially said. Mae could hardly fault him for keeping secrets, however, when she was sitting on her own knife-induced vision of the red velvet flag.

An hour before their landing, someone wisely put the champagne away, and the atmosphere grew more subdued. The Arcadians wouldn't actually allow the plane to fly into their airspace, so Mae's party was landing at a base on the Gemman side of the border. They would cross by land (and water, since there was a river along the border) and then be taken to the Arcadian capital, Divinia. Mae felt herself growing tenser as they neared their destination, and a glance at her fellow praetorians told her that they too were on edge as their implants warmed to the potential danger.

They received an enthusiastic welcome at the Gemman base, and Lucian paused for smiles and a brief talk with the soldiers there. After all, they were all potential voters who could influence their home senators to vote for him in the consular election. The soldiers seemed thrilled at the attention he gave them, but Mae was pleased to see them snap into business mode when it came time to escort her party to the border. Even with the water barrier, this was a dangerous post, and these soldiers had undoubtedly learned caution.

They took a military craft across the river, where a complementary Arcadian base awaited them—complete with a contingent of green-coated soldiers openly holding guns. Not counting the undercover women and base escort, Mae's party had fifteen soldiers, most of whom were praetorians wearing the regular gray and maroon military uniform. The Arcadian "welcoming party" had more than four times that.

"Senator Darling." A large uniformed man stepped forward from the throng, once the Gemman party was on Arcadian soil. His jacket was bedecked with medals and marks of rank that identified him as a general. "Welcome to Arcadia."

If Lucian felt any nervousness about the situation he was walking into, he didn't let it show. "You must be General McGraw. It's a pleasure to meet you." He strode forward confidently and extended his hand, which the general shook without hesitation. Unless Mae was mistaken, there was a collective sigh of relief from both sides. So far, so good.

"Well," said McGraw, "the real pleasure won't begin until you're in Divinia. I'm here to dispense with some necessary evils, which I'm sure you can understand."

"Absolutely," said Lucian. "Let's do what needs to be done."

The "necessary evils" referred to a series of identity and security checks of every person and his or her luggage. The Arcadians had received advance notice of the names of those coming in the delegation and first ascertained that everyone matched his or her dossier. Mae's picture and name were accurate, but she'd been given a fabricated bio to hide her true profession. According to the records the Arcadians had, she was a professional pianist. In Mae's eyes, that was a generous estimate of her musical abilities, but she could understand that her people would fabricate a background with some connection to reality, and she *had* studied music in her tertiaries.

The Arcadians merely glossed over the bios, however, and put their main effort into searching the Gemman military who were staying in the country. Atticus had explained that the Gemman soldiers could bring arms that they'd be allowed to carry at certain times—which he'd read as "never." And as Mae watched the Gemmans turn over their weapons, she could understand why they'd chosen to bring out-of-date models. No one wanted to give the Arcadians a tactical edge by letting them study advanced weaponry while it was in their "safekeeping." It made Mae a little uneasy to know their party was unarmed, but that was to be expected. Even with their weapons, their soldiers were outnumbered. It was up to her and the other praetorians, who were weapons in and of themselves, to handle defense if needed.

Once the soldiers were cleared, the Arcadians did a more thorough check of the Gemman diplomats and "concubines," scanning them with both metal detectors and physical pat-downs. Mae had a moment of fear that they'd pick up her implant on their scanners, but, as she'd been assured in the RUNA, the implant was buried too deeply in her arm and contained a small enough amount of metal to slip by. Her knife, however, was a different matter.

"What's this?" demanded the Arcadian soldier who pulled it from her boot. The Arcadians spoke English with an accent that drew the vowels out more than the Gemman dialect did.

"Mine," she said, momentarily stunned.

"Why would a woman need a knife like this?" he demanded.

"Actually," said Justin, moving to her side, "it's mine. I gave it to her."

The soldier turned his incredulous gaze on Justin. "Same question. Why would a woman need a knife like this? This is a weapon."

Mae felt her heart clench, and the implant spun her up into fight-or-flight mode. *They're going to seize it,* she thought in a panic. *It's my only guide to my niece, and they're going to take it from me.*

Justin, however, remained remarkably calm. Derisive, even. "Why? For protection. Don't think I didn't see. You enjoyed that pat-down a little too much. I don't want anyone coming near my woman if I'm not around. We haven't even been here an hour, and you're already leering over our women."

Mae's gut instinct was to chafe against "my woman," but a wiser part of herself warned, *Just stay still and be quiet. He's getting you out of this.*

And apparently he was. Mae hadn't thought much of the pat-down, but the sudden crimson in the soldier's face lent credence to Justin's accusation. McGraw, having overheard the exchange, strode forward and took the knife from his soldier. "Here." The general handed the knife to Justin. "You keep it, not her. Your women have nothing to fear while under our hospitality." There was something in the tone of his voice that made Mae think that last statement was more for the Arcadians under his command than the Gemmans.

"Thank you," said Justin, slipping the knife into his coat as though he did it on a regular basis. When the attention was off them, Mae gave him a small nod of thanks that he returned in kind. The dagger was still accessible to her, at least.

When all the security checks were done to McGraw's satisfaction, the soldiers from the base departed, and Mae's party was truly on its own. She and the others were escorted onto a large, armored bus with narrow windows that reminded her of something used to transport prisoners. It had enough room for all of the Gemmans, as well as several armed Arcadian soldiers. McGraw came on board to see them off but wasn't riding with them.

"It's about three hours to Divinia," he said. "These soldiers will make sure you arrive there safely for your welcoming festivities. It's been a pleasure to meet you all, and I'm sure I'll be seeing you again soon." With a curt salute to his men, he departed.

"Really?" murmured Val, sitting with Lucian in the seat in front of Mae and Justin. "*That* wasn't the welcome? Can you imagine the media spectacle this would've been if the situation had been reversed and we were receiving them? There'd be champagne fountains and dancing girls."

"I'm sure they have plenty in store for us," said Lucian pleasantly, never losing that camera-ready smile. But as Mae studied his profile, she could see the lines of tension and knew that no matter his glib talk, he was well aware of the possible danger if this trip went badly. Keeping him as a hostage could be a powerful bargaining chip for the Arcadians, if they wanted to force something from the Gemmans. Mae wondered if that put the rest of them—who weren't as important—in better or worse positions.

"That's right," said Justin, loudly enough for some nearby Arcadian soldiers to overhear. "Rest up on this ride. I'm sure the hospitality and wonders of Divinia will be overwhelming."

"Divinia," repeated Mae. "Was that always its name?"

"No," said Justin, making himself comfortable in the stiff seat. "Before the Decline, it was called Montgomery."

# CHAPTER 9

# CULTURAL ADJUSTMENTS

Justin couldn't help but keep thinking of Val's comparisons of how things would have been different if it were an Arcadian delegation visiting the RUNA. She was right about the media spectacle. There would've been more journalists than the Arcadians had soldiers, documenting every mundane aspect imaginable, even before their guests' feet hit the ground. No one would've been smuggled around in an armored bus, and while the Gemman security would have been just as thorough, they would've been so in a more discreet and tactful way.

*We would parade them around,* Justin thought, *because we love novelty. That, and we love to feel superior, and every single eccentricity of theirs that could be shown on air would serve as evidence for how much better we are than everyone else.*

*Are you saying you aren't?* asked Horatio.

*Of course not,* said Justin. *Ours is the superior civilization. The Arcadians want their people to believe the same of their country, and their tactic is to do so by not offering—or showing—them any other options. Their media, such as it is, is highly censored. Whatever gets broadcast about us will be full of propaganda and make us out to look like the immoral country they think we are.*

*At least the Gemman media portrayed you pretty well,* offered the raven.

*It doesn't matter, so long as something positive comes out of all of this diplomatically. That's the point of it,* Justin reminded him.

Horatio was skeptical of that proper response. *I thought the point was to get on Mae's good side.*

Justin glanced at her out of the corner of his eye. They'd covered her up in that smock of a dress and hidden most of her hair under the hat, but there was still no concealing her beauty. She was on good behavior for the Arcadian soldiers, face serene and hands folded elegantly in her lap as she looked ahead. Her gaze seemed to be focused on nothing in particular, but Justin knew she was taking in every detail and braced to spring into action if needed. The praetorian women had been strictly told a number of times that in the event of an altercation, they were to participate only as a last resort if their uniformed countrymen were present. Justin wondered how well Mae and the other women would adhere to that. Following orders was second nature to them . . . but so was defending others.

Signs of urban civilization eventually began to show through the slitted windows. Buildings appeared and grew closer together, though their state of repair varied wildly. The roads smoothed out. Then the scenery grew rural again as they passed out of the city proper, and the bumpy bus ride at last came to an end. The Gemman delegation was escorted out and found themselves standing in front of a wide colonial estate house that was certainly among the nicer ones they'd passed. Its pillared porch was crowded with people, and despite the house's upkeep and affluence, it didn't exactly feel modern. Glancing around, Justin saw a number of other buildings on vast, dusty acreage and realized they must be at the compound that was hosting them, the one Atticus had shown them satellite images of. The people on the porch were mostly men, all in suits and wide-brimmed hats, and from their sweaty skin and clothing, they looked as though they'd been standing there for a while. All of the men in the front, on the porch's steps, were Justin's age or older. Those in the back were younger, some even children. Also in the back, slightly apart from the others, were about a dozen women, wearing the long dresses and hats favored by Arcadian women in public.

A portly man in his fifties, with thinning hair and a bushy white beard, took off his hat and stepped forward to shake hands with Atticus. "Mr. Marley," the man said, "it's a pleasure to receive you at my home."

"It's a pleasure to be back in Arcadia," returned Atticus warmly. "And to be truly in Arcadia, not just skulking on the border in clandestine meetings. This is the kind of get-together we've needed for a long time, if we truly want to make progress." He stepped back and ushered a politely waiting Lucian forward. "Senator, may I present our host, Carl Carter, director of the Committee of Foreign Affairs and special assistant to the president. Director Carter, this is Lucian Darling, senator now and possibly our future consul."

"Just Carl will do." Their Arcadian host vigorously shook Lucian's hand and seemed sincere in his enthusiasm. "I'm delighted to welcome you on behalf of our president and show you our great country's finest hospitality. You'll get to meet him tomorrow when you tour the capital. Tonight, we thought you'd like to rest a little outside the city."

Lucian was in full show mode. "It's an honor to be at your home, and I look forward to whatever you have to share with us."

*Everyone's so polite and so happy to be here,* Justin noted to himself. *Listen to the word choice. "Honor." "Pleasure." "Delighted." You'd never guess our two countries' soldiers are constantly skirmishing along the border.*

*Would you prefer that here?* asked Magnus.

*No,* said Justin. *I'd prefer to be inside.*

Even in early evening, the temperature was high, the air hanging stagnant and humid around them. The bus had had nominal air-conditioning, but there was nothing to protect them now from the heat as they stood in the dusty yard. The comfort of indoors seemed to be a ways off, however, as both sides went through formal introductions of their important officials. A number of the Arcadians were familiar to Justin from his briefings, and he mentally linked up these real-life faces to what he'd read in the bios. As they'd expected, none of the Gemman women were given introductions. Of the twelve Arcadian women, three were introduced as Carl's wives, with another five being the head wives of other officials. That meant the four who weren't introduced were Carl's concubines, something Justin found staggering.

*He's got seven women. Should I be jealous?* he asked the ravens. After an assessment of the women, he decided he wasn't. Carl's youngest wife and one of the concubines were somewhat attractive, but the others were heavily marked by Cain.

*Some of the Arcadians are jealous of your women,* noted Horatio.

Justin had noticed that as well. The older officials had given the Gemman women once-overs, some of them clearly quite intrigued. But these men were disciplined and focused on the task at hand enough to do little more than that. The younger men, most of whom were Carl's sons, were less subtle as they openly stared at Mae and the others. Carl hadn't introduced any daughters-in-law, which Justin understood was quite common around here. The polygamous practices left a shortage of women, and most men couldn't afford a wife until their midtwenties, at least. The country's religious dictates had strong stances against premarital (or preconcubine) sex, and although Justin wasn't naïve enough to believe it didn't happen, it probably didn't happen nearly as much as it should have.

*If ever there was a group of guys who needed to get laid, it's that one,* Justin thought, watching as the young men shifted restlessly in the heat. *This is a system ready to explode. The old men hoard all the women for themselves. Some of Carl's wives and concubines are younger than his sons.*

The leaders of both groups made more speeches and performed more posturing, and at last, Carl declared that everyone should come in for dinner. Grinning broadly, he gestured his guests inside and then barked a sharp command to some of his sons.

"Their bags are in that second bus. Take them out to the guesthouses."

None of the sons protested outright, but the expression on their faces suggested this was an unexpected request. Carl flushed at the defiance.

"All the women are busy with supper," he hissed. "Takes all of them to feed this many."

"Why can't *their* women do it?" asked the youngest of the sons, whom Justin guessed to be around fourteen or fifteen. The oldest looked to be about ten years older, and he lightly cuffed the youngster, aware that they had an audience.

"Come *on*," he said, urging the other four on.

They traipsed off, and Justin breathed a sigh of relief as he stepped into high-powered air-conditioning. The Arcadians, though they had many technological capabilities, had mixed ideas about when that technology should be used, based on their god Nehitimar's commands. Justin was grateful climate control met with divine approval.

The estate's main house had a dining room large enough to hold a table that seated both countries' officials and Carl's sons, as well as a smaller table off to the side, to which the Gemman women were directed. The Gemman soldiers, they learned, would eat on the back porch. No mention was made of where the children would go, but presumably they'd get fed too.

"Interesting," murmured Atticus, pitching his voice so that only Justin and Lucian could hear. They were waiting to be assigned seats at the main table. "For formal events, women and men don't eat together. They've brought that table in just for us."

"Is that a good thing?" asked Lucian.

"Possibly. It means they're showing us a courtesy since they know we do eat together." Atticus chuckled softly. "It's deeply unsettling for their women, though."

He was right. The women's table was pushed to the far side of the room, with more chairs at it than it could comfortably hold. The women of Carl's household were too busy to sit yet, but the other Arcadian wives were sitting with the Gemman women and kept casting uncomfortable looks around, at both their tablemates and the men across the room. Justin wondered if it was strange for them to be eating in front of men who weren't family or if they were more disturbed at being seated with foreigners. Or maybe, judging from how busily Carl's women were scurrying to get beverages and food to the tables, the other Arcadian women just expected to help.

Justin had no time to ponder the women's fate, not with plenty to occupy him at his own table. He knew what was expected in situations like these and was as adept socially as Lucian and Atticus. George and Phil were more subdued but always responded appropriately when engaged. The Arcadians had a similar mix of personalities, and between them all, they were able to prevent awkward silences and keep to friendly cross-cultural topics as the women painstakingly brought out dish after dish.

The local cuisine looked fine to Justin, and he was surprised to find how hungry he was after the long day of travel. Mae's expression was neutral, but she and the other praetorians had to be famished. When Carl's women finally went and stood behind the chairs at their table, Justin's fingers itched to reach for his silverware, but he kept a close eye on the other Arcadians first. Their hands stayed in their laps, and conversation went silent as their eyes fell on the one empty seat at Justin's table. Moments later, a man dressed entirely in gray entered the dining room. He looked to be in his forties, and all hair had been shaved from his head and face. The rest of the Arcadians stood at his entrance, and the Gemmans quickly followed suit.

"This is our local priest, the Venerable Jeremiah. He's come here especially to meet you and perform our dinner prayers," explained Carl.

"We're honored," said Atticus gravely.

Justin had witnessed many religious services in his time, but this was the first in which he'd ever technically been a willing participant, if one looked at it that way. Even so, he still found himself studying the priest with a servitor's eye, analyzing every gesture and intonation as the Venerable Jeremiah began a long litany of prayers and thanksgiving.

*If he's one of the elect, I don't sense anything,* Justin told the ravens. *Maybe he's hiding it.*

*Hard to say,* said Horatio. *Not all who serve the gods truly have a connection to the divine or some special ability. That's as true here as in your own country. Plenty are simply ordinary people fulfilling mundane functions.*

Still, Justin scrutinized Jeremiah for some indication that he might be a player in the game. But after fifteen minutes of prayers, Justin lost interest in guessing the other man's motivations and began to wonder simply when they were going to eat. The food was going cold.

"Amen," Jeremiah said at last. The other Arcadians echoed him.

*That right there is reason enough not to be involved with a god,* thought Justin.

*Odin would let you eat whenever you want,* said Horatio helpfully. *In the old days, the Vikings would have happily dived in before everyone was seated. Feasting and drinking is very important to him.*

Cold or not, the food was excellent, and Justin had to bite his tongue to keep from complimenting any of the women on it when they came to check for refills and additional helpings. Here, compliments went to the man of the house. Justin tried to imagine Cynthia's reaction if he were the one praised for her hard work. He couldn't say for sure what would happen, but it seemed likely that thrown crockery would be involved.

"You work in religion, Dr. March?" asked Jeremiah. It was an unexpected question, seeing as the priest had mostly been silent since his long prayers.

"Yes, in a manner of speaking." Religion was not a friendly, cross-cultural topic, and Justin was cautious in his response.

Carl's oldest son, Walter, looked up at that. "Are you a priest too?"

"No," Justin told him. "I only study religion in an . . . academic way. I don't practice it."

Walter's face was blank. "I don't understand."

"I do it for the sake of knowledge, not faith," said Justin, knowing he probably wasn't clearing things up. "And to help me with the rest of my job."

"It wouldn't be a bad thing if our young people studied our god's laws more, regardless if they were entering the priesthood," rebuked Jeremiah gently. "Dr. March is more like an examiner."

"Ah," said Walter in understanding. "You hunt down heretics."

Justin drew on his knowledge of Arcadian religion. Examiners were empowered to find and even use lethal force on those who committed an offense against Nehitimar. "Not exactly. I find those whose religious practices are a danger to our country. I do it for the government—not for any god."

"If Dr. March is like most Gemmans," said Jeremiah, "I'm guessing he has no god."

"Correct," said Justin, uncertain if that was a lie. If so, the ravens let it go.

This was clearly a radical concept to some of the younger people at the table, but the government officials were prepared for it. "Not a bad system, your servitors," chuckled one of them, a presidential secretary named Matthias. "Anyone not worshipping Nehitimar is a danger. Now if you only had his teachings in your country, you'd be all set."

"Now, now, that's enough of that," said Carl. He had his host's smile on, but a tension in his eyes said he was well aware that they were straying from easy small talk. "Dr. March will hear much wiser words from the Grand Disciple than he will from any of us when they meet tomorrow."

"Will we?" asked Justin, startled. The Arcadians' highest religious authority hadn't been listed on any itinerary. "I thought we were meeting the president tomorrow."

"You are," said Carl. "And then the rest of these gentlemen are going to tour some of our famous monuments in Divinia while you go to the temple and meet with the Grand Disciple."

"It's a great honor," said Jeremiah gently. "Few are granted a personal audience with His Piousness. You alone have been asked from your party. No soldiers, I'm afraid. It's forbidden for outside warriors to set foot in the temple. But you'll be well treated."

Justin nodded, still a little stunned. "Thank you."

"We've also made some arrangements for your women," said another Arcadian. His name was Marlin, and he seemed to be particularly active in managing the Gemman itinerary outside of Carl's home. "Naturally, they won't come to the presidential luncheon tomorrow. They can stay here and help out Carl's family. I'm sure his women will appreciate the extra help. But afterward, we can have them join you for the city tour if you think they'd like to see some of the sights."

Sightseeing over household work back here? Yes, Justin was pretty sure they'd like that.

Atticus leaned forward, face thoughtful. "Will Justin's concubine be able to go with him to the temple?" It was a surprising question until Justin realized that their diplomat was uncomfortable with Justin's separating from the group to meet with the Arcadian head of religion. Atticus's earlier expression when the visit had been brought up suggested that it wasn't something he'd known about either.

The Arcadian men looked astonished at the suggestion. "Whatever for?" asked Matthias.

Even clever Atticus hesitated over that. He certainly couldn't say he wanted extra protection. Justin jumped forward as insight hit. "Sometimes she acts as my secretary. Takes notes when I'm in the field. There's a lot I'd love to learn from the Grand Disciple, and I'd hate to be distracted with menial work."

Some of the Arcadian officials exchanged glances, and Justin waited to see if the ploy would work. Arcadian women rarely held professions, but Justin hoped use of the word "menial" would make what she did seem suitable for her gender. He also hoped none of them were savvy enough to the Gemman bios to ask why a so-called musician was fulfilling that function.

"Perhaps we could supply a secretary," suggested Matthias.

"We're aware of the differences in our customs," said Marlin delicately. "And we are trying to accommodate some of yours. But you must understand that there are some things even we can't change. Women naturally go to the temple, but it's very irregular for a woman—any woman—to actually be in His Piousness's presence. They are a distraction."

"Of course," said Lucian smoothly. "But I'm sure she could be unobtrusive."

Marlin looked uncertain, but it was the Venerable Jeremiah who unexpectedly spoke up. "The Grand Disciple is very eager to speak with you, Dr. March, and he's a very understanding and compassionate man. We certainly want you to be as comfortable as possible during your audience. Let me contact him tonight and see what arrangements can be made. There might be no problem at all if she goes Cloistered."

"Which one is she?" asked Carl's second-oldest son.

"Jasper," snapped Carl. "It's irrelevant."

"I don't know." Jasper's gaze drifted over to the women's table across the room. "I'd keep them all Cloistered if they were mine."

The mix of shock and discomfort on the Arcadians' faces made Justin think they were dancing along a dangerous topic, but he had to ask the obvious question. "What does Cloistered mean?"

"If a woman continues to be a source of temptation and strife for men, Nehitimar decrees that she must be punished by going Cloistered. It refers to a head-to-foot veil that wraps around her, obscuring her body and features," explained Matthias.

"And it's a punishment?" asked Justin, seeking clarification. He chose his next words very carefully. "Is it brought on by willful actions on her part to cause, uh, temptation and strife? Or is she punished just for . . ." He nearly said "being attractive" but thought better of it. "Her presence?"

"Both," said Jasper.

"Don't think of it as a punishment in the case of the temple," said Jeremiah. "Merely a precaution. Those who serve Nehitimar need to keep their minds on holy things, not the baser temptations of women."

*Incredible,* Justin thought. *They punish their women for what sounds like male weakness to me.* But he couldn't let his mind linger on that for too long, not when there was an opening at hand.

He put on what he hoped was an easygoing smile. "Do I need to dress up or wear anything special? I've seen pictures of the Grand Disciple, and he's a pretty imposing figure, with the robes and that staff of his. There's some kind of bird on it, right? An eagle?" Lucian looked up sharply, surprise lighting his features.

Jeremiah nodded gravely. "The eagle of Nehitimar. It's one of the Grand Disciple's most holy objects. He only brings out that staff on high feast days and holidays, when he addresses great crowds. The robes of state . . . well, it's hard to say if he'll be in full regalia or not. If so, you needn't feel intimidated. What you're wearing now is perfectly acceptable. The Grand Disciple is used to overshadowing us ordinary men."

Silence fell at that, but Lucian was too good to let it last. "Well, I'm thrilled that Justin's going to get to meet someone so exalted— it's an honor for all of us, really—but I confess, I'm just as excited for myself to finally get to see some of the wonders of your country. What's on the sightseeing schedule?"

Tourism was a safer topic than women or religion, and everyone gratefully transitioned. Justin listened with half an ear while his mind wandered. When Geraki had mentioned the golden eagle being a threat, Justin had assumed it was some sort of symbol. The picture he'd seen on Mae's ego, with the Grand Disciple holding the staff, had furthered that idea. It made Justin think the golden eagle was symbolic of the Arcadian religion, which was so deeply tied to the Arcadian government and a threat in and of itself.

But now, Jeremiah's words made Justin wonder if something more literal was happening. *Is that eagle staff itself dangerous?* he asked the ravens. *Could that be what Odin was warning Geraki about?*

*Possibly,* said Horatio. *It could be some sort of divine artifact, which would be a rare and lucky find for the Grand Disciple—and give him and his god an edge in the battle going on.*

*Not that rare,* argued Justin. *I've seen other believers possess objects from their gods. That guy Mae fought in the death temple had a knife from the Morrigan.*

*Those are objects blessed by a certain god, which only have power and meaning for the user who believes in that god,* Magnus told him. *If the Grand Disciple possesses one of the great artifacts—which would capture Odin's interest—that would be something different altogether. There are objects in this world of great power, far more powerful than a simple blessed object, and that power transfers to whatever god controls it. They have their own intrinsic abilities that they impart to that god's servant. Said objects can be critical in the fight for divine control and can only be touched by those of the strongest faith.*

*How do we find out if this staff is one of the great artifacts or not?* asked Justin.

*If it is, it will have some very noticeable effect when in use,* explained Magnus. *Find someone who's witnessed it.*

When dinner finally wrapped up, the men adjourned to a separate sitting room for cigars and scotch. That at least was something Justin could get on board with, and he took some pleasure out of watching his fellow countrymen's shock at smoking real tobacco. It was rare in the RUNA, where smoking was itself a rare habit and only done with safer substances. They were told that the women would "tend to matters" back in the kitchen, and Justin had a feeling it was one of those things best not questioned.

He got his answers later that evening when he was finally allowed to retire to his room in one of the outlying guesthouses. Lucian, Atticus, George, and Phil were also in the same house. Each of them had his own bedroom, which was adjacent to a common room and bathroom. Gemman soldiers were stationed inside the house's door, and Arcadian soldiers were outside it "for everyone's protection." One of them escorted the women in, and Mae threw herself onto Justin's bed as soon as the door shut in his bedroom.

"Do you see this?" she asked. She held up her hands, which mostly looked the same as ever to him. "I've been scrubbing pots and pans with a homemade sponge for the last two hours!"

Justin sat beside her and took one of her hands in his. Up close, he could see that they were pink and water swollen. "Not much manual labor growing up in the old Koskinen homestead, eh?"

She pulled her hand back. "I've done plenty of manual labor! What's ridiculous is that this was to 'build character' and eradicate sin. Harriet explained it to us—that's Carl's head wife if you didn't catch it. Women are naturally evil, and hard labor helps keep that at bay."

"That's an idea based in a number of religions that their god—Nehitimar—embraced wholeheartedly and then took to a whole new level when his followers took over the government last century," Justin explained, knowing he wasn't really helping.

She sat up and shook her head in disgust. "It's appalling. They have the technology for plenty of domestic conveniences—like dishwashers and vacuum cleaners—but purposely don't use them in order to 'help' their women. None of the men do it, of course. Val scrubbed the dining room floor with a brush smaller than my hand!"

"I don't want to play 'I told you so,' and I'm certainly sympathetic about what you had to do," he said, "but I *did* warn you this place was messed up. And I don't think we've seen the half of it. Regret coming?"

Her gaze turned downward as she considered his question. "No." She offered nothing more, and he had to fight with himself not to badger her over why she'd wanted to come.

Instead he said, "Well, I can't guarantee there won't be more character-building labor tomorrow, but you will at least be able to get out of the house—to see the city or a temple, I can't say yet. I also can't say for sure that it won't be weird in a totally different way." He brightened. "But hey, at least the food was good. You've got to appreciate that."

"We didn't eat the same food," she told him ruefully. "Ours was a lot blander and in smaller portions."

"Really?" He'd had no idea. "More character building?"

"That, and it's important for women to remain attractive to their men. So Harriet tells us."

Justin scoffed. "And yet apparently not too attractive."

"She and the others couldn't believe we didn't have children," added Mae. "They've got Cain—lots of it—and it was unbelievable to them that five of us who were free of it hadn't reproduced at our age. When Val mentioned birth control . . . well, that got us some looks."

"Birth control's illegal here," he reminded her.

"This is a strange place," she sighed.

Justin thought ahead to his upcoming meeting with the head of a religion so powerful, it dictated what the government did. With a sigh of his own, he put an arm around Mae, unsure if it was more for her comfort or his own. "Hang in there, because it's going to get stranger."

# CHAPTER 10

# DAPHNE DEFINES
# THE TRUTH

D aphne held true to her word about signing a statement re-
linquishing any claim to Tessa's life story. She wasted no
time in getting started with the internship either, showing
up at the house on the second day after Justin had left. Tessa faltered
at the door when she answered it, remembering Justin's admonish-
ment about letting Daphne back in the house. Daphne hadn't known
about that, though, and neither did anyone else. So, while Tessa got
some wary looks from Cynthia and Rufus as she led Daphne in that
morning, nobody strictly prohibited the reporter's being around.

"Let the school know you're off doing fieldwork today," Daphne
said, noticing Tessa's uniform. "We've got a hot story to work on."

"Do we?" asked Tessa, a bit startled.

"We're interviewing someone today and need to finalize my research." Daphne settled herself at the kitchen table, moving away
empty breakfast plates and setting up a tablet on a small easel.
"Grab your own tablet or use the living room screen. I need another set of eyes."

Rufus, watching her with crossed arms, asked, "Don't you have
an office?"

"North Prime feels its reporters can work just fine without the
physical constraints of an office," she replied primly.

"Right, right," said Rufus. "I forgot you're freelance and not sal-
aried."

"You also forgot that you're hired help," snapped Daphne, angling her body toward Tessa. "Now then. Let's get started."

Cynthia cleared the rest of the dishes and chased Quentin from the table. "What's the story?" she asked, in a rare moment of curiosity.

Daphne's eyes lit up. "A girl—sixteen—got pregnant over in Burnaby. Her parents claim the implant was faulty, but there's evidence they belong to some weird religious group and might have purposely tampered with it."

"Sixteen," murmured Cynthia, looking appalled. "She's a child."

Tessa had known plenty of girls having children that young back in Panama, but around here, where contraception was compulsory until age twenty, sixteen was unheard-of. Daphne's kohl-lined eyes narrowed thoughtfully as she studied Cynthia more closely. "Shocking, isn't it?"

"Ghastly," said Cynthia. "That poor girl. Her poor parents." She glanced at the kitchen clock. "Time for Quentin and me to go. Have you seen where that praetorian went?"

"Pacing outside," said Rufus. He'd made himself a sentry between the kitchen and living room.

Daphne watched as Cynthia left and then turned to Tessa. "Did you see her reaction to hearing about that girl? That's what you want as a journalist—that deep, visceral response that sucks viewers in."

"I thought journalists wanted facts," said Tessa.

"Who says you can't have both? Now, I've got to double-check the time line on when they reported that she was pregnant, and I need you to look up what you can on their religion." Daphne skimmed her tablet. "Some god named Demeter. Find out if he'd be against fertility restrictions. Find out if their local chapter's even still licensed. That'll tell us right there how crazy this group is. Too bad your servitor skipped town on us. Even if the group's licensed, the servitors always know more dirt."

"Something tells me Justin wouldn't be too excited to help us if he were here," remarked Tessa wryly.

"Of course not," said Daphne, rolling her eyes. "Why would he be troubled by something so mundane, when he could be off on glamorous trips with our next consul? How did *he* pull that off? Is it true they used to be roommates?"

Tessa thought back to Justin's tone and expression whenever he'd spoken of the trip. Despite all his assurances that it would be safe and easy, Tessa hadn't been able to shake the vibe that he wasn't actually looking forward to it. "I'm not sure he really pulled anything off," she said at last.

"They were roommates," confirmed Cynthia, returning with Quentin and her assigned praetorian of the day. "Luck of the draw in the university housing system. I used to visit sometimes."

"I bet that must've been a sight." Daphne's tone was light, but Tessa noticed a shrewd look in her eyes.

Cynthia shook her head in a mix of amusement and disapproval. "Typical college life, I guess. Especially for two guys. Their place was always a mess, and I swear they spent more time at parties than in class. Yet look at them now."

"Did you ever think back then they'd end up in their current positions?" asked Daphne.

"I wouldn't have imagined servitor exactly for Justin," said Cynthia after a few moments of thought. "But I would've guessed something high-profile that allows him to be an expert and spout his vast knowledge, whether it's wanted or not. So I guess this fits."

"And Senator Darling?" Daphne prompted. She almost seemed to be holding her breath in anticipation. "Was he politician material back then?"

"When do you guys have to go?" interrupted Tessa. There was something in Daphne's line of questioning that she didn't like. It was too eager, too calculated for casual curiosity.

Cynthia glanced at the time and grimaced. "Five minutes ago. See you later."

She hurried her entourage out, and Daphne watched them with a frown. Tessa almost expected chastisement for scaring Cynthia away, but Daphne's features soon smoothed as she returned to the task at hand. Despite her initial misgivings, Tessa found herself caught up in the work. Research on the vast Gemman media stream was something that Tessa actually liked and could have done just for fun. Daphne was right about there being no official government records on Demeter's followers, but Tessa learned that Demeter was a goddess, not a god, and had strong ties to fertility. Tessa gathered all the pertinent information she could find and formatted it all in an organized way that allowed quick access and earned Daphne's grudging approval.

"Damn," she said. "I should've gotten an intern a long time ago."

A couple hours later, they set out for Burnaby, with Rufus in tow, to make the scheduled interview. Daphne fell silent as they rode, rereading her notes and touching up her heavy makeup, which, to Tessa's eyes, hadn't budged. When they got off at their station, they found a young man waiting for them with a camera case. Daphne introduced him as Felix and said that he'd be filming the interview for her.

The family they were visiting lived in a working-class suburb, nice but not as affluent as Tessa's. The mother was a petite, mousy woman who greeted them at the door and seemed surprised to find more than a lone reporter outside.

"My associates," said Daphne breezily. She shook the other woman's hand vigorously. "It's a pleasure to meet you, Mrs. Lin, and help you tell your side of the story. As soon as word of your lawsuit gets out, everyone will know what's going on and start making all sorts of assumptions. Best to have the truth on the record." Daphne gave a calculated pause. "You, uh, haven't begun your lawsuit yet, have you? Gotten in touch with a lawyer?"

"We've spoken to a few," said Mrs. Lin nervously. "But we haven't contracted with one yet."

Daphne's smile broadened. "I'm so glad to hear that. For Helene's sake. It means we have time."

Tessa knew that Daphne was much gladder for her own sake, since probably no lawyer would've let the family speak with her. Mrs. Lin led them to a modestly furnished living room, introducing them to her husband and the aforementioned Helene. Mr. Lin looked as meek and mild as his wife, and Helene looked like any ordinary girl that Tessa might see at school. All looked uneasy. Daphne chatted away about light topics and tried to make them comfortable as she and Felix set up the living room. It turned out he'd brought two cameras, one that would stay unmanned and fixed on Daphne and another that he would control in order to get the best shots of the Lin family. Tessa, remembering this was all supposed to be a learning experience, stayed out of the way with Rufus and tried to pay attention.

Daphne began by getting the family's backstory—what the parents did for a living, what Helene's hobbies were, etc. Daphne then moved on to Helene's relationship with a boy at her school. They'd been dating for six months, and no one seemed particularly surprised that sex had been an outcome. The pregnancy was the shocking part, and that was what Daphne soon homed in on.

"Why do *you* think you got pregnant?" asked Daphne.

Helene shot her parents a nervous look. "The implant was faulty."

"They're rated for ten years of use," argued Daphne. "Have you had yours that long?"

"Four," said Helene, flushing.

And then Daphne went in for the kill: "Is it or is it not true that you actually disabled your implant in tribute to your goddess Demeter and her cult of fertility?"

"No!" gasped Helene.

"Did your parents ask you to do it? Did your parents do it themselves?"

"Of course not," exclaimed Mrs. Lin.

"Why don't you tell me about your faith then," said Daphne. "Describe it and your goddess in your own words."

Mr. and Mrs. Lin, on the defensive now, attempted to paint a picture of their religion and did so in bits and pieces. A lot of it corroborated Tessa's research, and it was almost impossible to talk about Demeter without mentioning fertility.

"But it's not just about . . . babies," explained an exasperated Mr. Lin, when Daphne pointed out the connections. "It's fertility in a larger sense. Growth and new life of all things—plants, ideas, art. There's a lot to it."

Daphne fixed him with her dark gaze. "As a goddess who supports growth and new life, how does she feel about contraceptive implants?"

"I . . . I don't know," he said.

"Your church encourages removal of the implants when legally allowable at twenty, correct?"

"Yes."

"Do you think Demeter is pleased or displeased at news of your daughter's pregnancy?" asked Daphne.

The family fell silent at that. When Daphne repeated it, Mrs. Lin said, "I'm sure she has better things to worry about than us."

"She's a great and powerful goddess," said Daphne. "I'm sure she keeps track of all of her followers. Would she or would she not approve of Helene's pregnancy?"

"I suppose . . . well, I suppose she'd approve," said Mrs. Lin. "But—"

But Daphne had what she needed. Through that and a number of other tricky questions, even Tessa could tell that Daphne could edit together a segment where the family inadvertently implicated themselves. It made Tessa feel slightly queasy, but to Daphne, it was a triumph she couldn't stop crowing about on the train ride back to Vancouver.

"I just wish I could get an interview with the boy too," she said. "Get his reactions to being a pawn in a zealot family's plans to breed children for their goddess. His family wouldn't let him talk to me, though."

*Smart,* thought Tessa. Out loud, she said, "Isn't that a leap—breeding children for their goddess? They never said anything like that. You kind of just put it together from circumstantial evidence."

"Of course they're not going to say it," said Daphne. "And if they're truly innocent, I'm sure this'll all settle out legally."

"But your story gets attention in the meantime."

Daphne grinned. "That's how this business works. If it soothes your moral sensibilities, though, it *is* incredibly rare for contraceptive implants to fail."

"Yeah, but is it easy for the average person to disable one?" asked Tessa.

"I don't know. I'm no engineer."

Tessa thought about that for several moments. "Why don't you ask one? Get more facts for the story?"

"Because I need to edit and file this with North Prime while it's still hot," said Daphne. "I couldn't get an expert to talk to me on such short notice."

"What if I could?" asked Tessa. "I know someone—I mean, he's more like Justin's friend. He helps Justin out with cases. But his main job is at a contraceptive company. I bet he'd talk to us."

Daphne's earlier expression of smug triumph had transformed to razor-sharp focus. "Justin's friend? Is he local?"

"No . . . but recently, he's been spending time up here. Normally he's in Portland. But his company has offices in Vancouver, and he's been doing other government contract work."

"Fine," declared Daphne magnanimously. "See if he's around. If we can get in today, we can talk to him."

Leo Chan was surprised when Tessa called but not unfriendly. He'd always been kind to Tessa, and so had his husband, Dominic. She hadn't seen Dominic in a very long time, though. The few times they'd visited Leo in Portland in recent months, Dominic had always been away. It was around the same time Dominic had first left that Leo, who'd sworn he was firmly entrenched in the countryside outside Portland, had begun venturing back up to his favorite city. Luck and chance found him in Vancouver today, at Estocorp's downtown offices, and he agreed to talk to Tessa when she told him she needed help for a school project.

"You didn't mention you were bringing a reporter," Rufus remarked quietly to Tessa as they waited in the lobby to meet Leo. "One day with her, and you're already getting selective about what information you give."

Tessa blushed. "Leo's not as paranoid as he used to be, but he sometimes reacts badly to strangers. Though it kind of depends on the type of stranger. He was always nice to me. Not so much to Mae. I don't think he likes praetorians."

"Praetorians are intimidating," agreed Rufus. "But she's pretty enough to put a lot of people at ease—especially men."

"Leo has a husband," Tessa pointed out.

Rufus chuckled at that. "Ah. Well, then, yes, I suppose she wouldn't be so effective on him in that case. You've probably seen her turn on that charm with other men, though."

"Not really." Tessa reflected on her experience with Mae. "But I've never seen her around that many men, I guess. Just her friends. And Justin—but they always seem to be mad at each other. I've never heard her talk about a boyfriend or anything."

"Praetorians are rarely lonely," said Rufus, but he seemed pleased at Tessa's response.

Leo, however, was not so pleased when he met them and found out what he'd gotten into. He led Tessa's group into the elevator and took them up to a corporate lounge, saying bluntly, "I'll answer whatever factual questions you have about birth control, but I'm not going to be filmed as part of your efforts to smear some poor family."

Daphne, standing half a foot over slim and immaculately dressed Leo, beamed down. "Why would you think we'd want anything other than facts?"

And to Tessa's pleasant surprise, Daphne did simply ask for facts once they were all seated. She verified the functioning stats of contraceptive implants and asked for Leo's opinion on the brand of Helene's, which turned out to be one of Estocorp's competitors. Leo answered truthfully.

"It's a decent product. We've all got to meet government standards, especially that ten-year mark. Defects happen, though. Could've happened to them."

"Is it possible the Lin family could have tampered with it?" asked Daphne.

"It'd be difficult," he said. "They'd have to physically harm it, dig into the arm with a knife, maybe. That'd show up on the implant if they examine it, not to mention the girl."

Daphne looked unhappy at not having clear-cut evidence to support her theory. "I've heard of people remotely programming implants."

Leo smiled and shook his head. "Not a contraceptive one used by the average consumer. Military implants can be programmed remotely. Praetorians, for example, can have their implants' instructions modified. Female praetorians have contraceptive functions rolled into their military ones, so yes, you could theoretically tamper with one remotely in that case, but I'm guessing your victim—I mean, interviewee—wasn't in some secret junior praetorian program."

Daphne nodded in acceptance. "Thank you, Mr. Chan. I'll take this into consideration." Tessa, however, doubted anything that didn't back up Daphne's sensational angle would ever see airtime.

"Happy to help my little friend here, even if she is keeping surprising company," said Leo, giving Tessa a wry look. "Glad you've got a school you like, though."

"How do you want to be credited if I do cite you?" asked Daphne, taking out her ego. "Tessa said you work here and for the government."

"Government stuff's freelance and unrelated," said Leo. "Just use my Estocorp title—lead engineer."

Daphne nodded and made a note. She then looked up at him with a sly smile. "If you have done work for SCI, I'd love to get your opinion on the religious nature of this."

He held up his hands. "No way. I wouldn't even dream of commenting on that stuff. Everything I've done for them has been in a technical capacity. I have no expertise on the rest. Badger Justin for that."

Tessa hugged him and thanked him for his time. Daphne, eager to begin her editing and get the jump on any other reporters, accepted defeat in getting more out of Leo and waited impatiently at the door with Felix. "Well?" she asked Tessa. "Ready to see how editing makes magic?"

"Uh . . . sure," said Tessa, quickly taking out her ego as she fell into step with the others. "I just need to send a message to Darius. I didn't think we'd be out this long, and I'd told him I'd meet him for lunch."

"Lunch was three hours ago," Daphne pointed out.

Tessa smiled. "He's working a weird shift at the senate today. So he has a weird lunchtime."

Daphne came to a halt by the elevator and gave Tessa a long, searching look. "Go on," she told Felix after a few moments. "We'll catch up later." When he was gone, she turned back to Tessa. "Your castal friend works at the senate?"

"He has an internship," said Tessa uneasily, not liking the shift in attention. "Justin helped him get it. Through Lucian."

Daphne's eyes narrowed. "He works for Senator Darling?"

"I don't know who he works for exactly. I mean, probably not Lucian since Lucian's not in the country."

"But his work still carries on," Daphne murmured. She stared off into space for several seconds, and Tessa could practically see the wheels of scheming in the other woman's head. "Don't cancel plans on my account. Keep your lunch date."

"It's not a date," said Tessa quickly. "Not that kind of date."

Daphne continued as though Tessa hadn't spoken. "And while you're there, see if your friend's come across one Dr. Nico Cassidy."

The name meant nothing to Tessa. "Who's he?"

"A person of interest," said Daphne, after a bit of consideration. "Someone who spends an awful lot of time with Senator Darling's political party."

"Maybe he's their doctor," suggested Tessa.

"He's not a medical doctor. He's their wellness counselor—if you believe that."

"Well, there you go. That's why he spends so much time with their party." Tessa might have been getting more out of this internship than she'd expected, but jumping on board with every conspiracy theory still wasn't her style. The RUNA's health-care system required psychiatric evaluations every few years, along with citizens' normal physicals. Those deemed to be in stressful or high-profile professions—like the military or politics—received them more frequently, and unlike in Panama, mental health issues had less of a stigma here. A political party having its own therapist on hand to monitor members was standard practice.

Daphne clearly thought otherwise. "There's something weird about this guy. I've tried to research him, and he's been remarkably difficult. I had a source that suggested he might be involved with a religious group, but I haven't been able to find any other leads."

"Maybe there are none," said Tessa. "Maybe your source was wrong. And besides, not everyone involved in religion is newsworthy."

"They are if they're advising a major political party," Daphne countered. "Especially one that's carrying the next consul. The people have a right to know the truth, and if you care anything about this country, you'll use your inside connections to find out more about Dr. Cassidy."

Tessa somehow doubted Daphne was as concerned about the country as her career. "Sorry. Unless he walks right up to me and tells me his story, you're out of luck. There's no way I'm going to make Darius abuse his position to get us a story. It's wrong."

Daphne shook her head in exaggerated disappointment. "And here I thought you had the makings of a real journalist."

Tessa tried to ignore the jab as she and Rufus made their way to the senate. She believed in the truth, but that didn't mean taking the immoral routes Daphne always seemed to suggest.

"Darius can only sign in one guest," Tessa told Rufus as they approached the senate steps. "Do you mind waiting? There are a few cafés around here."

Rufus frowned. "I'm not supposed to leave you."

"It's just like leaving me at school," she explained. "You trust their security. It's probably better here."

He paused and surveyed the line of black-uniformed praetorians standing guard out front. Tessa knew most of the actual security screening took place inside, but they were still a formidable array. "I suppose," Rufus admitted gruffly. "Though at your school, I know I can come in at any time. Call me as soon as you're ready to leave, and I'll meet you back here."

Tessa agreed and made her way into the senate alone, feeling surprisingly free, as though she were getting away with something after being shadowed these last few days. Darius met her at the main security checkpoint, where she was screened and checked for weapons before he was allowed to bring her in with a visitor's pass.

"I'm so glad you could make it," he told her, eyes shining. He was wearing a suit and tie that looked a little too big for him. "In just two days, I've learned so much."

"That's great," she said, trying not to gape. Even in late afternoon, the senate was abuzz with activity. Tour groups viewed the public areas while lobbyists, politicians, and aides hurried back and forth through the crowded corridors, everyone intent on his or her destination. She couldn't help but share a little of his awe at the wheels of the Gemman government turning around them. Darius gave her an informal tour of the building parts that were open to her and then led her to the cafeteria.

"This is only one of them," he clarified. "There's another more exclusive one that the elected officials use, but a lot of them still come down here to eat with us workers. Isn't that great?"

Tessa wondered if that was truly out of a desire to bond with ordinary people or more for show. She then wondered at what point during her time in the RUNA she'd become so jaded.

She wasn't that hungry but followed him into a serving line, one that advertised various grilled sandwiches. It was one of the longest lines, so presumably it was good. He happily chatted away about his day's goings-on as they waited, and she found herself charmed, in spite of herself. Suddenly, he gasped and clutched her arm. "Do you know who we're standing behind?" he whispered.

Tessa didn't and shook her head. All she could see of the two men in front of her were their backs.

"That's Magnus Mercado. He's the chair of the Citizens' Party."

She knew the name. It was hard not to. Lucian Darling might have been poised for greatness, but at the moment, Senator Mercado was the most powerful person in their party, elected by its members. Since Darius had gained his internship through Lucian, she knew his work here involved a lot of errands for that particular party, but she got the impression Darius rarely dealt with its high-ranking members. His starry-eyed look confirmed as much.

Mercado glanced back just then, causing Darius to gulp. The senator was a striking man, handsome even in his early fifties, with a bit of silver almost artfully touching his black hair. He smiled a showman's smile as his dark eyes fell on an awestruck Darius.

"Well, hello there. Demetrius, right?"

"Darius, sir. But I mean, you can call me D-Demetrius if you want, sir."

Mercado gave a great booming laugh. "Ah, I love a sense of humor. I hope you're settling in nicely? Everyone's treating you well?"

Darius, who clearly couldn't believe the senator even knew he was alive, nodded vigorously. "Yes, sir. Very much, sir."

"Good, good. We were just talking about the importance of to-day's youth showing interest and involvement in our country." Mercado turned his smile on Tessa. "Hopefully you're recruiting more for the cause."

Even Tessa couldn't help but feel a little flustered under that powerful gaze. "I'm just visiting today, sir." Hoping she wasn't being too forward, she offered her hand. "Teresa Cruz."

Mercado took it graciously. "It's a pleasure to meet you, Miss Cruz. Do you mind me asking where you're from?"

She blushed, not from the attention so much as realizing that no matter how good her English was, she still hadn't shaken her accent. "Panama, sir. A family friend helped me get a student visa, and I go to school at Creative Minds now."

"Her friend knows Senator Darling," piped up Darius. "He's the one who helped get me here too."

Mercado's attention was on Tessa, though, and he nudged the man beside him. "You hear that? Creative Minds is a great school. It's a long trip to there from the provinces. You're living the Gemman dream, Miss Cruz."

"Thank you, sir," said Tessa uncertainly.

"You should have her come speak to your kids." Mercado had turned his attention back to his companion. "I think it'd be highly informative for them."

The man, who was younger than Mercado and had typically plebeian features, nodded in agreement and gave her a charismatic smile. "I think so too. They're all enthusiastic, but I think it's important for them to talk to others of different backgrounds."

"Forgive me," said Mercado. "I'm speaking over you. Tessa, Darius, this is our wellness counselor, Dr. Nico Cassidy. When he's not listening to us bemoan our problems, he runs a youth group for those interested in politics. Secondary and tertiary aged. It'd be a great favor to us if you'd consider visiting it sometime. You too," he added to Darius, clearly as an afterthought.

Tessa nearly dropped the empty tray she was carrying, and it had nothing to do with being extended a personal invitation by someone so powerful. Nico Cassidy. This was the man Daphne had told her about, the one who possibly had ties to a religion. Looking at him now, Tessa saw nothing particularly sinister about him. He might not have been a politician, per se, but he had that same polished feel that everyone else in this field seemed to radiate.

"It would be an honor, sir," exclaimed Darius. Then, seeming to realize Tessa and her exotic background were his ticket in, he glanced at her. "Right? Wouldn't you like to go, Tessa?"

In truth? Not really. Tessa had too much on her plate with Daphne and school to take on some extracurricular activity. But the pleading in Darius's voice was unmistakable. She also couldn't shake Daphne's reminders about her being a good journalist and the public's right to know the truth. Even Tessa's own words came back to haunt her, about how she wouldn't use Darius to learn about Dr. Cassidy. *Unless he walks right up to me and tells me his story, you're out of luck.*

Well, Tessa had technically walked up to him, but here he was, inviting her to learn more about him—and Darius seemed more than eager to help, though his motives were obviously different from hers. In fact, she didn't even know what her motives were. She still wasn't sure she bought Daphne's conspiracy theory, but if ever there was a time to investigate, here it was.

"Tessa?" Darius prompted.

All three men watched her expectantly, and she mustered a brave smile. "Sure," she said. "I'd love to."

# CHAPTER 11

# SPIRITUAL COIN

A knock at the bedroom door woke Justin out of a surprisingly sound sleep. The accommodations they'd given him weren't fancy, but they were clean and functional. Even a stiff bed was better than no bed after yesterday's mentally and physically exhausting day. Pushing aside the covers, he sat up and wasn't surprised to see that Mae was already at the door. She opened it unhesitatingly, and through his sleepy brain, he noted that the knock had been done in a pattern the Gemmans had established among themselves.

"Pardon me, ma'am." A young Gemman soldier in gray and maroon stood outside the door. "There's an Arcadian at the other door who says she's here to collect you and the other women for breakfast. To make breakfast," he amended, blushing. It looked like it was killing him to deliver such humiliating news to someone he considered a superior.

"What time is it?" asked Justin. They'd left their egos at the Gemman base, and there wasn't even a manual alarm clock in this room, let alone the sophisticated system he had back home that would tell him the time, weather, and news with a voice command.

"Oh-four-hundred," said the solider apologetically. "Local time."

The early hour meant little to sleepless Mae, and from the looks of her, she must have grabbed a shower and clean change of clothes overnight. Whatever resentment she might have felt about the tasks at hand, she pushed it down with soldierly discipline and even managed a parting smile for Justin. He fell back asleep almost immediately after she left and was awakened again later by the same soldier at the door.

"It's six, sir," he said when Justin staggered to answer it. "Daily meeting in a half hour, then breakfast."

Justin managed to yawn out his thanks and then made his way to a shower. The guesthouse held two of them, and he was lucky enough to find Phil just finishing up. The water was hot and plentiful, even with so many people at the estate, and as Justin slowly woke up, he found himself thinking again about Mae's words and how the Arcadians were perfectly advanced when they wanted to be. Afterward, he put on one of his best suits and wandered back to the common area, just as the others were sitting down to the first of their daily check-ins while here in Arcadia.

"All clear," said George, taking a seat beside Lucian. Along with the five main delegates, three of the commanding officers from the Gemman soldiers were also present. "No listening devices."

"Good," said Lucian. Cleaned and dressed, he too looked as though he'd had a solid night's sleep. "Let's get started since we're all here."

"Not all of us are here," grumbled George. "The praetorian women were supposed to be part of these meetings, not off degrading themselves with household labor."

"They knew what they were getting into, and it's not degrading," insisted Atticus. "I mean . . . it is, since women are expected to suffer and have harder lots, but they aren't singling our women out. Besides, it's just housework. I'm sure they'd rather be doing that than risking their lives in a border battle."

"You obviously haven't spent much time around praetorians," said Justin.

Lucian leaned forward in his chair and rested his chin on folded hands. "If you ask me, we're degrading the women by even suggesting this is a problem. They're smart. They're competent. They can handle this, so let's get on to the rest of the day's itinerary and hope we're just as successful."

Atticus was only too happy to jump into his paperwork. The presidential luncheon had been planned before their arrival, so many of the details were familiar. Lucian would be the superstar, with the others playing supporting roles.

"The tour afterward should be straightforward," continued Atticus, scrolling through his itinerary on a very basic reader. "George—I doubt they'll take us anywhere too sensitive, but keep your eyes open. And as for you, Justin." Atticus set the reader down and looked up. "Meeting with the Grand Disciple's a pretty big deal. Not sure what brought this about, but be careful. Even in Arcadia, the president has to go through the motions of the law. But the Grand Disciple . . . well, his word is kind of its own law."

"In other words," said Lucian, "don't piss him off."

"Wouldn't dream of it," said Justin. "Any idea why he's asked for this meeting?"

Atticus shook his head. "He may just be curious. And we have to remember that having religion and politics mixed is absolutely normal for them. It may just be a matter of us having never considered that a priest would be involved in a state visit."

After going over a few more points, Atticus wrapped up the meeting, just as an Arcadian soldier came to fetch them for breakfast. Justin had the impression they weren't a normal fixture in Carl's household, but during this Gemman visit, they were serving as regular go-betweens. The soldier took them out to the same dining room, which only had one table, for the men, this time. The women, Justin was told, would eat on their own later and would work now to feed and serve the men. It was something of a relief to him that only Carl's household women did the actual serving. He wasn't sure he could've handled the awkwardness of Mae or Val being subservient, faked or not.

Their host was in good spirits, delighted to hear that everyone had slept well and found the accommodations satisfactory. Lunch with the president wasn't a normal occurrence for him, so he was equally puffed with pride to be playing a role in that and help out the undersecretary who'd come to school the Gemmans in any additional pieces of etiquette. Atticus had done a pretty thorough job, and by the time the meal was finished, Justin found himself surprisingly calm about going off to meet the secular leader of one of his country's greatest enemies. That would mostly be Lucian's show anyway.

The Gemman women were allowed to see them off as the rest of the household women began trickling into the dining room to quietly clear dishes. None of the praetorians looked the worse for wear, and Justin reminded himself that there was some truth to Atticus's earlier words: A little domestic work was nothing compared to the type of warfare they normally engaged in, even if they preferred the latter.

"Did you make the pancakes?" Justin asked Mae softly when she came up to him.

"I was in charge of putting jam into those little individual serving dishes everyone had," she returned. "Did you notice those?"

"Oh yeah," he said, as Lucian strolled over to them. "We were just having a big discussion about how artful they were, weren't we?"

Lucian favored her with a grin. "Absolutely. Never seen anything like it. Is it selfish of me to hope you'll be out touring with us, even though it's probably better you go with Justin to the temple?"

Mae's amusement faded. "Do we know anything more about that?"

"No," said Justin. "Atticus is still looking into it and will let you know after we—"

A cracking sound jolted the three of them out of conversation, and they turned to stare as Carl's second-oldest son, Jasper, stood over one of the household women. Running through yesterday's introductions (or lack thereof), Justin was pretty sure she was one of the concubines, the youngest of the lot. She sprawled back on the floor, and an angry red mark on her face indicated she'd just been hit. Carl stormed over.

"What's going on?" he demanded.

Jasper pointed an accusing finger. "That whore was brandishing her legs for them!"

Carl's face turned even redder than hers, and she cowered under his scowl. "The strap on my shoe got caught in my skirt, and I had to push it up to fix it so that I wouldn't trip," she said meekly.

"Next time, you trip and break your ankle," growled Carl. Then, to Justin's complete and utter horror, Carl struck the girl too.

Beside Justin, Mae jerked, and he held her hand, pulling her back. Anger filled her teal eyes as she fixed her gaze on him.

"It's not our fight," he said, his voice barely a whisper. "Let it go."

"It's savage," she hissed back. "Someone should do something."

He tightened his hold, knowing if she truly wanted to get away, she could. "Not us. Not this time."

Mae looked as though she might still act and then finally gave a reluctant nod. Justin nearly relaxed, and then, suddenly, Jasper lunged for the girl without warning. He was fast—but not nearly as fast as Val, who put herself between him and his victim, catching hold of his wrist as it came down for another blow. Jasper's eyes widened, his jaw dropping as he struggled to form words.

"What," he gasped, "do you think you're doing?"

In the few seconds that passed, Justin could read the story unfolding. He was about to turn his fury on Val, and if he did, there'd be no stopping her from tearing him to pieces. Gone was the normally lighthearted woman Justin saw. There was a predator in her place, one who didn't take well to seeing innocents abused.

"Val!" boomed Lucian. "Step away immediately!" He managed to sound as outraged as any good Arcadian man would in such a situation, but Justin suspected fear was actually the senator's dominant emotion at the moment.

It was Mae who resolved things, however, by abruptly pulling Val away. From the look in Val's eyes, she was probably the only one who could have.

Atticus hurried forward and immediately began uttering apologies. Carl didn't look too happy about the turn of events, but he was too sensitive to the political balance at stake. His son, however, had no such qualms.

"Father," he exclaimed, pointing an accusing finger at where Mae still held Val, "are you going to let her get away with that?"

"*They* will deal with that," Carl said. He turned toward one of the older women. "And we will deal with *her*. Make sure this doesn't happen again." The older woman gave a curt nod and dragged the girl on the floor from the room. When they were gone, he turned a stiff smile on his guests. "Embarrassing. It's what I get for saving money and going to one of the country salons. Don't worry— Harriet'll take care of things. Let's go."

"Father—" Jasper tried again.

"Enough," warned Carl.

Lucian wisely sent the praetorian women away as well. They went without protest, but Justin could see the anger in their eyes as they left.

*This is what sets them off,* he thought. *Not painstakingly filling little cups with jam. They're trained to be the strongest and the best, to fight their enemies and defend those weaker themselves. We're asking them to stand aside.*

*Will following orders trump their instincts?* asked Horatio.

That was a question for later, Justin supposed. For now, he had to continue on with the public relations game and their day of touring. Carl led the Gemmans out cheerfully, as though the incident hadn't happened, but a slight cloud hung over Justin and his colleagues. No one was naïve enough to think domestic violence didn't happen in the RUNA, but it certainly wasn't openly accepted—especially over the baring of an ankle.

Everyone did their best to have their social masks back in place when they reached downtown Divinia, which displayed the same mix of affluence that Justin had observed on the bus ride. Government and religious buildings were well maintained, but more common dwellings and businesses reflected Arcadia's patchy economy. Justin was happy to see the original capitol building still stood and had been restored after the chaos and destruction that had swept Arcadia following the Decline. A number of less elaborate buildings flanked it, modern establishments that had been added on to carry the administrative burden of running an entire country. The original building made a prettier backdrop, though, and that was where they focused a lot of photo ops before going inside. Justin also finally got to see what passed as the Arcadian press. Considering that the government censored its media, he supposed it shouldn't have been a surprise that they got by on a handful of journalists, rather than the RUNA's horde.

The Arcadian president, Enoch Campbell, had earned his office through a fixed election and looked pretty much like every other politician Justin had ever met. Apparently that was something universal across cultures. President Campbell and Lucian smiled and simpered at each other as they toured the capitol building and made grandiose claims for the future of their countries. Some of those claims were even lightly touched upon at a pre-lunch reception, when the two leaders—with assistance from economic expert Phil—brought up the potential export of Arcadian oil to the RUNA. Considering Arcadia's oil-rich southwestern borderlands were those the RUNA was constantly encroaching on, Justin supposed trade over invasion could be another promising outcome on this trip.

No one expected him to participate in that negotiation, however. He worked the room of government officials and made small talk, complimenting the country's food and beauty. More of the same came when he was seated for lunch later that afternoon. They served cordials with lunch, and his tablemates were particularly fascinated to hear about his trips to various provinces. Discussing the tensions between their own countries might have been taboo, but the provinces provided a safe third party that Gemmans and Arcadians alike could mock. All the while, Lucian and Campbell stayed thick as thieves, supposedly doing great things to usher in peace.

*He needs more than pictures,* Justin told the ravens. *He needs those too, but he also needs to walk away from this trip with one concrete souvenir in place, whether it's a trade agreement or something else.*

*And he also needs to survive so that he can actually walk away,* added Horatio.

*That's not even an issue anymore. They're dancing on eggshells as much as we are. As long as no one does anything too stupid, we'll all walk out of here just fine.* Justin glanced around the banquet room. *This really isn't any more dangerous than the corporate training getaways SCI used to send us on, except with weird accents and no women.*

He'd been told the lunch had been prepared by women, but they were far removed from this space, with all the serving being done by teenage boys from prestigious families. That made Justin's mind wander to Mae, and it was a relief when the presidential activities disbanded and he and the other Gemmans were sent on to their next stop. They found the praetorian women in the capitol's lobby, waiting to join in on the tour of the city. Mae wasn't with them.

"She's waiting for you in a car outside," said Val as Justin approached. A grin lit her face. "She's, uh, something else."

"She always is," said Justin.

But when he reached the waiting car and slid into the backseat, he immediately discovered what Val had meant. Mae—at least he assumed it was her—was literally covered from head to toe. It looked as though she had on a long Arcadian dress that was thick even by their standards. He couldn't see many details because a long veil of heavy material hooded her and wrapped around her body, all the way to her feet. It had at least been done in a way that gave her partial use of her arms and hands, which were gloved. A thinner material, but still opaque, hung over her face, and he hoped she could see out of it better than he could see in.

"I thought it'd be black for some reason," said Justin, "Maybe that'd be too chic." The color—if one could call it that—was a muddy mix of gray and brown.

"They're going for as unflattering as possible," came her voice through the veil. "Just in case obscuring all feminine shape and even the ability to walk didn't do it."

The car merged into traffic, and Justin leaned forward to ask the driver how long until they were at the temple—in Mandarin.

"I beg your pardon?" asked the man, startled.

Justin switched to English. "Sorry. Wasn't thinking. How long until we get there?"

"Ten minutes."

No matter how often he visited the provinces, actual drivers instead of automated cars were still odd to Justin. It just didn't seem like a good idea to trust control of a bunch of large machines to humans alone. The RUNA and EA were the only places technologically advanced enough to have automated traffic networks or run their cars without fossil fuels. The smell of gasoline always grated on Justin. Still, he felt smug as he settled back in the seat.

"Oversight on their part," he told Mae, switching back to Mandarin. Although it wasn't used regularly in the RUNA, all children learned it in school, just as EA children learned English. "They should have a Mandarin speaker out with every Gemman on this trip."

"He could be faking," she said.

"I saw his expression. He wasn't, but I'm sure at least one of the soldiers wandering Carl's halls knows it."

"Probably," she agreed. "Most of them took an extended break once you guys left, by the way. I guess they didn't see us as much of a threat."

Even with the language protection, Justin found himself lowering his voice. "How is that girl? She's one of the concubines, right?"

"Hannah," said Mae. "And yes, she's his newest. From what I gathered, she's been with their family six months, and this isn't the first time Jasper's had a problem with her."

"You mean not the first time that she's wickedly lured him with her charms?"

Mae's expression was obscured, but Justin guessed she was scowling, judging from the way her gloved hands clenched into fists. "From the way he watches all of us, I'd say anything female lures him. He just stands there while we're working—kitchen, dining room, whatever. Claims he's 'supervising,' but there's no question what he's really thinking about. Sounds like his older brother—Walter—used to have issues too, but he's mellowed out since getting engaged. I guess the promise of sex'll do that."

"No wonder. These guys are sexually frustrated, and their dad is hoarding all the women." An alarming thought occurred to Justin. "He hasn't threatened any of you, has he?"

She shook her head. "I don't think he'd dare, at least without serious provocation, which we haven't given him. Hannah's the easier target. She seems to know it, as do a couple of the other women. They go out of their way to make sure she's not alone. If something happened, and Jasper raped her, the blame would be put on her shoulders. She could be beaten, sold, or—in extreme cases—put to death. It's disgusting. This whole place is."

Justin said nothing because there was nothing to say. He couldn't lie and act like things would get better. Reminding her she'd wanted to come here wouldn't help either. Further conversation was put on hold anyway when they reached the temple, which left both of them speechless for entirely different reasons.

Although the RUNA technically allowed freedom of religion, most practitioners knew they were expected to be discreet. Those whose facilities actually looked like temples and churches kept them out of urban centers. Those within populated areas usually opted for brisk, modern business suites that didn't draw too much attention. The largest religious facility—if it could be called that—was the Church of Humanity, which was actually a secular institution that held services and sermons emphasizing the country's social values.

But even that was dwarfed by the Temple of Nehitimar. It was bigger than the capitol building, even with its additions, taking up more city blocks than Justin could see. He and Mae stood at the curb, gawking up at the temple's spiraling heights and rich embellishment. It was literally decorated with gold and jewels, contrasting oddly with some of the run-down buildings and bedraggled pedestrians nearby, but the heavily armed and cloaked temple soldiers surrounding the grounds must have been enough of a deterrent against any would-be thieves.

"What is all this space for?" Justin asked the driver in English. "It can't all be worship."

The driver nodded toward an approaching man. "Ask him."

"Dr. March?" The young man wore a gray and deep blue uniform, indicative of temple service. "I'm Deacon Hansen, here to take you to see His Piousness." The man did not appear interested in meeting Mae, and Justin didn't attempt an introduction. Instead, he repeated his question as Hansen led them up the temple stairs.

"The temple has all sorts of uses," Hansen told them. "Worship space, school, the priests' homes. Nehitimar's work requires a lot of space."

He paused in his explanation and glanced back, realizing his guests had fallen behind. Mae's tightly wrapped dress and veil made it impossible for her to take anything but the smallest of steps. Justin, not caring if she felt coddled or not, linked his arm through hers as she made her way along, half-afraid she'd topple over. If the Arcadians had wanted to eradicate any sign of alluring female movement, they'd succeeded. They'd all but hobbled one of the most graceful and athletic women Justin knew. Hansen looked displeased, but whether that was simply because a woman was going to see the Grand Disciple or because Justin was helping her, it was hard to say.

Justin soon saw that Mae wasn't the only woman there that day—just the only woman going into the inner depths of the temple. When they cleared the grand main doors, they found themselves standing in a huge open lobby with vaulted ceilings and a fountain nearly two stories high. Icons of various figures from the Arcadian religion decorated the walls, with Nehitimar himself always portrayed as largest and grandest. Worshippers knelt in front of the images, leaving offerings of various types behind—candles, flowers, incense, even bread. In a far corner, vendors in temple uniforms sold the offerings to long lines of petitioners.

"Offerings left to Nehitimar and his holy host must be sanctified and appropriate in order for blessings to be received," Hansen explained, seeing Justin stop and take it all in. Hansen nodded toward an icon of a woman in a flowing dress, with a wide-brimmed flowered hat, kneeling at the feet of Nehitimar, who was depicted as more than twice her size. Several Arcadian women knelt before the image, setting down piles of white orchids. Although modestly dressed, none of them were Cloistered. Justin also noted their attire was rougher and much less well made than that of Carl's women. His family was among the Arcadian elite. This was the average citizenry.

"That image is Nehitimar's wife, Hiriana the Fruitful," Hansen continued. "She was rewarded with many children and can put in a good word with Nehitimar to share the blessing of fertility for those who show the proper respect."

"With that orchid," said Justin. "What happens if someone brings a different flower?"

Hansen looked shocked. "They wouldn't consider it. It'd be sacrilege. They'd be removed, and Hiriana might very well ask Nehitimar to curse them. No one would take that risk."

"Understandable. But that kind of orchid is rare and expensive, even where I come from. It must be difficult for some people to bring them."

"That's why we make it easy on them," said Hansen, his features smoothing again. He nodded toward the vendors. "They may purchase the flowers here. In fact, the temples are the only places that sell them in the country, appropriately blessed and ready for offering."

Justin nodded in agreement. "Very convenient."

*Very convenient for the temple,* he thought. *I'll bet the other requisite offerings for the holy host are only available for sale here too. Nice way to turn a profit, that and the fee for even entering.*

*You got in free of charge,* said Horatio. *What are you complaining about?*

Thinking Justin was satisfied with the answer, Hansen led them through the rest of the foyer, to a door marked CLERGY AND TEMPLE PERSONNEL ONLY. It was smaller than the larger, grander doors that indicated the entrance to the public sanctuary and was labeled NO WOMEN BEYOND THIS POINT.

Hansen led them through a winding series of hallways used exclusively by those who served the temple in some capacity. They passed a few people who seemed startled by Mae, but Hansen was apparently a well-known enough figure that no one questioned anything. These corridors were as richly decorated as everything in the public areas, but Justin didn't find himself awed by it so much as the infrastructure that it was connected to.

*All of this is public, authorized, and accepted,* he thought with a chill. *No worship in the shadows. We have nothing like this in the RUNA. The Morrigan had a fraction of this, and her servants had incredible abilities. What kind of power does this god have, when he has such a foothold in the mortal world?*

*Wait and see,* responded Magnus grimly.

Their journey ended before another set of heavily embellished doors, ones that were also guarded by openly armed temple soldiers. They nodded when they saw Hansen and stepped aside, allowing him to push open the doors. Justin followed him inside and had a surreal moment, feeling as though he'd left the temple and stepped into someone's luxury penthouse back in the RUNA. They stood in another entryway, this one just as opulent as the temple's main entrance, if smaller. Only, whereas that had attempted to create a sense of ancient awe and majesty, this was all done with modern sensibilities.

Secular art from a famous EA artist Justin recognized hung around them, and the works appeared to be originals. They were juxtaposed with a modern flat screen hanging near the doorway, apparently to entertain guests who had to wait for further instructions. Arcadian news scrolled across it, none of it mentioning the Gemman delegation. A voice called for them to enter, and Hansen beckoned Justin and Mae forward through a doorway.

They entered a living room with more expensive art and leather furniture, including a narrow wooden bench near the back where Hansen made a sharp gesture for Mae to sit. The room's focus was a breathtaking picture window that looked out over the city, taking up almost all of one wall. A man stood gazing out it with his back to them, and here, old and new worlds clashed again. Because while the apartment was modern, this priest—or Grand Disciple, to be more accurate—was straight out of the pages of some mythology textbook. He wore floor-length, purple brocaded robes embellished with more of the gold and jewels this place loved to buy with its offering profits. When he turned, Justin got a full view of a two-foot-high golden crown. The man's hands were clasped together, hidden within voluminous sleeves, and the ornamentation even went so far as to extend into his salt-and-pepper beard, which had tiny jewels woven into its ends. He carried no golden staff, nor was there one on display that Justin could see.

But none of that bejeweled splendor was what took Justin's breath away. It was the wave of invisible power that rolled off the man when he faced Justin. Justin had never encountered it, power with such a tangible force that he felt like he was trying to keep his balance in a boat on choppy seas.

*He's one of the elect,* Justin thought to the ravens. *Or is he something more? I've never felt anything like this.*

*Because the scattered cults in your own country are but candle flames to this bonfire,* said Magnus.

*He's not making any attempt to hide what he is,* said Justin.

*Why should he?* countered Magnus. *He has no rivals here.*

A panicked thought hit Justin. *Can he sense me? Will the charm hold?*

*It'll hold,* said Horatio, who didn't sound nearly as convincing as Justin would've liked.

"Your Piousness." Hansen fell to his knees before the Grand Disciple and kissed the proffered ring. "I've brought you Justin March, from the Lost Lands."

Justin almost smiled. He knew that was what Arcadians called the RUNA behind closed doors, though everyone on this trip had been very careful not to use the term around him and the other Gemmans. Many Arcadians found "Republic of United North America" offensive, seeing as they clearly weren't included in the *united* part.

"Thank you, Timothy. You may leave us." Hansen nearly trembled at the use of his given name, and Justin wondered if the deacon's faith was just that strong. It would have to be, to work in a place like this.

*That*, added Magnus, *and a powerful elect has that effect on one of the uninitiated.*

Hansen left with no introduction for Mae, who seemed content to remain a veiled shadow in the back of the room. Justin approached the Grand Disciple, uneasily wondering if he was expected to kiss the ring too. When the Grand Disciple extended his hand, however, it was for a handshake between equals, not a sign of obeisance.

"It's a pleasure to meet you, Dr. March," the Grand Disciple said. Justin had researched as much as he could on Arcadian religion before the trip and knew the man's real name, but it seemed it wouldn't be used today. Those who served Nehitimar believed his Grand Disciple gave up all personal identity . . . if not personal luxury.

"You honor me," said Justin, getting acclimated to that elect aura. The man's presence was still intimidating, but a lot of it now was psychological. Justin had just spent the first part of the day with the country's secular leaders, yet combined, they didn't wield the power of this one man alone.

"I'm sorry to receive you in such humble accommodations," the Grand Disciple said.

Justin glanced at the lush surroundings in surprise. "Begging your pardon, but we must have different cultural interpretations of 'humble.' These apartments are lovely."

"Indeed, but this is my home in the temple. I have a much more hospitable residence on Holy Lake that I prefer to receive guests in, when time and duty permits."

"I'm more than honored to be received here," Justin assured him.

The Grand Disciple smiled, revealing a tightness in his skin that suggested Cain treatments, something the Arcadians claimed was a sign of vanity. He gestured for Justin to sit down on one of the leather armchairs. The priest himself settled into the center of a love seat, spreading out his robes so that they took over in a magnificent and sparkling display. A remote control rested on the love seat's arm, and he pushed a few buttons. The soft classical music vanished, and the entire panel of the giant window slid down, opening up the top section to the outdoors.

"We have air-conditioning, of course, but I love fresh air, especially in the evening. All the technology in the world can't make up for what our creator's already given us sometimes." The Grand Disciple smiled again and nodded to a decanter of wine on the low glass table between them. "Please, help yourself. It's imported from Argentina. You're probably pretty familiar with their wines after your stay in Panama."

Justin returned the smile, albeit stiffly. So. He wasn't the only one who'd done research. "I am indeed. Sometimes it was the only drinkable stuff I could get ahold of."

The Grand Disciple poured himself a glass when Justin had filled his own. "I'd like to visit the provinces, but I don't know if my vocation will ever allow it. There's much to do here."

"Running this temple alone must be like managing a city," said Justin. "I can't imagine how much work you have to do for the rest of the country."

"Nehitimar has called me, so I must do the best I can. And he's very generous in the many other servants he's provided to assist me."

Justin thought about all the temple staff and priests he'd witnessed walking in today. "Very generous," he agreed.

"Does this bother you?" the Grand Disciple asked. "Talking so openly about a god? Talking about a god as though he's real? I know you Gemmans don't believe in such things."

"Our country maintains an open policy toward religious belief." The words were automatic. A servitor's mantra.

"Some of your scattered citizens do, perhaps, but not people in your profession. And don't get me wrong." The Grand Disciple paused to sip his wine. "I respect what you do. We have our own branch of the priesthood dedicated to weeding out heretics in our midst. It's important to keep the faith pure."

"I don't think I have very much in common with your Examiners."

"Even so, you have a good eye for what's important to your country, as do I." The Grand Disciple set down his wine and leaned forward, ringed hands clasped together over his knees. "Do you know why I asked you here, Dr. March? Because believe me, Enoch didn't initially approve of this meeting."

The priest was on a first-name basis with the president, naturally. "Would that have really stopped it?" Justin asked.

That brought another smile to the Grand Disciple's face. "No, but this country runs much more smoothly when Enoch and I are in agreement—or at least when he thinks I'm in agreement with him. You see, no matter what suspicions you might have, Enoch actually would like to establish peaceful relations with your nation. There are things he thinks we need. More efficient fuels. Medical technology. He believes that commerce will be the key to ushering in peace between us, but he's only half-right. It's not currency of the material world your nation needs, but rather, spiritual coin. And that's why I brought you here today, to seek your help in a great endeavor that will unite our countries in a harmonious future."

Justin had no idea what was coming, save that he probably wasn't going to like it. "What endeavor is that?"

"Sending missionaries of Nehitimar into the RUNA."

# CHAPTER 12

# TEMPTATIONS

M ae didn't need Justin's deafening silence to know what an outlandish suggestion the Grand Disciple had just made. Her initial offense at being wrapped in these restrictive garments and discarded in the back of the room had long faded once the weird conversation was up and running. This was not her field of expertise, and she was glad to be ignored. Let Justin navigate these diplomatic waters.

Nonetheless, she dutifully made notes on the exchange that had just taken place, since her ostensible reason for being here was to be Justin's secretary. Before leaving, Hansen had slipped her a small notebook and a pen, which would've almost been comical in any other situation. Everyone in the RUNA typed or used styluses with tablets that would transpose handwriting into neat text. In a situation like this, no one would've bothered with notes. A recorder would've been used. Apparently, this was another instance in which the Arcadians wanted to remain low-tech, and she supposed she should be glad Hansen hadn't given her a scroll and quill.

Justin didn't stay down for long. Per his way, he quickly recovered from the shock of the topic. "You make a valid point that a cultural exchange may be just as valuable as a monetary one," he said carefully. "But I'm not sure this is the best place to start. If you wanted to discuss art or literature, possibly some exchange of students—"

"For us, our religion *is* our primary means of cultural exchange," the priest gently interrupted. "It permeates every part of our society. If we are to be understood, to truly connect with your people, it's important to us that we share our faith. And you just told me yourself that the RUNA is open to different forms of religious worship."

Mae could just barely see Justin's profile and a bitter smile at having his words thrown back at him. "That's true, but we allow those beliefs with certain conditions. One is that we maintain a distinct line between government and religion. And while crossing that line has worked well for your country, I'm afraid it's just something ours isn't ready for."

Justin was being more than diplomatic, Mae thought. For starters, the RUNA was never going to be ready for that kind of theocracy. And to say that it had "worked well" for Arcadia was certainly an exaggeration. The atrocities she'd witnessed in Carl's household were proof of that, let alone the countless reports Gemman intelligence had collected of barbaric justice committed in the name of Nehitimar's religion. Even today's drive into the city had highlighted Arcadia's economic woes, with its wild disparities between rich and poor.

"We have no interest in your government," said the Grand Disciple, voice filled with amusement. "We would rather talk to ordinary people, let our missionaries come and simply explain about Nehitimar to those who will listen."

"Missionaries and public proselytizing are both illegal in the RUNA," Justin told him, in an apologetic way that reminded Mae of when he would tell religious leaders their licenses were being revoked. He managed to sound as though he were legitimately sorry.

The Grand Disciple stayed firm. "I'm not suggesting they convert people on the streets, just that we find a way to let our people communicate with yours about what's most important to us. Perhaps it could be in the context of a larger cultural exchange as you suggested, a series of university lectures about Arcadia, with our faith featured as part of it. We could simply send a group of diplomats and lecturers." Something in the way he spoke made Mae think these all-purpose "lecturers" sharing Arcadian culture had been his original goal but that he'd opened with the far more dramatic suggestion of missionaries to soften the blow.

"I'll take it back to my people and see what they think tonight," said Justin.

"I appreciate that," said the Grand Disciple. "Though I'm sure that, ultimately, they'd defer to your opinion on such matters." He rose to his feet, and Justin immediately followed suit. "Come, I won't keep you any longer. I know you've had a long day and would probably like to rest. If you'd like to speak to me again, simply let your host know, and we'll make it happen."

The two men walked toward the doorway, passing by Mae. The Grand Disciple came to a stop and regarded her with a look that managed to be both fond and condescending. "So this is your secretary? Nehitimar has commanded us that women are best subdued as servants of the home, though Enoch likes to keep telling me that a day may come when we must turn some of ours out to other jobs if we wish to compete globally." He held out his hand for Mae's notebook. Having nothing to hide in it, she handed it over wordlessly. He grunted in approval as he skimmed the pages. "Excellent penmanship. I'd been led to believe Gemmans were so dependent on machines that you could barely spell your names."

Justin leaned in to look at the notebook. "Well, hers is certainly better than mine. She comes from a culture that values such, uh, art forms."

It was true. The castes didn't cling to antiquated technology like the Arcadians did, but there was an emphasis on cultivating skills viewed as signs of civilization. Handwriting, even in an age where devices could do most of the work for you, was one such skill. Mae had spent many hours being drilled in writing letters over and over.

The Grand Disciple glanced up sharply at Justin's words. "Is she from one of the patriarchies?"

Justin looked uneasy at the sudden interest. "Yes. Nordic."

The priest fixed his gaze on her with such intensity that she felt as though he could see right through the veil. Then, most astonishingly of all, he reached toward her face, letting his hand hover there as he shot Justin a questioning look.

"May I?"

Justin appeared understandably confused, his eyes darting to Mae as though he might get some sign from her, but she was equally puzzled. "Yes," he said at last.

Slowly, carefully, the Grand Disciple lifted the semi-opaque veil that hung over her face, removing the black haze from her vision. With equal care, he pushed back the heavier grayish-brown scarf that had been wrapped around her head and obscured her hair. His breath caught, and he let his hand return to his side as he scrutinized her. Mae wasn't easily intimidated, but something in those dark eyes made her skin crawl. That, and there was just something about being near him that made her feel ill at ease. It was like nothing she'd ever felt before, and although she couldn't pinpoint any specific danger, her implant responded accordingly to her discomfort.

"Exquisite," said the Grand Disciple, leaning close. "We have lovely women here, you know. But many of them—and many of us—carry the marks of what you call Cain."

"What do you call it?" asked Justin, sounding curious in spite of himself.

"Nehitimar's justice. The virus that devastated the world was part of his plan, to remind those who, in their arrogance, had forgotten who was truly ruler of this world. It was a righteous punishment that we bore gladly, and those who've inherited the marks wear theirs with pride as well."

Not all of them, apparently. This close, Mae could see where the priest had had treatments done and knew Justin must've noticed as well.

"Your country accepted the vaccine when ours invented it," said Justin lightly.

"Well," said the Grand Disciple, shooting Justin a wry look, "I wouldn't say 'accepted' so much as purchased at exorbitant rates—and that was only when your country was willing to sell, which certainly took a while. But believe me, you wouldn't have 'invented' it if it hadn't been Nehitimar's will. We had served our penance, and he'd determined our time was up. We did not try to skirt our punishment by whoring out our population in unholy pacts with other nations—no matter how attractive the results."

Mae knew that genetic swapping was one of the points of contention that had driven the RUNA and Arcadia apart. The Arcadians had refused to entertain the idea of aggressively mixing their populations with those of Asia, even though early evidence had shown those of heterogeneous backgrounds had greater resistance to Mephistopheles and Cain. She had not, however, known the Arcadians described it in terms of "whoring out" and "unholy pacts."

"But you." The Grand Disciple fixed his attention back on Mae, resting his hand on her cheek. She froze. "You aren't the result of sullied blood and breeding. And to be so unmarked . . . you must come from a blessed lineage." He abruptly turned to Justin. "She's yours?"

Justin's eyes were on the Grand Disciple's hand, still on Mae's cheek. "In a manner of speaking."

"Leave her with me tonight, and I'll make you a wealthy man. Gold and jewels exchange easily in both our countries."

Justin made no jokes, no diplomatic quips. His answer came swift and sudden, with a harshness that astonished Mae. "No."

"It's quite common with concubines here," the Grand Disciple said. "Nehitimar has decreed that their bodies may be freely shared among the faithful—or even the unfaithful, as the case may be." When no response came, he sighed. "I suppose this is where you loftily tell me Gemman women aren't for sale."

"No," said Justin evenly, "this is where I tell you *I* don't share."

For a moment, the whole room was still. Then the Grand Disciple removed his hand and laughed uproariously, an unexpected sound that startled Mae. He straightened up, and some—but not all—of the tension went out of Justin.

"I can't say that I blame you, and I'm not going to quibble over a mere woman when the more important task of spreading Nehitimar's message is on the line." He gave Mae one last lingering look. "But you'd best cover her before you leave this space."

By the time Hansen arrived to escort them out of the temple, Mae was sufficiently Cloistered again. After flowery farewells from the Grand Disciple, she and Justin left, neither saying a word to the other until they were in the car.

"Are you okay?" he asked in Mandarin.

"Are *you*?" she returned. "You looked like you were ready to—"

He shook his head. "Wait until we're back."

Mae bit back her questions and turned her gaze out the window as the car drove through downtown Divinia. She was looking forward to getting back to Carl's, even if it meant more housework, so that she could finally move freely and see without the veil's smoggy haze. Their car stopped at a light in one of the city's more depressed areas, and suddenly, something made her do a double take and break her silence.

"What's that?" she asked Justin.

He followed where she pointed, to a small building on a corner with a red velvet flag hanging over the door. There were no windows or markings of any other kind.

"A salon," he said.

"Where they keep girls . . . for sale."

"When the red's out, it means they have girls available who've hit puberty. They can't be sold before then, and they have to be at least thirteen."

"Thirteen? Is that supposed to be some kind of safeguard?" she asked in disgust.

"It's the best the government can do to show some sort of responsibility. And I've heard that in a few of the more remote and rural salons . . . well, those rules aren't always enforced."

Mae had been unable to tear her gaze from the building, even as the car began moving, but his words suddenly snapped her attention to them. "How many salons are there?"

"In Arcadia?" Justin shrugged. "Countless. I'm sure there's a dozen in this city and its suburbs."

For a brief second, as Mae had stared at that ramshackle salon on the corner, it had so vividly reminded her of the dream that she'd been certain her niece might very well be beyond those walls. But if what he said was true . . . a dozen in metropolitan Divinia? Let alone the rest of the country? A wave of nausea swept through her at the thought. The vision had shown her niece in one of these establishments but had given no indication where. Arcadia was a big country. Mae had no assurance that the salon she wanted was in this city . . . or that her niece was even in one of the so-called civilized ones that "protected" girls until they were thirteen.

At Carl's house, the rest of the Gemman delegation was still out on their city tour. Carl was out as well, though his sons and wives stared as Justin and Mae made their way across the compound to the guesthouse, including Carl's head wife, Harriet. She was carrying buckets of water from the well, another backward practice that the Arcadians employed to build character in their women. Their technology was perfectly capable of modern plumbing. In fact, the bathrooms were fully equipped with it. For cooking, however, household women had to lug water across the property and run it through the kitchen's filtration system, which was in itself pretty sophisticated, only making the whole exercise that much more ridiculous. Mae had yet to engage in the chore, though Val had had plenty to say about her time with it when they were in private.

Harriet stopped in their path now, angling her body from Justin and keeping her eyes turned deferentially away. "Forgive my interruption," she said. That was for him, though the rest of her message was clearly intended for Mae. "Once you've made yourself fit again, we need you to help with dinner preparations. None of the others are back yet, and Hannah isn't able to pull her share." Then, not quite accusingly, she added, "It's a lot of work to feed this many extra mouths."

"Yes, of course," said Mae, glad her face was obscured. "I'll be there as soon as I'm able."

Harriet's sour expression said she was used to more groveling responses, but she accepted that one and went on her way, after a curt nod to Justin.

When they reached the relative security of their room, Mae had one of those fleeting moments she sometimes got as a praetorian, where she wished for sleep. She wanted to throw herself on the bed just then and pass eight hours in a slumber where red velvet flags and "character-building" labor didn't exist. But instead, she began the painstaking process of unwrapping her layers of clothing, so anxious to get out of them that she even let Justin help her. Considering it had taken two of Carl's wives to help her put them on in the first place, she wasn't all that surprised she needed extra assistance. He shook his head in disbelief when they finally got down to the bottom layer, a calf-length shift in that same muddy color, now soaked with sweat.

"Unbelievable," he said, settling down on the bed. "I had no idea there were that many layers under there."

Mae ran a hand through her damp hair, wishing she could shower. It seemed pointless if she just had a night of hard labor ahead. "I guess it takes quite a barrier to protect these people from the evil powers of lust."

His expression darkened. "Well, that still apparently wasn't enough for 'His Piousness.' That guy was one step away from having his hand down his pants. Or robe. Or whatever."

"And you looked like you were one step away from starting an adolescent fight," she chastised. "I appreciate the chivalry, but you didn't really think my virtue was in peril, did you?"

To her surprise, he didn't smile at her joke. "Mae, that man is part lunatic, part genius, and he runs the network of lunatics that runs this country. I know someone like you has never had to worry about being forced by a guy, but believe me when I tell you, if he'd wanted it, he could've gotten a dozen lackeys in there to hold you down and sing hymns to their god while he had his way with you."

It wasn't the graphic image that made Mae wince internally. It was the casual remark about her never having to worry about being forced that momentarily drew her up short. Justin was almost right. Throughout her life, she'd maintained complete control in her sexuality and related choices—with almost one exception.

Her ex-boyfriend, Porfirio Aldaya, had once tried to rape her after their ugly breakup. He wouldn't have called it rape, of course. Mae had fought him off with, unknowingly, the help of the Morrigan, the Celtic goddess who'd tried to control the first part of Mae's life. Even now, Mae wondered if she would have been able to save herself without divine intervention. Porfirio had been stronger than her, trained with the same praetorian skill. And as memories of the terror and feelings of powerlessness swept her, Mae wondered if she would consciously choose divine help to protect herself again, knowing what she knew now.

This was one of the few secrets that not even Justin knew, however, and she kept her troubled feelings off her face as she dismissed his concerns. "We've been saying this whole time the Arcadians don't want an international incident. If he's as much of a genius as you claim, he won't risk the peace over a woman, no matter how much power he can toss around."

Justin looked her over and finally relaxed enough to smile. "Well, you're not just any woman—even in that god-awful scrap of fabric. Don't underestimate these guys' desperation, even the powerful ones." His amusement was fleeting and quickly dried up. "And trust me when I say his power's something else altogether."

She'd started to rummage through her suitcase for a clean dress and paused at his words. "I think I know what you mean," she said slowly. "When we were in there . . . I felt . . ."

Justin leaned forward, holding his breath. "Yes?"

"I don't know how to describe it. It made my skin crawl. Maybe it was nerves. . . ."

"You felt it. You felt that he was one of the elect." He exhaled and sank onto the bed. "I didn't think you could. I don't know if that says more about him or you. You still have the charm?"

She reached under the neckline of the shift and held up the wooden charm, still on its string.

"Good," said Justin. "Don't ever take it off around here. This is a dangerous place to be noticed by the gods." Seeing that she was about to change, he politely turned away. She gratefully rid herself of the shift.

"What will you do about his request to bring in missionaries? Or cultural experts?"

"Take it to Lucian and the others, then give my recommendation," Justin said simply.

"Which is?"

"No fucking way. Nehitimar won't have the power at home that he has here, but letting servants of a god like that into our country is a bad idea, politically and spiritually. Even if they say they're only lecturing about Arcadian culture in general, you know religion will be the real focus."

Mae finished buttoning up the new dress and walked over so that she was in his line of sight again. "Spiritually?"

He nodded. "Things are crazy enough with a bunch of fledgling gods struggling for control. We don't need one that's already established."

Mae left him soon thereafter, stopping by one of the other outlying guesthouses in the hopes of finding Harriet and tonight's instructions. The house showed the signs of overcrowding, with makeshift beds in the halls and common areas for those who'd been displaced by the Gemmans in Mae's building. Even the children were gone, however, and Mae was starting to leave the foyer when she thought she heard what sounded like sobbing. She hesitated only a moment about intruding into someone's personal quarters before making up her mind. The house's layout was similar to that of the one she was staying in, and in the third bedroom, she found the source of the sound.

"Hannah?"

Carl's young concubine sat huddled in a corner of the room, wearing a shift similar to what Mae had worn earlier underneath her Cloistered wrappings. It wasn't that that was so startling, however. It was the sight of uncovered, bleeding lash marks on the girl's back that made Mae catch her breath. At the sound of her name, Hannah hastily wiped her eyes and staggered to her feet.

"I'm sorry," she said. "I shouldn't be sitting around. They must need me."

"I . . . no, no one sent me," said Mae, catching the misunderstanding. "I was just, uh, passing through. Can I help you?"

The young woman regarded her with wary eyes in a face that was pretty but gaunt with malnourishment. It was sickening, considering the way the men around here gorged themselves at meals.

"I'm supposed to be Cloistered," Hannah said at last. "But I'm having trouble doing it."

Mae was even more horrified. "On those wounds?" The restrictive clothing had been uncomfortable enough in good health, let alone Hannah's condition. "Who did that to you? Carl?"

"Harriet did. It's her duty as head wife to keep us in line. She decided I should spend some time Cloistered to help me correct my sinful ways and stop tempting men."

A thousand comments sprang to Mae's mind, none of which, she knew, would be appropriate. Instead, she took a deep breath and said, "I can help you. Are you allowed to dress the wounds first?" Surely even these savages were mindful of infection.

Hannah gave a hesitant nod, and a quick search of the house turned up some basic first aid supplies. There was nothing in the way of antiseptic, but Mae hoped simple cleaning and bandaging would be good enough.

"Does Harriet do this often?" she asked.

It took several long moments for Hannah to answer. "Only when I deserve it." She sighed. "If I could only get pregnant, Carl might make me a wife. Then my sinful nature might be kept more in check. But Nehitimar hasn't deemed me worthy."

"I don't think Nehitimar has that much to do with it," said Mae, the words slipping out before she could stop them. With a gasp, Hannah suddenly turned to her.

"One of your men . . . would they take me?"

"Take you home?"

Hannah shook her head furiously. "Take me . . . in the way men take women. I would give myself to them, any of them. All of them. They're all healthy. It's obvious they've been blessed. There's an underground exit in your bathroom closet that I could sneak in through tonight. It would be a great sin, of course, but I could do penance later, and if it got me with child—"

"I don't think so," said Mae, feeling stunned. "I mean, I'm sorry for your trouble, but it's not something they'd really—"

"Of course," interrupted Hannah, looking away. "They wouldn't have any interest in me, not with you Gemman women on hand."

Mae tried to protest that the issue was more complex than that, but Hannah had shut down by that point and only wanted to expedite the Cloistering. In truth, Hannah was one of the prettier women around here, but that had only led to her troubles. And when she was finally wrapped up in that ridiculous getup and ready to help, Mae walked with her to the main house, wondering how much labor Hannah would be able to do so constrained. Harriet had plenty of ideas, however, and was quick to set them to work.

Mae had the mindless task of peeling and chopping potatoes, giving her time to ponder the day's developments. Her encounter with Hannah had only darkened her mood. Was that the kind of future her niece had? The picture Mae had seen had shown a pretty girl unmarked by Cain, no surprise since her unknown plebeian father's genes would've helped stamp it out. Would she be destined for a life like Hannah's? Coveted by men and despised by other women? Even if she was made someone's wife—at thirteen—that was no protection from beatings and other "character-building" behaviors. Anger kindled in Mae the more she thought about it, anger toward her family for their part in shipping the girl off with no thought but to protect the illusion of their bloodline.

A deep breath settled her, and she pushed all thoughts of her mother and sister away. There would be time to deal with them later. Right now, Mae's niece was the priority. Mae was here, closer than she'd ever been, and she needed to locate the girl before the opportunity was gone. But how could she when the country was filled with those salons?

The knife.

As the night progressed, she accepted that truth. It all came down to the knife. She listened patiently when Val and the others came back, describing their day, but the image of the amber hilt was never far from Mae's mind. Even after dinner and the evening wrap-up, when Justin related his discussion with the others about Arcadian missionaries, Mae still found herself unable to stop thinking about the knife. It had brought her this far. It would take her the rest of the way. It had to.

Resolved, she made her decision.

# CHAPTER 13

# THE RUNA'S BEST
# AND BRIGHTEST

D aphne couldn't have been happier to hear about Tessa's new involvement with the Young Citizens' Council.

"I knew it!" whooped Daphne, when the two (plus Rufus) met for coffee near Creative Minds that week. "I knew you wanted to hunt down the truth."

Tessa grimaced. "It wasn't quite like that. Dr. Cassidy just wanted me to participate in his group so that I can tell the other kids how great the RUNA is. I didn't even have to do anything."

"So much the better," declared Daphne.

"I really just did it because Darius wants to be part of it so much," added Tessa with a sigh. "But the thing is, he can't even make one of their meetings right away. His intern schedule conflicts. So I'll probably just wait until he's free to—"

"No," interrupted Daphne. "Absolutely not. When's their next meeting?"

Tessa thought back to the multiple messages she'd received from Dr. Cassidy since telling him she'd attend the YCC. "Early this evening. It's geared toward students in high school and college who are busy in the day. But I'm not going to—"

"What? That soon?" Daphne's eyes, which seemed to have even more kohl than usual on, widened. "Of course you're going. Tell Cassidy you are so he knows to expect you. Damn." She finished her coffee in a gulp and stood up. "We've got to get you a wire."

Tessa stayed where she was. "What? Is that legal?"

"Perfectly," said Daphne. "Especially for a group that's allegedly educating kids on politics. No one's going to even think to check you. And if they did . . . well, in some ways, that'd be evidence unto itself. Now, come on—we'll go get one at North Prime."

Tessa reluctantly finished her own drink and followed. Rufus trailed them as always and remarked sweetly, "I'm surprised you don't lend her your own wire, Miss Lang."

Daphne cut him a look. He'd found her hidden microphone the first time she'd come to the March house, and she hadn't bothered wearing one since. "I might need it. Besides, the kid should have her own in this kind of work—especially if she's going to be hanging out in political company."

"It's just a youth group," insisted Tessa. "They do volunteer work and teach about the Citizens' Party. He's not going to be openly giving them subversive messages."

"'Openly' is the key word," said Daphne. "But you'd be surprised what gets slipped into the message when impressionable youngsters are involved. That's not for you to worry about, though. I'll review the data. You just have to gather it. Look cute and hopeful for the future of this country. Participate in any conversations that seem controversial."

"Yeah, because that won't seem suspicious at all," grumbled Tessa.

Daphne led them down to the subway station. "It won't, actually. You're provincial. In some ways, that means you should be cautious about what you say to fit in. At the same time, others won't be surprised if you say something uncouth."

"I'm not going to make myself seem like some backward barbarian, just to get you a story that probably doesn't exist!"

"Don't be so dramatic." Daphne chucked Tessa's chin. "You're a smart girl. You'll know what to look for and what to say. Just pay attention to everything, and I'll help you figure out the rest. I thought we were out of leads when Lucian left the country, but this may be bigger than talking to him directly."

A loud train rushed by, forcing Tessa to wait before responding. "What do you mean talk to him? Did you have an interview lined up or something?"

"Not exactly," said Daphne, with a small grimace. "But I was working on it. Look, if you don't think it's worth uncovering Senator Darling's and his party's possible ties to religion, that's fine. But think on this. Senator Darling's shown a lot of favors to your friend Dr. March. If you were hiding secret religious membership, wouldn't it be a smart thing to be on the good side of a servitor if things go bad?"

Tessa gaped, thinking of friendly, open Lucian, who was always so kind to her when he came over. "You think he's using Justin?"

"Not yet. But a politician like Darling has to think ahead. If he got outed for being in a cult—"

"By someone like you," interrupted Tessa.

"Or by anyone," said Daphne, "then having a servitor in his pocket would be very handy for damage control. A servitor going on record and stating that you weren't a threat or even disavowing your religious involvement would save a future consul's career. Don't you think Dr. March should know the truth—that the reason the senator pays him these visits and gives internships to his friends is so that *your* friend and benefactor will be obligated to help in a cover-up someday?"

"I thought Lucian did all this stuff because they were friends," insisted Tessa, though she could hear the doubt in her own voice. "And because Lucian likes Mae."

Rufus looked up sharply at that. "What do you mean 'likes' her?"

"If that's all there is, then great," said Daphne mysteriously. "But wouldn't you like to know for sure?"

She refused to say anything more about it after that and simply let Tessa's own ruminations run wild. Down at North Prime's main office, they had boxes of hidden microphones available for check-out, and Daphne soon had Tessa ready to record. In the meantime, Tessa sent Nico Cassidy a message saying her schedule had cleared and she wanted to attend the day's meeting. He wrote back right away, expressing his delight and welcoming her to join them.

The Citizens' Party owned a suite of offices in a secure downtown high-rise, and it was here that the YCC held their meetings. It didn't take Tessa long to figure out how things worked. There were student political groups all over the country, but this one, directly run by the Citizens' Party, consisted of handpicked individuals from a demographic similar to that of Tessa's classmates. They came from money and families with connections. Most didn't have free-form schooling like her, however, so they had meetings outside of classes that gave them lots of photo ops and provided good references for future academic and work applications.

Dr. Cassidy, as it turned out, ran the student meetings only about a third of the time and usually left them to an assistant of his, a young aide named Acacia. He was there today, however, and all smiles for Tessa. "Welcome," he said, guiding her inside a conference room. "We're so glad to have you here."

She cast a fleeting look at Rufus, waiting just outside the door, more because she'd gotten used to him for mental security than anything else. Facing this group alone was suddenly like reliving any of her past failed first days of school. There were two dozen other students gathered around tables in the room, all watching with bright eyes and questionably sincere smiles. Dr. Cassidy introduced her to them, earning surprised looks, and assured them they'd get a chance to ask her questions later. First, he let Acacia start them off in their regular business, giving Tessa a moment to relax and observe.

The YCC had two big projects coming up. One was a fund-raising concert geared toward young constituents. It involved a well-known local band and had the dual goals of both raising money for the Citizens' Party and spreading awareness of its candidates and policies to those in attendance. The group's other big endeavor was handing out electronic pamphlets when the election grew closer in the fall. Paper was a rarity in the RUNA, but canvassers could stand on designated street corners and transfer information about various people and causes to the egos of consenting passersby.

Tessa watched as the group set to their tasks with genuine enthusiasm. There was some talk that Lucian might be able to stop by the concert and speak, which was setting many of the YCC's members—especially its female ones—aflutter with excitement. Lucian's youth and strong opinions were hugely appealing, and the hero worship he inspired was an almost palpable thing. One girl politely tried to involve Tessa by asking if she knew who Lucian was, and Tessa suddenly found herself the center of attention when she admitted to having met him multiple times, in a home setting.

"You're so lucky," said another girl. "If he came to my house, I'd be like, I don't know. I'd totally pass out or something!"

Others agreed, and while Tessa hadn't had quite that reaction to meeting Lucian, she suddenly recognized an opportunity for herself. *You're a smart girl,* Daphne had said. *You'll know what to look for and what to say.* Tessa put on an adoring smile. "I know! When he came over that first time, I couldn't even get two words out. I just stopped and stared." Encouraged by the others' expressions, she added, "If we'd had someone like him in Panama, we'd have made him king or something!"

They loved that, and Dr. Cassidy used it as a chance for the others to engage Tessa in conversation about her background, bringing up a line of questioning she was well familiar with. Knowing what they hoped to hear from her, she made it a point to emphasize how amazing everything in the RUNA was compared to the provinces. She also made it a point to highlight those Gemman issues that were of particular relevance to the Citizens' Party's beliefs. She saw that pleased Cassidy and Acacia but knew Lucian was still the big draw for the others.

"You're so lucky," said another girl. She lit up with inspiration. "You should join us—like on a regular basis. It's only right, since you're a family friend and all."

A guy who was chairing the concert committee and had hair

styled suspiciously like Lucian's nodded in agreement. "We'd love to have you help at the concert. It's a lot of work—but it's a lot of fun too."

For a moment, Tessa was too flustered to respond, and it had nothing to do with the fact that she hadn't really planned on doing much with the YCC beyond this meeting. The remarkable thing here was that she couldn't ever remember receiving such a warm social welcome. She never would've thought to find it among a group of elite students hoping to pad their résumés with political connections. Dr. Cassidy smiled at her and the others, mistaking her silence for shyness.

"Now, now, let's not pressure Tessa on her first day. I know she has a lot of other things going on." He glanced at the time. "Now would be a good chance to discuss current issues and what's been going on in the news."

Everyone took out their egos and began looking up the day's headlines. "The New Republic Party wants to make some cuts to the ration program," said one boy disapprovingly. "They say it'll cut taxes and can be fed back to the employment program—but *of course* they'd say that."

The group tackled the issues, and Tessa listened with interest. She was impressed that Dr. Cassidy and Acacia attempted to discuss the reasoning of opposing sides, but ultimately, the group resolved every topic in a way that aligned with the Citizens' Party's principles. No one seemed to expect her to participate—until they reached the last topic of the day: a recent push by religious-freedom lobbyists to lighten restrictions and regulations on those who wanted to openly worship. Although the Citizens' Party had been courted by said lobbyists, Tessa knew they had no official position yet and was surprised when Dr. Cassidy turned toward her.

"Panama has freedom of religion, doesn't it?"

Tessa flinched at the unexpected shift in attention. "I suppose so. I mean, there's no real law for or against it. People just do it. Or don't."

"And has chaos resulted?" he asked mildly.

Tessa thought of her homeland, with its armed gangs and puppet government. "Not from religion."

"But it's still a much less advanced place socially and technologically," argued one girl. "We can't rule out that the pervasiveness of religion in that society plays a role in its not being up to our level. No offense, Tessa."

"And," added someone else, "we know from our own history that warring religions create disaster. That's where the Decline came from."

"That's the thing," said Tessa, surprising herself. "In Panama, there aren't really competing religions. Those who belong to one are usually Catholic."

"Interesting point," said Dr. Cassidy. "So what do you all think? Could religion be more openly practiced—if there was just one unifying faith and not a bunch of squabbling?"

"Arcadia does that," said a boy sitting near Tessa. "And they're not really a model country."

"How would you determine which religion is superior anyway?" This was the girl who'd claimed she would've passed out if Lucian came to her house. "And we're not like Panama or Arcadia. There are *tons* of little religions here—all kept in check by the servitor's office. If you lifted the restrictions, would one emerge superior? Or would they all just start fighting for control?"

"This is a different era," someone insisted. "Our society is advanced and civilized enough that people could freely believe without us degenerating into chaos."

"Tessa," interjected Dr. Cassidy, "did you belong to a religion in Panama? Did you get something out of it?"

It was a surprising question, one she hadn't been asked before. "Yes, I did. I still do, I suppose. As for what I get out of it . . . I mean, there's comfort in knowing there's a higher power looking after you. That there's a meaning to everything we do." Those were dangerous words in the RUNA, and she suddenly wondered if she might lose all her goodwill.

"Yes, but how do you know?" insisted the guy by her. "What

proof is there that your god is out there looking after you? Do you see miracles? Answered prayers?"

She shook her head. "Most of it's taken on faith."

"I need miracles," he insisted. The mood lightened as he flashed the others a grin. "Give me a god who shows some power, and I'll be right out there with those lobbyists."

Dr. Cassidy laughed as well, though Tessa could sense a controlled quality to it. "Well, if those lobbyists gain traction, we'll know who to appoint to the head of the outreach committee, eh, Laurence?"

More laughter followed, and an end was called to the meeting. The others gathered their things and stood to leave. Tessa wondered if she might be able to slip out quietly, but it was Dr. Cassidy who held her back, rather than any of Lucian's fan club.

"I wanted to thank you for taking the time to come today. I'm sure it's a bit overwhelming, but I think you offered the others some very useful information."

"I learned just as much as them." She nearly made a polite farewell, but Daphne's words came back to her, about how Lucian might be using Justin in case a religious agenda went bad. Putting on what she hoped was a starry, provincial expression, Tessa said, "I never thought much about religion in the RUNA. I haven't really been involved with it since coming here. No church or anything. Just my own prayers. I haven't really felt like it's right for me to go out openly anywhere."

"I'm sure those prayers are still very meaningful," he replied.

"Do you think religion could be more openly practiced here?" she asked. "By important people? Not just a minority?" The brazenness of her question unnerved her, but she tried to remember what Daphne had said about how people might not be surprised by an uncouth provincial girl's bluntness. Feeling bold, she added, "I mean, the Citizens' Party is still listening to those lobbyists, so you must see some potential, right? And I know Senator Darling wouldn't consider anything harmful to the country."

"Senator Darling wants all citizens heard, certainly," said Dr.

Cassidy. He was careful not to commit on anything in the religion issue, Tessa noticed, but he didn't seem displeased by her comments. "It's a complex matter, one we're considering from all sides."

Tessa nodded eagerly. "Oh, I'm sure. That's what I love about being here in the RUNA. So many sides and opinions get listened to. It's such an amazing country that offers those kinds of opportunities to its citizens. You're all very lucky." She added a note of wistfulness into her voice, hoping to make her act convincing, but it achieved more than expected.

"Would you like to be a citizen someday?" he asked.

"I . . . I haven't thought about it," she said, caught a little off guard. "Mostly I've just been focusing on my education."

"Of course, of course, but if you'll forgive my saying so . . . I don't know how much use you'll get out of it in Panama. But if you stay here, Creative Minds could launch you into an outstanding university, and then . . ." Dr. Cassidy spread his hands magnanimously. "Well, who knows what? Your possibilities are endless."

Tessa stayed speechless, less for effect than from the fact that she truly hadn't thought that far ahead. Her silence seemed to empower him.

"I know you're not sure about joining the YCC, but I think you'd be an excellent addition. And I'll be honest with you, if you really do want to apply for citizenship—something not easily or often given to outsiders—involvement in a mainstream political party will look excellent on your record." He beckoned Acacia over. "I'll tell you what. Why don't you start small? No one expects you to jump in and start chairing committees. In a couple of days, I'm having a fund-raiser of my own at my house, and a few of the other YCC members are helping out—little things like running errands, bringing drinks. Just enough to meet the potential donors and show them our role with today's youth. You could help out and see what you think."

Tessa could already imagine the scene he was describing. It'd be a repeat of what she'd gone through tonight, with her answering prompts about how great the RUNA was and how grateful she was that it—especially under the leadership of the Citizens' Party—was helping her find her way in this shining new country. Cassidy would reap as much benefit as she'd be getting. Part of Tessa balked at being used . . . yet, at the same time, she could already picture Daphne's reaction to this opportunity. Tessa could have access to answers beneficial to Justin . . . and the country.

"Acacia can give you all the details," Dr. Cassidy continued, when Tessa didn't answer. "She's helping organize it."

"Okay," said Tessa, beaming back at them both. "I'd love to."

# CHAPTER 14

# ROLE-PLAYING

When Justin fell asleep later that night, Mae took out the dagger from his luggage and moved as far away from his bed as possible, hoping that whatever mixture of prescription sleep aids and Carl's liquor he'd taken would keep him knocked out for a while. She didn't know for sure how to activate the knife's powers and could only make a best guess at it, based on the happenstance way things had transpired before. After one last, anxious look at Justin's sleeping form, she gripped the knife's hilt in both hands and made a silent plea.

*Whoever is master of this, please complete the vision you showed me before and help me to find my niece.*

She had no idea if that was the right way to address a god. Justin had taught her a great deal about the academic aspects of religious studies but had little to say about practical worship. For all she knew, maybe the dagger's deity couldn't even hear her in Arcadia, where Nehitimar reigned supreme. Nothing happened, and she started to despair until a burst of inspiration hit. Opening her eyes, she drew the blade across the palm of her hand, watching as a line of red appeared . . .

. . . and the world dissolved around her.

The walls of the guesthouse melted, and she stood outside, on the land of Carl's now-dark compound. Then that shifted, and she stood in the middle of an empty road that looked vaguely familiar.

Yes—it was the country highway that led into the city. She recognized it from the car ride that morning. Again, the world went fuzzy, and now she stood next to a nondescript rural building with no noticeable features—except a red velvet flag, its color barely discernible in the fading light. Thick trees stood around it, and she saw no other buildings or notable landmarks. Then, in her peripheral vision, she caught sight of a light that went away as quickly as it had come. The highway! She hurried in that direction, afraid the vision would fade. As she got closer, another car went by, its lights briefly illuminating a sign stating that Divinia was ten miles away.

Frantically, Mae tried to convert that to kilometers and then contrast that with what she knew about the distance from Carl's place. The intersection wasn't that far from where she was staying. How was this possible? What crazy coincidence had landed her this close to the salon that might be holding her niece? As the vision materialized back into Justin's room, Mae heard a female voice say, *You're too entrenched in mortal thinking if you think this is a coincidence. Don't you know I'm looking out for you?*

Mae's heart was racing as she stared around the darkened bedroom. Her hand was smooth and uncut. The moon, visible through the outside window, hadn't shifted far, so she hadn't lost as much time as before. It wasn't even midnight yet. Based on what she'd seen in the vision, it might take her . . . what, an hour to walk to the salon? If she could get out. Hannah's desperate words came back to her: *There's an underground exit in your bathroom closet that I could sneak in through tonight.*

Was there? Mae quietly slipped out of the bedroom and out to the common area. There were three bathrooms adjacent to it, and a search of the second one found what she needed: a small door in the back of a linen closet. The door was unlocked, revealing a cramped tunnel, low enough that Mae had to duck when she entered it. At least she didn't have to crawl. The walls and floor were packed dirt, and she had no lights to guide her, only touch. She followed it to its end, discovering an earthen wall with ladder rungs that led up to a trapdoor. Cautiously, she climbed up and lifted the door to get a peek. It opened up outside, underneath some dried brush someone had packed on top for concealment, in what appeared to be the back of Carl's property. After a few more moments to get her bearings, Mae slipped back down and returned to Justin's bedroom.

He still slept deeply, allowing her to sort through his clothes and put on pants and a three-quarter-length coat. It was too big for her but clearly masculine, which was what she needed. She pulled her hair up into a tight knot and added a wide-brimmed Arcadian-style hat Carl had gifted each of the Gemman men with. No one would mistake her for a man up close, but she hoped that in the dark, the illusion would hold. Her last task before leaving was to scrawl on the notepad she'd used at the temple. It was a quick note, in Mandarin, one she hoped would calm Justin if he woke up but not alert anyone else: *Wait for me.* With that, she set out.

The back of Carl's property was flanked by an electric fence, and in the distance, she saw a man patrolling with a dog. Whether it was a son or hired help she couldn't say, but she thanked her luck that he was too far away to notice her. An overhanging tree gave her the opportunity to climb up and drop down on the other side of the fence, which would have been a jarring fall for anyone else. Her ramped-up implant let her handle it easily, and she soon got her bearings and headed for the country highway that led into the city.

She kept to the side of the road as much as possible, again hoping anyone in a passing car who noticed her would think she was male. Her calculations proved correct, and after an hour of brisk walking, she saw the sign from her vision and the small road that branched off from the highway. Down it, she spotted a building identical to the one in her vision, save for one thing: no red velvet flag. Justin's words came back to her: *When they've got some girls "for sale" that have reached puberty, they hang a red velvet flag outside their door.* The vision had shown the salon for what it was, but in the real world, the girls must still have been of an age where they were safe—if anyone was safe in one of those places. She left the road and traveled through the woods, approaching the back of the salon. The proprietors had opted for slightly less sophisticated security than Carl's: a thick perimeter of nasty barbed wire. They'd also had the foresight to trim away any overhanging trees. Mae had no tools to cut the fence and instead had to take the unpleasant but inevitable approach: climbing it by hand.

The upside to that too-big coat was that it provided fabric to protect her hands, and the thick-soled shoes kept her feet safe. The trick was patience, and she finally managed to land on the other side with only minor discomfort. Unlike at Carl's, there didn't appear to be any dogs, which was a blessing, but she soon found another obstacle to getting inside. Aside from the front door, there were no other points of entry. Was that to keep the girls in or intruders out? It was hard to say, but Mae hoped they never had a fire.

She crept up to the front door, which was actually open. A second, screened door kept insects out while allowing air in. Peering inside, she immediately realized these people lived in a much different demographic than Carl's family. The walls were rough wood, the floors concrete. Aside from basic electricity, the house lacked even Carl's modest nods to technology. At a knotty pine table, she saw two men playing cards, with an arsenal of weapons lying within arm's reach around them. The sight of the guns was a jolt until she reminded herself that Arcadia didn't have nearly the weapons laws her homeland had. The guns the men had lying out were older, but her hand still itched for the feel of a trigger. It would have solved a lot of her problems.

*No. No violence. I just need data.*

But how could she get it, with those men in her way? She needed access to the rest of the house. As she was puzzling this out, one of them gave a harsh shout, and a young woman entered through one of two doorways. Mae winced, more from surprise than anything else. The girl—who looked to be in her late teens or maybe early twenties—was wearing a ragged dress and had some of the heaviest Cain scarring Mae had seen in Arcadia so far, or ever, really. Cain rarely ran that strongly in the RUNA anymore, and in the rare cases it did, corrective surgeries were readily available to help tone down the worst of the defects. That, of course, wasn't acceptable here.

The man who'd shouted for the girl set down his gun and approached her, coming to stand provocatively close. She kept her gaze fixed downward as he touched her cheek and said something Mae couldn't hear that made the other man snicker. The standing man took the girl's hand and led her from the room. Once they were gone, the remaining man peered back at the doorway they'd used for several moments and then, satisfied he was alone, pulled a flask from his pocket. He took a couple of long swigs and then fixed his attention on a newspaper. It was a paper one—a novelty to Mae—and he used both hands to hold it, forcing him to disarm.

If a distracted guard was the best she could hope for, Mae would make do. He was angled slightly away from the door, and after a quick analysis of the distance between him and her, Mae headed back outside to find a rock. She returned with one the size of her palm, paused for a moment to collect herself, and then struck. The man never saw her coming. She opened the door with almost no noise and moved faster than he could turn around. The rock slammed into the back of his head, with precisely enough force to incapacitate but not kill. She even managed to do it without drawing blood, though he'd certainly have a lump on his head later. Carefully, she eased him down so that his head rested on the table, the flask sitting beside him. It'd be lucky for her if his companion thought he'd passed out from drinking, but she wasn't counting on it. Fortunately, she planned on leaving no other sign of her visit tonight. Maybe they'd figure out there'd been an intruder, but they'd have no indication of her identity or that she'd disturbed the house's women or contents.

With one exception. The array of weapons called to her, and after a heartbeat of hesitation, Mae scooped up a handgun. It was an older model, with only six shots, but it was fully loaded and would be effective if her attempts at subterfuge didn't go so well tonight. Feeling more secure with a weapon in her hand, she strode toward the two doorways, only to hesitate once more.

One door led to what looked like a primitive kitchen, and here Mae found the other guard. His back was to her, and all his energy was going into the marked woman, who stood bent over the counter with her long skirts hiked up. Mae's lips curled in disgust, and the gun was heavy in her hand, the urge to aim at him over-whelming. Once again, she had to remind herself she was only here to observe, not take action. At least the girl looked like she was of consenting age, though "consent" was probably a dubious term. Whether the girl was a lawful concubine or a ward being taken advantage of, Mae doubted she'd ever admit to doing something she didn't want. It made Mae's stomach curl.

*This is the room she came from when called,* Mae tried to tell herself. *And she's older than girls usually are in these salons. Most likely she is a concubine or a servant being used. There's no reason to think those animals do this to all the girls here. They prize virgins in this country. Surely the others are left unmolested.* That didn't change Mae's desire to save this girl, and it took a cold, logical voice in her head warning that she needed to use this distraction to finally move again.

The other doorway led to a narrow stairwell, and she trod lightly, trying to avoid squeaks. The stairs opened up to a hallway with five doors, three of which were closed. The two open ones turned out to be a bathroom and an office. Based on the outer dimensions of the house, she assumed the other three doors led to bedrooms, which—she realized belatedly—might be locked. It seemed like the kind of sadistic thing these guys might do.

But the first knob opened easily and quietly, and she stepped inside, pleased to find a nightlight dimly illuminating the space—probably so this salon's keepers could do night checks. Four girls ranging from what looked like ages six to twelve slept soundly in narrow beds with threadbare covers. Despite their gaunt faces, the girls didn't look like Arcadians. Mae saw no sign of Cain on any of them. Their features were regular and healthy. She also recognized the telltale signs of mixed heritage that characterized so many of her countrymen but weren't very common here.

*These are Gemman girls,* she realized. *Stolen Gemman girls.*

The second bedroom revealed more of the same, though one of the girls had a slightly darker complexion than the rest and fragile-looking hair indicative of mild Cain. *Stolen from a province,* Mae guessed. The third room held what looked like another provincial girl and two more Gemmans . . .

. . . one of whom was Mae's niece.

There was no question she was the same girl from Emil's picture. And even if Mae had never seen the picture, the family resemblance would have confirmed it. Blond curls—nearly white in the poor light—framed a little face that was still lovely in spite of malnourishment. A swell of emotion burst in Mae's chest, fed by the implant's need to increase her adrenaline and endorphins. The instinct to carry the girl away was so strong that Mae had to physically step back to stop herself from reaching out.

*No action. Just information,* she reminded herself.

And yet . . . even though she'd come here wanting to find her niece, Mae wasn't prepared for the reality. It was one thing to come in saying she would only observe and another to obey that when faced with not only her niece but these other girls who were victims from her own country. And after witnessing these rustic living conditions, not to mention the poor servant downstairs . . .

Mae closed her eyes and took a deep breath, forcing calm as her free hand touched the amber dagger in her belt. *The dagger brought me here. Against all reason, it helped me find this place. Surely it has a plan for me to do . . . something.*

What that something was, however, remained unknown for the moment. Mae was unprepared and would have to return with a concrete course of action later. Right now, she needed to leave. For all she knew, the man in the kitchen had finished and found his partner unconscious. His first action would be to immediately check on the girls he was shoddily guarding, and Mae had no avenues of escape up here. And so, with one last wistful look at her niece, Mae crept out of the slumbering room and back down the stairs.

Sounds from the kitchen told her things were wrapping up there, and the man she'd struck was still immobile. She left the same way she'd entered—keeping the gun with her. She could stash it in the tunnel back on Carl's property.

The walk back to his house went much more quickly than her initial one. Her mind was so busy spinning with plans that she hardly noticed the time passing. Unfortunately, no matter how much she tried to puzzle it out, she didn't know what to do. How could she save her niece? How could she save the others? The Gemman government had to know its girls were sometimes stolen. What would it do if she offered definitive proof of where some were being held? Would it do anything? Or would her leaders turn a blind eye in the name of political diplomacy?

*Lucian,* she thought. *I should ask Lucian.* And yet, no matter how captivated with her he might have seemed, Mae didn't think his affections would go so far as to risk an international incident—especially since she'd never really returned his attention. It didn't matter, she soon decided. Even if she had encouraged him, his attraction to a Nordic patrician wouldn't trump his career goals. She would have to rely on her own actions. And the dagger.

When she reached Carl's property, she was faced with a new problem, more easily solvable. The tree she'd used to leap the fence was no use to her from the outside. Fortunately, she found another growing on the exterior, and although it didn't hang nearly as conveniently over the fence, it nonetheless gave her enough clearance to make a leap that put her back within the compound's boundaries. When she landed, it took her a moment to gather her bearings and figure out where both her guesthouse and the tunnel's entrance were. At last, she had her orientation figured out and hurried off in the direction she needed.

Inconveniently, she found an obstacle in the form of Carl's older sons stumbling drunkenly along, arms slung about each other as they returned from a night of carousing. She quickly ducked into the shadow of a shed, silently cursing when she heard one of the young men say, "Hey, did you just see that? There's someone there."

"One of the guards," said another of the brothers.

"No, no," said the first, whom Mae recognized as Jasper, the particularly obnoxious one. "I swear, I saw someone else." He came staggering forward around the side of the building to her hiding spot. Discovered, Mae sprang up before he could see her face and took off across the yard. No point in pretenses now.

"There!" yelled Jasper. "He went that way."

"Doug!" yelled one of the other brothers. "Get the dogs—there's some guy breaking in!"

More shouts followed, and Mae ran, confident in her ability to keep ahead of all of them, though less confident about where to actually go. She was moving in the opposite direction of her goal, and the only saving grace was that the property was so big that she could keep out of sight from most of her pursuers—for now. It wouldn't take long for the whole compound to wake up, and eventually, her hiding spots would dry up.

Carefully keeping track of the sounds of those coming after her—who weren't being quiet in the least—Mae managed to double back and finally go in the direction she'd initially wanted. She paused halfway there and was pleased to hear that the others were still going off where they'd seen her. She could pull this off after all. And she might have—if Jasper hadn't stayed behind.

She encountered him in almost the same spot she had before. All the others had left. He drunkenly lurched after her, and she easily dodged him, sidestepping around him to continue her escape. Unfortunately, the maneuver briefly put her in a patch of light, and his eyes widened.

"You!" he gasped. He looked as though he were about to shout for the others, and with no other options, Mae swung out and clocked him with the handgun. He keeled over, and she didn't wait to see if he was unconscious or not. She ran the rest of the way to the trapdoor hidden at the back of the property and, after first ascertaining no one was around, disappeared down it. The narrow tunnel slowed her a little, and she didn't use nearly the care she had in her exit of it. She abandoned the gun just before she reached the bathroom's closet and paused before emerging. Everything in the house sounded silent, but she could hear the activity outside—and it was getting louder. Louder and closer.

As silently as possible, she shut the closet door and slipped out of the bathroom and back to Justin's bedroom. He was sitting up in bed, looking as though he'd been abruptly wakened—probably by the exterior noise. He stared at her as she shut the door and leaned against it, as though she might keep her pursuers out by sheer will-power alone. He gave her a once-over, and she realized her clothes were covered in dirt from the hasty trip through the tunnel.

"What have you done?" he asked.

Her answer was preempted by the sound of pounding at the guesthouse's exterior door. "They're looking for me," she blurted out. "But only one actually saw me."

Justin sighed and pulled back the covers. "Take off your clothes and get over here."

Mae didn't hesitate. She shed everything in the corner and was in bed with him by the time she heard voices just outside their door. To her astonishment, he pulled her down in a kiss, his body covering hers as he rolled her onto her back. A surreal mix of feelings took hold of Mae as she instinctively wrapped her arms around him, her hands touching his bare flesh. Fear, of course, was her primary emotion. But her body was so on edge, so amped up with the churning of endorphins and other chemicals, that it also responded quickly to the feelings of desire being stirred up by having his body against hers. She entangled her legs with his and parted her lips, taking in more of his tongue and mouth. His hands gripped her tighter, and as her heart pounded like some caged animal seeking escape, she couldn't say if it was from panic or desire.

The bedroom door burst open, shattering the confusing spell. Justin jerked away from her with a look of outrage so convincing that she wasn't sure it was entirely faked. "What are you doing?" he exclaimed.

A group of Arcadian men poured into the room, flinging on the lights, and Jasper pushed his way through them, a prominent welt on the side of his face. "Where's your woman? What is *she* doing?" he demanded, coming to an abrupt halt.

"Where does it look like?" roared Justin. He climbed out of the bed, pulling most of the covers off Mae in the process. He'd been sleeping in boxers and crossed his arms over his chest as he strode forward to address Carl, who'd come to join Jasper. "What are you thinking, coming in like this?"

It took Carl a few moments to form any words. "My, uh, son says he saw your woman outside. . . ." But as his eyes drifted to the bed, it was clear he wasn't buying it.

"Does she look like she's outside?" Justin demanded. None of them answered right away. They were all dumbstruck, staring at her, and as uncomfortable as their attention made Mae, she knew Justin uncovering her in front of this sexually repressed crowd had been an effective distraction. Goal achieved, he turned on her with an expression as furious as any Arcadian man might have had in his situation. "Cover yourself!"

Mae obeyed meekly, wrapping the covers back around her, though her hair and shoulders were still uncovered. Jasper finally dragged his gaze from her and looked between Justin and Carl.

"It was her. I saw her outside." He pointed at his face. "She did this to me."

Justin leaned forward to get a better look and scoffed. "*She* did that to you? With what, her fist?"

"I . . . no . . ." Even Jasper looked uncertain now. He started to turn toward Mae again but caught himself. "She had something. A gun, I think."

"A gun? Where the hell would she get a gun?" Justin fixed his fury on Carl now. "Is this what passes for hospitality around here? Is this some kind of elaborate scheme to see her naked? Don't think I haven't seen how you all look at her—especially him!" Justin pointed accusingly at Jasper. "How am I supposed to feel secure, now that he's seen her? How do I know I can leave her alone? How do I know he's not going to be secretly—or not so secretly—lusting after her and planning something?"

Jasper paled. "Father, I swear it was her—"

Carl backhanded him, causing the young man to stagger back a good two feet. "Shut up. Don't say anything else, you drunken idiot. You've embarrassed me enough for one night—*and* you probably let the real prowler get away by wasting our time with this!" He gestured angrily toward the bed and then turned to Justin. "Your woman is safe. You have my word. No one will bother her. Now come on—all of you."

The Arcadian men filed out, leaving Justin and Mae alone. For a few heavy moments, neither moved nor spoke. Then, exhaling deeply, Justin came and sat beside her on the bed. All his bravado and bluster was gone, and to her astonishment, she found he was shaking. She was too, but it was from the implant's normal letdown as the endorphins were metabolized by her body. She rubbed her hands together out of habit, feeling a prickling sensation along her skin as she did.

"I hope," Justin said at last, "that whatever you did, it was worth it."

# CHAPTER 15

# THERE'S ALWAYS A COST

Mae didn't answer Justin right away. Instead, she surprised him by putting her arms around him and resting her head on his shoulder.

"Thank you," she breathed. "Thank you for that."

As they pressed together, he could feel the rapid beating of her heart and realized she must have been legitimately scared. What had she done? Had she really managed to get a gun? And how had she even gotten outside without detection in the first—

The spiral of questions in his mind ground to a halt as she suddenly lifted her head and brought his mouth down to hers. Her lips were warm and impatient, filled with an urgency that hadn't been there earlier when they'd kissed for the benefit of the Arcadians. He felt himself fall into that kiss, his hand entangling in her hair as he pulled her closer. She'd been sweating from her earlier exertion, and the feel of her bare, damp skin against his was intoxicating. There was no resistance from her, none of the walls she usually put up. She was yielding and eager—*very* eager—and the temptation to lay her back and lose himself in her was almost overwhelming.

But he didn't. And for once, it wasn't the fear of divine consequences that made him pull away.

*She's too keyed up on the implant right now,* he realized. *She's churning with all those chemicals, braced for a fight. Getting all*

*that aggression out with sex instead isn't such a leap from battle,
and I just happen to be the most convenient outlet.*

*Is that a problem?* asked Horatio.

To Justin's surprise, it was. He'd spent a good part of the day
trying to reconcile his feelings over the Grand Disciple's offer to
"buy" Mae. It had bothered Justin, not just because it was barbaric,
but because he didn't like the idea of anyone thinking they could
take possession of her. Her throwaway lovers were meaningless.
None of them held any sway with her, and the problem was, he had
a feeling he would be no different from them if he gave in now. The
sex would be great, he didn't doubt that in the least. Animalistic,
passionate . . . those weren't adjectives he normally had a problem
with. But just then, he didn't want Mae to look at him as a convenient lover. He wanted her to look at him as . . .

*Me,* he thought. *I want her to make love to me because it's with
me, not because of the act itself.*

It was a startling revelation, and not just to Justin.

*Did you just use the term "make love"?* demanded Horatio. *I'm
pretty sure that's not your usual word choice with women.*

Justin gently broke from Mae, experiencing a weird sense of
déjà vu. How many times had they been in this moment? How
many times had they, against all reason and assertions to the contrary, found themselves on the edge of physical consummation?
And how many times had they backed off?

*Maybe that should tell you something,* said Magnus. *Maybe you
keep coming back together for a reason.*

*Maybe,* Justin agreed reluctantly. *But we aren't going to come
together like this—not in this place and not for these reasons.*

Mae looked momentarily confused at the interruption, and
then before his very eyes, he saw her walls starting to go up. When
he'd stopping their escalations before, he'd usually done so in the
most obnoxious and insulting ways possible, even going so far as
to tell her she held no interest for him in bed a second time. It had
been a lie then, and it would've been a lie now. Maybe making her
angry would've been a smart tactic to prevent these moments, but

he found himself smoothing things over instead as he held her hands in his and kept his distance.

"You can't play me like those undersexed savages," he said lightly. "I need to know what happened. What trouble did you get into? And don't try to get out of it by distracting me with your feminine wiles."

Especially because he wasn't sure how good his resistance would be if the barely-there sheet disappeared again. But his approach worked, both the joking and the attempt at appealing to her reason. And really, that last one wasn't even entirely faked. He did need to know what had happened tonight. His muddled relationship with her might have been a charming mess, but their dealings with the Arcadians were no game. If there was more trouble to come, they had to start preparing, and he could tell from her chagrined face that she knew this.

Before she could speak, however, a knock sounded at the door. It was the Gemman knock, no doubt one of their countrymen coming to see what had happened. "Just a minute," Mae called, springing up. Justin was treated to a few moments of that glorious body before she quickly pulled on one of the Arcadian dresses and moved for the door. Lucian stood there, with a crowd of others behind him.

"What in the world was that all about?" asked Lucian.

"Sounds like Carl's sons got drunk and saw—or thought they saw—some intruder on the property." Justin shook his head in disgust. "One of them swore up and down it was Mae—the one's that's obsessed with her and everything else female—and had some crazy-ass story about how she attacked him with a gun."

The other Gemmans had trickled into the room, and Atticus groaned. "Great, just what we need. Anything I'm going to have to deal with in the morning? No fallout? No injuries?"

"Not to us," said Mae coolly, arms crossed as she struck up a defensive position along the wall. "But whoever that kid did get in a fight with gave him a pretty nasty blow."

"You don't think this intruder has anything to do with us, do you?" asked George. "Some spy?"

Justin nearly considered nixing that theory but thought better of it. Not only would it throw them off the scent of what Mae had really been doing, it would also be a good way to put Carl on the defensive by suggesting he wasn't adequately protecting them. "I don't know," Justin said simply. "Like I said, those guys were trashed. It's hard to say who was out there."

"I'll talk to Carl about it first thing," said Atticus. "We've operated on the theory that the Arcadian officials don't wish us harm, but we haven't given much thought to rogue factions who might want to make a statement against our government."

He and George began talking strategy as they and the other Gemmans began trickling from the room. Not everyone was buying the story, Justin noted. Lucian, though looking as agreeably pleasant as always, had a thoughtful glint in his eyes as he walked out. Val, the last to leave, also looked uncertain, possibly because she knew Mae best of all. "You sure you're okay, Finn-girl? Your hair's a mess."

It was actually—a sexy, tousled mess that Justin kind of wanted to run his hands through again. Only half of it was his doing. The rest was from when Mae had hastily yanked off her hat and hairpins before getting into bed. She laughed easily now and brushed it away from her face.

"I let it down for the night, not knowing we were going to get invaded. You should've seen their scandalized faces, Val." Mae's words were glib and natural, as good as anything Justin might do. Val still didn't look entirely convinced, but she smiled and gave Mae a hug and Justin a nod before exiting the room.

Mae shut the door, and the light expression she'd put on for Val vanished. "Okay," Justin said. "Start talking before anyone else bursts in."

Indecision played over her features, and he found himself holding his breath in fear that she might not actually tell him what had happened. What stung the most wasn't simply the lack of knowledge—though Justin hated that too—but more the idea that she didn't trust him. After a few more moments, though, she took a deep breath and said, "I found my niece."

She then proceeded to tell him an incredible story about how she'd sneaked out through an underground tunnel, walked down the road to a salon, subdued a man, stolen a gun, verified her niece was there, and then managed to get back inside mostly without detection.

"I know it sounds crazy," said Mae. "But I know it was her. The resemblance to Claudia is all over her. If we could manage a genetic test, I'd prove it. And almost all of those others are Gemmans too."

"It *does* sound crazy," admitted Justin. "But that's not the craziest part here." He was actually a big believer in gut instinct, and if Mae believed this girl was her vanished niece, he could almost buy it. The problem was—and it took him a moment to put his finger on it—Mae's story was missing a few critical components. "What I want to know is how we came to be staying within walking distance of where she was being held and how you knew it."

The look on Mae's face was almost comical, like she was fully aware of that gap in logic and had hoped he wouldn't notice—but knew that he probably would. She walked over to the pile of clothes she'd discarded earlier and returned with her amber knife.

"This," she said simply. "This is how I knew. I . . . I had a vision."

Her next story was almost more unbelievable than the first . . . except that in recent months, Justin had found there was little he didn't believe anymore. This, however, was testing his limits. Mae was communicating with a god! After being born into a cult she'd had to battle her way out of, she'd willingly sought out union with a new deity to achieve her goals. At least, he hoped it was a new deity.

*You've said before you don't know where the knife came from,* Justin reminded the ravens. *You still sticking to that story?*

*It's not sacred to the Morrigan, if that's what you're suggesting,* said Horatio. *Remember that Mae used the blade to defeat her.*

*Then who? Who's helping Mae?*

*Once again, we must remind you we aren't all-knowing,* said Magnus wearily. *But thank you for the compliment.*

"Tell me everything you know about this . . . being who sends you visions," Justin told Mae. "What's he asked you to do in return for this help? They *always* want something."

Mae sat cross-legged on the floor, clasping the dagger in her hands. "It's a she . . . I think. Whenever I hear a voice, it's a woman's. She makes me think of . . . I don't know. Sunshine. And life. And plants. And . . . desire. But she's never asked for anything. I mean, except my blood. I have to cut myself to make the visions work."

"Sounds like a fertility goddess," he said. "Though a dagger isn't exactly what I think of as something that'd be sacred to one. Maybe a cup. Or flowers."

Mae smiled at that. "A knife's more useful. I suppose a cup could be. But what good are flowers? Just decorations."

*Decorations in the hair,* Justin thought with a start. To Mae, he said, "Has she ever mentioned a crown of flowers? And, uh, stars?"

"No, but I—" Mae stopped. "Wait. She—the voice—once talked about the crown looking more fragile than it was. And in one of the visions, I had a wreath on my head made of different flowers that kept changing."

Justin leaned forward. "What did she say? Exactly what did she say?"

Mae's brow furrowed in thought. "Just that the crown looked fragile but wasn't. That it had power, and then something about making life being more powerful than taking it. I think."

"You think or you know?"

"Damn it," she exclaimed, "I'm not like you! I don't memorize things word for word. That's as close as I can remember."

Justin took a moment to calm himself, breathing deeply. Mae was having visions of some of the things that had haunted him. He didn't like that. He didn't like that at all. Whatever great destiny

Odin had planned was much easier when it had been one-sided. Justin didn't need Mae getting actively involved now too.

"I'm sorry," he told her, hoping he could hide his panic. "I've just seen how it is dealing with gods. It's dangerous, and while there isn't much I don't think you're capable of contending with, this worries me."

She accepted his apology with a small nod. "What do I do then? What do I do about those girls? About my niece? Should I talk to Lucian?"

"I don't know," he said. "I wouldn't. Not yet, if only because you don't want to explain the supernatural connection. But honestly . . . I don't know what he could do. Wait for now. And *don't* use the knife again. You can't trust it."

"It gave me answers."

"It's dangerous," he repeated. "There's always a cost to these things. Forget the knife. I'll think of something."

The smile she gave him was amused, maybe even a little wistful. "Will you really?"

Sleep was difficult after all the excitement, not to mention the new problems Mae had presented to him. Muddling it all was that somehow, even with the brevity of their fumbling, she'd left the sheets smelling like her. The scent reminded him of what had almost been—and perhaps what might be if he were brave enough to take a gamble—so he finally sought sleep with one of his sedatives. It worked, but taking it so late left him groggy in the morning and no closer to finding solutions to what faced him.

Mae left early to help with the other women's morning chores, and Atticus went as well to do damage control from the previous night's shenanigans. He returned to the guesthouse lounge a little while later with Mae, both of them looking frustrated.

"Well, Carl swears they scoured the grounds and that it was just a random prowler, nothing for us to be concerned about." Atticus flounced into a chair beside Lucian.

"You believe that?" growled George.

"We have to," said Atticus. "That and it's in the government's best interest to keep us safe. I think he's at least upping his night-time security, so that's something."

Mae remained composed, but Justin saw a flash of dismay in her eyes at that comment. No doubt added security would interfere with future excursions.

"Our newest complication is that Carl thinks it best if Praetorian Koskinen is kept out of Jasper's sight," continued Atticus. "They want her to go Cloistered for the rest of our stay."

"Unacceptable," said Justin swiftly. He'd seen how miserable one day of those confining clothes had made her.

"I agree," said Atticus. "I watched how they made that other poor Cloistered girl of his shuffle around doing household work, and I said there was no way we'd subject any of our women to that. I gave them an ultimatum. If they want her to help, she goes about in her normal—well, normal Arcadian—attire. If they can't handle that, then she can stay confined to this guesthouse, unless we're all going out in some planned activity, at which point she'll put on that costume."

"Seeing as she's here," said Lucian, "I'm guessing they opted for the latter?"

Atticus nodded. "They're not happy about it, but Carl's being more accommodating, since he still feels like he might have lost face over the security incident. That, and apparently she's just too much of a temptation for Jasper. Carl really doesn't want them crossing paths."

*Carl probably doesn't want to cross her path either,* Justin thought. *He wasn't unaffected last night. He's just a little better at keeping control.*

George snorted in contempt. "Seems like if all these women keep 'tempting' Jasper, they'll eventually realize maybe it's him, not them."

"You forget where we are," said Atticus simply. "Now then. Let's talk about the day's itinerary."

It was more of the same as yesterday, sightseeing and meeting with important officials about trade and other peaceful negotiations. Justin, still preoccupied with Mae's dilemma, was tuning out of most of it when he suddenly heard Atticus say, "Oh, and Justin. They want you back at the temple."

Justin started. "What, today?"

"Tomorrow. The Grand Disciple wants to have brunch and get to know you."

"And find out if he can send in missionaries," said Justin darkly.

"Would it be so bad?" asked Phil, who usually stayed quiet in these discussions. "I mean, the attempts at religious conversion are, obviously. But if we were able to do it the way he said, as a cultural exchange, some university lecture circuit of Arcadian speakers . . ."

Justin shook his head. "It's a bad idea. You brought me here for expertise? Here it is. Don't let that religion in under any pretense. It's dangerous. There's no gray area here. I've spent years searching for hidden threats in religious groups, and this one's not even hiding it."

"If we don't walk out of this with some trade negotiations or peace terms for the border, a reciprocal Arcadian delegation visiting us would still be a win," said Lucian. "We shouldn't dismiss it. It'd be a huge step for progress."

Justin cut him a look. "I'm not risking our country's well-being for you to gain some laurels that'll buy you the election."

He expected a rebuke for that, but instead, Lucian turned unexpectedly thoughtful. "Maybe you can find a way to stall him and avoid giving an answer on this trip then. Act enthusiastic, like you'd do it if you could but other factors are getting in the way back home." A little of Lucian's earlier levity returned. "It should be easy for you. Pretend he's a woman you're trying to avoid a second date with."

"I still don't think it's a big deal," Phil argued. "Getting a couple of Arcadian scholars or whatever they call themselves to come talk about their country would be great for all of us."

"Not if Justin thinks there's a risk," said Lucian, getting to his feet. "Now, let's head out and at least maintain good relations by showing how much we appreciate their breakfasts." He paused to glance at Mae, who stayed where she was. "When do you get to eat?"

"She'll have leftovers here," said Atticus.

"I'll deliver it myself," Lucian told her solemnly.

That earned him a smile from her, one that faded once he was gone. Mae caught Justin's sleeve, holding him back from the others. "Lucian backed down awfully quickly about letting the Arcadians in. Is it possible he knows what you do—about SCI's secret missions?"

"I was wondering the same thing," Justin admitted. "I mean, I'd like to think he just instantly values my opinion when I give it . . . but let's face it, if he's positioned to be one of the greatest leaders in the country, the odds are good he knows about SCI's agenda and the 'game' being played—and my role."

"Which," she mused, "means he probably does value your opinion."

"Only because he's been tipped off to just how dangerous the forces at large are—or, well, how dangerous the forces he's been told about are. I doubt he knows as much as I do about this."

Hope lit Mae's features. "Maybe you should talk to him about it. Let him in on what we know. Maybe he could help with my niece after all—"

"No," said Justin swiftly. "Even if he knows there really are supernatural powers scrambling in our country, it's better my involvement—and yours—stays under wraps. Don't worry. We'll figure this out."

As he left to join the others, Justin wished he felt nearly as confident as he'd sounded. He was still blown away that a divine vision about her long-lost niece—brought about by a knife, of all things—had been the driving force for this trip. It had been much easier to think she'd wanted to join this expedition for the adventure of it.

*Easier to think, but easier to* believe? asked Horatio.

The raven had a good point. Mae might have thrived on action, but it had been foolish of him to think she'd go to the trouble of coercing him to come simply for her own selfish gratification. That wasn't how she operated. She was a good soldier. She put the greater good of her country and commanders over her personal wants—except for this. Trekking out on her own last night had been a considerable risk. Mae could've caused irreparable diplomatic damage if she'd been caught—not to mention personal damage. The status of a concubine might have been fragile, but it still meant one had the protection of a man. Justin knew—if Mae didn't—that being captured out on her own might've been read as a forfeiture of male protection in Arcadian law, meaning she'd be anyone's for the taking. He doubted Carl would've pushed for that, though his crackpot son might have.

As it was, Jasper was all scowls this morning as he sat in sullen silence at breakfast. His face was bruised and swollen, both from Mae's attack and from what Justin guessed was some further "parental authority" on Carl's part. Justin was glad Mae was going to be out of the Arcadian's sight for the rest of the trip, and not just because it would spare her the humiliation of shuffling around and serving men in those ridiculous clothes, like poor Hannah. Everyone else might have believed that Jasper had been drunkenly mistaken—Jasper might have even admitted to it—but his dark expression said he still knew who he'd seen.

Mae and her niece had to be put on hold as Justin's attention shifted to his other problem: the Grand Disciple and his missionary-scholars. Carl kept bringing up how great it was that Justin had been invited back the next day, as did other officials whom the Gemmans met with later in the afternoon. Justin's feeling of dread increased as he realized how much Arcadian expectation was building around this, even if Lucian had technically given him approval to stall.

*I wish I was like Mae,* Justin thought. *Able to break out and daringly conduct my own reconnaissance. I'd love to know just what the Grand Disciple is really planning for us and if his god is part of the game being conducted.*

*So get out there and look,* said Horatio.

*How?* demanded Justin. *Shall I come up with some brilliant dis-*

*traction at brunch tomorrow to lure him away while I rummage through papers in his suite?*

The raven sighed in irritation. *You need your information before you see him.*

*Yes, well, if you have suggestions on how I can get to the temple and gather that, I'm all ears. I'll take Mae's tunnel and scale the walls. How does that sound?*

Magnus joined the conversation: *Or you could fly.*

Justin was almost ready with a snippy retort, but something in Magnus's tone held him back. Magnus was usually more serious than his counterpart.

*Explain,* ordered Justin.

*I wouldn't have to if you'd been more diligent about studying Odin's path,* said Magnus. He might have been more serious, but he could also be more difficult.

*I've learned the runes. I've learned all their basic uses.*

*You've scratched the surface. You think it's just memorizing runes? Anyone could be a priest if that were the case,* chastised Magnus. *You were called because you have the potential for other powers. You think you know Odin, but you don't truly* know *him.*

*What does this have to do with me "flying" to the temple?* asked Justin, thinking he was getting just another variation on the lecture so often given by Geraki.

*I'll show you tonight,* Magnus told him. *Skip dinner. Don't eat anything. Tell them you don't feel well, then have Mae guard your room from anyone else entering.*

The ravens offered no further elaboration, and as more diplomatic dealings and small talk called for Justin's attention, he had no chance to question his feathered companions. But when the day wrapped up, and they returned to Carl's estate, he followed the birds' bidding and stayed behind while the rest of the Gemmans (except ostracized Mae) went off for dinner. Lucian shot him a look almost as skeptical as the one he'd given the previous night, but if he had doubts or suspected an ulterior motive, he kept that to himself, saving Justin from lies or explanation.

Mae was another story.

"What's going on?" she demanded, once the two of them were alone in his room.

"I'm not sure," he said. "Maybe nothing. Magnus supposedly has a way for me to gather intelligence about the Grand Disciple."

"Didn't you lecture me last night on the dangers of supernatural involvement?" she asked. Pointedly.

"Yes, because you're dealing with an unknown variable. I know mine."

"You said there's always a cost."

"One I pay daily," he shot back. "I'm sparing you from a similar fate. Are you in or not?"

She sighed. "You know I am. What do you need?"

Per the ravens' instructions, Justin stripped down to his boxers and sat cross-legged on the bed. "Mostly they say just to stop anyone from interrupting me. Don't let anyone come through that door. Oh, and open the window."

Mae looked up at the small window at the top of the wall. It was big enough to allow light but would provide difficult egress for an adult, especially without a ladder to get up there in the first place. But she was still able to open it by standing on the bed before moving over and striking a defensive position against the door.

"Now what?" she asked.

"Now your guess is as good as mine."

*Relax*, Magnus said. *Expand your senses. Think of me. Think of becoming me.*

*You're going to turn me into a bird?* Justin asked him.

*Not exactly. Just try to let go of your own body. Focus on mine, on wings, on flight, on my essence.*

It wasn't easy, and not just because of the metaphysical nature of the task. Justin had never seen Magnus physically—well, not since a brief glimpse on a smoky night. But Justin did his best to focus on that memory and what he knew of the raven now, of his personality and nature. Magnus talked him through it, guiding Justin's mind and breathing until time and his surroundings faded away. A strange euphoria began to fill Justin's body, an indescribable power like nothing he'd ever felt, though it reminded him of the high brought about by some of the sketchier drugs he'd taken in his life.

Suddenly, Justin had a sense of emergence, like he was breaking through a barrier or bursting from water. The room snapped into focus, clearer and more vivid than before as he looked down on it . . .

. . . and himself.

There he was, still on the bed. His body sat in the same cross-legged position, but his blank, staring eyes were like those of someone stoned or comatose. The weirdness of it started to break Justin's control, but Magnus talked him back.

*That's only your body, your common physical form,* the raven said. *You're sharing mine now. The parts of you that matter, your soul and your essence, are in this form. You're safe. You'll return to your body . . . eventually.*

Justin looked around the room again and became aware that he was circling it, gliding and hovering on large, black wings. By the door, Mae stared up at him with wide eyes, and while she didn't look scared, per se, she certainly appeared a little disbelieving.

*She can see us,* he told Magnus.

*Yes. We're in my physical form. You don't have the strength or power to go in my invisible form, unfortunately.*

*What is that . . . joy I feel?* Justin asked. *That bliss? Is it just that awesome being a raven?*

*Well, yes,* said Horatio.

*Are you in this body too?* Justin asked, startled.

Magnus answered. *No, but we are always joined. Thought and memory cannot be separated. As for that bliss, that is what it feels like to open yourself up to Odin. Now come. You won't be able to stay in this state all night, and we need to go.*

Justin flew toward the open window, leaving a gawking Mae behind, unsure whether he or Magnus was the one fully in control. At times, as they flew through the darkening twilight toward the lights of downtown Divinia, Justin felt as though he were indeed the one powering those strong wings. Other times, it seemed as though he were merely a rider. Regardless of who was in control, that glorious feeling remained, burning within him.

*You've spent your whole life seeking the next best high from drugs or the arms of a woman,* Magnus told him. *When all along, all you had to do was surrender to the god who wants you. Easier, isn't it?*

*That's questionable,* Justin responded. *I can control when I take the drug. I can walk away from the woman. Something tells me that once I give in to Odin, there's no going back.*

*You won't want to,* Magnus assured him.

The rest of the journey passed in swift silence. Even if Justin hadn't had the benefit of the raven's better vision, one didn't really need special sight to spot their goal. If you could find the city, you could find the glittering temple. It dominated its dreary landscape, easily visible from above. Less obvious was which of the many windows led to the Grand Disciple's apartments, but Magnus had apparently retained a good sense of that and skillfully guided them around the numerous angles and towers of the temple's exterior.

*The question is if he still likes fresh air,* said Magnus. *Otherwise, this journey—while full of compelling conversation—has been a waste.*

They circled one corner of the temple, and the rush of wind against Justin's feathers—feathers?—slowed as they prepared for a landing. A large window that he now recognized as the magnificent picture one he'd seen yesterday loomed before them—and it was halfway open again. Magnus's body deftly swooped in and landed on top of the glass pane, pausing so they could get their bearings.

Justin experienced that same disorienting sense of power that told him a strong elect was nearby. The Grand Disciple sat in the same living room once more, though his body was angled away from them, so he hadn't seen the raven's quiet landing. The room was in shadows, lit by candles, and the odds seemed good the priest wouldn't notice his feathered intruder with the light fading outside as well. Unfortunately, Justin wasn't sure there was much they could actually observe, save that the Grand Disciple looked much more like an ordinary man when wearing a black silk dressing robe instead of his jewel-laden regalia. Magnus might have provided a clever entrance, but the raven didn't have the capacity to rummage through any personal possessions, and the priest didn't seem like he would start talking to himself either.

Justin was about to express his frustration at their inability to learn anything useful when a soft chime sounded. "Enter," called the Grand Disciple. Several moments later, the screens leading into the room parted, and a young man in a temple uniform entered with a Cloistered woman.

The woman was a mystery, but Justin soon recognized the man as Hansen, the deacon who'd let them in earlier. He knelt and kissed the Grand Disciple's ring while the woman held back, much as Mae had earlier.

"Your Piousness," Hansen said. "I've brought her, as you asked."

"Excellent, Timothy," intoned the priest. He gestured Hansen to his feet and looked past him to the woman. "Unveil."

The woman did as bidden. She was no one Justin recognized, but she was lovely, especially for an Arcadian. Her dark hair, though pulled back, was still clearly thick and luxurious, and neither it nor her skin showed any sign of Cain. She looked to be about eighteen and kept her eyes lowered, as was proper. The Grand Disciple grunted in approval.

"You may wait for me in the bedroom," he said. The girl gave an obedient nod, and Justin watched as she slipped out of the room. Glancing back at the priest, he saw a lascivious expression cross the older man's features. So much for his being above the distractions of women.

*You're not watching the right person*, said Magnus.

For a moment, Justin was confused, then he focused on Hansen, who, after watching the girl leave, glanced back at the priest—with undisguised contempt. The expression was fleeting, and when the priest turned back, Hansen's face was smooth and subservient once more.

"Your Piousness," said Hansen carefully, "I've saved enough money to make Elaina a proper wife now. How much longer will we have to wait?"

The Grand Disciple gave him a patronizing smile. "Patience, Timothy. It's not about money so much as Nehitimar's will, and right now, the god wills that she remain a concubine."

"But why?" blurted out Hansen. He immediately looked chagrined for daring to ask.

"Because if she is your wife, then she must keep her body only unto you. As long as she is a concubine, I am able to continue giving her my blessing. That pleases Nehitimar. Doesn't it please you as well?"

*"Giving her my blessing"? That's what he has the audacity to call it?* Justin wondered.

*It may please their god,* noted Magnus. *But it doesn't please Hansen.*

The raven was right. Even as the young man murmured his agreement, Justin could see the angry glint in his eyes. The Grand Disciple was either too full of himself to notice or—mostly likely—didn't care. No surprise coming from a man who lived in splendor and excess while much of the country remained impoverished.

"You know how difficult my work is," continued the Grand Disciple. "Nehitimar requires many sacrifices of me, and I must take my pleasures where I can to continue his work—even if that requires sacrifices on the part of others. You understand."

"Of course," said Hansen.

*Hansen would punch him right now if he could,* Justin noted.

"Don't worry," said the elder priest. "If all goes well with your mission into the Lost Lands, Nehitimar will undoubtedly reward you with marriage. And I of course will look after Elaina while you're away."

"Thank you, Your Piousness."

The Grand Disciple strolled around the room, hands clasped

behind his back. "Have you found an acceptable group to go on the expedition?"

"I'm finalizing it," said Hansen, seeming more at ease discussing business than Elaina. "If the Gemmans will allow us to enter as you plan, I'll make sure to have some of Nehitimar's best spokespeople go, along with those you've trained to disable the Gemman media stream."

It happened so quickly that Justin was almost certain he'd misheard. *Wait, what did he say?*

*Shh,* cautioned Magnus. The scenery around them flickered slightly in Justin's vision, and he forced himself to focus back on the two men in the room.

"It's just . . ." Hansen started to continue but stopped.

"Yes?" asked the Grand Disciple. Again, Justin's vision flickered.

"Even if the country is plunged into as much chaos as you say it will be, can a handful of our best missionaries truly effect change in that godless land?"

"It's okay for you to have doubts, Timothy. You can't even begin to imagine the extent to which their society rests on their media. It's not as simple as television here. Everything is wired into one system: entertainment, news, security, identity. Disable that, even for hours, and you'd throw off their world order. If we can keep it down for a few days as planned, it will be like bringing back the Dark Ages. Some will be scared. Some will listen to our people, and the seeds will be planted. In the meantime, the lapse will allow our military to strike and seize back some of our most prized borderlands—lands which may have women even more beautiful than Elaina." The Grand Disciple gave him a knowing smile. "You might have a greater reward than her ahead of you."

"I only want her," insisted Hansen with a frown. "And I'm dedicated to this mission. You know that. It just seems like if so much is riding on this media stream, it won't be easy to take down."

"That's why our people have been studying it for so long," explained the other man. He wavered in Justin's vision, and the disorienting sensation made it hard to follow the conversation. "Cowlitz and his men know what they're doing. But they truly need to be within Gemman borders to make their plan work. The president and his advisers support us, if we can only find our opening."

The priest started to say more, but Justin couldn't follow it any longer. *What's happening?* he asked Magnus.

*You've been out of your body too long, and your control is slipping.* The raven lifted up from the window's edge and flew into the night. Whereas before Justin had felt like he was one with the bird, he now had the sensation of clinging on for dear life.

*No!* he insisted. *Go back! We need to hear more. They're talking about taking down the fucking media stream! Do you know how serious that is?*

*All I know is how serious getting you back to your body is,* countered Magnus. *If you aren't rejoined soon, bad things will happen.*

*How bad?* asked Justin.

Magnus's voice was grim. *The kind of bad where your soul is permanently severed from your body and wanders the earth forever.*

# CHAPTER 16

# GOOD PROVINCIAL GIRLS

Tessa got her hair cut just before Dr. Cassidy's event, much to Daphne's dismay.

"You've lost your rustic provincial feel," Daphne exclaimed, as she adjusted the tiny microphone hidden in Tessa's collar. "That's half your appeal."

"Thanks," said Tessa dryly. Her hair was still long by Gemman standards, reaching her shoulder blades. She'd gotten it edged and layered in a more modern way that helped lighten some of the weight. In Panama, most girls her age wore their hair elaborately up or braided, so length and blunt edges were the goals there. "And I actually think it's going to help me. Dr. Cassidy wants to show me off as some kind of poster child for Gemman assimilation. Looking the part—and not like I just came in from the provinces—will convince them how great the RUNA's been for me."

Daphne made a noncommittal grunt and stepped back to survey Tessa. "Maybe," was all the acknowledgment Daphne would give. "But you don't want to come off as *too* worldly and sophisticated. If you get caught doing something you shouldn't be, you'll want to play up that provincial naïveté."

"I'm not going to do anything except what I'm asked," Tessa told her, for what felt like the hundredth time. "I'm not cracking safes or hacking encrypted files."

And Daphne responded with the same refrain she'd been giving

Tessa for the last couple of days. "You're going to be in the man's house! This is a golden opportunity, better than we could have hoped for. You've got to maximize that. You might end up being president of the YCC and never get a chance like this again."

Tessa shook her head. "No. I'm not doing anything like that. I'll try to stick around the donors as much as possible so you can get some good sound bites, but that's it. Besides, *if* Dr. Cassidy really does have some involvement with a religion, and *if* he is consequently getting the rest of the Citizens' Party involved, it's not like there's going to be one document I can seize that's got it all laid out for you to exploit."

"No," Daphne agreed. "And it's also unlikely we'll be lucky enough that this group of donors is made up of cult leaders giving us the story we need. All the sound bites in the world will be pointless if there's nothing in them."

"Because maybe there's nothing here at all in the first place." Again, it was an argument Tessa had made many times. Daphne was familiar with it and shook her head with a mix of what seemed like amusement and exasperation.

"Go," she said, pointing at the door. "Find me something good."

They were at North Prime's offices downtown, in order to make sure the surveillance equipment was working. Tessa had already dressed at home before coming out, in a black skirt and white blouse as requested, and had only a short trip to make back to the YCC's building. There, she met up with Acacia and three other lucky chosen members who were helping out at the event tonight. Dag was her bodyguard of the day and accompanied them on the car ride out to Dr. Cassidy's house, per arrangements Tessa had made earlier. At first, Acacia and Dr. Cassidy had been uncertain how to deal with Tessa's protective arrangements, but upon learning she might have a praetorian in tow, they'd been quite charmed with the idea and asked that Dag come in uniform. Tessa would still go about her tasks at the party while he stayed stationed at the door, adding further gravitas to the affair. Dag had had no problem being on display, so long as he could be sure Tessa was safe and that he would be given dinner.

Being a political party's therapist must have paid pretty well, judging from the size of Dr. Cassidy's house and lawn. Although it was dinnertime, the summer evening still offered plenty of light and warmth so that he was able to host his guests out on an expansive patio and terrace area. There were about twenty couples invited, spread out among small round tables set with perfect linens and crystal. Hired waitstaff and caterers handled the most intense labor, while Tessa and her student colleagues ran errands and took on small tasks. Tessa herself was on champagne duty, going from table to table to check on glasses, after Acacia had assured her that tipsy donors were generous donors.

"Tessa," Dr. Cassidy called, as she passed by him at one point. "Come here a moment."

He'd hardly sat down all night and had instead flitted around to interact with his tables of guests. He stood beside one such table now, and Tessa hurried over to him, her champagne bottle poised for refills.

"Set that down for a moment," he told her amiably. "I'd like to introduce you to some people."

She and the other YCC students had already been introduced to various guests throughout the night, so this was something she was prepared for. She and the others, under Acacia's tutelage, had perfected their roles as upstanding youth greatly benefiting from the Citizens' Party's guidance. Tessa expected more of the same here, but when Dr. Cassidy highlighted one of his guests specifically, she suddenly knew why she'd been invited tonight.

"And this is Adora Zimmer," he said, indicating a middle-aged woman sitting to his right. "CEO of Garnet Industries. That's not even the most interesting thing about her. Adora has a background much like yours, having come to the RUNA in her youth and earning citizenship. Adora, Tessa's with us from Panama and attends Creative Minds—when not helping me pour champagne."

"That's wonderful," said Adora. She bore no trace of an accent, and Tessa could only guess at some European ancestry, based on her surname and appearance. "I love success stories of other provincials finding greatness in our country—and clearly you have! I have a colleague whose daughter goes to your school. It's not easy to get into."

"Tessa's quite an exceptional student," Dr. Cassidy quickly said. "That, and she's fortunate to have a benefactor who's an old friend of Senator Darling's. And you all know how concerned the senator is about seeing young people develop their full potential. His aid's helped Tessa in her Gemman journey."

That wasn't exactly true. Tessa's student visa and enrollment at Creative Minds had been the result of Justin's finagling, but she knew better than to ruin Dr. Cassidy's performance and simply skirted the subject of who could claim credit for her. "I'm so lucky to be here," she said. "In Panama, all my education came from home tutors, and the subjects were pretty limited. It was nothing compared to what I've been able to learn here." She gave Adora a shy smile. "It's especially inspiring to meet someone like you, Ms. Zimmer, knowing that no matter where I was born, I can succeed if I make use of all the Gemman opportunities being offered to me."

"Of course you can, dear," said Adora, face softening. "People like us have to work extra hard, but if we persevere, we can achieve anything we like. I help fund a group that's been instrumental in lobbying for more immigration opportunities for provincial youth with outstanding potential. A good provincial girl is exactly the kind of role model I'm always talking about."

Dr. Cassidy nodded in agreement. "And you know, Adora, that several members of our party—including Senator Darling—have been very interested in discussing your group's cause. I look forward to enabling you all to speak more about it."

Adora scoffed. "I'd much rather talk to this young lady. Let me borrow her for a few events, and we'd bring a change of heart to all those paranoid people who think letting in more immigrants will lead to another Decline."

"I thought that's what the religious-freedom lobbyists were doing," joked a man across the table. "Haven't a few of them been courting the CP too?"

"The Citizens' Party has only been talking to those religious lobbyists who have demonstrated responsible, stable groups," corrected a woman beside him. "Those are exactly the kinds of groups people need to see more of. The only time religion's ever in the news is when there's animal sacrifice or arson."

This sparked a lively debate among the table's occupants, one put on hold when Dr. Cassidy turned his smile back on Tessa. "Okay, we won't bore you with all of this. I'll let you get back to your assignment, and don't worry—I'll drive a hard bargain with Adora before she can 'borrow' you."

Tessa actually wasn't bored and would've liked to see how a religious debate panned out with the Citizens' Party's wealthy supporters. It might also have given her the sound bite she needed. But standing around and listening was out of the question, especially when it was clear Dr. Cassidy was so pleased with her for charming his immigration-supporting donor. Tessa didn't want to ruin that rapport, and after a polite farewell, she visited other tables.

As the night progressed, she tried to pay attention to other conversations and linger near any tables discussing things relevant to Daphne. Not much came of it, though. Religion was rarely brought up. Taxes and the economy were more often than not the big topics, and mostly what she heard were variations of common arguments posted on media stream news channels.

As dessert was being served, Acacia summoned Tessa for another task. "We're losing too much light, and the lanterns aren't doing enough for us. Go inside and grab some candles from the dining room. It's on the opposite side of the house. Just walk straight, cut right, and you can't miss it."

Tessa obeyed, entering the mostly empty grand estate, with only a few harried waiters and caterers rushing past her. She reached the opposite side of the house and found a Y-shaped hall, with the right-hand branch going off to what was obviously a dining room. The left-hand branch went off to what appeared to be an office, and Tessa hesitated.

Here, she knew, was where Daphne would have told her to do some investigating. If people were going to hide incriminating records, an office was a likely place for it. Of course, as Tessa had told Daphne many times, "hide" was the key word. Whatever connections Dr. Cassidy had were going to be well concealed, and Tessa was in no position—nor did she have the talent—to break into someone's electronic files. Still, she found herself taking a few steps forward, lingering in the doorway to the office. Its French doors were open, further confirming that nothing untoward was going on. Dr. Cassidy would hardly leave his study exposed while guests were around if it were hiding anything nefarious. And from the looks of it, this wasn't even a real office that saw much use. It had no screen or computer and was filled with antique paper books and all sorts of artwork.

"Tessa?"

She jumped and spun around to find Dr. Cassidy himself. He looked as friendly as ever and only mildly curious. "Can I help you with something?"

She felt herself flushing and opted for a version of the truth. "Acacia sent me to find candles in the dining room, but it looks like I went the wrong way." Realizing that didn't explain why she was standing in the office's doorway, she hastily added, "I was about to leave but was drawn to that, uh, statue and just had to stop and look at it. Sounds silly, I know. I'm sorry, sir. I'll go find the candles—"

"No, no apologies necessary," he said, strolling into the office, touching the sculpture Tessa had chosen at random. It was one of several varied types on the desk, a statue of a man with robes made of what looked like actual gold. His skin was made of some precious blue rock. "Were you really drawn in by this?"

"Yes," Tessa lied. "It's beautiful. I've never seen anything like it. I . . . I just couldn't stop looking at it."

Dr. Cassidy nodded. "I'm not surprised. Of all the pieces to draw the eye, this one probably has the most power. Do you know who it is?"

"No, sir." She studied the lines of the statue and hazarded a guess. "It looks Egyptian."

"You're right," he said, beaming in approval. "I got this in a very competitive auction. This is Osiris. Does that mean anything to you?"

She shook her head.

"He was a powerful god, worshipped in ancient Egypt. According to the myths, his brother killed him—cutting him to pieces— but Osiris's wife restored him to life and had a son with him. Osiris then went on to become ruler of the underworld, judging souls." Dr. Cassidy's gaze rested on the statue, and then he turned back to her with a small laugh. "Forgive me, I get caught up in my folktales. That probably sounds silly to you."

Tessa's heart was pounding heavily. She could feel she was on the edge of something but didn't know how to properly attain it. Justin teased her that she was his protégée, able to pick up on small observations and details that others missed, just as he did. And Tessa could tell that this statue represented more than just a charming myth to Dr. Cassidy. Unfortunately, she hadn't picked up Justin's ability to win people over and get what he wanted from them. He could do it with men and women alike, but the means of achieving that were still a mystery to Tessa. She wasn't antisocial by any means, but she'd never developed enough social ease to finesse people.

"It's not silly at all," she said at last. "It's kind of like the religion I was raised in. There was a god brought back from the dead there too." Seeing appreciative surprise in Dr. Cassidy's eyes at the connection, she tried to go farther. "Is Osiris kind of the same? Offering release from death to his followers? Or resurrection?"

Dr. Cassidy hesitated before responding. "In some ways. He and his family do certainly have ties to rebirth, though in a different way from the religion you're referencing. The ancient Egyptians believed he ruled in the underworld. Here, among the living, the kings—or pharaohs—were linked to his son, Horus. It was very inspiring for them to think of their leader having divine connections in order to make wise judgments on earth."

"I can see that," said Tessa, improvising. "As much as I like learning about the political world, it gets a little wearying, with all the donors and lobbyists. It cheapens things. It'd be nice to know whoever's in charge is doing so not just because of money . . . but, well, because of some higher calling or power."

She thought she'd gone too far when he caught his breath, but a moment later, she knew she'd said exactly the right thing. "I forget how different your background is from the others'," he said at last. "It gives you a more open-minded perspective. But it's because of your background that I shouldn't even be telling you these stories." He laughed again, and this time, there was a forced quality to it. "People will accuse of me corrupting a young girl with religion. You saw the reaction it stirred up out there at dinner. If you do want to apply for citizenship, don't learn about this kind of thing. Keep avoiding attending the church you were raised in. If you want to return to it after you're a citizen, well, then by all means go forward. But until then, you need to walk a straight and narrow line, and I'll do my best to help, not hinder, you. Come on." He stepped out of the office and shut the doors, his affable persona back. "Let's go find those candles. Helping with this dinner *is* the kind of appropriate activity that looks good on a girl's citizenship record."

Tessa followed obligingly, saying little as she pondered what she'd just learned. The dinner soon wound down, and Acacia made sure all the YCC members were taken back to their homes. As Dag walked her inside, Tessa wanted nothing more than to dive into the media stream and start looking up all she could on Osiris. She wished more than ever that Justin was in town, because he would've probably instantly known what was relevant. All that research had to be put on hold, however, because she'd made plans for Darius to come over. He'd been elated to hear about her opportunity tonight and wanted all the details in person.

He jumped up from the kitchen table when she entered. "How

was it? Anything exciting happen? Did you meet anyone who—"
He paused, jaw dropping slightly. "Wow . . . your hair. It's so pretty."

"Thanks," she said, collapsing into a chair. Mental energy aside,
the effects of being on her feet all night were now taking a toll.
"And nothing too exciting happened."

"Did they feed you?" asked Cynthia. "I can get you some leftovers." She was at the table too, along with Quentin and Rufus. The
four of them were engaged in a game of mah-jongg, something that
everyone kept trying to teach Tessa but that she didn't have the
knack for yet.

"Yeah," said Tessa.

"But I'll still take your leftovers," said Dag cheerfully. Seeing
Cynthia start to stand, he waved her off. "No, no. I'll find them."

She settled down, but Rufus stood up. "You should take my
place, Tessa. It's ridiculous that you don't have this mastered yet.
And my shift's almost over anyway."

Tessa wasn't in the mood for games or even pleasant conversation, but before she could offer a protest, the doorbell rang. Dag
jerked his attention from the refrigerator to a small screen in the
kitchen that was connected to cameras at the front door. His jovial
face hardened at the potential threat, and then when he actually
saw who was at the door, his expression turned to one of disbelief.
"Well, I'll be damned," he said, hurrying off to the door with no
other explanation.

Tessa, curious, got up to look at the screen and was swiftly
joined by Rufus. "Do you know her?" asked Tessa, seeing his look
of astonishment. He immediately smoothed his features and shook
his head.

"No. Just expecting someone more formidable from Dagsson's
reaction," he said gruffly. And yet, when Dag nervously ushered
their guest in, Rufus couldn't take his eyes off her.

She was no one Tessa knew, a plebeian woman of average height,
with dark eyes and wavy brown hair pulled into a haphazard pony-
tail. Her clothes were casual but showed a body that, although
small, was muscled and toned like that of someone who engaged in

regular athletic activity. For half a second, Tessa wondered if this was another backup praetorian, except there was a slightly dazed look in the woman's eyes that Tessa didn't usually observe in those supersoldiers.

"This is, uh, Drusilla Kavi," said Dag, who seemed uncharacteristically uncomfortable. "She's a . . . colleague. A praetorian."

Quentin was the only one who didn't seem to pick up on the weird vibe in the room. "Are you here to help too?" he asked brightly.

"I'm looking for Mae," said Drusilla, voice dreamy. "She isn't returning calls, and I've looked everywhere. I went to her home, but she wasn't there. Then I found out she's been at IS and went there—except I don't have access to the building anymore. When I heard she's been hanging out here, I thought I'd stop by." Drusilla glanced around with a small frown. "But she doesn't seem to be here either."

"Mae's on a mission and not able to take calls," explained Tessa.

"Ah," said Drusilla. "That explains it."

Dag cleared his throat. "I, uh, didn't know you were out of the hospital, Kav—Drusilla."

"I'm still staying there," she told him. "But I get day passes. I'm doing much better. I'm sure I'll be out and back on duty in no time."

"I'm sure," murmured Dag.

"Are you certain you have permission to be away?" asked Rufus, still regarding her curiously.

The smile she gave him was as spacey as the rest of her, but there was a wry tone in her voice. "Do you really think I could leave if the military didn't want me to, Mr. . . . ?"

"Callaway," he said. "And I suppose not."

"They've taken very good care of me," continued Drusilla. "They take good care of us all—don't they, Linus? Do you still have your implant?"

Dag looked startled at the question. "Of course. Don't you? I mean . . . I'm sure they turned it off while you're, uh, recovering, but you must still have it."

She shook her head. "The doctors thought it best to remove it. Just until I'm better. It's helped . . . a little. Some things haven't gone away, though. Like my hands." Looking down, she rubbed them together. "Do you get that? The pins and needles?"

Dag looked completely baffled . . . and like he wished he were somewhere else. Or that she were somewhere else. If Tessa weren't so equally weirded out by their guest, she would've taken pleasure in seeing her normally cocky tormentor so off his game.

"Uh, no. I don't get that," he said. "I'm not really even sure what you mean."

Drusilla nodded in sad resignation. "I guess you're lucky then. The meds help with some things . . . but that never seems to go away."

Awkward silence fell, and at least now, Tessa had some explanation for what made this woman behave so weirdly. Whatever her "meds" were helping with, it had to be significant to justify this haze she lived in.

"Well," said Drusilla. "I've taken up enough of your time. When did you say Mae was getting back?"

"I didn't," said Dag. "It's a mission. We don't know."

"Right, right. Well, I'll just keep trying her, and maybe I'll get lucky. She visited me once in the hospital, and I think I was kind of out of it." Drusilla gave a shaky laugh. "I wanted to make amends now that I'm with it again."

As she moved toward the doorway, Rufus hurried forward. "How about I help you get back. I'm not sure you should be out walking alone this late."

Drusilla laughed again. "I'm a praetorian. Nothing can hurt me."

"Let me. I might be going your way anyway," he insisted.

"You're going to the base's hospital?"

Rufus exchanged looks with Dag. "Uh, as it turns out, I am." It was obvious to everyone but Drusilla that he was lying. He turned to Cynthia. "Okay if I go early?"

"Fine with me," she said.

"Then I'll make sure Praetorian Kavi gets back safely."

Dag nodded. "Better you than me."

"You're very kind, Mr.—um, I forgot your name already," Drusilla said apologetically.

"It's okay. Just call me Rufus." He guided her toward the door. "Let's get you back."

Drusilla followed, giving the others one more distracted smile. "It was nice meeting you all. Nice seeing you, Linus."

"You too," Dag said stiffly. When the front door closed, he sat down at the table and shook his head in exasperation. "I owe him. He's right—she shouldn't have been out alone, but I'm not sure I could put up with that all the way back to the base."

"Who was she?" asked Cynthia. "And what was wrong with her?"

"Just another praetorian. One injured in—well, it doesn't matter, but she's taken a long time to recover. And honestly, I'm not even sure what she's recovering from anymore," he said.

"Something that seems to require a lot of medication," suggested Tessa. Dag nodded in agreement.

Cynthia returned her attention to the game and began reassessing her tiles. "Well, I hope for her sake she gets better, but in the meantime, I've just got to say I'm glad she doesn't have an implant. I mean, she doesn't seem that dangerous, but anyone that out of it has no business with performance-enhancing technology. Your turn, Darius."

# CHAPTER 17

# GEMMAN GODS

Seeing Justin go immobile as a raven appeared out of thin air had been startling to Mae. And yet, that was nothing compared to when the raven suddenly returned without warning, bursting in through the small window in a flurry of squawks and dark feathers. It circled once around the room and then flew straight at Justin, as though it might attack him—only to vanish an inch before it made contact. The moment it did, Justin began gasping and sputtering, like a drowning man finally able to breathe air again. It was the first movement he'd made in an hour.

Mae sprang from her position by the door, moving instantly to his side. She put an arm around him as he coughed and was surprised to feel that his skin was burning up. He halfheartedly tried to push her away and sputtered out, "Going to be sick . . . get something . . ."

There were no bowls or trash cans in the room, so she grabbed the next best thing: the hat that Carl had given him. Justin dry-heaved into it a couple of times, and Mae left him for the guest-house's bathroom, returning with a cup of water. His stomach settled, he accepted the water greedily but only took a few sips before handing it back to her and collapsing onto the bed. Mae had some experience with battlefield wounds, but illness was beyond her—particularly one with a supernatural cause.

"What happened?" she asked, smoothing back his sweat-soaked hair. The fever had come on instantly.

His eyes glittered brightly as he stared through her. "The touch of the god," he said. "And the downfall of the stream . . . but they can't, right? Too much redundancy. No one can take it down. The god . . . he will know what to do. . . ."

Mae managed to get him to take another sip of water, and then he sank into a heavy sleep. She made a wet washcloth for his face and let him rest his head in her lap as she stared around the room helplessly, wishing the ravens that pestered him so much would come talk to her.

"I don't suppose you'll pop into my head and let me know what's going on?" she said aloud. But no response came. She didn't have the benefit of answers from supernatural entities. All she had was a knife, but she certainly wasn't going to use it now and risk losing time, not when Justin might need her in his current state. He'd warned her of the price for supernatural involvement. Was this what he was talking about? Her impression had always been of a greater, more metaphysical cost, not something so acute and immediate.

He remained warm to the touch, but his breathing grew even and regular, and she hoped that solid sleep would cure whatever this ailment was. A knock at the door an hour later forced her to gently remove him from her lap and admit Lucian into the room. He handed her a plate of food as his gaze drifted to Justin's sleeping form.

"He really is sick," said Lucian. "I thought maybe . . ."

"You thought what?" prompted Mae when he didn't continue.

He shook his head. "It doesn't matter. Is there anything I can do? Do we need to find a doctor?"

Mae set down the plate and handed Lucian the hat that Justin had been sick in. "You can get rid of this," she said. "And make apologies to Carl."

Lucian wrinkled his nose and promptly set the hat outside of the room. "Noted. Anything else? Anything else I can do . . . for you? I hate that you're locked away like this . . . though, honestly, I don't want to see you suffocated in all those scarves either."

There was legitimate concern in his voice, and it occurred to her that the unvoiced thought he'd hinted at might be that Justin had faked being sick in order to arrange some sort of liaison with her. *I've given so little encouragement,* she mused. *And yet he remains interested. What should I do to be clearer?* That was followed by a more startling thought: *Should I be clearer?*

Mae had never played the games other girls of her caste and social status had seemed to love so much. And as an adult, her dealings with men had generally been straightforward as well. She ended things that needed to be ended and didn't lead others on for her own gain or ego gratification. Justin had told her not to mention her niece to Lucian, but she now wondered if that was really the best course of action. Surely there might be a way to approach this that didn't bring up the supernatural aspect at all.

"This is a hard country for women," she said, choosing her words carefully. "I'm glad I wasn't born into it and feel sorry for those who were—especially since they don't know any better. I've heard stories . . ." She paused to glance away, as though too overcome to go on. "I've heard of them stealing women and girls, not just from the provinces but from the RUNA too. Is there any truth to that?"

"In my experience, you can't put anything past anyone," he told her grimly. "Anything's possible—but if it does happen to us, it doesn't happen very often. Our border's too locked down. It's not easy for them to sneak over and snatch girls."

*Unless castals are just handing them over,* Mae thought bitterly. To Lucian, she said, " 'Not very often' is still too often. Is there anything you could do to get them back?"

He shook his head. "Finding them would be next to impossible."

"Physically, it might be obvious," she said. "Less or even no Cain. And then all you'd have to do is a genetic test to match their parents to our registry."

"They'd have to be in the RUNA for that. We don't have the

means to test here, and the Arcadians certainly aren't going to let us bring them back based on a hunch over physical appearance. Even if we had some kind of hard proof that someone was a Gemman national, the politics of it would be sticky—especially if she'd been here long enough and was brainwashed into this system. An Arcadian wife with four kids isn't going to want to come back, especially since they're all taught that we're godless servants of evil."

Mae wondered if the same would hold true for a girl of eight. She made no response, but her face must have given away her dismay. Lucian gently touched her arm and drew her nearer.

"I understand your concern," he told her. "I don't want to see anyone stuck in this system, born to it or not. If there was something I could do, I would, but it's out of my control."

Mae smiled, though she didn't feel much good humor. "You're going to be one of the two most powerful people in the RUNA. Is anything going to be beyond you?"

He gave her a long, level look, and when he answered, she wasn't sure if they were still talking about the girls. "Some things just might be."

Behind her, Justin groaned in his sleep, and she hurriedly moved back to the bed. "I should sit with him," she told Lucian. "I'll let you know if he gets worse, but hopefully he'll just sleep it off."

"Ah," said Lucian. "It's one of those things."

Mae realized he'd misunderstood and thought Justin had overdosed but decided not to clarify. Better for Lucian to think Justin had popped one too many of his daily stimulants than know that he'd been communing with supernatural forces.

She sat by Justin's side until morning, when his fever finally broke. He woke up, face drawn and exhausted but eyes much clearer than they had been. She helped him sit up and brought more water, waiting until he'd had his fill before broaching what had happened.

"Do you remember anything?" she asked. "You were kind of out of it."

"In more ways than you can imagine," he said with a grimace. "I was out of my body . . . and in Magnus's. We flew to the temple and spied on the Grand Disciple." Justin suddenly straightened up. "Fuck, Mae. That nut wants to take out the media stream. He actually thinks he can send hackers or something with those missionary lecturers to do it and then launch an invasion."

She blinked in astonishment. "You said something like that . . . but I thought you were just delirious. You also said there's redundancy built into the stream, which is true. It's nearly impossible to take down."

"Then why was he so confident?" Justin raked a hand through his disheveled hair, his face lined with thought. "They have nothing comparable to that in their infrastructure. Nothing. Even if they had programmers from the provinces—hell, even the EA—they wouldn't have the knowledge needed to crack our system."

"Maybe you should tell the others."

"With what proof?" Justin sighed. "I mean, I guess it's all a moot point if I find a way to stall the Grand Disciple's request. But then . . . should I? If they really do have intel, then that's something we need to find out. If only there was a way to—"

Someone knocked at the door, and when Mae called a greeting, she saw Val's face appear. The other praetorian grinned upon seeing Justin sitting up. "Well, well, you are alive. Barely. The senator's report wasn't so upbeat the last time he saw you."

"I can't promise I'll be my normal sunny self for a little while," said Justin, "but yes, it looks like I'll survive another day."

Val nodded. "That's what we figured. Lucian had them send word this morning that you wouldn't make brunch because you were sick. The temple just sent some guy here to check on you, I guess to make sure you weren't faking. But we can tell him you're out of commission until further notice."

"Wait," called Justin, seeing her back out. "Did you get his name? The guy they sent?"

"Hansen, I think."

Justin went still, and Mae could practically see the wheels of thought spinning behind his eyes. "Tell him I'll talk to him here in—I don't know, fifteen minutes. Give me a chance to clean up first."

He moved to the edge of the bed and winced when he tried to stand. Mae quickly intercepted him and slid her arm around him for support. "Like hell. You need to rest."

"I need to talk to Hansen," Justin insisted. "Tell him, Val. Mae'll get me showered."

Val slinked away, muttering something about how some people got all the good jobs. Mae helped Justin to the door but hesitated before leaving. "Are you sure about this? You're really in bad shape. What caused this?"

"Magic I wasn't prepared for," he said. "This is the physical toll for being part of such power when I wasn't trained enough. But we found out what we needed."

Mae lowered her voice. "You said something else when you got back . . . about the god's touch. What was that all about?"

He didn't answer for a long time. "Something else I wasn't prepared for. Something glorious."

That was all he'd say, and she guided him out to one of the guesthouse's bathrooms. He managed to make it in on his own, and she sat outside as he showered, listening for the sound of falling. He managed to avoid disaster but still looked exhausted when he emerged. Even when he was dressed later in clean clothes, it was obvious to anyone that he'd been sick. Once he was propped up comfortably on the bed, though, Mae began hunting for her hairpins. She didn't have to be Cloistered for Hansen like she did Jasper, but she still needed to be Arcadian proper.

"Don't," said Justin, seeing her start to pull her hair up. "Stay like you are. Just brush it down."

"Are you crazy?" she asked. "You know how these people are."

"Yes," said Justin. "Yes, I do."

That was all he'd say until Hansen was shown in. The Arcadian did a double take when he saw Mae, but it seemed to be more out of surprise than uncontrollable lust. He accepted the chair offered to him near Justin's bed and paid little attention to her after that as she sat near the door.

"Dr. March," said Hansen awkwardly. "You've been ill."

"I'm on the mend," said Justin. "But I hope your master will understand why I can't make it today."

"Of course, of course," said Hansen. "I'll let him know, and perhaps you can reschedule if you recover before your trip ends. Let us know if there's anything we can do. I'll keep you in my prayers."

Justin smiled and shook his head. "There's nothing anyone can do—well, except my god. This is his doing, the price I gladly pay for wielding his power."

Mae might have thought she'd misheard, but Hansen's startled look told her otherwise. "I'm sorry, did you say your god?" he asked.

"Yes," said Justin, like it was the most natural thing in the world.

"B-but Gemmans have no gods," stammered Hansen. "You persecute those who do."

"Some of us have gods, gods capable of great things. Gods who truly make their followers earn power and reward those who serve faithfully." Justin paused and gave Hansen a long, scrutinizing look. "You're a faithful man. If you served my god, you would've married Elaina long ago."

Hansen froze. "How do you know about her?"

Justin spread his hands. "Because my god's power is great, and he's given me knowledge about many things. I know that you do much of the temple's work but that the Grand Disciple takes all the credit and rewards—other things, not just Elaina. I know you hate him for it."

Mae didn't know any of the context, but she could see that Justin had struck a nerve. Hansen shook his head, almost frantically. "No. I serve him faithfully. I gladly share what I have. He is a great man who deserves much—"

"Like the woman you love?" asked Justin knowingly. "How can you say that? If you won't admit to your own feelings, think about hers. Does she enjoy it? How does she feel each time he makes you bring her to his bed? Does she like getting his 'blessing'?"

Hansen stood up, face flushed. "I'm leaving—"

"To do what? Crawl back to him and tattle on me because I know that he's sleeping with your concubine? So that he'll reward you with another shit errand that you'll get nothing for?" Justin pointed at the chair, and despite his pale face and signs of sickness, there was an authority in him that Mae was completely unprepared for. "Now sit down and shut up. I'm going to help you change your life."

Hansen sat.

"My god also knows about your plan to take down the RUNA's media stream," continued Justin.

Hansen's jaw nearly hit the ground. "There's no way you can know that!"

"Haven't you been paying attention? My god can do anything. You think Nehitimar's the only player in town? You're wrong. Mine sees everything and can do things yours can only dream of. And this media stream plan? It's a dream. No self-taught hacker can take it out. The Grand Disciple's setting you up for failure."

"They aren't self-taught," said Hansen, regaining a little composure. "They were trained by a programmer who defected from your country a few years ago. He swears he still knows the protocols and says that if the stream is attacked from at least three different points, it can be temporarily disabled."

Justin said nothing but simply gave the other man a hard stare. Despite that, Mae had a feeling Justin was as surprised as she was. He'd said not even an EA programmer could crack Gemman networks . . . but a defector trained in them? It was possible, possible enough to give the theory a little more consideration. And Mae knew enough to know that the media stream was backed up and run out of several points throughout the country, exactly for the purpose of avoiding crashes. Simultaneous knockouts could have had an effect, but she didn't know enough of the technicalities to say for sure. Justin probably didn't either, but he was doing a good job of acting as all-knowing as the god he claimed he served.

"It won't work," he told Hansen. "You and the others will fail. And you'll be caught and trapped in our country. And the Grand Disciple and your president will disavow all knowledge of your plan, claiming you worked alone. And then they'll leave you to rot in a Gemman prison. Don't worry, though. I'm sure Elaina will be well taken care of."

"What do you want?" asked Hansen, through gritted teeth.

"It's what you want, not me." Justin pointed at Mae. "Look at her."

Hansen, seeming reluctant to do so, turned and looked.

"She's not my concubine. She's not my wife. I have no legal claim to her, no force that keeps her by my side, but she chooses to stay with me anyway. Would Elaina do that for you, if no laws bound her to you?"

"Yes," said Hansen instantly. "She loves me."

"Can you imagine that?" Justin lost some of the command in his voice and was now going into wheeling-and-dealing mode. "Having your beautiful woman free and uncovered, for all to see, with everyone knowing that she's with who she chooses—you—and that no one else, no matter how much they want her or lust for her, can lay a finger on her." He focused on Mae. "Tell Hansen what you studied in school."

She wasn't expecting the question and presumed he wasn't talking about her military training. "Music," she said.

Hansen, however, was one step behind. "You went to school?"

"All our women do," said Justin. "They can learn what they want, take on what professions they want, and be with the men they want. We don't cover them up either. We let them show off their beauty. And we don't let men who are full of themselves crush others who've done the work. A man who serves gets his rewards. They aren't snatched up by others."

That was perhaps a bit of an exaggeration, Mae thought. There were certainly power inequalities in the RUNA, but compared to Arcadia? Yes, her homeland was every bit the paradise Justin was describing.

"And your god allows all these things," said Hansen wonderingly.

"Well," corrected Justin, "our country does. But . . ." He studied the other man carefully, and Mae could guess Justin's thoughts almost as if he was explaining them out loud to her. Hansen might have been dissatisfied with what his god had given him, but he'd been raised in a world with gods, and that was what he understood. "My god makes it possible. It's the kind of world his followers live in. He could make it possible for you. And Elaina."

Hansen turned away from Mae and looked back at Justin. "How?"

"By defecting." Justin leaned forward. "We let the Grand Disciple go forward with this plan, send your party over. You keep us informed about their actions and let us know when they plan to make their move. We'll stop them and catch them, and you'll stay in the RUNA."

"Without Elaina," said Hansen flatly. "I'll be there. She'll be here. None of it means anything without her."

That was obviously an obstacle for Justin, but he waved it off. "I'll make sure she's there."

Hansen looked dubious, and Mae couldn't blame him. "How?"

"Haven't you been listening?" exclaimed Justin. "My god can do these things. He can heal this." Justin gestured to his body. "Ask the Grand Disciple to reschedule our meeting for dinnertime. I'll make a full recovery, you'll see. My god will make sure I can do his work."

"A full recovery?" echoed Hansen.

"Yes," said Justin firmly. "Make it happen. And I'll get Elaina to the RUNA. The hackers are predetermined . . . but the others, the missionaries posing as university lecturers or whatever. You're in charge of selecting them, yes?"

Hansen nodded.

"Are there others like you? Others abused by the Grand Disciple that Nehitimar has forsaken?"

The Arcadian man didn't answer, but once more, his expression gave him away.

Justin looked pleased. "If you can control those who'll go with you, make it happen. Bring them. My god will offer them a new life as well if they help us catch the programmers."

"You have to get Elaina," insisted Hansen. He looked Justin over. "And actually make it to dinner tonight."

"I'll make it," said Justin. "You'll see. You'll see what it's like to actually have a god who delivers." With what seemed to be great effort, he stood up and held out his hand. After a few moments, Hansen shook it.

"I'll talk to His Piousness," he told Justin. "We'll see you tonight."

Hansen started to leave, but Justin suddenly called him back. "Wait—do you know anything about a staff the Grand Disciple has? One with an eagle on it?"

"Of course," said Hansen. "It's believed to be a sign of Nehitimar's favor that he sent it to this Grand Disciple."

Justin frowned. "What do you mean 'this' one?"

"His predecessor didn't have it . . . his predecessor also didn't have nearly the power. I mean, Nehitimar's worship has been strong in Arcadia almost since the country's founding. It was a rallying point after the Decline. But when this Grand Disciple took over, there was something different . . . a different feel to him that caused people to flock to him in a way never felt before. I feel it sometimes, especially when he's carrying the staff. It's this overwhelming feeling of the god's glory and power. It makes it very difficult to oppose him."

"Is that why things happened like they did with Elaina?" asked Justin gently.

This caused Hansen to grimace. "No. When he wields the staff, the Grand Disciple is glorious and formidable. But even without it, he's still a hard man to oppose."

"I didn't see the staff in his temple apartments. Where does he keep it?"

"Probably at his retreat on Holy Lake." Seeing Justin's puzzled look, Hansen explained, "It's north of the city. Very secluded and well guarded."

"I would imagine so," Justin murmured. "Thank you."

Once Hansen was gone, Justin sprawled backward onto the bed and tossed an arm over his eyes. "What on earth have you done?" Mae asked him, not understanding half of what had just transpired.

"That," he groaned, "is an excellent question."

"How much of that was true?" She came to sit beside him, leaning over so that when he uncovered his face, he was forced to look her in the eyes. "I've seen you charm and fool people . . . that was all an act, right? You don't have a god."

"Depends on how you look at it," he said, not sounding happy in the least. "I mean, last night, I did have an out-of-body experience where I merged with an otherworldly raven that serves a god who wants to claim me."

"Yes . . . but *you* don't serve that god." She studied him more closely when he didn't comment. "Do you?"

His response came hesitantly. "No. But I'm more involved with him than I've led you to believe—though not by my choice."

Mae nearly brought up his earlier usage of "glorious" when describing the touch of this god but then decided they had bigger concerns for now. "Can you do all those things? Get that woman he wants into Arcadia? Get yourself out of bed? No offense, but you still look like crap."

"Stop with the flattery."

She gave him a small shove. "I'm serious! You're risking a lot on something you don't know you can make happen—and this is a big deal. Trying to take out the media stream's an act of terrorism when our own people talk about it. From these lunatics, it's a declaration of war. Our entire infrastructure's tied into the stream. The country would stop running. Chaos would break out."

"Which is why we can't risk tipping our hand yet," said Justin. "We need to let them think they might get away with it. We need the control, so we can find out what they know. If they find out we're onto them, this whole conspiracy will blow away in the wind."

"One of them already knows you're onto him," Mae pointed out.

Justin tugged the covers over his body and rolled away. "Which is exactly why I'm going to reel him in. And to do that, I need to sleep some more. After that, food. See if Lucian'll lend me his makeup. They wouldn't let you guys bring it in, but I know he must have some for his photo ops. It'll have to do to hide any remaining dark circles, and Exerzol'll do the rest to make me look lively."

She groaned. "You're not going to do yourself any favors if you get sick from taking too much of that."

"I can be sick as much as I want tomorrow. I've just got to show the power of my god tonight."

Mae moved toward the door and paused. "Can you at least tell me what that part about the staff was?"

Justin had started to close his eyes but opened them again. "Possibly a weapon, from what the ravens are telling me."

"Like my knife?"

"Much more powerful. They claim it's a threat to us and our country, but I don't know how we can get ahold of it. Even if we knew where Holy Lake was—and I'm sure that wasn't its name pre-Decline—getting there would be nearly impossible." He sighed and closed his eyes. "We'll have to be content with pulling off one heroic act in our country's defense and let that one go."

Mae left him after that, feeling troubled at the thought of another potential threat waiting for them but concurring that there was little to be done when they had so many other issues to deal with. The other praetorian women had been invited out on a sight-seeing expedition with the Gemman men, one she would've been allowed to go on as well, save that she didn't want to leave Justin. He woke up later in the afternoon and actually did look better, though he insisted on another shower. He made it to the bathroom unassisted, which was promising, and she went out to the main house to find him some food.

It required putting on the Cloistered getup, which was a pain in theory but proved useful when she passed some of Carl's sons on the way to the kitchen. They lingered in the hallway, barely giving her a second glance. Mae realized they'd mistaken her for Hannah.

Even Harriet did when Mae found the older woman tidying up by the kitchen stove, and it wasn't until Mae asked for a plate for Justin that Harriet realized who she was talking to. Mae stayed out of the way as the plate was made up, standing close enough to overhear the men—and an unexpected conversation.

"You better get Father to put a hold on one of Pittsfield's girls. He's moving his salon any day now." It was one of the younger sons, whose name Mae couldn't remember.

"Since when?" demanded Jasper.

"There was a break-in the other night at his place," explained the first speaker. "He doesn't think it's safe there. Wants to find a more secure location until the girls are of age."

"That's exactly the problem," said Jasper. "Why would I want one? None of them are old enough."

"He's got the best-looking girls in the city," said a voice Mae recognized as Carl's oldest son, Walter. "Of course, they're illegals, but that won't matter once he sells them—if he can sell them. No wonder he's hightailing it out. If he loses them before they're sold, he's out a lot of money. He's probably got at least three more years until they're ready."

Jasper's voice was petulant. "I don't want to wait three years, no matter how good-looking. I want a woman *now*."

Mae didn't pay attention to the rest and barely noticed when Harriet handed her the plate. The Cloistered costume allowed Mae to walk unbothered past the brothers again, and her mind spun out of control as she hurried back to the guesthouse. There was no way they could be talking about any other salon but the one she'd broken into. She'd suspected her visit wouldn't go unnoticed, but it had never occurred to her the owners would take off as a result. She wanted to scream in frustration. Fate had sent her to a location right by her goal, and she was about to lose it through her own actions. Any day now. What did that mean? When was the salon moving? What could she do in so short a time?

She longed to speak to Justin about it, but he was too preoccupied with his upcoming task at the temple. He chatted a little about it as he ate the food, and it was a sign of his focus that he didn't notice how troubled she was.

"If this god really is on my side," he remarked, bright and alert from his first Exerzol dose, "I'll come back to you tonight with good news."

Mae jerked herself out of her troubled thoughts. "What do you mean come back to me? I'll be with you."

"No need this time," he assured her. "As long as the Grand Disciple wants to bargain with me about this missionary visit, I'm in no danger. And I don't really want to watch him leer over you the whole time either."

"I can handle it," she said, crossing her arms.

"Yeah, well, I can't." Justin set his plate down. "Besides, if Hansen sells me out after all, I don't want you anywhere near where those freaks might get ahold of you."

"If he sells you out, then you'll need me more than ever!" she exclaimed.

"No. You stay here. I'll be fine." He looked her over. "I'm serious. You and your implant can settle down."

Her implant had spun up, raising all her endorphins, though it had been triggered long before this by the news of the salon. "How do you know my implant's up?" she asked.

Justin gave her a wry smile. "Because you always have that same tension and predatory look when the implant inspires you to proposition me. You'll have to find some other outlet tonight, though. I've got to keep my strength up."

Mae felt blood rush to her cheeks, but he'd already turned away from her and was trying to make sense of the makeup kit they'd pilfered from Lucian's room. As Justin experimented with under-eye concealers, she simply sat around dumbfounded, replaying his last words. Did he think that was why she'd tried to take him to bed after the Arcadians burst into the room?

*Was* it the reason?

She could admit that her libido did ramp up when the implant was activated, and it certainly had been after she escaped from

Jasper. But as she thought back to the details of that night, it hadn't just been the surge of chemicals that had drawn her to Justin. It had been . . . him. And not just the feel of his body either—though that hadn't been without its effects. There'd been something powerful in the way he'd stood up for her. Not that she was looking for rescue. Mae didn't expect that from anyone. It was more about the trust between them than the actual act of helping her. He'd had no idea what was going on, yet he'd unquestioningly stood by her. He always did. In Mae's life, trust was a tenuous thing. She trusted her fellow praetorians because they'd been trained to have each other's backs, and she knew she could count on them. Mae realized she placed just as much faith in Justin as she did Val or Dag or any of the Scarlets . . . without any of the same concrete reasons. There was something intangible that bound her to Justin, something that burned with both loyalty and a deeper attraction that she didn't know how to articulate.

In fact, she didn't know how to articulate any of this. And as she continued struggling to come to terms with her own tangled emotions, she felt the moment to act or say anything more about them slipping away. Justin grew caught up in his task, and before long, the other Gemmans returned home and wanted updates. Lucian was understandably surprised to hear Justin now saying he wanted to encourage an Arcadian cultural delegation without elaborating on why. Mae lost any other chances to speak with Justin alone until the others left for dinner, just as word came that a temple car had arrived for Justin's pickup.

"Are you sure I can't come with you?" she pushed, standing alone with him in their guesthouse's common room.

"I'll be fine. This is all on me, and I'll feel better knowing you're safely back here under boring house arrest." He certainly looked capable of making anything happen. He'd made a remarkable recovery and was back to the same outgoing, dashing mode that Mae knew so well. "And when I get back, we'll figure out this business with your niece."

"I thought you'd forgotten," she said, legitimately surprised. It had never left her mind—especially in light of recent developments—but she'd thought it had slipped his.

"I don't forget anything," he teased. "Especially something like that. Wait for me, and we'll talk."

A surge of emotion swelled within her chest, muddled by her earlier fears that he thought she only came to him when she was amped up on endorphins. Of course, he had his own share of bad behaviors in their history of fumbling romantic attempts, ones she'd heard no good excuses for. But as she allowed herself to accept that he'd misunderstood her recently, she also came to terms with the idea that she'd maybe misunderstood him. The how or why—especially in light of some of the things he'd said to her—was still a mystery, but enough weirdness surrounded them these days that she understood that there were very possibly factors at work that she had no knowledge of.

Yet again, expressing all of these things was beyond her. Words were Justin's gift, not hers. And so, bereft of any other immediate options, Mae leaned forward and kissed him—a long, lingering kiss that didn't say "I want to take you to bed" but that hopefully conveyed some of the depth of what she was feeling inside. It was the best she could do. Whether she was successful or not, she couldn't say, though he certainly looked surprised when shouts from outside about the waiting car forced them to part. He looked as tongue-tied as she felt and only managed to say, "Wait for me," before slipping away.

Mae returned to his room and tried to find some distraction that wouldn't leave her obsessing over him or the risks he might be facing. The sight of the amber knife reminded her of her own problems and the clock ticking on the salon. Justin had said he'd help her tonight . . . but that was assuming he got back in a timely enough manner to do anything. Picking up the dagger, running her fingers over the amber inlay, she knew instantly what she wanted to do, no matter his warnings about the supernatural. The knife had led her to her niece, who was about to be taken away again. Justin had said he'd help her tonight, but what harm was there in being prepared with more information? The more they knew, the better prepared they'd be. The only risk she faced was if she didn't come out of the knife's trance before the other Gemmans returned from dinner. A check of the clock in the main sitting room told her she had at least two hours, if not more. Resolved, she summoned a prayer to the unknown goddess and sliced her palm with the blade.

The expected vision came, showing unexpected things. Mae saw what was happening with the salon and what she had to do. When the vision ended, and she returned to her senses in the bedroom, she discovered two things. One was that only an hour had passed. The other was that she had a mark left on her skin from where she'd cut it. Before, the wound had always healed by the time the vision ended. It still didn't look fresh now by any means—more like it had happened a couple of days ago—but she was startled to see any residual mark at all. A voice sounded in her head: *You can't keep asking for much without giving a little.*

Mae had no time to ponder that, though. Not after what she'd seen. Time was more critical than she'd realized. *Wait for me,* Justin had said.

But as Mae began stripping off her Arcadian dress, the unfortunate reality hit her. "I can't," she said aloud. "I can't."

# CHAPTER 18

# ODIN'S PRIEST EARNS
# HIS KEEP

J ustin knew he looked good. The mirror and Mae had told
him as much. Did he feel good? That was a different matter. He could've easily slept another six hours, and he had
a feeling he might more than double that once the current Exerzol
high wore off. As long as he could get through this upcoming
meeting, though, it would all be worth it.

*You could've warned me about the aftereffects,* he told Magnus, as
the temple car drove into the city. *Or maybe that soul-severing part.*

*It's been a long time since I've done that for a priest,* explained
the raven. *I knew there'd be some consequences but didn't think it'd
be this bad. But you've recovered nicely, and next time, we'll make
sure you're better prepared.*

Justin didn't appreciate the assumption. *No one said there'll be
a next time.*

*Won't there?* asked Magnus. *Don't you want to feel that communion with Odin? Not that you need me for it. If you embrace your
calling, you'll find maintaining that connection on a daily basis is
easy.*

Justin wasn't sure if he wanted that either. Yes, he could freely
admit that it had been pretty thrilling, but as he'd learned from his
lifetime of substance abuse, a high wasn't always worth what you
paid for it. The potential to lose control was too great. He'd discovered that with drugs on more than one occasion and wasn't sure he

could win if he tried it with a god. The hypocrisy of his having warned Mae away from such things wasn't lost on him either.

And then there was Mae herself.

For a sweet moment, the weight of human and godly concerns lifted from Justin, and he was left only with the memory of that kiss. What in the world had brought that about? Concern for his safety? Gratitude for his help with her niece, help he still really wasn't sure how to give? There'd been no question the feel of her lips made his blood burn and hands long to touch her . . . but that parting kiss had been about so much more than just sex and desire. What that more was remained to be seen.

"Because my life needs one more complication," he muttered.

"Excuse me?" the driver called back.

"Nothing," said Justin.

Hansen met him at the temple steps again, and even Justin was proud of the poker face worn by the young priest. Hansen gave no sign that the two had any connection outside of this escort service. In fact, the young Arcadian did a good job of looking as though this were just another irritating errand. He brought Justin back to the Grand Disciple's apartments and then left with a bow when dismissed.

The Grand Disciple was decked out in his bejeweled regalia once more, which he apparently needed to convey power when dealing with underlings and diplomats, rather than young girls brought to him without choice. He had a chilled decanter of white wine that Justin actually found nauseating after his recent malaise, but etiquette and keeping up with this farce required a good show. He'd sworn he'd be in perfect health tonight and didn't want word getting back to Hansen of any weakness.

"I trust you're feeling better?" asked the Grand Disciple. "I was so distressed to hear you'd taken ill. I said many prayers for you."

"Thank you." Justin made himself comfortable on the love seat and accepted a glass of wine. "I think I've just overindulged in too much food while I've been here. I don't get this kind of cooking at home. In fact, I usually skip meals."

"That's half your problem. We never do that—in fact, our dinner should be here in an hour. You Gemmans don't marry nearly as much as you should. I'm sure you wouldn't skip meals if you had a wife to take care of your needs," said the priest.

"I have a sister who tries to," Justin said. "One who gives me plenty of grief when I slack off."

The Grand Disciple arched an eyebrow at that, probably because no Arcadian woman gave any Arcadian man grief about anything. "Well, just so long as you're feeling better. I feared we wouldn't have a chance to discuss my proposition before you left."

Justin took what he hoped was a polite sip and set the glass down. "Well, you're in luck. I've actually talked to my people about it, and they're in favor of it—with some modifications."

"Oh?" asked the Grand Disciple, not sounding entirely surprised. Justin could imagine he was expecting all sorts of restrictions, so what came next was undoubtedly astonishing.

"You see," Justin began, "I don't know how much you know about our media or politics, but image is everything over there—especially to guys like Lucian. Senator Darling. He's up for election, you see, and this trip is going to go a long way to help his image, showing how proactive he is about peace between our countries. And while a trade negotiation or promise of a future reciprocal trip would look good, it's not going to have the impact of immediate action that Lucian wants. He's got his heart set on a big impression, and he wants us to return later this week with something that'll make people stop and stare. He wants us to come back with Arcadians."

The lies came easily, and if it all worked out, Justin hoped he'd be able to sound just as convincing to Lucian.

"This week?" asked the Grand Disciple.

Justin nodded. "He's afraid if we leave with only verbal promises of something, then someone will get cold feet later. But if we can come back with a delegation, your people ready to share with ours, just as we've shared with you . . . well, he thinks it's going to seal the election. That's what he's got his heart set on, even though I told him that's probably not enough time for you to get together the kind of scholars you wanted to have come teach us about your culture."

The idea had come to Justin after talking to Hansen. If they were going to catch a potential Arcadian plot, then time was of the essence. Justin didn't want to leave things hanging with promises of a visit that might go awry. He didn't want to leave enough time for Hansen to change his mind—or get caught. From what Justin understood, the defector-trained hackers were already selected and ready. It would just be a question of whether the Grand Disciple was ready to let them go sooner than expected in order to aid Lucian's alleged dreams of power.

"It might be possible," the Grand Disciple said at last. "Certainly it would disrupt the plans of some of the individuals I'd thought to send, but I'm sure they'd be accommodating in the goal of helping diplomatic relations. To be honest, I expected a long drawn-out battle over this . . . you'd sounded so uncertain about anyone speaking about Nehitimar in your country."

"Ah, yes." Justin put on a sheepish look. "There *is* one other slight complication. Some people in our party are still concerned about the idea of anyone teaching about your religion—even academically. And, unfortunately, there are also those who haven't forgotten tragic military, uh, entanglements between our nations. They're afraid that a group of men coming in might reinforce harsh images—even though I've told them that's just how things are done. The men do business here. So what Lucian was wondering was if we could soften the image of your people by having your delegates' families or wives accompany them. They wouldn't be active in any of the real diplomatic work, of course. They'd have peripheral roles, just as our women have had here. See some sights, stay well chaperoned. But the hope is that by showing that side of your culture, it'll warm up public perception of you—which Lucian naturally hopes will warm up public perception of him."

Justin gave a small laugh at that, hoping that it sounded like he and the Grand Disciple were in on some private joke together. *Poor*

*Lucian,* he thought. *I almost feel bad for all the things I'm claiming he's said.*

*The thing is,* noted Horatio, *that setting aside the conspiracy against your country, the rest of the logic might actually appeal to him. It would be good press for him to show up with an Arcadian peace delegation.*

The Grand Disciple's face was lined with thought, but it seemed to be more about solving a problem than refusing. "That would be highly irregular—and also difficult in such a short time frame. It's already tight enough just getting our men together in a few days' time. You're certain—and Senator Darling's certain—that your government would allow this? These are big promises to make, and he hasn't been elected yet."

It was a fair point, and Justin could only hope that—once he'd convinced Lucian of this madness—the senator would have enough connections back home to get the Arcadians admittance at the border. It was a big gamble.

"He can do it," Justin stated. "But if this is all too much for you, I can tell him—"

"No, no." The Grand Disciple got to his feet. "All things are possible in Nehitimar, and this may be the god's way of expediting something I've long hoped for. We'll get our lecturers together—and most certainly their concubines, if not their wives—in time, but it's something I'll have to start work on immediately." He glanced at an ornate clock on the wall. "You've got me so worked up, I nearly forgot dinner is coming. How impolite. We can do that—then business."

"No, no," said Justin, welcoming the chance to escape small talk with the priest. "This is more important, and it might do me good to go easy on the food."

The two of them hashed out a few more logistical details, like the number of the party and how they'd be distributed throughout different cities in the RUNA. Justin made up more grand claims from Lucian and uneasily hoped he'd be able to return to Carl's soon, because the senator was going to need a heads-up about this sooner rather than later. That, and Justin's Exerzol was wearing off. He wanted to get out of show mode and seek the comfort of his bed. He could talk to Lucian in pajamas.

Hansen arrived to take Justin out, and the Grand Disciple brightened upon seeing his assistant. "Excellent. As soon as you've taken Dr. March to the car, we can discuss some very exciting plans."

"Ah. Forgive me, Your Piousness." Hansen bowed low. "But the driver's sick, and I haven't had time to find a replacement. I was going to take him myself. But if you have need of me . . ."

The Grand Disciple frowned, though it was obviously no fault of Hansen's. "No, take him, and if he needs to pick up any food on the way home, do so. I can talk to Cowlitz first."

"Cowlitz?" asked Hansen politely.

"Yes, yes. Looks like we have some exciting news. The delegation I've long hoped for to their country will be going forward—much sooner than we expected. I'll need Cowlitz to make sure his people are briefed, and you'll need to finalize yours, so be thinking about that tonight. Young Hansen here is one of those who'll be coming with you," the Grand Disciple explained to Justin. To Hansen, he continued, "Additionally, the parameters of the trip have changed, and our delegates will be bringing their wives."

"Some of us don't have wives, Your Piousness," Hansen reminded him.

"Then you'll bring concubines. I'm sure Elaina will enjoy the trip. We'll discuss it later." The Grand Disciple was so caught up in his plans now that he didn't notice the transformation that took place in Hansen's face at the mention of Elaina. "Now, get Dr. March home, and hurry back. There's much to be done."

Hansen didn't say a word to Justin as he led him out, and it wasn't until they were alone in the car that the younger man exhaled in relief. "You did it. You really did it."

"My god did it," said Justin, remembering the role he was playing.

Hansen nodded eagerly as he started the car. "I knew that . . . somehow, even though my logic said not to trust you, my heart believed. I knew that you—and he—would come through. That's why I went ahead and told the others."

Justin had started to relax, looking forward to his bedroom, but those words drew him up short. "The others?"

"You told me to find those who are dissatisfied to join us, and I did. I mean, I knew about them long ago, and now we're going to meet them. Your driver getting sick isn't a coincidence, I'm afraid, but you needing dinner is—a happy one. It'll explain why we're out so long."

"So . . . wait. Where are we going, exactly?" Justin suddenly wished he had Mae after all. There'd been no danger in the temple, but now, going off into the unknown with Hansen, Justin felt much less secure.

"To the home of a friend of mine," Hansen told him. "A great man. A priest retired from active service who wants to talk to you. He's almost right on the way back to your house, so it works out nicely."

Justin wasn't so sure about that, but he'd made an ally of Hansen and had to deal with the consequences. He just hoped the other man's love for his concubine would keep him loyal. "Who was the Cowlitz guy that the Grand Disciple mentioned?" Too late, Justin realized he should've known that if he was truly all-knowing, but fortunately, Hansen was too excited to notice the slip.

"The defector. The three men he trained will come with us and pretend to be lecturers like the others."

"So they're the actual threats here. The rest are your guys?"

"Yes. And they'll be thrilled to bring their women," said Hansen. "Thank you. Thank your god—I look forward to learning more about him!"

It occurred to Justin then that this plan involved letting a large number of Arcadian refugees into the RUNA. When he'd originally left Panama, he'd tried to get visas for all of Tessa's family and been denied. He had to hope Arcadians held more political value, or he would have seriously led poor Hansen and these "others" astray.

*Having regrets?* asked Horatio.

*No,* Justin told him. *If we stop them from carrying out a plot to take down our infrastructure, it'll be well worth the cost of a dozen refugees.*

He had nightmarish visions of being led to a shack in the woods, but the house Hansen took him to was a well-kept suburban residence with less of a farm feel than Carl's place had. And although the home had a fair amount of privacy from its neighbors, it was still in enough of a neighborhood to give Justin some sense of normality.

At least until he stepped inside.

There had to be nearly fifty people crammed inside the house's living room, something he'd been totally unprepared for since there were only three other cars in the driveway. While some wore higher-quality clothing reflective of the upper class, most appeared to be from Arcadia's struggling masses. He had no time to ponder the secrecy that must've gone into this meeting because they all fell silent at his and Hansen's entrance. More remarkable still, Justin noticed that a third of those gathered were women, and although they wore the traditional modest clothing and hovered near the crowd's edge, there was something fresh and different about the way they interacted with their men here, compared to what Justin had observed so far in Arcadia. These weren't just struggling Arcadians, Justin suspected. They were dissatisfied ones. An elderly man with snow-white hair came forward slowly, hobbling on a cane. The smile he gave them was kind, and he embraced Hansen warmly.

"Timothy, I'm so glad you made it—and so glad you brought our esteemed guest." The old man extended his hand to Justin. "I'm Gideon Wexler. Welcome to my home. If there's anything I can get you, don't hesitate to ask."

"He hasn't eaten," said Hansen.

Justin shook his head. "No, don't worry about that. Hansen, what's going on? I asked you to find others to go with us who thought like you . . . but all these people can't come to the RUNA."

"I know," said Hansen. "And they aren't all going. Just some of them. The rest know they have to stay here, but they want to meet you and learn from you before you leave."

The sea of faces swam before Justin's eyes, and he focused back on the two men closest to him. "Learn what?"

"About your god," said Gideon. "We've long been dissatisfied with our lots, with the way Nehitimar's power and wealth is abused by the temple and the government. We'd thought when revolution comes—and it *will* come—we'd either have to do it without a god or radically reform our worship of Nehitimar. Only, when we prayed and asked for guidance, we received none. Hopefully your god will answer our prayers. Teach us about him, and we will carry on his worship in secret after you and the others have gone."

Justin felt his eyes widening. "I just revealed myself to Hansen today . . . and you're already prepared to jump on board with another god?"

"We've been waiting for a sign for a very long time," said Gideon serenely. "This is it, and we aren't going to delay and waste it. Timothy told us of your miraculous recovery and the knowledge your god possesses."

"And he got the Grand Disciple to let Elaina come with me to the Lost Lands," said Hansen eagerly. "Those coming with me can bring their families too."

Murmurs of excitement rippled through the crowd, and Justin resisted the urge to pinch himself. "Okay, look, before we get any further, you have to stop calling it the Lost Lands. The RUNA, the Republic . . . any of those are fine. But not the Lost Lands."

Everyone around him nodded eagerly, as though he'd just delivered the most profound piece of wisdom in the world's history. Inside, he was reeling.

*What have you gotten me into?* he demanded of the ravens.

*This was all you,* Horatio assured him.

"Tell us more," said Gideon. "Tell us how we may worship your god. Tell us how you're connected. How do you serve him?"

"I . . ."

It was a weird position for Justin to be in, one in which he had no words or stories ready. If he had any sense at all, he would've denied all connection to the divine, but he could hardly do that after his sales pitch to Hansen. Keeping Hansen and his allies close was key to stopping the Arcadian plot. Justin swallowed.

"I'm his . . . priest."

Geraki and the ravens had called him that often, but it was the first time Justin had used the term aloud to describe himself, and he was surprised at the power it imparted. Gideon looked so overjoyed that Justin thought Gideon might sink to his knees in adoration. Instead, the old man took Justin by the arm and led him to a chair in the center of the room.

"Come. Tell us everything. Everything you can."

"I have a couple hours at most," Justin warned him. "They'll wonder what happened to me."

"Then tell us everything you can in a couple hours."

All of those gathered sat down, either on the floor or in chairs, and watched Justin with rapt eyes while he worked to keep his exterior composed. *What do I tell them? I don't know anything about worshipping Odin.*

It was a strange but true statement. He knew Odin's history academically, as any servitor would, and he'd learned a host of spells and magical rune meanings. The day-to-day worship of the god was nothing that had ever come up, though. Geraki had a collection of followers who met in secret, but Justin had never attended their services.

*You're Odin's priest,* said Magnus. *Your job is to lead the people and guide them into love and devotion to our god. Whatever ways you have of doing that will be correct. Worship of him evolves. You will define what that is now, in this place and in this time.*

Fatigue gnawed at the edges of Justin's consciousness, though adrenaline was currently keeping him as alert as it might a praetorian. To be safe, he reached into his coat pocket for his Exerzol bottle and popped another pill. Mae was right that he might regret it tomorrow, but only getting through the next two hours mattered.

"His name is Odin," said Justin at last. "And he's the king of all the gods."

There was a collective intake of breath, though one person dared to ask, "What other gods? Like Nehitimar?"

Someone tried to shush the speaker, but Justin waved it off. "No, no. Questions are permitted. Questions are encouraged. Odin is a god of wisdom and knowledge. The gods and goddesses he rules over are called the Vanir and the Aesir. Some are his relatives. Some are just, uh, associates. Some of them interact with humans."

"Goddesses?" asked a young woman boldly. "Gods can be women?"

Justin realized that in the Arcadian system, Nehitimar's wives didn't hold divine status equal to his. They weren't human exactly, but they also weren't full-fledged gods.

"Yes," he said firmly. If ever there was a group that needed female empowerment, it was this one. "The goddesses are on equal footing with the gods. One of them—Freya—is especially powerful. A match for Odin. Some people say she and Frigga—his wife—are aspects of the same deity, but that's a more complex mystery for later. Let's get back to him."

What unfolded in the next two hours was a mix of everything he'd scraped together about Odin, a recitation of Gemman ideals of social and gender equality, and some of the greatest improvisation of Justin's life. What surprised him immensely was how much they loved the stories in which Odin faced hardship. He told them about how he'd sacrificed his eye for wisdom, how he'd grieved when his son Baldur was killed. Yet, Justin always brought it back around to make Odin triumphant, and they loved that too.

*Nehitimar is cold and unyielding,* Justin thought. *He makes no sacrifices; neither do his high priests. They take and take while the people give and give. That a god might be relatable is blowing their minds. Not too relatable, of course. They still want to look up to him, but hearing about his weaknesses is just making him seem that much more powerful to them.*

The ravens silently agreed and offered no comment when Justin began outlining ways the people could worship him. He had nothing on which to base any ceremony and used a mix of elements observed from other gods' worship, as well as what he knew about the nature emphasis of old Norse religion. The Arcadians liked that although Odin required respect and fealty, he didn't require the wealth and heavy taxation of Nehitimar's worship. Justin taught them *ansuz*, the rune most associated with Odin directly, and had a feeling many would be secretly wearing *ansuz* pendants when he left. Gideon in particular seemed to find deeper understanding as Justin briefly outlined the rune's higher meanings.

*He truly is a priest,* noted Magnus. *He's one who could grasp the runes and their secrets. You must make sure he knows what he needs to know before you leave.*

*I don't even know what he needs to know!* Justin snapped back. *I'm making half of this up as I go along.*

*And you're doing a great job,* said Horatio. *All-Father is pleased.*

In conversing with the ravens, Justin had fallen silent. Seeing the curious looks of the Arcadians, he turned apologetic. "Sorry. Odin speaks to me through his ravens, Huginn and Muninn. Thought and Memory. Normally, they stay with him, bringing him the world's knowledge, but he's blessed me by allowing them to advise me."

*I don't think "blessed" is a word you've ever used with us,* said Horatio. *We're touched.*

*Hush. These people need some signs and wonders. Feel like making an appearance?*

That caught the ravens by surprise, a rarity Justin had little chance to appreciate. *Are you sure?* Magnus returned. *You know what it's like when we manifest, and you aren't in great shape to begin with.*

Yes, Justin knew. The ravens were so bound to him after all these years that if they left his mind and took on corporeal form, he was left with a splitting headache. But in his state, he wasn't sure he could pull off any rune spells. One of Justin's most frustrating issues with the religions he'd investigated was that they were all talk and little action. These people deserved action.

*Do it*, said Justin.

There was a *poof*, and like that, Horatio and Magnus appeared out of thin air, causing gasps and screams from the assembly. They beat their huge black wings as they sought a place to land, and instinctively, Justin held out his arms, offering a perch to each one. They accepted, and although his head *did* feel like it was going to explode, there was a rightness to having the ravens there.

After that, the people were his.

He gave them everything else he could think of to carry on a fledgling worship of Odin, including naming Gideon as an interim priest. "Pray and do your best," he told the old man. "Odin may come and guide you further in your dreams."

The crowd was equally awed when Justin made the ravens disappear, and they followed him to the door when Hansen finally said he could leave. One tug on Justin's sleeve caught his attention, and he saw it was the same girl who'd spoken to him at the beginning. This truly was an unusual group if they allowed their women the right to talk and question.

"Thank you for speaking to us," she said shyly. "I wish we'd been able to learn more about that goddess—Freya. Or would . . . or would that make Odin angry?"

The girl's face was heavily marked by Cain, but there was an intelligence and strength in her eyes that Arcadian discipline and lack of formal education hadn't diminished. "No," he said. "She is his equal, and they can exist together. You can worship her and pray to her as well."

*Way to advocate for the boss*, said Horatio, sounding more amused than upset.

*These people need to see a female face on the divine*, Justin insisted. *It does no one any good to just have Odin slip into Nehitimar's tyrannical role. Odin will be better served by empowered, freethinking people, men and women alike.*

The gravity of that thought, that he was pondering what might best serve Odin, drew Justin up short and left him momentarily at a loss for words. The Arcadian girl tilted her head and studied him curiously.

"Are you okay?" she asked.

Justin put his show face back on and tried to smile reassuringly. "Absolutely."

She smiled tentatively in return. "Can you tell me anything else at all about Freya? Anything about what she's like?"

Justin lacked some of the more spiritual insights about Freya that he did Odin, but his mental encyclopedia of most gods was still at the ready. "She governs love, sexuality, and fertility . . . but also war and death too. She rides into battle as fiercely as any other warrior but still remains the most beautiful woman in the world. Beauty like that is shown, not covered up or left to be ashamed of."

The girl's eyes were wide. "What does she look like?"

Justin was on the verge of offering some esoteric answer about how one couldn't describe the beauty of a goddess but instead found himself saying, "Her hair is gold, like sunlight on a winter's day, worn long and unbound with a crown of flowers on top."

"What kind of flowers?" asked the girl breathlessly.

"Apple blossoms." Then, turning back to Norse canon and away from his own images of divine beauty, he added, "And she wears a cloak of feathers and an amber necklace."

As the words left his lips, he again found himself doing a mental double take. *Is it more than coincidence and my own unresolved feelings that are muddling Freya and Mae together? Is there a connection I've missed?* The girl was too awed to say more, and with Hansen pulling him to the door, Justin had no chance to cultivate the small fear beginning to grow in the back of his head. Everyone else wanted to make their good-byes, especially Gideon. Justin felt dizzy by the time he made it to Hansen's car, but whether that was from the stories he'd just spun or sheer exhaustion, he couldn't say. There was also the possibility he was reeling from something else, a feeling of exhilaration and lightness that had been building in him as he spoke to the assembly and that seemed to fill every part of his being with power.

*Odin's presence,* affirmed Magnus. *Your words brought him to this place tonight. Do this often, and you will always enjoy the touch of his power.*

*I don't think it's anything I'll be doing again soon,* Justin countered.

The raven didn't buy it. *Won't you, priest?*

Hansen was high and thrilled in his own way and chatted the whole way home about how Justin had changed his life and how all those who'd heard him tonight would hold true to Odin and not betray Justin. Justin hadn't thought that much about betrayal until now and realized, with a sinking heart, that it'd only take one slip from one person to reveal what he'd done. Promoting worship of anyone other than Nehitimar was high treason in Arcadia.

*That group seemed pretty caught up in the excitement of it all,* said Horatio. *So long as they don't start doubting for three more days, you should be fine.*

*In fact,* added Magnus, *you could probably go after that staff in your free time.*

Justin was incredulous. *Free time? I need to lay low and not do anything else to cause attention until we go home. The staff is out of our reach.*

*It could be a powerful weapon for you,* said Magnus.

*For me or for Odin?* asked Justin.

*Does it matter? What Hansen described sounds like something that creates a glamour, or aura of influence, around the bearer. Imagine the things you could achieve with that kind of asset.*

*My own personality does that for me,* Justin joked.

The raven was stern. *Not like this. This object may have been instrumental in the Grand Disciple's rise to power and why he's able to exert the control he does not only over his followers but his government as well. Find it and take it, and you would bring a great asset to Odin—and deal a harsh blow to Nehitimar*

Justin was unmoved. *I already am, in thwarting the Grand Disciple's plan to tear apart our infrastructure! Mortal concerns like that are much bigger to me right now than nebulous immortal ones.*

Justin ignored the ravens' further badgering and longed to discuss the night's events with Mae when he arrived back at Carl's estate. He was troubled by the priestly role he'd so easily slipped into, as well as some suspicions he was gathering about another godly influence. Mae was the only one who could understand, and Justin was grateful that socializing and post-dinner cleanup had detained the rest of the Gemman party. He was able to slip back into the guesthouse undisturbed and go immediately to Mae in his bedroom. The question of that surprising parting kiss was also still fresh in his mind.

She was sitting on his bed when he entered the room, which was unusual for her. Usually, she had a more predatory position staked out near the door. Her back was to him, though, and she flinched slightly at his entrance.

"Man," he said, tossing his coat to the floor. "Am I glad to see you. You will not believe the fucked-up night I just had."

He noticed then that she was fully covered in her Cloistered getup, which was also weird since she wasn't obligated to wear it around their guesthouse, especially in his room. Putting the rest of his ruminations on hold, he walked around to face her, growing increasingly troubled by her stillness and odd behavior.

"Everything okay?" he asked, kneeling in front of her. "What's going on?"

She said and did nothing for several moments, and then slowly, almost nervously, she removed the opaque veil from her face—a face that wasn't Mae's. It was Carl's young concubine, the one who'd been beaten and reprimanded. Justin stared at her dumbfounded, suddenly remembering a story Mae had told him about Hannah asking if one of the Gemmans could impregnate her.

"What are you doing here?" he demanded. "Where's Mae?"

"I am Mae," said Hannah simply. "At least for the rest of your trip I am."

# CHAPTER 19

# ACT OF FAITH

Sneaking out of Carl's compound during dinnertime wasn't that much more difficult than when Mae had done it late at night. He'd upped his security since that incident, employing the bulk of it when darkness fell. With the sun still lingering in the sky and the family up and active, the patrolling security guards were few and far between. The only edge they had was better visibility, so Mae had to be extra conscientious of their positioning when she climbed the tree and swung out over the fence. Returning would've been a much more complicated matter . . . if she'd planned on coming back.

No one bothered her once she was on the road, walking toward the salon in ill-fitting men's clothing. Seeing as Justin had ruined his wide-brimmed hat, Mae had "borrowed" Lucian's from his room, hoping he wouldn't mind. Honestly, once he and the others saw what she'd left behind, the hat would be the least of anyone's worries.

Even now, resolved on this course of action, Mae couldn't help but feel a pang of guilt for what she was doing to the others. On the surface, the transgression was obvious: She was violating orders and abandoning her mission. That would've been wrong in any situation, let alone one that required her presence for extra security. She'd left those who needed her protection and possibly endangered them further by creating a sticky political situation. The

Arcadians wouldn't take kindly to discovering that one of their Gemman guests had disappeared, and Mae could only hope her attempt at damage control would work.

The knife's vision had left her no alternatives. She had needed to act and act fast. Using Hannah had been a stroke of brilliance, though Mae regretted that the girl's unfortunate circumstances had led her to that point. Val had told Mae earlier that Hannah had been beaten again that morning, severely enough that she was out of commission for dinner. So, while the others ate, Mae had crept to the other guesthouse and given the young Arcadian woman a chance at freedom. Both of them were supposed to be Cloistered for the duration of the Gemman trip and were of close-enough heights that they were indistinguishable when fully wrapped up. Mae's only gamble had been whether the girl would accept the deal.

Hannah had, with equal parts vehemence and fear. She'd come back to the Gemman guesthouse—after first ransacking her own room to make it look like she'd packed in haste—and accepted Mae's assurances that the other Gemmans would help her once her identity was known. Mae didn't actually know that for sure but had to believe it was true. Once they discovered she was gone, it would be in their best interests to leave with as many women as they'd come in with. They'd cover for Hannah, who would hopefully be able to pass as Mae by staying Cloistered until the border. From what Mae had learned, runaway wives and concubines were rare, but surely it was rarer still for one to try to slip out of the country pretending to be a foreigner. So long as no one thought to lift Hannah's veil, she'd be okay, and the RUNA would give her refugee status once she was on their soil.

Mae's own fate was less certain, but that was a problem for later.

She studied her hand in the dusky light, wondering just how much trouble she'd gotten herself into. The mark from the knife was still there, a tangible reminder of her involvement in supernatural affairs. But she could hardly dismiss the knife's powers when she turned down the rural side road and found a scene exactly as the vision had shown her. Crouching in the trees, Mae quickly assessed the situation. A large truck with an open flatbed was parked outside the salon, and men were loading up furniture—mostly beds and tables—onto it. Near it was parked a large van, presumably what would be used to take the girls themselves. The knife had shown her immediate action was needed, and here the proof was, right before her eyes. If she'd waited one more day—or even until this evening, when Justin got back—her niece might have been gone forever.

And not just her niece. When Mae had traveled to the salon in the knife's vision, the goddess had spoken to her, that radiant voice echoing everywhere.

*Go and get the girl, and I will guide you to safety.*

*I have to get all the girls,* Mae had said. *Not just my niece. I can't take her and leave the rest to that fate.*

*You have no responsibility to them,* the goddess had reminded her.

But Mae had been thinking the matter over for a while and was firm. *Some are my countrywomen. All are my sisters. One way or another, I have a human responsibility to them. Is it beyond your power to save the rest?*

*Don't try to coerce me into acting by playing to my vanity. That's a human trick, one you don't need to play on me. I can and will help you, so long as you are up to fulfilling your part.*

*Yes, of course,* Mae had thought bleakly. *Justin told me there'd be a price. There always is. What will I owe you?*

*Faith,* the goddess had replied simply. *Something you give very easily to your masters in your professional life but a commodity you rarely share personally. If you want this to succeed, you will have to put your faith in me to guide you and know that you will not always immediately have the answers to your questions as you undertake this task. But if you have faith, I will guide you home and help you to thwart your enemies. Do you accept?*

Faith had sounded like both an easy and terribly high cost, as no doubt it was intended to. But Mae had agreed, for better or for worse, and now there was no turning back.

She watched the packing for a long time, something that grew more difficult as dusk fell and stole the remaining light. But by the end of her surveillance, she felt confident in her assessment of the situation. The two guards from her last visit were there, occasionally appearing outside for some task, though they weren't responsible for the bulk of the packing. That fell on two other men who seemed to be hired laborers. A fifth, older man paced the property and barked orders to everyone. Someone referred to him as Pittsfield, the same name Carl's sons had given to this salon's owner. Mae instantly despised him. Aside from these men, the only other person Mae saw was the marked woman from the kitchen, who must indeed have been a servant working for the salon, judging from the way she scurried about her tasks. None of the young girls, the actual merchandise, were visible.

*Probably locked away in their rooms,* Mae thought. Pittsfield and his cronies wouldn't have them on display with workers around, though something told Mae the girls probably never got outside, even without visitors. They were probably kept concealed at all times, with no sunlight or play, forced to listen to that horrendous religious rhetoric about how they were lesser beings only put on this earth to serve men. Anger began to kindle in Mae, and she forced it down. She needed a cool, collected head to pull this off.

An hour later, the packers finished, and the moving truck left. Pittsfield and one of the guards went inside while the other remained on the porch. It was almost completely dark now, and Mae was able to move about the perimeter more freely. She wondered what the delay was until the marked girl brought the outside guard a plate. Dinnertime. It made sense, feeding the girls before a trip, and Mae realized it was something she too now wished she had done for herself. No matter. Praetorians might have loved their meals, but they were trained to go without and withstand harsh conditions.

This was her last opportunity to plan. There was another car on the property, so most likely only some of the men would be accompanying the girls in the van. That didn't mean all three might not see them off, and Mae needed to start evening her odds. Creeping into a dark thatch of woods near the property's edge, she grabbed a large limb and struck it against a tree as hard as she could. The guard, illuminated on the porch, immediately set his plate down and aimed his gun in Mae's direction. He took a few steps forward and peered around, but the darkness was against him. She could guess his thoughts. The noise had definitely been made by something living . . . but was it human or animal? The guard cast a hesitant glance back and then, to Mae's relief, strode forward without seeking backup. He moved toward Mae's hiding spot, and even when he took out a flashlight, the advantage was still hers. She waited until he'd almost walked past her and then sprang on him from behind, clamping a hand on his mouth to muffle his cries as she wrestled him to the ground and choked off his air. When he was still, she eased up and shone his flashlight on him, revealing him to be the same guard she'd struck the other night. Bad luck for him. Ripping off a piece of his shirt, she made a makeshift gag for him and then tied his hands up behind his back with his belt, binding it as best she could to a small shrub. In the event he came to before she was gone, that would slow him down.

*You could always kill him.* The voice in her head was her own, not the goddess's, and Mae hesitated. It was true that killing the man would be the ultimate act of incapacitating him. There was no telling what atrocities he'd committed and would continue to do. Shooting him would make too much noise and give her away. Slitting his throat with the knife was an option, but she'd already used it once to kill, and Mae didn't want to link the blade to death again if she didn't have to. The Morrigan had been all about death. If Mae was getting involved with another goddess, she wanted this relationship to be as much about life as possible. For now, he would live.

She immediately seized his gun, adding it to the one she'd pilfered on her previous trip here, which now only had one shot left. She also took the man's lighter, his coat, and the real treasure: a set of keys, which she was pleased to learn unlocked the van. A quick check of it showed no extra supplies, save a few jugs of water that suggested they were going farther than just down the street, though perhaps not across the country. A folded-up map provided no clues to Pittsfield's destination, though it did give her a much-needed sense of the roads in the areas. No one had noticed the guard's absence yet, and she used the time to study their best escape route. Due west would lead her to the RUNA's border in less than a day and was by far the fastest. That particular border was a river crossing. In fact, the Mississippi River made up a huge portion of the Gemman-Arcadian border. It was nearly impossible to avoid. The river became bigger the farther south it went, and Mae had no idea how she'd get a group of young girls over it. If she went northwest, she might have an easier time crossing where the river narrowed, but her best chance would be going straight north, to a point where the border turned east and was strictly on land. Those points had the greatest clusters of soldiers, on both sides, and meant a longer trip, but if she could get close enough to the Gemman border, their technology would pick up her chip and at least get her countrymen's attention, if not their aid.

It was the best shot she had at a plan. The rest would have to be faith.

She stuffed the map in her coat pocket and then took the coat from the unconscious man over to the smaller parked car. Mae wasn't overly familiar with the mechanics of gas-powered cars, but she understood the basic principles and figured out the rest by doing a quick survey of the vehicle. No one else had come to check on the missing guard, and she used her opportunity to twist and tear the stolen coat into a makeshift fuse leading into the gas tank. Satisfied with her work, Mae used the lighter to ignite the end of the cloth, and then she ran as fast as she could to the far side of the house's property. She'd just ducked for cover when the car exploded spectacularly.

It took a few moments, but the response she'd hoped for came. Pittsfield and the other guard came tearing out, both armed. They ran the opposite direction from Mae, staring openmouthed at the fiery wreckage. With their backs to her, Mae was able to run right past them into the house, slipping in without their noticing. The entryway was empty, but the marked girl hovered in the doorway to the kitchen, cringing when she saw Mae.

"I'm not going to hurt you," Mae said, realizing that probably didn't seem convincing with her two guns. "Where's the emergency exit?"

Hannah had explained to her that many Arcadian homes, especially salons, had secret ways in and out similar to the tunnel Mae had used at Carl's. Arcadian men were covetous of their women and wanted them secured, but they still needed fire exits and other emergency paths out.

Mae's hope was that a household servant like this girl would know where the house's hidden exit was, and then Mae could smuggle the upstairs girls out while the men were distracted by the fire. It became immediately obvious that the girl wasn't going to help, however, when she began screaming.

"Shut up!" hissed Mae. The girl kept screaming, dashing any tentative attempt at secrecy. Desperate to regain some semblance of control, Mae leapt out at the girl and dealt her a blow to the head that rendered her unconscious. That brought a merciful return to silence, but Mae didn't know if it was a little too late. That, and it had also silenced a potential source of information unless one of the girls knew about the house's secret escape.

As it turned out, danger came not from outside but within. Mae had barely turned toward the stairs leading up when two unknown men came barreling down. Her implant, already on alert, surged to action, flooding her with adrenaline that made her act quickly and instinctively. She lashed out as the first assailant came at her, blocking his attack and flipping him over so that he landed hard on his back. At the same instant, she saw his partner draw a gun on her, and with no other means to dodge or attack the man directly, Mae deferred to her faster reflexes and shot him before he could shoot her. The man she'd knocked to the ground began to scramble toward her, and she shot him too.

"Damn," she muttered. If the men outside didn't know something had happened earlier, they did now. She'd been foolish to think that just because she hadn't seen more guards outside, there were none on the property. It made sense that Pittsfield would've had extra security after her previous visit, leaving those men directly with the girls while others ran errands outside. Done was done, and there was no point in beating herself up over the error. The question now was where she was going to make her stand.

She chose a spot just up the stairs to launch her defense, one that afforded her an angle on the front door but mostly kept her out of sight. When the other guard—the one who'd had sex with the serving girl that night in the kitchen—came through, he had only the briefest of glimpses of Mae before she shot him. Even if she'd had time for remorse, she wouldn't have spared it for him, not after seeing the earlier terror in the marked girl's face. That girl's entire life had been spent at the mercy of others, and he'd callously taken advantage of it.

A creak on the stairs behind Mae explained why only one man had come through the door—and also revealed the location of the emergency exit. She spun around and saw Pittsfield launching himself down the stairs at her. The secret way he'd taken must have wound through another staircase hidden within the walls that went up to the second floor. That edge of surprise allowed him to literally get the jump on her, and the two of them tumbled down to the main floor, landing in a heap that left them both momentarily confused. Mae, burning with the implant's chemical flood, recovered much more quickly, and its edge helped knock down whatever advantage his greater body size held, as did her youth and training. She soon gained the dominant position, disarming him and throwing him down on the floor again as she got to her feet. He started to follow, but the sight of her gun pointed at him made him freeze. Slowly, he held up his hands in a warding gesture.

"Let me go," he begged. "Let me go, and you can have whatever you want. Take the girls. They're worth a fortune in—" His mouth clamped shut, and his eyes bugged as he looked her over. "You . . . you're a woman!"

"Good catch."

He was still flabbergasted. "Wh . . . what are you doing?"

"I'm taking the girls."

"But . . . why?"

It was incredible, Mae thought. A moment ago, when he'd thought she was a male thief, he'd tried to barter the girls for his safety. Now he couldn't even fathom why she'd want them.

"To set them free."

The blank look he gave her told Mae he was still lost.

"You kidnapped them," she said through gritted teeth. "You took them from their homes so you could sell them into slavery and make a profit from it."

"Homes?" he spat. "I took them from heathen lands where women fornicate with demons and brought them here where they can live in Nehitimar's salvation. I did them a favor."

"By locking them up and selling them to men twice their age?"

Pittsfield's eyes narrowed. "You're one of them. One of *those* women. This is what happens when people stray from Nehitimar's grace, when women aren't taught their proper roles!" Emboldened, he tried to get to his feet. "I'll show you right now how a woman needs to—"

Mae pulled the trigger.

It wasn't entirely his irritating tirade that made her do it. Soldier or not, Mae didn't like to kill wantonly. He had presented no immediate threat, true, but she couldn't leave him here bound and gagged as she had the guard in the woods. He'd identified her as a woman and a foreigner, and when word of this got around, that might be too big a connection for someone not to pair with Hannah's disappearance. And although Mae didn't necessarily see herself as a dispenser of vengeance, there was no telling how many atrocities he'd been responsible for. She was only dealing with this crop of girls. How many had come before them? How many stolen and sold away? How many misused like the poor unconscious girl

265

in the kitchen? He was no innocent, and while Mae would've liked to walk away from this mess with no bloodshed, she wasn't going to lose much sleep over killing someone who profited from taking advantage of those who were weaker.

And now she needed to find those girls and get out of here. Although the salon was relatively isolated, it wasn't that far from the highway, and the odds were good someone would've seen or heard what happened. If she could get everyone out of here soon enough, the authorities would think enterprising men had stolen this prime catch of girls, never guessing that a woman was behind it.

Eager as she was, however, Mae moved cautiously when she went upstairs, in case more unknown guards were lurking. She didn't have to worry. All eleven girls were crowded together in one of the bedrooms, with no other men in sight. They only flinched a little when Mae burst in with her gun, looking more surprised than afraid. Guns weren't an oddity around here the way assertive women were.

"I'm not going to hurt you," she said, taking the approach she had earlier with the kitchen girl. "I'm here to free you."

This received almost no reaction, and Mae had to accept that she wasn't going to be welcomed as a liberating hero. These girls had no concept of freedom—not yet. They were used to force and orders, and for now, that was the approach she'd have to run with. She sighed and waved her gun toward the doorway.

"Come on, we're leaving. Move quickly and quietly in a single line."

They fell to it, trooping dutifully down the stairs, though some did display a bit of shock at the bodies there.

"Wait," said Mae. She gestured to two of the older girls and nodded toward the unconscious servant. "Drag her out. She's coming with us."

One of them frowned. "Why take her? She's not worth anything."

"I'm taking her for the same reason I'm taking all of you," said Mae. "To get you out of this hellhole." The servant woman wasn't a

Gemman, nor did she have the sympathetic story the provincial girls here did, but it didn't matter. No way would Mae leave her behind, and at this point, she was facing so many complications when—and if—she made it back to her country that tacking on one more hardly seemed significant just then.

The two girls obeyed, but another one was still skeptical as they walked out toward the van. "You aren't taking us to sell us?"

"I'm taking you to a place where you'll be free," Mae told them, eyeing the smoke from the burning car with dismay. That was definitely going to attract attention. The confused looks on the girls' faces said most still couldn't comprehend the concept of freedom, and she groped for an explanation as she hurried them into the back of the van. "You won't be sold off or made anyone's wife unless you want to. And if you do want to be a wife, then you'll get to choose your husband."

"There's no such place," insisted one of the younger girls. "Nehitimar wouldn't allow it."

"Nehitimar has no hold where we're going." Mae shut the door behind her. The girls settled into the back of the van, no doubt breaking a hundred of the RUNA's safety mandates, but Mae didn't care. She started to step past them and then paused when she saw her niece sitting quietly in the van, taking everything in with wide hazel eyes. "What's your name?" Mae asked her.

The girl cowered at having attention drawn to her, and Mae felt the earlier anger she'd tried to push down return. It wasn't directed at her niece but rather at the people and system who'd made her niece this way, docile and fearful, waiting to be told what to do.

"Ada," said one of the other girls, the one who'd wanted to know if Mae was selling them. "Her name is Ada."

It was a pretty enough name but not one Mae was familiar with, meaning it almost certainly wasn't part of the RUNA's Greek and Latin registry. "Not anymore. You'll have a new name in the place we're going to. Ava." It was the first Gemman name that came to mind that resembled "Ada," and even though Mae knew it was a harsh thing to tell a little girl who had no concept of what was happening around her, something in Mae couldn't help it. She was still angry at the forces that had dropped her niece here, and breaking free of at least their naming system seemed like a first step at freedom, even if the poor girl didn't realize it yet.

Mae had no more time to talk and took the driver's seat. She slipped the keys into the car's ignition but nothing happened. She pulled them out and tried again, only to get the same effect. "No," she groaned. Not this, not now.

"You have to turn them." The girl who'd told Mae her niece's name had quietly slipped into the passenger seat. "Haven't you seen a car driven before?"

Mae had both seen and driven one before—at least, she'd driven Gemman cars before. Most populated areas used automated cars, but military personnel were trained to drive manually since battlefield situations often required a human touch. Those vehicles—leagues more sophisticated than this one—started much more simply, with buttons or a key that sparked ignition the instant it was inserted. Heeding the girl's advice now, Mae fumbled with the key, finally managing to turn it in a way that brought the archaic-sounding engine to life. It was loud but steady, and she hoped it was in good shape.

The rest of the controls bore enough similarity to what Mae knew that she was finally able to get the van to drive with a little more trial and error. The girl beside her looked suitably impressed in the glow of the dashboard's controls, probably because she'd never seen a woman drive before. Mae managed to get them onto the main highway without pursuit and grew more accustomed to the van's operation, creating a less jerky ride that the scared and silent girls didn't seem to appreciate.

"What will my name be?" asked the girl beside her.

"Hmm?" asked Mae, attempting to adjust the rearview mirror.

"In the new land we're going to. Don't we all get new names?"

Mae hadn't really thought that far ahead. It would be a matter for those in the Citizens' Ministry who maintained the National Registry.

"It depends," she said. "What's your name now?"

"Cecilia."

"That's Latin. You won't need a new one."

The girl looked so disappointed that Mae immediately felt bad. "I mean, you could go by Cecily, I guess. Or Cecile. There's probably a few other acceptable variations from that root in the registry."

"Cecile," said the girl decisively, her face brightening. "I like Cecile."

It occurred to Mae that cultivating the one girl who didn't seem terrified of this journey she was taking them on might not be a bad thing. It was foolish to hope her niece—Ava—would immediately latch on to Mae, but that didn't mean she shouldn't seek allies in the others. She might need them to get out of here, them and the goddess who so far hadn't had to do much except show her a few visions.

"Okay, Cecile. Do you know if any others were coming by the salon tonight? Any other men?"

"I don't think so," said the girl. "I think we were getting ready to leave when . . . you came. We'd just finished supper, and Mr. Pittsfield told us to go upstairs and get the rest of our things. Then we heard that big boom. Did you do that?"

"I did," said Mae. "I needed to—oh no."

Alternating which hand stayed on the wheel, she'd been rummaging through her coat pockets in search of the map. It was gone. It must have fallen out during the scuffle with Pittsfield.

"I don't suppose you know the roads around here?" Seeing Cecile's astonished face, Mae almost smiled. "Never mind. We'll figure it out." She'd gotten a good look at the map and had enough of a sense of direction based on the sun to know her cardinal directions. It would have to be enough to get her to the northern border until something better came along.

"You should sleep if you can," she called back to the others. "We aren't going to be stopping for a while. And I'll need someone to be in charge of those water bottles. Everyone can have a drink every . . ." How long until the border? Mae couldn't have said for sure with the map, let alone without. "Every hour."

"I'll do it," said one of the older girls who'd helped carry out the unconscious servant. "But what will my name be?"

Some of them were starting to think this was a game, and Mae couldn't decide if that was a good or bad thing. It made some of them more agreeable, but at the same time, she kind of wanted them to take this seriously. Nonetheless, after a little discussion, her water volunteer was dubbed Monica. The girl took to the task happily, and she was also the one who calmed down the marked servant when she groggily woke.

"It's okay, Dawn," Monica told her. "We're just on our way to the new place. You had an accident. Rest."

Mae hoped there'd be no screaming when Dawn learned the truth of the situation, and fortunately, darkness and tension eliminated most conversation in the van. They had traveled north for about an hour when Mae came to a junction and signs indicating multiple destinations. East would take them toward downtown Divinia, where she most definitely didn't want to go. West was the route she wanted, both because of the lack of cities indicated on the sign and because that was where her mental map told her to go until she could turn north. What gave her pause was another small northerly route, marked as leading to Holy Lake.

Holy Lake. The Grand Disciple's words came back to her, how he'd bragged to Justin about having a private lodge and property there . . . and Justin's speculation that this was where the staff might be hidden. Mae knew the smart thing now was to turn west and put as much distance between her and Divinia as possible. Time wasn't a commodity she could spare just then. And yet, she was also fully aware of the complete stroke of luck that had brought her to this point. If she'd still had her map, she likely would've turned west already on one of the many smaller side roads they'd passed. She'd been uncertain until reaching this point but now had clear direction. Taking it was the logical choice.

And yet, Holy Lake had been Hansen's best guess for the staff, the staff Mae knew little about, save that it troubled Justin and might hold a threat for the RUNA. It was impossible to imagine anything posing a greater threat than the hacking conspiracy that Justin was already working on . . . but who was she to say for sure just how much damage the supernatural forces swirling around them could cause? She'd certainly witnessed enough to know the potential was there, and there was a very real possibility the knife's master had sent her down this path with the purpose of finding Holy Lake.

*If you have faith, I will guide you home and help you thwart your enemies,* the goddess had said. Mae had assumed at the time those enemies were the salon workers. Now it seemed very possible the knife's master was offering her the opportunity to thwart her country's enemies as well.

Mae was hardly in a position to cut herself and find out, but she was, according to the sign, less than ten miles from the lake. A quick check of the area would take no time at all. And so, knowing it might very well make an already dangerous situation worse, Mae merged onto the small road that led to the lake.

# CHAPTER 20

# ASCENDANT

R eligion might not have been a mainstream practice in the RUNA, but there was plenty of information about its many incarnations on the media stream for those who were interested. In some ways, there was almost too much. Following Dr. Cassidy's party, Tessa threw herself into research on Osiris and Egyptian mythology, coming up with more questions than answers.

"All of this is on ancient stuff," she complained to Daphne. "And there's no real record that details exactly how they worshipped. There's just a general set of beliefs."

"That's all there usually is for these modern revivalist cults," said Daphne. "Most of these groups based on ancient gods weren't around just before the Decline. They popped up afterward and pieced together new practices based on the old myths."

"But there's hardly any info on what those new practices are." Tessa knew she sounded whiny but couldn't help it. It was frustrating to have access to so much information and not actually get what you needed.

"The servitor's office probably has it," Daphne said. "Smart groups keep their practices secret. But that's not important to us. This is. And really, there's just nothing that damning." She tapped her ego, which had a transcription of the conversation recorded in Dr. Cassidy's office. Daphne had gone over it a hundred times, and while there were insinuations present, the recording contained nothing that concretely linked the man to membership in a cult. She sighed. "Smart groups also don't leave any public records of their members that we could possibly tie Cassidy or anyone in the CP to."

Tessa disagreed with Daphne that the practices weren't important. She couldn't shake the feeling that understanding the worship of Osiris would be instrumental in understanding Cassidy and his subsequent agenda. And seeing as his own words and the public record offered no conclusive results, it seemed to Tessa that investigating the religion itself was their only option.

"What about this?" she asked. She had a reading tablet propped up on the March kitchen table and turned it toward Daphne. "Dr. Cassidy mentioned Osiris's son and how the ancient Egyptians believed the pharaohs embodied him. It says here that his son's name was Horus and backs that whole idea up—about how sovereignty is linked to divinity. I think Dr. Cassidy believes that—I saw it in his face, that Gemman leadership would benefit from godly influence."

Daphne gave a scarlet-lipped smile and leaned back in her chair. "Sweetie, I would love that if it were true. If we had proof that the Citizens' Party was out searching for the next son of Osiris to lead this country, it would make both our careers. Unfortunately, 'seeing it in his face' isn't enough. You should appreciate that, since you're always such an advocate for proof."

"I don't think they're looking," said Tessa. "I think they've already found their Horus. You see the way they talk about Lucian. And the press has noted for a long time how unusual it is that the Citizens' Party rallied around such a young candidate for consul. Maybe it's not that weird if they believe that candidate's been marked with divine favor."

"Once again," said Daphne, "I would *love* it if that were true. We have no proof, especially with the good senator out of the country right now. Our best bet is to try to finagle an interview when he's back, and in the meantime, keep you on good terms with the YCC. When's your next meeting?"

"Today," admitted Tessa. "But I wasn't planning on going."

"Of *course* you're going," exclaimed Daphne. "It costs you nothing but time. And who knows? Maybe we'll get lucky and catch something unexpected. Don't forget this." She slid the microphone over to Tessa, who took it reluctantly.

"Dr. Cassidy may not even be there," she warned Daphne. "I get the impression his visits are rare. Makes sense since his main job's counseling party members. Acacia will probably run things."

Daphne nodded along, undaunted. "Yes, and she'll report back to him, which will reflect well on you."

Tessa had no arguments to make. She was caught up on her schoolwork and had no other plans that afternoon. So, with more of Daphne's blessings and advice, Tessa grudgingly took the train back downtown to the YCC's offices with Rufus. As expected, Acacia ran the meeting alone, which turned out to be a variation of the last one. They finalized project plans and had more discussions about current issues. The only surprising part came when, a few minutes before things ended, Dr. Cassidy himself actually showed up.

He nodded in approval as the group finished up debating a piece of education legislation that had been in the news that day and then bade each of them farewell when they started to disperse. When Tessa joined the others, he called her back.

"Just a moment," he told her. "I actually came by to ask you something." He let the others leave and told Acacia he'd lock up for the night. Tessa grew nervous at the dramatics, but his request turned out to be pretty benign. "I know you're still getting your feet with us, and I certainly don't want to pressure you into anything . . . but Adora Zimmer's been in touch with me, and you've made quite an impression on her."

Tessa thought back to the woman from the party. "Really? We only talked a few minutes."

He smiled. "Well, apparently that was enough. Immigration reform is something she's very passionate about, but it's a tough sell to a lot of people. The CP sees certain benefits to it, especially with such a compelling spokeswoman."

*Such a wealthy spokeswoman,* Tessa thought. Aloud, she said, "What would you like me to do, sir?"

"Adora's group has its own share of fund-raising and awareness events, and she'd simply like to meet with you to discuss possible future involvement. I know it's asking a lot," he admitted, looking truly apologetic. "Especially when you're just getting to know us and have your own work and projects, but . . ."

"It's a good cause," said Tessa, actually meaning it. After seeing the way she'd been treated in the RUNA, she was sympathetic to any mission that might help others in her situation. But she knew that wasn't Dr. Cassidy's biggest motivator here. "And it'd make the CP look good in her eyes if you lent me out," Tessa added.

"Don't think of it like that," he said, with a small chuckle. "We don't treat people like commodities around here. But yes—she's definitely someone we want to keep in good favor with, and not just because of her wealth. She's also very influential in business and has a lot of important contacts, whose endorsement could be critical to our cause. You haven't been with us that long, but I hope you've seen enough to understand that we really do have the best intentions for this country."

"I have, sir. And I'm happy to help. But, sir . . ." He'd lit up at her acceptance, and Tessa realized in that brief moment that she had an opportunity. Since that night at his house, she'd thought a lot about the charm she saw Justin work on others. It was still largely a mystery to her, but she'd realized that often when she witnessed him in action, he had knowledge of or power over something important to the other person. That was how he engaged others, by putting to use what he learned about them. Tessa might not have fully grasped the finer points of that art, but she could tell now that Dr. Cassidy was legitimately grateful and fond of her right now.

"Yes?" he asked, eyebrows knitting in worry. "Is everything okay?"

Tessa glanced around, ascertaining they were alone before bursting forth with the inspiration that had just struck her. "I don't know," she said, making her voice waver a little. "I . . . I'm confused about something. And I don't know if anyone can help, but I think you might be the closest person I can ask."

"Of course," he said. "Go on."

"Well . . . for the last two nights—ever since I saw that statue at your house—I've been dreaming of it." She dropped her voice to nearly a whisper for that last part. "But there was more. It wasn't just the statue I dreamed of. I saw a falcon too. A golden falcon. Only, sometimes, it seemed like the falcon was Senator Darling. Which doesn't make any sense. I mean, none of it makes any sense, right? It's just a dream. I wouldn't think anything of it, except that I had it twice, and it just felt so . . . so *real.*"

She held her breath as she studied him and waited to see how her story would sink in. It was a lie, of course. In her research, she'd found that Osiris's son, Horus, was often depicted as a golden falcon, and she'd mixed that imagery with her own speculation that any divine aspirations of the Citizens' Party would involve Lucian. For a small moment, she felt a pang of regret that she was doing something bad in making up a story about a god . . . but then that suggested they were dealing with a real god. Tessa had never given much speculation to the validity of religions outside her own and didn't have the time to now.

Dr. Cassidy paled. "Tessa, I can't talk to you about any of this. I'm sorry. It's for your own good."

"But it means something to you, doesn't it?" she insisted. "The falcon . . . Senator Darling . . . you know what it means."

His face confirmed as much, but as Daphne had said, that wasn't going to stand as hard proof. Tessa's gamble had paid off in some ways, but Dr. Cassidy was too smart to admit to anything. She supposed he couldn't have reached the point he was at now, advising one of the country's most powerful political parties, if he so easily confessed to his clandestine doings.

"Tessa, remember what I said the other night? About how there are things that could endanger your path to citizenship? These same things could endanger me as well. I simply can't talk to you about them."

"But I wouldn't tell," she insisted.

His face looked truly pained. "I can't be involved with this. I'm sorry."

Tessa felt a bit of desperation at possibly losing this opportunity and hoped it came through in her to add legitimacy to her pleas. "But what if I have the dream again? What am I supposed to do? I know it means something. It's not the kind of dream that fades away either. It stays with me all day. I can't stop thinking about it. Please help me."

She could tell he was on the edge of refusing again, but something finally held him back. "Hold on," he said at last. "There's someone I can call, a friend of mine who's an expert in Egyptian history and mythology, if you're interested in learning more."

Tessa started to say that wasn't exactly what she'd had in mind but then realized that was as close an admission as he was going to make. He might not have known she was recording him, but he was still cautious about saying anything that might be quoted back against him. She gave a small nod. "Thank you."

He took out his ego and strolled off to one of the small storage rooms adjacent to the main conference area. Although he shut the door, Tessa could still make out occasional snatches of conversation. ". . . don't know . . . one of the elect . . . young . . . would have to be in public . . . bodyguard."

Tessa waited as patiently as she could, with panic welling up inside her as she tried to school her face to neutrality. She hoped whatever nervousness she showed about her lies would just be read as anxiety about the recurring dreams. When Dr. Cassidy returned, his face was grim.

"Well, we've got a bit of luck, but I don't think we can take advantage of it. My friend is actually here downtown as we speak, finishing up dinner with another colleague. She says she'd be willing to talk to you, which is nice and provides the convenience of a public place to meet, but she wouldn't want your bodyguard around. Or even me. It's really best at this point if you just meet with her, so we'll have to find a time when you can be on your own to talk to her."

Tessa could feel the opportunity starting to slip away, and her gaze fell on the adjoining rooms. "Do any of those lead out?"

"One is shared with a neighboring conference room, so—no," he said with a groan. "No. I'm not going to encourage you to slip away from your bodyguard. Your family has that protection for a reason."

"It's my decision to make. Just tell your friend I'll be there, and tell me where to go." Seeing his reluctant face, she added, "There's been no sign of danger, and it's pretty unlikely tonight's the night some adversary followed us here and is waiting outside this building—on its very public street—hoping that I'll just happen to walk out alone."

Dr. Cassidy wasn't happy about the plan. The deception made Tessa feel guilty, and she had to remind herself that the greater good of the country might be at stake, not just Daphne's story. Really, when all was said and done, he was a pretty upright person and didn't want to be involved in the corruption or endangerment of youth. But it was also clear he felt her concerns and "dreams" needed addressing, and he took a chance on what he saw as the greater good, especially since his contact was relatively close and in a safe area. He showed Tessa the storage room that led to another conference room, which in turn was serviced by a corridor and elevator different from the one Rufus was currently waiting for her in. She sent Rufus a message saying she was staying late to help work on a project. He should have no reason to actually come look in the room to check on her, and if all went well, she could return later with him none the wiser.

Dr. Cassidy's contact was dining in a very upscale establishment, and Tessa was glad she'd followed the YCC's style of wearing dress clothes to their meeting. She still felt self-conscious as she stepped into the dining room, having to tell the hostess that she didn't even know the name of who she was looking for. All Dr. Cassidy had told her was to look for a black-haired woman with gold coins in her hair.

Tessa soon found her, dining at a corner table with a man whose back was to Tessa. The gold coins were part of barrettes used to pin the woman's thick hair into an elaborate updo. Tessa approached, and the woman glanced up. She said something to her companion that must have been a dismissal or farewell, because he rose and held out his hand to shake hers good-bye. Tessa reached the table and then froze as he turned to leave.

It was Geraki.

The one time they'd met, he'd been in jeans and a T-shirt, so it was surprising to see him in an expensive suit now, with his shoulder-length hair neatly pulled back. He looked equally astonished and then threw back his head and laughed.

"You, huh?" he said to Tessa. "I should've guessed you were the potential protégée Damaris was meeting. Justin seems so reluctant when we meet, and all the while he's been encouraging your calling. I knew his faith was greater than he let on. Enjoy the evening, ladies."

He gallantly offered his chair to Tessa, who took it nervously, as her stunned mind tried to fully process what he'd just said. The woman across from her had a serene, statuesque kind of beauty and smiled kindly at Tessa. "My name is Danique," she told Tessa, who silently noted that that wasn't the name Geraki had called her. "Our mutual friend tells me you've been troubled by dreams. I hope I might be able to help you."

Tessa spun out the same story she'd told Dr. Cassidy, feeling even more anxious than before. If Danique was some kind of expert, then surely she'd see the lie that her colleague had missed. But Danique's face remained calm and intrigued, showing no trace of disbelief or indignation.

"That's fascinating," she said when Tessa finished.

"I think it sounds silly," Tessa responded. "I'm worried I've wasted your time. And Dr. Cassidy's. It's just a dream."

"A dream that stays with you in the day and has left a lasting impression," clarified Danique. "There's nothing silly about that. There are some who believe the gods speak to us in dreams. Have you ever heard that?"

Tessa was a bit taken aback. Even though she'd hoped to insinuate supernatural involvement with her dream story, she hadn't expected it would be met with this sort of response. "No. I mean, not in seriousness."

"There are some who believe the gods have returned to us again and are now battling for a place in the world. Those who believe gods are active in the affairs of mortals also believe that only a few very, very lucky people have direct communication with those gods. Dreams are the preferred means of contact. Such people might think that you were sent a divine message."

"Do *you* think that?" asked Tessa, noticing that Danique was very careful to use terms like "such people" and "those who believe."

Danique's dark eyes glittered with amusement. "I'm not the one who sought out help. What do *you* think? Did your dream feel like something unusual?"

"Yes," said Tessa, again feeling bad at the lie. "But I don't really feel like it was a direct message."

"What does it make you want to do?"

Tessa groped for a response that would be both believable and further her goals. "It makes me want to learn more about the things I saw in my dream. I mean, I guess I already am learning more about Senator Darling—being with the YCC and all. It's the other stuff that pulls me but that I still just don't get. Like the falcon. And that statue of O-Osiris. That was his name, right? Dr. Cassidy said you're an expert in Egyptian stuff."

"That I am," Danique agreed. "And your conclusions seem logical. If you feel like you need to learn more about those things, then perhaps you should."

"I did!" exclaimed Tessa, not needing to feign exasperation. "I looked all over the stream and found lots of things . . . but nothing that seemed real. Nothing that reached me in here." Tessa touched her chest. "If you're saying a god reached out to me, then I feel like whatever response I make—if it's the right one—is really going to be something I feel."

"*I* never said a god was reaching out to you," Danique said craftily.

"You know more about this than the stream does," said Tessa. "You know about these gods—what's real and what's meaningful. Please. Tell me what it all means."

"Have you ever heard people referred to as 'elect,' Tessa? No? Well, let me see how best to phrase it. Some believe that there are people—humans like you and me—marked as special, often with notable powers or abilities, who are desired by the gods."

Tessa's breath caught. "You think I'm someone like that?"

"No," said Danique bluntly. "Well, I could be wrong, but I'm usually good at sensing that kind of thing, and I don't get that vibe from you."

Tessa had started to get caught up in her act enough that she was almost too disappointed at not being "special" to realize that Danique had slipped for the first time, admitting that she had some involvement with gods.

"Most people are simply worshippers, some fulfilling important functions in a church or temple, but not having that exceptional quality that marks the elect. There's another category, however, which some call the 'the ascendants.' Those are ordinary people, not initially marked like the elect, who nonetheless through re-markable cunning or dedication manage to rise in the ranks of godly esteem and nearly match the elect."

"You think I'm like that?" asked Tessa, again reminding herself this was all nonsense.

"I don't know," admitted Danique. "Usually, an ascendant has purposely sought out the service of a god and worked hard before getting any favor. But there are always exceptions. You getting summoned out of the blue would seem odd to believers, but gods are rarely predictable."

"What should I do?"

"If you think a god tried to reach out to you, then show your receptiveness. Keep researching—even if you don't think anything will come of it. Pray. Meditate. Seek wisdom, and maybe the shape of your dreams will change."

"But I can't talk to anyone who actively worships that god," said Tessa, not needing to hide her disappointment.

Danique's expression grew gentle. "This is a dangerous path for any Gemman, let alone one who isn't a citizen. Dr. Cassidy told me some of your background. As much as you'd like to learn more from others, solitary learning and contemplation is the best path for you right now. You shouldn't attract attention, not when you're so young and without citizenship. This counsel really is for the best. But know that people like me and Dr. Cassidy will be watching. If the time is right . . . well, who can say what will happen someday?"

A message lit up Tessa's ego, and she saw it was from Rufus: *WHERE ARE YOU?*

Apparently, he'd found a reason to come by the room. She wrote back: *I'm fine. I'll talk to you soon.*

She turned her attention back to Danique. "I have to go soon. Can you at least tell me what the other things meant? Why did I see a falcon? Why did it turn into Senator Darling?"

"You tell me," said Danique. "You said you'd researched. Did you find anything about a falcon?"

"The falcon is Horus," said Tessa. "Is Lucian Darling Horus?"

Danique blinked in surprise. She clearly hadn't expected that leap. "In ancient Egypt," she said, "they believed those marked with greatness became kings and rulers. Then they became the chosen of Horus."

"So he's not Horus yet," said Tessa. "Or won't really ever be. But he *is* special and will have Horus's blessing to guide and lead if he becomes consul?"

Another message from Rufus popped up: *If you don't tell me where you are now, I'll go to the police and have the GPS locator in your ego activated. What follows won't be pretty.*

Tessa quickly sent Rufus the name of a café across the street and stood up. "I have to go. But am I right? Is Lucian Darling one of the elect? And will he have a god's power to help guide the country?"

"I think you're wiser than you know," said Danique enigmatically. "And that you should think on what I said about ascendants."

"Thank you for meeting with me." Tessa started to leave, then remembered something. "That man who was here—Demetrius Devereaux. Geraki. Is he a, uh, expert in Egyptian mythology too?"

"No," laughed Danique. "He's an expert in another area. But we share many similar goals."

Tessa thanked her again and headed out to meet Rufus. She dreaded the chastisement to come, but Rufus wasn't her parent. He could only scold and turn her over to Cynthia . . . and what would happen then was anyone's guess. It was hard to be too worried, though, after everything she'd learned and heard tonight. Maybe she hadn't received any direct confessions, but she was certain that her microphone had recorded more than enough for Daphne to build a pretty incriminating case against Lucian.

The thing was, Tessa realized, there might also be a case against Justin.

# CHAPTER 21

# DETOUR

As Mae neared the outskirts of Holy Lake, the road split into two. One fork led to what was marked as a public camping and recreation area, something Mae found almost comical. It seemed ludicrous to imagine these hardened, devout people participating in anything like a lakeside picnic. The road's other branch had signs warning that it was private and was for authorized personnel only. Mae decided this was the most likely route to the Grand Disciple's residence and found a small pull-off on the road that kept the van concealed from any other traffic passing in the night. After a little maneuvering, she managed to turn off the engine and remove the keys.

"I have to step out for a minute," she told Cecile. "You're in charge. You and . . . who's the closest to a leader this group has?"

Cecile nodded toward one of the older girls in the back, who looked a bit startled at the attention. She'd regarded Mae warily back at the house, but Mae had long since discovered the pressure of responsibility could end up swaying someone to your side.

"You're in charge too," Mae told her. "Both of you need to keep everyone calm until I get back. Do not leave the van. There are dangerous things out there, and I won't be around to protect you."

It was a bit of an exaggeration, but Mae couldn't risk her prizes escaping or being detected. And if the Grand Disciple had lackeys in the area, it might not be an exaggeration after all. The girls looked properly cowed and had probably never been left on their own before. If the goddess did intend for Mae to accomplish something here at the lake, then hopefully that goddess would keep the girls together until said task was done.

Mae traded coats with one of the girls, wanting something more her size that would allow better movement than the bulky men's coat she'd worn earlier. Rather than wear the equally cumbersome hat, Mae also accepted a couple of collected scarves that she managed to wrap around her face and head. She wasn't sure what kind of surveillance equipment she'd run into and didn't want to risk any chance of her features being recorded. A glance at her reflection in one of the van's mirrors showed she'd ended up looking like some ancient bank robber, but at least she didn't look like herself.

A mile down the road soon brought her to what seemed like a pretty good possibility for the Grand Disciple's residence. The lodge was built into the side of a hill that afforded what was probably a stunning view of the lake. A fence enclosed a wide perimeter of gardens and ornamental trees around the house, and Mae could vaguely make out control panels that indicated the fence was probably electrified. Lights shone strategically on the grounds and in the house, but they were faint and seemed to be the type that were regularly left on when a house was vacant. She saw no signs of any other occupation, which made sense if the Grand Disciple was busy entertaining Justin.

Feeling confident, Mae scouted out a tree that would allow her to jump the fence, just as she'd done at Carl's. But once she was actually up in the tree, a look down showed her that there might be more danger than just the fence itself. Tiny, nearly obscured pinpricks of light on the fence's interior side indicated some secondary defense system. Mae jumped back down and approached one of the control panels on a fence post. Its display showed readings for more than just electric current in the fence: There was also a motion-sensing field being projected from the fence onto the grounds. If she jumped over, she'd promptly set off that alarm and give herself away.

The panel's display had a keypad ready to accept a security code, but Mae couldn't make any attempt at guessing that. She needed a more primitive solution. After a few moments of studying the wires and cords coming out of the control panel, she did a quick walk around the property and soon had a sense of how the fence's power was generated. It fed out of a large cord, which wound up a power pole into a control box, which was then connected to more wires feeding out to large power lines running along the road.

Exposed power lines were rare but not unheard-of in the RUNA, especially in more rural areas. Mae had seen a few on the outskirts of the Nordic land grant—and had also seen how susceptible they were to storms. Operating on the idea that Arcadian technology was faultier than her homeland's, she scoured the wooded area around the fence until she found the biggest fallen limb that she could reasonably carry up the pole with her. It made for a cumbersome journey, but the pole was designed for worker access and had hand- and footholds that made the task much easier than climbing the tree earlier. Wrapping her legs around the top of the pole, Mae swung the limb down on the wire leading to the fence—only to have the wire stay firmly connected.

So much for faulty Arcadian technology. Mae had seen power lines at home brought down by smaller limbs and had assumed this would be simple. She supposed anyone building and powering a residence out in the woods wouldn't have done so without reinforcing their power lines. Sizing up another swing, Mae struck the power line again and managed to put more of her weight into it. Doing so cost her her balance and secure hold on the pole's top, however. She managed to scramble at the last moment and save herself from plummeting to the ground, but her strike with the limb turned out to be more unwieldy than she'd intended. She not only hit the line running to the fence but also the one feeding into the house. Both fell, swinging down in a shower of sparks.

Mae clung to the pole and held her breath. Two things were very likely to happen. One was that a power outage would trigger some kind of backup alarm system, sending security forces out this way.

She'd have no way of knowing that until they actually showed, however. The other possibility was that losing the main power would trigger a backup generator, meaning her acrobatics had been for nothing. But as the lights in the house and on the grounds went out and continued to stay that way, Mae realized she might have gotten lucky on that, at least. In fact, as she climbed down, she wondered if she'd gotten lucky inadvertently knocking out the house's main power. After all, the house probably had a security system she would have had to deal with as well. Now there were no obstacles preventing her from going inside, so long as she could beat any backup coming.

Wasting no time, she ran up to the house's main door. A manual lock kept it closed, power or no power, but the absence of an active security system meant she could freely break a nearby window without consequences. There'd be tangible signs of a break-in, yes, but so long as she was gone in a timely manner, it wouldn't be connected to her—or, hopefully, the person who'd raided the salon. An ornamental garden urn proved a useful tool for smashing a large enough opening in the window, but once she was inside the house, Mae discovered her luck might be out.

"What was that?" she barely heard a voice say. It was followed by the sound of running feet.

So. Apparently the house was occupied after all, not by its main resident, but by security guards skulking in the dark. She'd seen no obvious movement in her initial observations and had been foolish to assume the Grand Disciple wouldn't leave a manual security system in place. Mae dove behind a large couch, using the shadows and darkness to her advantage as three men with flashlights came barreling into the room. They immediately ran toward the broken window, studying it with their backs to her. One of them tucked his flashlight under his arm and used his free hand to retrieve an old-fashioned radio communication device. Mae didn't know if he had on-site or off-site backup in mind, but she couldn't risk either. She sprang out from the couch, again using her gun as a blunt weapon, just as she had at the salon. Shooting would've been more efficient, but she didn't want to risk Arcadian forensics tracking the gun back to the salon. Tonight's altercations needed to seem unrelated.

She effectively took out the guy with the radio in one blow, aided by the element of surprise. His comrades took a little more finessing, but they too were caught unprepared and limited with hands full of guns and flashlights. Their eyes weren't attuned to the darkness like Mae's were, and she was too fast for them to initially get a good a fix on, though one managed a few futile shots. Within a minute, she had both of them knocked unconscious on the ground.

There were apparently others in the house, however, and the shots drew them to this location. Their feet and flashlights gave them away, and Mae hid in the shadows once more, using similar techniques to take each one by surprise as he came into the room. She had seven unconscious men down by the time the house truly and finally stayed silent. Someone still might have gotten out a call for backup, or the power failure might've automatically done so. Regardless, Mae wasted no more time and began exploring the house. She tucked the gun from the salon into her belt and took one of the fallen men's guns to hold in its place. She also retrieved his flashlight but didn't turn it on yet, instead relying on ambient light from the moon outside. She didn't want to give herself away as the others had done.

The house was the height of luxury, even by Gemman standards. Passing through opulent bedrooms and parlors, Mae wondered how much time the Grand Disciple spent here and how much entertaining he did. She also wondered if this was all paid for by his priestly salary or "contributions" from followers. But although each room was furnished with rich fabrics and artwork, she saw nothing like the staff that had been described to her. Conscious of the time passing while the girls waited for her, Mae was nearly ready to call the mission a failure when she flung open what seemed like a bedroom's closet door and found—another door.

A glowing panel on the door showed her that at least one part of the house was using a generator. After a little bit of study with the flashlight, she discovered the panel was a palm reader. Apparently, the Grand Disciple would take no risk of anyone guessing a code. Knowing she couldn't forge his palm, she studied the panel and door frame, looking for any sign of a power source that she might disable in a similar way. She found nothing, meaning it was too well concealed or possibly kept in another part of the house. Before she could decide whether to go after it, she heard more voices and movement.

"Sir! Don't go in until we know what happened here. Someone could still be inside."

"If they are, I know exactly where they'll be," said a voice Mae recognized. "You—come with me. The rest of you check the remainder of the house and call someone to get the power back."

Mae's heart rate sped up. The Grand Disciple was here. From the sound of it, his arrival might very well have been coincidental, meaning his retinue might be small. It didn't sound like it would stay that way, and Mae intended to leave before the others showed up. As it turned out, however, the place the Grand Disciple knew any intruder would be was the very room she was in. He and a guard appeared in the doorway before she could get out. Mae froze as a flashlight illuminated her, and the guard trained his gun on her.

"Don't move!" yelled the guard.

"Don't shoot him," warned the Grand Disciple. His eyes were wide as he studied Mae in the flashlight's glow. At first, she thought he'd recognized her but soon discovered something else had caught his attention. "Who do you serve?" he demanded. "Who sent you? I've never felt power like this . . . not here in my own country, at least. . . ."

Mae didn't dare answer, not when her voice would possibly give away her identity and most certainly her nationality. She didn't want to bring trouble to the other Gemmans. Knowing her speed was superior, she fired on the guard, moving at the same time to make sure she was out of the line of fire of any return shot. Before he'd even hit the ground, she grabbed hold of the Grand Disciple, who put up zero resistance as she dragged him to the closet door. Maybe he was too stunned by this turn of events . . . or maybe he just didn't know how to overpower people without the full weight of his office.

She forcibly pressed his palm to the scanner. It turned green, and the door unlocked. As soon as she had it open, she slammed him down hard, so that his head hit the wall and he slumped to the ground.

On the other side of the door, she saw a small room containing only a table. And on that table was a golden staff with an eagle perched on top, just as she'd been told. Mae sprang for it and heard a voice croak out behind her: "You'll never be able to touch it. You'll—"

Her hand closed around the staff, and a shock ran through her, like static electricity. The staff shimmered before her eyes, then twisted and changed shape. Moments later, she was holding not a staff but a torc, an open-ended neck ring worn by ancient Celtic and Nordic peoples. It was still made of gold, but rather than an eagle, the torc's two ends now displayed dragon heads.

The coat she wore had large pockets, and Mae carefully tucked it inside one. Her blow was keeping the Grand Disciple down, but he was still conscious enough to stare in gaping disbelief. "How . . ."

Mae stepped over him without a word or glance. She could hear a commotion in the rest of the house and knew more guards were coming. Rather than go back out through the house itself, she used an end table to break the bedroom's window and create an escape onto the roof. Not looking back to see if she was being followed, she darted outside and managed to deftly leap over the various eaves of the lodge until she found a low enough point to safely drop to the ground. If anyone had followed her, none would be able to conduct that roof walk as skillfully, which gave her a lead. And as she ran off into the woods, two cars pulled up in the house's driveway, showing her that for now, at least, the attention was on the house.

Pumped full of adrenaline and emotion, she ran back to the van in nearly half the time it had taken her to get to the house earlier. All the girls were still inside, many recoiling in fear when she burst in and immediately started the engine. "We have to get out of here," she said, as though her frantic actions didn't make that clear.

She tore off for the main highway, knowing that if she could do it without passing anyone on the lake's road, they'd be safe. If there were more responders coming, her van would be suspect, fleeing from the scene. Either luck or the knife's goddess was with her, because she made it back to the highway, heading south toward the junction without incident. Mae didn't allow herself hope, though, until she reached the westbound road going off into the Arcadian wilderness. Even then, she didn't entirely relax but knew that she had eluded immediate pursuit from those looking for whoever had robbed the Grand Disciple's lodge. For all she knew, however, patrols were out monitoring these roads in search of the salon's raider. Even if no one knew a Gemman woman had attacked the salon, the word might still be put out that kidnappers were on the loose in a van matching this description.

But as one and then two hours passed, Mae saw no signs of pursuit or patrol. Either no one monitored these hinterlands, or else she'd been too fast for her crimes to catch up with her. Mae was starting to think she'd actually pulled off the impossible—twice—tonight when the van began to sputter and tremble. Mae felt the motor choke up and finally stop altogether, forcing her to guide it off to the road's shoulder.

"I knew this thing sounded bad," she muttered, staring bleakly at the instrument panel. Cecile leaned toward her.

"I think it's out of gas," she said, pointing toward a dial aimed at the letter *E*.

"We haven't been on the road that long," protested Mae. "Even with the detour." Admittedly, she hadn't checked the fuel gauge when setting out. She hadn't thought to. Gemman cars, even most of the manual ones, ran on solar power or highly charged batteries. Those that did use fossil fuels were so efficient that she would've expected even half a tank to last longer than this. The cars themselves also would've told her if they were running low on fuel. "I don't suppose there's any way of knowing where we could buy gas," she said. They'd passed a place on the main highway when starting out but had seen nothing in some time.

"No woman would ever go buy gas anyway," said Cecile. Although she was fascinated by Mae, she'd also picked up quickly that there were some things Mae just wasn't savvy to.

Mae got out of the van and stood on the side of the dark road. Night insects chattered around her, and a humidity reminiscent of what she'd grown up with dampened the air. They were surrounded by fields scattered with trees and had no other landmarks or signs of civilization. Looking up, however, Mae found guides in the sky. It was a perfectly clear night, filling the sky with more stars than she could remember having seen at once. Her father used to stargaze with her when she was younger and had taught her the basic constellations, many of which she could see now: the great bear, the small bear, the dragon. One in particular caught her eye, Cassiopeia—the queen. Mae remembered her father teaching it to her on a small tablet, which had overlaid an image of a crowned and enthroned woman across the stars. There was probably an old myth behind that constellation, one that Justin would know.

He lingered on her mind for a moment, but as Mae gazed at the cluster of stars and thought of that crowned woman, it was her guiding goddess who soon dominated her thoughts. This time of year, the queen was almost directly to the north. Now, it would seem, was the time for faith and divine favors.

Cecile came up beside her, with Monica and the girl whose coat Mae had borrowed not far behind. "What are we going to do? Some of the little girls are getting scared."

"And they want to use the bathroom," added Monica.

The girl Mae had traded coats with held out something. "This was tangled in your old coat," she said nervously. Mae took it and saw Justin's charm, the one that obscured her from being recognized as one of the elect. So. That explained why the Grand Disciple had reacted as he had. She fastened the necklace back on and couldn't spare any extra worry for what the consequences of that slip might be.

Instead, Mae's eyes focused on the stars a few seconds more, and then she fixed her attention on the dark shapes of the two girls beside her. "First, some of you are going to help me push this van off the road and out of sight. After that, we're going home," she said. "On foot."

# CHAPTER 22

# A LONG TWO DAYS

Hannah's disappearance wasn't discovered right away, giving Justin some time to brief Lucian that their world had just been turned upside down. Ironically, Mae's raiding of the salon down the highway caused enough of a stir that first night that no one in Carl's family spared a thought for Hannah.

"They said it must've been a whole team of guys," Walter told Carl. It was late, and most of the household would've normally been in bed if not for the breaking news. Walter and some of his other brothers had just returned from a local tavern where they'd gotten the scoop. "Everyone shot dead except one, all the girls taken. Heard there was a fire or something too—like maybe they tried to burn the place down to cover their tracks."

Justin was lounging in a stuffed armchair in Carl's study, trying to appear casual, though anyone looking closely would've noticed the death grip on his untouched scotch. After the exhausting evening with Hansen's followers, Justin couldn't have stomached the alcohol if he'd wanted to, and the latest developments had only reinforced the need for sobriety. Across the room, Lucian's drink was equally untouched, and his eyes met Justin's at the mention of "a whole team of guys." A whole team—or one Mae.

Justin almost felt bad for Lucian. Justin had at least been semi-prepared, knowing about Mae's last secret visit to the salon and her niece. That didn't make tonight's developments any easier to handle, but Lucian had had it much worse when Justin had essentially told him in sixty seconds that Mae had run off to liberate stolen Gemman girls and left a fugitive Arcadian concubine in her place.

"Damn," said Carl, stamping a cigar butt into his ashtray. "Pittsfield had some fine girls there too."

"Is this common?" asked Phil, legitimately curious. He was, as of yet, blissfully unaware of the disaster unfolding in the Gemmans' laps.

"Not usually around here, this close to the city," said Carl. "Out in the real country . . . yeah, you'll get all kinds of barbarism. People stealing their neighbors' daughters. It's savage. Makes me sad to see it happening here."

"Someone must've thought it was worth the risk," said Jasper, leaning forward with clasped hands. "Figured they could make a lot of money—or maybe they wanted to keep the girls for themselves."

"What's so special about this group?" asked Atticus.

Carl leveled a warning look at his sons. "Just a particularly pretty group. Smart thing would be to sell them. They lose half their value once they're bedded."

Justin felt mildly ill, but it was getting difficult to tell if it was from Arcadian gender politics or his continuing recovery from divine powers.

"Do they just raid salons?" asked Phil. "Any chance that prowler you had here the other night was connected? You said that place is relatively close, and I'll come out and say it: *Our* women are a particularly pretty group."

Carl frowned, not liking the suggestion but unable to deny it. "I already upped the security, but I'll have the boys do some extra watches too." Said boys didn't look thrilled about this but offered no complaint.

Lucian, however, had plenty to say afterward, once the Gemmans had retired to their guesthouse for the night. He ordered Justin to his room and immediately turned on him, after politely asking Val to step outside.

"If they increase security, Mae's going to have a hell of a time getting back in here," said Lucian.

Justin shook his head. "Didn't you follow what I said? Mae's not coming back."

"No!" exclaimed Lucian. "And that's the problem. I didn't follow half of what you blurted out earlier. Why would Mae do that? Why would she abandon the mission to raid a salon and—so help me—kill a bunch of Arcadians! We're supposed to be here to promote peace!"

"The salon was holding Gemman girls," said Justin, trying to make a logical argument for something he knew was illogical. "Girls stolen from our country."

"Mae couldn't have known that," argued Lucian.

"Come on, you only have to look at them to know! Plus . . . one of them was her, uh, niece."

That took Lucian aback, and Justin sketched a hasty explanation of the Koskinen family's sordid history. He blurred the details of how Mae had obtained her intelligence, though, citing a vague connection to the Swedish mafia, which wasn't entirely a lie since Mae had once tried to work with them.

Lucian sat down on the bed, looking about as far as possible from the dazzling and cheerful politician Justin usually saw. "You know, she mentioned that she was looking forward to this trip, and I dared to hope—well, it doesn't matter. She's out there now, and I don't know how the hell she's going to get back home."

"She'll find a way," Justin insisted, not that he had any idea either. "And in the meantime, there's another situation you should know about."

Lucian's head jerked up. "Really? Something worse than one of our soldiers going rogue and forcing us to smuggle a defector back home, in order to save our asses?"

Justin considered that. "I guess it depends on how you define 'worse.' You know I had that meeting with the Grand Disciple, right? Well, it looks like Hannah isn't the only Arcadian we're going home with. I made arrangements for the Arcadian cultural lecturers to visit us, uh, immediately."

For a moment, it almost looked like Lucian thought there was some joke going on, and Justin couldn't entirely blame him for the mistake.

"You said they were missionaries in disguise and that letting them in would be a terrible idea," Lucian reminded him.

"Turns out I was wrong," said Justin. "They're actually hackers in disguise who want to stage an act of data terrorism."

And so, he delivered his second bombshell of the night, about how they'd be escorting a group of Arcadians back home, half of which were defectors while the others harbored plans to usher in an attack upon the RUNA. Again, Justin did some serious editing, leaving out Odin and playing up the Arcadian defectors' motivation to start a new life in the RUNA in exchange for selling out their countrymen.

"You should probably let Atticus know soon," added Justin helpfully. "You guys are going to need to get in touch with the people back home to get that delegation into the country."

Lucian was quiet for so long that it actually started to become disconcerting.

*You might have really done it,* Horatio told Justin. *Here's someone who deals with tough situations and scrutiny on a daily basis without cracking his smile, but you may be what finally breaks him.*

"How?" began Lucian at last. "How could you and Mae possibly wreak this much damage in only a few days? I mean, I know we've had our ups and downs, but did you really want to get back at me for something this badly?"

Justin sat down beside him. "You can't think of it that way. Think of it as an opportunity."

"An opportunity for what?"

"Greatness. You said you wanted this trip to prove something to the people." Justin held his hands up in the air. "Can't you see it now? Lucian Darling, the senator—the *consul*—who uncovered a plot to undermine our country *and* who secured the release of innocent Gemman girls stolen from their homes. Imagine how happy their families will be. The RUNA's never been in better hands."

Lucian thought about it for several moments. "The odds are good some of those girls were sent away, just like Mae's niece. Are their families going to be happy?"

"The media doesn't need to know that. All we'll need is confirmation of their genes in the registry and then an adorable photo op with you."

"Goodwill with my own people is going to worsen things with Arcadia."

"The Arcadians don't vote, and they're the ones who've worsened relations with this media stream plot," said Justin, warming up to all the spin potential. "And when they're caught, their government's going to disavow all knowledge of those hackers. We'll let it be known that the girls were recovered through the assistance of our new defector friends and leave out the part about a rogue soldier killing Arcadians. The government here's going to be so concerned about backpedaling and keeping us from retaliating on the data stream conspiracy that they'll let the girls slide. So, really, we come out looking good, and relations aren't that much worse than before."

Lucian gave him a long, scrutinizing look. "How do you do that? How can you talk people into anything? Do you think of this stuff in advance, or does it happen on the spot?"

"Are you impressed?" asked Justin.

"Kind of terrified, actually. But glad you're not in politics."

*Perhaps now would be a good time to ask if he'd like to learn about Odin,* said Horatio. *You're on a roll.*

Justin ignored the bird but felt a little unnerved that in many ways, he was doing now exactly what he had back at Gideon's house: spinning tales and converting hearts and minds. He wasn't really sure if it was genius or trickery.

*It's both,* said Magnus, almost affectionately. *And this is why our god has chosen you.*

"This dream plan only works if Mae gets those girls in without being caught," warned Lucian. "That border isn't easy for anyone, on either side, to cross. If the Arcadians find her, *we're* going to be the ones having to do a lot of disavowing. And if it happens before we leave the country, there's no way they'll let their delegation come with us. Hell, who knows if we'll be able to leave."

Justin thought back to his last encounter with Mae. He'd had no sign that she was planning anything of this magnitude. Her concern had been for him, and if he would've let her, she'd have gone to the temple too. Something must have happened, something must have driven her to act. Something that probably had to do with that damned knife. And if that was the case, he had to believe she wouldn't do this without a concrete plan to get back to her own country. What that plan was, he couldn't fathom, but he believed in Mae. He had to.

"She won't get caught," Justin said firmly. "She's been thinking about this. She's got a plan, and we'll see her back in the RUNA. That being said . . . life will be a lot easier for her when she gets back, even if she's victorious, if you come out telling our government that you authorized her actions. They'll spin a cover story for the media, but she'll still have a lot to answer for behind closed doors."

"*I'll* have a lot to answer for," protested Lucian. "I'm not consul yet, Justin. I don't know why you think I have that kind of power."

"Because your star's going to be so high after we sort out this mess that there's no way you won't be consul. And no matter how many regulations have been trampled on, no government official's going to punish you for helping one soldier who's responsible for a heartwarming victory. No one will come after you when you've got that much public love. They'll grumble, and that's it."

"A consul leads the senate and upholds the law." Lucian sighed. "You're basically telling me I can throw all that away if I'm popular enough."

"Pretty much."

Lucian sighed again. "Then we'd better go tell the others what to expect."

Justin had to give his friend credit. Lucian might have needed a fair amount of convincing, but by the time he pulled himself together and called the other Gemmans for an impromptu meeting, it was as though Lucian had personally orchestrated everything from the very beginning. He did a fair amount of editing himself, smoothing out some of the parts where he'd clearly been in the dark, in order to inspire confidence in the plan. He stood by Mae, leaving out the part about her niece and insisting her actions had been on his orders. He made everything sound easy, so much so that Justin almost wanted to let go of his own doubts and forget that there were actually a million things that could go horribly wrong.

Atticus, their diplomat, had the biggest problem with it. "This is a disaster," he exclaimed. "There's no way this can end well! We'll start a war."

"If what you say is true, they're already trying to," said George, who seemed to be taking the proposed conspiracy personally. "Why wait to catch their hackers in a sting? I say we start dropping bombs as soon as we get home."

"Because we need proof," said Lucian patiently. "We need to find out how much they know and how much they learned from that Gemman defector—what was his name?"

"Cowlitz," said Justin.

George actually looked impressed. "I've heard of him. He was pretty high up on the tech side. Had no idea he ended up here. Me, I'd go to South America."

That outside verification of Cowlitz's history soothed Atticus a little, but it was clear his mind was still spinning with all the potential diplomatic fallout. "It's going to be very hard getting that Arcadian woman back in with us."

"We're going back in with the same number of women we left with," said Lucian. "So long as we can keep them away from her for the rest of this trip, there shouldn't be any problem."

Atticus groaned. "We've got a long two days ahead of us."

The group finally dispersed to get what sleep they could, and

Val caught Justin's attention before he retired to his room. "You and the good senator painted us a very rosy picture back there," she said softly. "How much of it was true?"

"All of it," Justin assured her. "We're going to return to the RUNA as heroes, uncovering international plots and freeing young girls. Hope Dag's finally ready to make an honest woman of you, because you're going to be hip-deep in suitors after this."

Val rolled her eyes. "And you're hip-deep in bullshit. Both of you. How much trouble is Mae in?"

"None, not so long as she succeeds."

"Succeeds in getting a group of girls through a hostile country and through a highly protected border, you mean?"

"Yes." Justin started to turn away, and Val pulled him back.

"I'm serious," she said. "Please tell me Mae has more to go on than a wish and a prayer."

"A prayer? I never took you for a religious woman, Val."

"After what you guys told us?" Val shook her head. "I just might have to become one if it's the only way to get us out of this mess."

Back in his room, Justin was spared any awkwardness with Hannah since she'd already fallen asleep curled up on the floor. Or at least, he assumed she was asleep. It was hard to say, with all the concealing clothing. He would've let her have the bed if given the option, but without it, he gladly sank into the covers, fully dressed, and fell asleep almost as soon as his head hit the pillow. Too much physical and mental exertion, not to mention the Exerzol crash, sent his body into a much-needed slumber . . . that unfortunately only lasted a few hours.

He knew what was happening as soon as the shouts outside woke him up. Hannah, sitting bolt upright, did as well. "It's okay," he told her, hoping it was the truth. "Everything's going to be okay."

"They'll find me," she whispered. "There's nowhere to go."

"You're going with us." Justin made a halfhearted attempt to smooth his wrinkled shirt, then wondered why he was bothering. A few seconds later, a Gemman knocked at the door, and he found one of the praetorians there.

"They're searching the entire compound," she said, face grim. "One of the concubines is missing." He assumed there were Arcadians within listening distance.

"We'll be right out," Justin replied. He took Hannah's gloved hand and squeezed it. "It'll be okay."

In the guesthouse's common area, the other Gemmans were congregating by gender, and Justin led Hannah to a spot beside Val before joining the men. The Cloistered attire was useful for a lot of things, he decided, because he was pretty sure Hannah had a terrible poker face. Concealed as she was, all she had to do was stay quiet and still and hope that no one thought to have her reveal herself.

"What's going on?" he asked, stifling a yawn.

"They lost one of their women and want to make sure she didn't wind up in any of our beds," said George.

Carl strode in, overhearing the comment. "We didn't lose anyone. She was taken."

"Or she ran away," said a smirking Jasper, following behind his father. "I always told you she was an insubordinate bitch."

"She was taken," Carl repeated, though it was clear even he didn't really believe that wholeheartedly. "None of my women would run away." He glanced over the Gemmans to make sure they were all accounted for and then directed his sons to search the bedrooms. The young men took to it with relish, turning over beds and chairs, possibly hoping to find some sort of illicit treasures hidden away. Justin noticed Carl giving quiet directions to Walter, and a moment later, the young man disappeared into one of the bathrooms, presumably to search the emergency escape tunnel they didn't think the Gemmans knew about.

After an hour, they declared the building Hannah-free, and Carl stormed out muttering, "I'll kill her." Apparently he was having to face the reality that she might very well have run away. It would've been far easier on the ego to accept abduction, Justin supposed.

None of the Gemmans slept well after that, and things grew

increasingly weird the next morning when a messenger came from the temple demanding to know everyone's whereabouts the previous night. Justin was the only one who'd been out, but he had Hansen as an alibi for part of the time and had apparently checked back in at Carl's during whatever time frame was of concern to the messenger. At first, Justin wondered if they were under suspicion for the salon raid, but something in the messenger's manner made Justin think this inquiry stemmed from a different matter altogether. Whatever it was, he was never enlightened, and the messenger left without finding any answers.

Justin and his companions soon found themselves falling into the long two days that Atticus had warned about. Hannah's disappearance was a personal problem for the family, one they spoke little of to the Gemmans, though it poisoned the atmosphere for the rest of their stay. Of course, Justin knew he and his party wouldn't have been all that comfortable regardless, what with their complicity in the matter. The Gemman men continued the scheduled diplomatic events, and the women went on with their mix of chores and regulated outings, except for Hannah, who, posing as Mae, was excused from the former. She wanted to stay behind and hide in the room during the women's outings too, but Justin pointed out that this wouldn't be in character for Mae, plus he wanted to minimize any chance of someone speaking to her alone.

Meanwhile, arrangements were made on both sides for the Arcadian diplomatic group to return home with them, and Hansen visited once to brief Justin on the public details, confirming that all was in order. When they had a private moment, the Arcadian man also let Justin know that all was well with his handpicked group of delegates and that those left behind were still keeping the faith with Odin.

*What have I done?* Justin wondered after Hansen left. *What have I gotten these people into, only to abandon them?*

*You did good work, but don't think they'll flounder without you,* chided Magnus. *All-Father has been connecting with his followers since long before you came along. There will be other priests, other dreams.*

Hansen also reported that no one suspected a setup was taking place and that Cowlitz's men were still going to attempt their disabling of the media stream. Lucian looked relieved when Justin relayed that, meaning the senator was on track to get his public accolades when the plot was revealed. The other half of Lucian's hoped-for fame, Mae's rescue, remained shrouded in mystery, and all they could hope for was that no news was good news. When Justin tentatively asked Carl about the raided salon one day, the Arcadian simply shook his head and said, "Looks like they got away with it."

The day before the Gemmans were scheduled to return home, Justin asked the ravens something that had been on his mind for a while: *You'd tell me if you knew which deity was helping Mae, wouldn't you?*

*If All-Father allowed us,* said Magnus.

*What's that mean?* asked Justin. *You do know and aren't telling me?*

*No, we don't know, and that's why we aren't telling you.*

Justin wasn't sure he could buy that. *Or maybe you're not telling me because the goddess helping her is an ally of Odin's, and this is all terribly convenient for you guys and part of some setup.*

*That would be very convenient,* said Horatio. *Which ally do you think it is?*

*You know which one. Freya. Freya's a fertility goddess known for her amber necklace. Mae's being helped by an amber knife sacred to a fertility goddess.*

*Amber's important for half of European religions,* Horatio argued. *Go look it up on the media stream when you're home—if it's still there.*

*I just can't shake the feeling I'm being played,* Justin said.

*Well, if you are, then it's not by us. We didn't send the knife. We don't even have opposable thumbs.*

That was true. He and Mae had never figured out where that

knife had come from, and Justin supposed that would provide the first set of answers. A human servant was needed to use the Gemman postal system. His initial suspect, Callista, denied involvement, and her patron goddess was more about magic and moonlight than amber and fertility. Odin and the ravens had talked about Mae's being crowned in flowers since before Justin met her, and it made sense they'd be referring to a fertility goddess in their own pantheon.

Somehow, despite all the complications tormenting him internally and externally, Justin survived those long two days. On that third morning, his party packed up and made their farewells to Carl's family. The cloud of Hannah's disappearance still hung over everyone, but Carl's initial swagger and pride at hosting important foreigners was still going strong. And really, for those not privy to the dark underside of it all, the trip had been a stunning success. Quiet Phil had managed to work on a favorable trade negotiation, and Lucian had endeared himself to the Arcadian president, who promised to further open lines of communication. Along with touring Divinia, they'd made a number of day trips to other important sites and cities, ultimately accomplishing what no Gemman in history had.

"Now if we can just make it out alive," Atticus muttered to Justin, as they boarded the bus that would take them back to the border. Justin was pretty sure the diplomat was going to start drinking heavily once they were back on their native soil, and honestly, Justin couldn't blame him.

The Arcadian delegation coming back with them took separate transportation, no doubt to receive their last, covert orders. Lucian and Atticus had been in contact with the Gemman government, gaining permission for the group's ostensible purpose: Arcadians visiting and sharing their culture. Lucian hadn't dared communicate any hint of knowledge of the conspiracy while in Arcadia, but he'd assured Justin that once they were safely within the RUNA's borders, they'd make sure the hackers were set up and discovered quickly.

"We don't want them sitting around, gathering more data," Lucian had said. "We'll act like we're going along with the cultural exchange and conveniently set them up in locations most accessible to the media stream's way stations. Once they take the bait, and we get your defector friends to testify about the plan, this'll be a done deal." Lucian had then paused to give Justin a long, level look. "And they really *are* your friends. That Hansen guy adores you. How'd you pull that off?"

"He just wants to live the Gemman dream, that's all," Justin had replied glibly.

The Gemman dream and worship of Odin. When Justin's bus reached the base on the Arcadian side of the Mississippi, they found Hansen's party of men and women were already there. Hansen approached Justin with a formal greeting and then, once others were away, murmured, "I expect things are going to be a little . . . hectic when it all comes out. But I hope once matters calm, and Elaina and the others and I have settled down, we'll be able to meet with you regularly to learn about *him*."

"I look forward to it," Justin replied, feeling a sinking sensation in his stomach.

The Arcadian soldiers searched the luggage of everyone, Arcadian and Gemman alike, and performed more pat-downs to ensure nothing was being transported illegally. None of the soldiers suspected a woman might be smuggled out, and none of them dared ask a Cloistered woman to uncover herself. The Gemmans and the Arcadian delegation were given permission to leave and ushered onto a boat that would take them to the other side of the river. As the shore drew closer, Justin could see the familiar gray and maroon of the regular Gemman military waiting for them, along with a welcome sight: the RUNA's flag.

He experienced a strange emotional surge at the sight of it, the maroon and dark purple field adorned with a golden circle of laurel leaves, that reminded him of his return from Panama. The RUNA's motto, *Gemma Mundi,* echoed in his mind, and he wondered if Hannah had any idea of the extraordinary opportunity those words and that flag offered her. Did she realize that her world was about to open up? Sitting quietly beside him, unreadable in her thick clothing, Justin couldn't guess at her feelings. Probably she was terrified at being caught, which perhaps wasn't that unreasonable a fear since they hadn't crossed the Gemman border yet.

Having her here reminded him of Mae, who *should have* been here beside him instead. Where was she? Surely they would've heard if something had happened to her. The not-knowing was maddening, and Justin kept thinking back to their last meeting, to the kiss he still couldn't understand and how he'd promised her he'd help with her niece. Was there something he could have done differently? If he'd helped her sooner, could they have avoided her disappearing with those girls?

*I'm going to give you some relationship advice,* said Horatio, interrupting the endless questions.

*I don't have a relationship,* Justin replied promptly.

*Shut up and listen anyway,* ordered the raven. *You and she work well together, no surprise since you're meant for each other—and I don't just mean in the romantic way you keep botching up. You're a team, a good one. You watch out for each other, and that's good. But that doesn't mean you're meant to do every single little thing together. Yes, you have a shared destiny, but you also have an individual one, and so does she. The reason you didn't think of anything sooner to help her is because that wasn't your task. That was hers, and she found something and acted. Your task was to uncover the Grand Disciple's conspiracy and bring these people to Odin. Be content with the knowledge that you're both fulfilling the duties you're supposed to.*

*It's hard to feel content when mostly I'm worried I'll never see her again,* said Justin. *I don't know how I could get by without her.*

*Well, then,* said Horatio, *maybe you should tell her that the next time you see her.*

The boat docked at the Gemman base, and a group of Arcadian soldiers waited to make sure both the Gemman and Arcadian diplomats crossed over safely. There was no press here—they'd face that in Vancouver—but there were enough Gemman soldiers watching to make Justin feel like he was already being broadcast on the stream. It made him uneasy, especially knowing anything could still go wrong, but the spotlight was Lucian's natural habitat. He thrived on it and made a pretty speech to the Arcadian soldiers at the boat, thanking them for their service and hospitality. He then strode forward to an officer waiting with a chip scanner, making it a point to be the first of them to officially return home.

Justin was close behind him and watched as Lucian rested his hand on the scanner. It was a formality for Gemmans, so common that they did it without conscious thought most of the time. And, Justin realized with a pang, it might be Hannah's undoing.

The officer—a captain, from his uniform—glanced at whatever information popped up on the small screen facing him and gave a small nod. "Welcome home, Senator."

"Glad to be back," boomed Lucian in his show voice. "Though I am disappointed I missed the Hamaki Cup finals. Tell me the Comets won, and you'll make me a happy man."

The man's stiff face broke into a smile. "They did, sir. Three—two. Great game."

Lucian whooped with joy and shook the man's hand, much to the delight of the watching soldiers. "See? You've already got this homecoming off to a great start. I love this country." Still shaking the captain's hand, Lucian leaned close and dropped his voice so that Justin could barely make his words out. "And keep smiling, because you're also going to help save this country. There's a woman who'll be coming through who won't have a chip, and you will give no sign of this when you scan her. You'll wave her through, without breaking ranks, and I swear to you as senator and soon-to-be consul that your career will benefit greatly for doing this." Lucian's smile increased as he clapped the soldier on the back and said in a louder voice, "I hope we can get a recording of the game on the plane—and you better not have been playing me."

The captain's smile had faded, and he looked understandably bewildered. He scanned and sent Justin through without a word, then did the same for all the other men. The Gemman women came next, still grouped in gender order from Arcadia. Justin watched beside Lucian, who was still beaming like a king surveying his kingdom, but both of them were tense under their happy masks. If the soldier called out anything irregular about Hannah while the Arcadian soldiers were still watching, things might still end very badly.

The women came through one at a time, and Justin saw Val lean forward and murmur something to Hannah, likely instructing her how to play along with the scanning. Val probably thought Lucian had managed some prearrangement long before this, not knowing he'd had to do it on the fly. As with the hackers, Lucian hadn't been able to send word of Mae's mission into the RUNA while they were still in Arcadia.

Hannah's turn came, and Justin found himself holding his breath. He hoped no one noticed how pale the captain looked. The poor guy was a soldier, one used to following regular orders, not impromptu ones that came down from unverified sources. But his faith in Lucian must've been strong, because he nodded at the screen as though normal chip information had popped up. He welcomed Hannah home and greeted the next woman in line. Justin exhaled and resisted the urge to sink to the ground in relief.

The entering Arcadians had a different process, a much lengthier one involving visas and paperwork to match their identities, which had been sent in advance by Atticus. Once they were in, the Arcadian soldiers finally left, getting back on their boat and sailing for the other shore.

"I can't believe it," Justin muttered, falling in step with Lucian as an aide led them all to the plane that would deliver everyone to Vancouver. "We made it. We're here."

When he and Lucian started to board the plane, a voice behind them calling Lucian's name gave them pause. Justin turned and saw the captain who'd scanned everyone waving his hand and hurrying forward. Lucian smiled at the Gemman and Arcadian delegates and stepped aside from the stairs going into the jet.

"You all go ahead," he said grandly. "And cross your fingers that score wasn't wrong."

He walked across the tarmac to meet the captain, and Justin followed, his earlier tension returning. What was going to go wrong now?

"Sir," said the captain breathlessly, "I did what you asked. I—"

"Yes, yes," said Lucian, clapping the other man on the back. "You did, and believe me, you'll be rewarded. I know it was an irregular thing to ask, letting her through, but trust me when I say you've played a role in one of the biggest events of our time. I'll be in touch with your superiors as soon as I'm in Vancouver, and all of this will be cleared up."

The captain nodded. "Yes, sir. I believe you. I don't know who that woman is, but if you say she needs to be here, then I believe you and trust what you're doing. The thing is, sir, I know who she's not." He lifted up a small tablet that appeared to be full of names. "Everyone's been accounted for in your original party and in the visiting Arcadians'. With one exception. Senator . . ." The man looked nervous and then hardened his resolve. "If you can't tell me, then so be it, but I still have to ask: Where *is* Praetorian Mae Koskinen?"

Lucian exchanged a pained glance with Justin, and here, away from all the other eyes, Lucian was no longer the swaggering leader-to-be. Mostly, he looked beaten down by all the lies he'd become enmeshed in.

"Captain," he said wearily, "I wish I knew."

# CHAPTER 23

# TESSA DEFINES
# THE TRUTH

Tessa deliberated for a long time on what to do. In the days following her meeting with Danique, she best coped by putting off meeting with Daphne. Tessa went about her normal life, returning to a somewhat regular schedule at school and spending time with the Marches and Darius after class. She also still maintained contact with the YCC and promised to attend future meetings, just in case that turned out to be a connection she wanted to further.

Tessa was finally able to make her decision the day she found out Justin was back in the country. Cynthia told her moments before the news channels all broke the story, and Tessa soon discovered she also had a message from him. Based on the time, he must've sent it pretty soon after crossing the Gemman border. There wasn't much to it, but something about the gesture moved Tessa: *Back in civilization. I'll never make a joke about Panama again. See you soon, sweetie.*

He hadn't had to send her anything. Even if his and the others' arrival wasn't a public spectacle, he'd have known that Cynthia would pass along whatever he sent to her. Yet, he'd still written to Tessa personally, and she knew why. To him, she was family, and this showed it in a way that all the student visas and fancy schools never could have. The indecision that had been knotting inside Tessa eased, and she finally knew what to do about the volatile information she'd learned. Resolved, she called Leo, who looked surprised—and a little wary—to hear from her when his face appeared.

"You aren't coming to see me with another reporter, are you?" he asked.

"Nope. I need to know if you know anything about a . . ." Tessa paused to lift up the tiny microphone she'd worn recently. "A model RXM73200-XS microphone."

"Not specifically," he said. "But I know a little about them and their type. What do you need?"

"I need to know how to erase what's on it—in a way that won't actually show I erased it. And so that the data can't be recovered."

Leo raised an eyebrow at that. "You aren't in some kind of trouble, are you?"

"No . . . I'm just having ethical qualms about some stuff I've recorded for Daphne." It actually wasn't that far from the truth and also appealed to Leo's paranoid nature.

"Well," he said, "lucky for you, you can do it at home. Go find Cynthia's radiant warmer."

"Her what?"

"You use it to keep food warm at parties. I guarantee someone like her owns one. It uses a kind of low-level radiation that'll wipe that microphone's storage unit clean, if you get it close enough."

He explained it in further detail, and when Tessa ended the call, she found that he was right and Cynthia did indeed own such a device. Tessa followed the directions he'd given and then tried to transfer the microphone's data to her ego, as she and Daphne had done in the past. Nothing happened. Satisfied, Tessa then made another call.

Daphne arrived an hour later, in high heels and red lipstick, giving her usual eye roll when Rufus checked her for her own surveillance. "It's about time," she told Tessa, once he'd finished and went off to another part of the house. "Where have you been these last couple days?"

"Busy," said Tessa, sitting down at the kitchen table. "With schoolwork and stuff."

"*I'm* your schoolwork," snapped Daphne. "Now tell me what happened at your last meeting."

Tessa took deep breath. "A lot. I may have met with some sort of religious leader—some priestess or something—who has ties to Dr. Cassidy and, by extension, the Citizens' Party."

If Daphne's eyes had gotten any wider, they might have been in danger of popping out. "You did *what*?"

Tessa launched forward with a retelling of the story, edited of course. Many important parts remained, like how she'd convinced Dr. Cassidy she was having dreams about his religion and how he'd referred her on to Danique.

"Danique didn't outright say anything too incriminating or admit to her full involvement, but the guy who was with her just before I got there called her Damaris. I did a search on those two names and found a reference to a Damaris Chu, who goes by the alias Danique, who's been investigated by SCI a few times for religious suspicions but was never found guilty of anything. Of course, the exact details from the servitor's office weren't public record, so it's hard to know what exactly they looked into her for, but I'm sure we can—"

"I'll be the judge of all this," said Daphne, who was practically salivating. "Where's the mic? Let me hear this myself."

Tessa shifted uncomfortably. "Well, that's the problem. I went to upload it, and I got an error. There's nothing recorded. It's like the microphone wasn't working that night."

The idea was so ludicrous, it was clear Daphne couldn't take it seriously enough to panic. "Of course it was working! We'd just tested it. It was on when you left me. Even if you turned it off—you didn't, did you?—there'd be something there."

Without another word, Tessa handed over the microphone and watched as Daphne repeated the attempt to pull its data. Her condescension turned to disbelief and then to outrage. "This is impossible! We tested it. I'll take this back and see if one of the tech guys can do anything. Shit." Daphne slouched back in the chair, arms crossed in anger. "It figures. We finally get something, and *this* happens! Tell me again what you heard. Everything."

Tessa complied, again leaving out the same key parts—like how, along with looking up Damaris Chu, she'd found a similar report about Demetrius Devereaux on the stream, one that linked him to unspecified religious investigations that had never been conclusive. Daphne couldn't know about him. Tessa had realized the reporter was thorough enough to do a similar search and draw the conclusion that he too was tied into some underground religion—and that judging by Geraki's words, Justin had some involvement that didn't sound like normal servitor behavior. Tessa didn't know if it was innocent. She knew Justin had met with Geraki a number of times over the last few months, but she'd always assumed it was SCI business. It might very well still have been—or it might not. Geraki had made a comment about Justin's "faith," and although that was impossible for Tessa to imagine, she couldn't take the chance of that insinuation falling into the hands of someone like Daphne. Tessa would protect Justin, as he had protected her so many times, by erasing the recording. If there'd been a way to just pull out the parts that incriminated him, Tessa would've done that, but some tech person at North Prime might have uncovered that there'd been an alteration.

"I'll go on record with any of this," Tessa told Daphne. "Whatever you need me to swear to—I mean, so long as it was something that happened."

Daphne grimaced. "I'd rather you didn't. I'd rather we had the recording, but if this doesn't pan out, then a teenage testimony will have to do. Not nearly as credible."

"Well, then," said Tessa, feeling pleased to succeed in her ruse and to see that Daphne was actually pursuing facts instead of speculation, "I'll keep going with everything else—the YCC and all that. Maybe it'll give us leads. And it will look good for citizenship—if I decide to go after it."

"Of course you will," said Daphne dismissively. She stood up, microphone clutched in her hand. "I'll take this to the guys downtown and see what we can salvage." She glanced around, noting the mostly empty house. "I heard the news today. Call me when your guy gets back. Especially call me if he brings Lucian Darling around so I can finally get an interview. I was annoyed at first when he left the country, but the delay might have been for the best, in light of all this other stuff that's been uncovered. This internship panned out . . . just not how I expected."

"Delay . . ." Tessa frowned as she processed Daphne's words. "Delay in getting an interview with Lucian? Were you expecting one?" Daphne had hinted as much before.

Daphne grinned. "Of course. What's the point of having a well-connected intern if I can't make use of it?"

Tessa followed her to the door, trying to piece meaning together with the time line she knew. Something didn't feel right, but she couldn't put her finger on it yet. "You didn't know I was connected—that Justin was connected—to Lucian until the Arcadian trip was announced." There it was. Tessa put it together. "No, you did. Didn't you? You knew all about me before you approached me at school. You knew all about my family and Justin being friends with Lucian."

"So? What if I did? I wouldn't be much of a reporter if I didn't research the person I was approaching for a once-in-a-lifetime internship, now, would I?"

"But you said . . . what about all that stuff about wanting to see a girl like me rise above my background?" exclaimed Tessa.

"That's true too," said Daphne, who was clearly having trouble understanding why Tessa was so upset. "There are lots of pieces to this."

"But Lucian's the biggest one, isn't he? Did you even want an intern? Or were you just looking for a connection to him?"

Daphne turned and leaned against the front door. "Look, I've been chasing this lead with Darling, Cassidy, and the whole idea of religious involvement in the CP for months without getting anywhere. Someone like me couldn't get an interview with either of them—at least not through normal channels. So, I started looking into abnormal ones. Any connection—or one-off connection—that might get me an in to talk to the senator. I went with his friends, his friends' friends, his friends' family . . . and then through a stroke of luck, I found his friend's ward needed a mentor in journalism. It was a long shot, but it was the best opportunity I'd had in a while. So I went with it." Daphne sighed in frustration when she saw Tessa was still upset. "If it makes you feel better, you actually have been a million times more useful than I ever expected. When I found out Lucian was leaving, I thought my chances of talking to him were leaving too. But this work we've done . . . well, it's been kind of amazing. You've got a real knack for this stuff, kid."

"Not anymore," said Tessa, surprised to feel herself on the verge of tears. "I'm done with all of it! I'm especially done with you. I'm not going to be part of any more games."

"Uncovering religious motivations in one of the country's political parties isn't a game," insisted Daphne. "And you backing out of that just because your feelings are hurt is childish. What does it matter if my intentions with you changed, when we've gotten so close to uncovering the truth?"

"Because the intentions and methods you use matter," said Tessa calmly. "I got so caught up, I lost sight of that. And now you're nowhere near uncovering the truth because you've got a dead microphone, and I'm *not* going to go on the record about what I saw."

Daphne's smugness vanished. "Tessa! You can't do that. If they can't recover this microphone—"

"Then I guess you're out of luck." Tessa turned and raised her voice. "Rufus?" The stocky bodyguard appeared within moments. "Daphne and I are done for the day. Please make sure she gets out okay."

Rufus looked as though he wanted to do nothing in the world more than just that and swiftly opened the door, giving Daphne a pointed look. "Tessa . . . ," she tried again, but Tessa wasn't paying attention anymore.

She walked away, leaving it for Rufus to sort out. All the while, Tessa's heart threatened to beat out of her chest. Had she ended things soon enough? Was it possible Leo was wrong and the microphone might be salvageable? No, Tessa felt confident in his advice, if nothing else. He wouldn't have given her a household remedy if it wasn't foolproof. The question now was if Daphne could do any damage based simply on what Tessa had told her. When Tessa had invited Daphne over, selling out Lucian hadn't seemed like such a big deal. Tessa liked him well enough, but she had no real personal stake in his career, and the people *did* have a right to know who they were electing. But now, knowing the full extent of Daphne's machinations, Tessa realized the reporter likely wouldn't have stopped there. Tessa could only hope that in refusing to help anymore, she'd protected Justin and his secrets.

Of course, that still meant Tessa herself had to reconcile the idea that Justin—who spoke out against religion both professionally and personally—was involved with it at a very deep and covert level. And yet . . . did it really change anything between them? Tessa herself clung to loose religious ideas, and he'd always said hers were harmless and she shouldn't feel bad about holding on to them. If Justin wanted his own, she could accept that.

But as the day progressed and she waited for news of his return, one question continued to burn in her mind: If Justin wasn't sharing his beliefs with her and the rest of the family, did that mean they weren't so harmless?

# CHAPTER 24

# LONGER DAYS

Once, on a campaign in an Asian province, Mae and some other praetorians had trekked cross-country for almost a week. They'd subsisted on bare-bones army rations, and without the need for sleep, they'd marched practically day and night. It had been one of the most taxing missions of Mae's life, but as she began her third day of leading eleven girls and one woman through the Arcadian wilds, she was starting to look back on that Asian trip with new fondness and respect.

Mae knew it was wrong to hold the girls responsible for their group's slow progress. Ordinary soldiers couldn't have matched her pace, let alone civilian adults. To expect a group of sheltered children to keep up with a praetorian was ludicrous. Mae told herself that constantly, but the experience still proved challenging. And it wasn't just because the girls were slower and weaker. Mae's protective nature made her sympathetic to that. She wanted to help them because no one else ever had, and she was glad to do it. Her frustration mostly came from a sense of urgency and pressing danger. Even though the route they were taking bypassed most populated areas, they still always ran the risk of being spotted and reported. The Arcadian authorities could easily send ground troops and helicopters in, and all of Mae's covert work would be for nothing. Would the authorities go to such extremes for a group of runaway girls? Possibly, especially since there'd been murder tied to their disappearance. Would the authorities go to such extremes for a soldier from an enemy country? Almost certainly.

And that was the question that ate at Mae during those long hours of traipsing across fields, of keeping watch while the girls slept. Today was the day the Gemmans would've returned home. Had they? Had Hannah gone undetected these last couple of days, and if so, had Justin gotten her into the RUNA? There was no reason for anyone to suspect Mae was responsible for the salon raid and therefore no reason for anyone to suspect Hannah had assumed her identity. The whole purpose of Cloistering a woman was to keep her out of sight. No one should have any reason to investigate her.

Guilt and worry still plagued Mae. She felt as though she'd abandoned her friends. She felt as though she'd abandoned Justin especially, not to mention sticking him with a lot of problems to patch up. If anyone was clever enough to fix the mess she'd left behind, it was him. She just wished she'd been able to give him more warning, particularly since he had his own mess with the Grand Disciple's conspiracy.

*He'll take care of it all,* she thought firmly. *And hopefully afterward, he'll forgive me.*

He was on her mind a lot, and some of her musings about him were deeply personal, far removed from these political snares. She wished she'd been able to express her feelings more clearly to him before they parted and vowed to try when they saw each other again. That quiet promise drove her even harder, as did the constant knowledge that if she failed in this task, she'd not only end up in potentially lethal trouble herself but also implicate her country in hostile actions against Arcadia.

"Miss Mae?" Monica hurried up to her side as they walked through a barren field that looked like it had once grown corn. "Octavia and Maria say they need a bathroom break."

"Again?" exclaimed Mae. "We just stopped an hour ago."

Monica shrugged helplessly. "That's what they say."

Monica, Cecile, and a couple other girls had taken to Mae relatively quickly, appointing themselves her unofficial assistants. Interestingly, it was the girls in the middle age range, around nine or so, who were most eager to help her. Monica was the only older girl intrigued by what Mae offered. The others, having been programmed for too many years, were still too put off by Mae's strangeness. The younger girls, including Ava, were a mix. Some were fascinated, some too cowed to stray from what they'd been taught. They all were used to responding to authority, however, which was what kept them going on this endeavor.

"Well, then," said Mae, "they're going to have to—" Her sharp ears picked up the faintest of buzzing sounds, and her implant surged to life. "Airplane! All of you—run to those trees, now!"

Several of the girls immediately complied, heading for the field's edge at a hard pace. Some of the younger girls tried but couldn't move that fast. Mae scooped up two of the smallest ones and took them most of the way, depositing them close to the trees before heading back for other stragglers. One person, however, was making no attempt at hurrying her pace. Dawn, Pittsfield's long-suffering servant, strolled along as though she were walking casually through a park. Mae picked up a struggling Ava and then jogged over to Dawn after first ascertaining that the airplane—which was growing louder—wasn't in sight yet.

"Move!" Mae yelled. "Run!"

Dawn regarded Mae with blank eyes. In the last couple of days, Dawn had tried to run away twice and had generally been difficult to manage. At first, Mae had thought she was mentally handicapped, but it was becoming clear that Dawn simply wanted a return to her old life. She was too shaped and beaten down by her world to embrace what Mae was offering, and running away from her masters *with a woman* went against every sense of the natural order Dawn had. Mae would have gladly left her behind, if not for the fact that her capture would prove too dangerous for the rest of them.

Juggling Ava with one arm, Mae pulled out her gun and pointed it at Dawn. "Move," Mae repeated. For a moment, it seemed the other woman wouldn't respond to that either, but there was familiarity in force apparently, and Dawn finally began a halfhearted jog. Their group made it to the tree line as the plane came into sight. Mae was relieved to see it wasn't a military craft and didn't circle back after passing overhead. They hadn't been discovered.

She gently set Ava down, then realized the gun was still out. Feeling self-conscious under the little girl's gaze, Mae put the gun back in her belt. "I wouldn't have hurt her," she said. "I wouldn't hurt any of you. But other people might hurt us if we're discovered. Do you understand?"

The little girl nodded, but whether it was from a need to please, Mae couldn't say. Ava scurried off to join her friends, and Mae watched with a pang. This wasn't exactly how she'd envisioned their meeting, but she had to remind herself that Ava knew of no connection between them. They were strangers, strangers who'd been raised in very different environments. Mae had to comfort herself with the knowledge that all would change once they were safely in the RUNA.

"We might as well rest and take your bathroom break here," Mae told her charges. "But it won't be long, so make the most of it." That last part was met with glum faces. They were tired of this march too, and she could hardly blame them.

"When can we eat?" asked one. Several others nodded with interest.

"Soon," Mae said automatically.

Food had been a constant struggle on this trip, one she hadn't foreseen. They'd set off into the wilderness with no supplies, the effects of which were becoming greater and greater each day. It was still high summer, and this part of the country was in a drought, which had proved a blessing in some ways. They were spared the effects of rain, and evenings were warm enough that they didn't require blankets (though those might have helped keep mosquitoes away). The lack of rain meant natural sources of water were running scarce, and it had been a stroke of luck when they'd found a nearly dry creek yesterday to refill their water jugs. The jugs were glass, awkward to carry but capable of withstanding the temperatures needed to boil the creek water. That process had taken a while, but it and a strict water schedule (that the girls still complained about) had gotten them by.

They'd need more water by tomorrow, and food was an entirely different matter. The drought wasn't supporting much in the way of plant-based food sources, and what little there was had been picked over by birds and animals. Drawing on the survival courses she'd taken, Mae had shot and cooked a rabbit yesterday, which hadn't gone far between Dawn and the girls but had at least given them some protein. Mae had abstained, as she had from most of the food sources they'd scavenged. Praetorian metabolisms craved constant nourishment, but they could withstand deprivation if needed. For a while.

As the girls rested, Mae made a desperate decision. She pulled Cecile and Monica aside, telling Monica to keep watch on the others and come find Mae if there was trouble. Mae took Cecile with her farther into the woods, until the others were well out of sight. A large stone made a makeshift chair, and Mae settled down on it, taking out the amber knife.

"I'm not exactly sure what's about to happen to me," she told the girl. "I think I'll go into a trance and just sit and stare. I don't know how long it'll last. Don't bother me or talk to me. Stay here and keep watch. The only circumstances under which you should try to get my attention are if Monica comes and there's some kind of problem—a *real* problem. If the others are bored or hungry or whatever, then do what you can to get them through. Only bother me if there's actual danger. Do you understand?"

"Yes," said Cecile solemnly. What Mae didn't tell her was that she didn't know if someone could wake her out of a trance, but hopefully, they wouldn't have to cross that bridge.

Wasting no time, Mae slashed the blade across her palm. Cecile gasped and then faded away. The forest shimmered like the scene might change, and then it stabilized and remained as it was. No—

not exactly as it was. Everything was more intense—the colors, sounds, smells. It was like Mae was now in a more idealized version of the woods.

*No,* said that majestic voice she'd come to know. *It's just that when you open yourself up like this, you're more in tune with the natural world.*

*I need to be in tune with it now so I can find food and figure out how far we are from the border. Can you help me?*

*Spread your wings and see for yourself,* said the goddess.

Mae felt herself rise in the air and looked down to see feathered wings, like a falcon's or hawk's, where her arms had been. Higher and higher she went, her vision becoming sharper and clearer. Soon, the landscape spread out before her like the map she'd left behind, and she tried to superimpose what she saw now over the memories in her mind. There, to the west, was the ribbon of the Mississippi. They were paralleling it as she'd hoped. In fact, if her knowledge of other natural features was correct, following the con-stellation had put them on the trajectory she'd hoped for, toward a northern land-bound border. Guessing the distance was trickier. On her own, Mae could've done it in a day. With the girls? It would take at least two, maybe three.

*We're going to need food before then,* Mae thought. She de-scended from that lofty height, back toward her rock in the forest. Before she reached it, though, the vision slowed, showing her a change in the tree type a few miles ahead. There, in what appeared to be a dormant orchard, was a small shack.

*So we're thieves now?* she wondered.

*I told you I would provide you with the means to make this jour-ney. You must make the most of them,* the voice told her.

She returned to the rock, and the world's brilliance dimmed back to reality and a nervous-looking Cecile, who shot to her feet when Mae blinked.

"You're back!" exclaimed the girl. "I mean, you weren't gone, but I thought—"

"I know," said Mae, getting gingerly to her feet. The sun told her a little over an hour had passed. At least the girls couldn't complain about getting a long enough break. "And I'm sorry if I—"

She cut herself off and stared in amazement at the hand she'd sliced. The wound hadn't healed. In fact, it didn't even have the scabbed-over look from last time. The cut had congealed and wasn't openly bleeding but still looked fresh and wet, as though it had indeed happened that day. Mae had no explanation nor time to find one and instead hastily wrapped it in a piece of cloth torn from her shirt.

She gathered up the girls, pleased to see there'd been no crisis in her absence. They continued on through the woods, finding a relatively cleared trail that confirmed the habitation shown to her in the vision. A little less than a mile from where she expected the house to be, she called another halt, something none of the girls had a problem with. Mae pulled aside her three leaders: Monica, Cecile, and a girl who'd made her Gemman name Clara.

"I'm going to get us some food," she told them. "Stay here, and do the usual. Keep them in line. Keep an eye on that water. I'm taking one of the empty jugs in the hopes of getting a refill, but there are no guarantees, and we're running low."

"Shouldn't one of us come with you?" asked Cecile.

Mae grimaced. "Not for this. I'm hoping it'll go smoothly, but if not, I don't want any of you nearby." Seeing the fear that struck in them, she attempted a lighter tone. "But everything'll be fine, and we'll be eating tonight."

She left them behind and set off down the trail, which soon led to the old orchard and shack from her vision. Mae's secret, improbable hope was that someone had left a feast behind and would be gone for days, relieving her of the guilt of taking their food. In the event of a face-to-face confrontation, she was hoping for a peaceful negotiation. She'd found some Arcadian currency in the van, and although it wasn't much, surely it was enough to buy scant rations.

As she approached the house, she found an older man chopping wood. His back was to her, but there was no way she could sneak into the house unseen. Negotiation it was.

"Excuse me," she called.

He spun around with impressive speed, axe poised menacingly as he regarded her with wild eyes. Mae was a bit more startled than she'd expected. His face was almost completely covered in Cain acne, and yellow and brown teeth only added to the monstrous appearance. *Not monstrous,* she told herself. *Just a man who hasn't had access to adequate medical care.*

"I'm sorry to bother you," she said, "but I was hoping to buy some of your food. I have money." She held out the currency and waited. When he didn't speak or move right away, she wondered if he could understand her. There were slight accent differences between Gemman and Arcadian English, and it was possible they were more pronounced away from the country's urban centers.

Then, with a roar, the old man came charging at her with the axe. Mae easily sidestepped him and continued dodging his subsequent attacks. Finally, frustrated, she put distance between them and pulled out her gun.

"Enough," she said. "Don't move. I don't want to hurt you."

The man halted his attack.

"Drop the axe and walk inside the house. Slowly."

Again, there was hesitation, but he complied, so at least communication was working. "I have no intention of harming you," she reiterated. "I'm going to pick out some food, and then I'll leave money behind for you."

The shack consisted of only one room, containing a cold fireplace, straw pallet, and table. Dried herbs hung from the ceiling, but aside from those and the picked-over bones of some small animal on the table, she saw no other signs of supplies.

"Where's your food?" she asked.

By way of response, the man grabbed a knife from the table and charged her again. The close quarters prevented her from completely dodging the attack, and they wrestled briefly. Shooting him would've been simple, but Mae didn't want to kill him if she didn't have to. He didn't seem like the kind of person who had much out-side contact and was likely to report on seeing her, and even if he did, a lone woman wouldn't raise the red flags that one with a host of girls in tow would.

She was easily stronger than him, but the flailing of his wild attack made it hard to immediately disengage from him. At last, she threw him off her, toward the far side of the room. Her throw wasn't *that* hard, but he landed wrong, his foot slipping on a wet spot on the floor. Fumbling, he tried to get his balance but instead fell against the fireplace—the back of his head hitting a jagged stone in its border with a sickening crack.

"No!" yelled Mae, running over to the hearth. Blank, staring eyes met her from that hideous face, and she swore in Finnish. For someone who'd wanted to achieve this rescue with as little death as possible, she seemed to be causing it everywhere. After ascertaining there really was no hope of resuscitation, she left him there for the time being and performed a more thorough search of the premises. Her examination concluded two things: He lived alone, and there was no extra food.

What had he done? Had he just hunted as needed? Had he been about to journey to civilization and obtain some food? Or was there a cache hidden away somewhere? He had no answers to give, and Mae tried to work off her frustration by digging a shallow grave for him with a shovel she'd found. It wasn't what he deserved, but it was all she could offer for what had fallen out between them. The one bright spot on the property was an active well, and Mae wanted to bring the girls here to resupply and sterilize new water. That would require getting him out of sight.

The crude shovel wasn't that efficient, and by the time she'd buried the man, she was covered in sweat, and her cut had opened and begun bleeding. She'd have to use the thin blanket she'd seen on the pallet as a bandage and then do a thorough washing. Before heading off to retrieve the girls, she made one more sweep of the property, just in case she'd missed something.

She hadn't, and that realization made her anger grow. She was tired and hungry, weighed down by an impossible task that she'd been promised divine help on—and hadn't received.

"You promised me food!" she yelled to the dormant orchard. "Where is it? How am I supposed to feed them? How are we supposed to make it to the border without food?"

No answer came, but of course it wouldn't, she thought furiously. Gods didn't like to talk directly to mortals. They did it in dreams and other inconvenient ways—like blood-induced trances. Mae stared at her bleeding hand, but apparently it had already served its purpose. Fully aware she was acting out of frustration, Mae cut her other palm with the amber knife and demanded, "Here's what you wanted, right? You said I had to give something to get something. Where are my answers? Where's the help you promised?"

No answers came. No vision came either. *This is what it comes to*, she thought. *This is why gods are no good for humans. They only let us down. Justin was right about everything. I shouldn't have gotten involved.*

A wave of dizziness struck her, and she put her freshly cut hand out to support herself on a tree, wincing at the pain. She pulled her hand back and then stared openmouthed at what she saw. The tree's trunk was scaled and corroded with disease. That and drought had prevented the tree from producing fruit this season. But where her blood touched the trunk, the scaling disappeared, and a healthy patch of bark spread out, stopping when it was about twice the size of her palm.

*I'm hallucinating.* It was the obvious explanation . . . but it didn't stop her from unwrapping her other hand and placing both bleeding palms against the bark. A sense of warmth and lightness spread out from her, through her hands, and through her blood, sending her life into the dying tree. It was a heady, exhilarating feeling, reminding her of the sensation she sometimes had in the goddess's presence in her visions, that glorious feeling of being alive and connecting to all things living. At the same time, it was an excruciating feeling, drawing on every bit of Mae's core of strength, a core that had been tapped considerably these last few days through both mental and physical hardship.

Despite that exertion, she kept her palms on the tree and continued focusing her energy. The healthy bark spread farther and farther until it consumed the entire trunk and branches. Green leaves burst into life, soon followed by delicate pink and white blossoms. The world reeled around Mae, and she nearly let go.

*No, no,* she thought. *The cycle isn't complete yet.*

The blossoms grew and then fell apart, showering her in fragrant petals, far sweeter and richer than any perfume of hers could manage to be. And in the flowers' places, fruit began to grow, starting small and green and soon developing into full, red apples that weighed down the limbs. It was then that Mae finally broke away, gasping at the strange mix of pain and pleasure coursing through her. There was blood on her palms and blood on the tree, but it was alive and healthy, ready to feed a group of hungry girls.

The goddess's voice reverberated in Mae's head: *This is the kind of power you have in service to me, the power of life and love and fertility. As my priestess, you will bring life where you choose. As my warrior, you will bring death when necessary. You will bring comfort and healing. You will ignite desire. And always, always, I will have my hand upon you, empowering you.*

Mae staggered back, and black spots danced before her vision. Praetorians might not have slept, but they could certainly pass out from injury, and she fought for consciousness. All of this would be for nothing if she couldn't get the girls here. Not bothering to rewrap her hands, she stumbled down the path back to where she'd left her charges. The journey was unwieldy, and she had to stop a number of times to catch her breath. At last, she reached the clearing she'd left them in, where they sat waiting in a small, nervous cluster. Cecile and Clara ran to her side, faces shocked at her appearance.

"Come on," Mae said, gesturing them forward with bloody hands. "I have food."

Not waiting to see if they followed, she turned back toward the

shack and plunged down the trail, vaguely aware of others following in her wake. Each step was harder than the last, but Mae refused to rest until she was back at the tree.

*If I didn't imagine it,* she thought with a panic. In her current
state, barely able to stand, with the world spinning, it seemed possible the entire thing had been a hallucination. But when she
reached the ragged orchard, the thriving tree was still there. At
least, she thought it was. She turned to look at the girls hurrying
behind her, and their overjoyed faces told her that this was indeed
a reality.

"Your dinner," she declared grandly. And then she passed out.

She came to a couple hours later, as sunset was darkening the
sky. She was lying in the grass beside the tree she'd revived, and
someone had made a makeshift pillow out of a coat for her. She
tried to sit up, and Clara hurried to her side with a jug of water.

"Drink this," she said. "We got more from the well and boiled it
inside while you slept. Probably it was fine, but—well, just in case."

"Smart thinking," Mae managed to say hoarsely. After a few sips
of the water, she pulled herself upright and took in her surroundings. A crude ladder that must've belonged to the dead man was
propped up against the tree, and Mae counted at least three girls
up in the limbs, picking and throwing down apples.

"We can leave some for the owner," said Monica, coming to sit
down. "But we thought we should get as many down as we could.
And, uh, we didn't really ration them at first. We just kind of went
on a binge."

Mae smiled weakly. "That's okay. Get your fill now. We'll ration
when we leave." An apple descended from the tree and rolled
toward her. She picked it up and bit into it, pleased that it was indeed a real apple and not something insubstantial. When she finished, she ate a second but turned down the third when Clara
offered it to her.

"It seems like a lot right now, but these need to get us through
at least two more days, and thirteen mouths is a lot to feed," Mae
explained.

The two girls exchanged uneasy looks. "Twelve," said Monica. "Dawn ran off while we were waiting for you back there. We tried to stop her, and then we didn't know if we should follow her or stay where you'd left us."

"No, you did right," said Mae. "She didn't want to be here anyway."

One less mouth to feed lightened Mae's load, but Dawn was a witness to what had happened. It was a cruel thought, but as inept as she was at living off the land, Dawn very well might not survive to find anyone to tell her tale to. Or, if she found someone like Mae had encountered, Dawn might find herself caught and forced to be some hermit's wife. Again, not a pleasant thought, but one that would make Mae's life easier. For now, there was no further point in worrying. Getting to the border was all that mattered.

They spent the night there, eating apples and drinking from the well unchecked. Everyone was in better spirits in the morning, and even if not all of them had come around to trusting Mae, they at least responded more favorably now that she'd tended to their basic needs. Their final count gave them eighty-seven apples, which initially seemed like a bounty until Mae looked ahead to their next two days. They split the apples up between some supply sacks found in the shack and then, with newly filled water bottles, set out on the rest of their journey. Mae gave the apple tree one last, lingering look, etching its details into her memory, wondering if she'd ever create such a thing again. Wondering if she'd want to.

The orchard gave way to more deciduous forest, and by the end of the day, they were back in bedraggled open grassland. That made Mae nervous, but the failing light would help obscure them from aircraft, as would some of the taller vegetation. She'd regained a lot of her strength, something made easier by keeping to the girls' lighter pace. They did a respectable job that day, due largely to the rest and nourishment. She hoped for the same progress tomorrow and finally called a rest by a cluster of scraggly trees near a dried-up pond.

The girls curled up together on the ground, settling themselves for sleep, and Mae watched with fond protectiveness from her spot against a thin tree. To her surprise, Ava came and sat beside her, her fair hair gleaming in the moonlight.

"How come you never sleep?" asked the girl.

"I slept yesterday in the orchard," Mae reminded her.

"Yeah, but you don't sleep when the rest of us do."

Mae thought of how to explain it, not really sure the Arcadian-raised girl was ready to learn about Gemman military implants. "I'm a soldier. Part of my training was how to get by without sleep."

Ava seemed to accept this and move on. "I didn't know there were woman soldiers."

"There are lots of them where I'm from. Where I'm taking you."

"Why are you taking us there?"

"Because it's where you belong," said Mae fiercely. "You were taken from there when you were young. It's your home."

"Dawn says you're a demon."

Mae laughed at that. "Dawn's gone. Do I look like a demon?"

Ava shook her head. "Will we live with you in the new country?"

"I don't know," said Mae. Certainly the other girls wouldn't, but Mae didn't know how Ava's custody would fall out. The Nordics wouldn't take her, but there was a chance Ava's plebeian father might want her, once she was identified. Mae had no clue what kind of man her sister had had her fling with but felt confident of one thing. "Wherever you end up, it'll be better than where you came from. You'll be safe. No one will hurt you, and you'll have all the choices in the world. Now, go get some rest."

The next day was less upbeat. Strict rationing took its toll once more, as did the mental exhaustion of these long, arduous days. The landscape didn't change, remaining open grasslands with scattered clusters of small trees. It left Mae on pins and needles, especially since the number of aircraft increased—and she was almost certain they were military machines. The upside was that the more frequent aircraft and her calculations strongly supported the idea that they were nearing the border. Further confirmation came that night when the girls had made camp again near the best group of trees Mae could find, which wasn't saying much. She hadn't seen anything before the sun went down, but now, in darkness, she could make out lights on the horizon.

A chill ran through her. The border.

She gathered Monica and three of the oldest girls. They didn't have the zeal of Clara and Cecile, but they'd warmed up to her, and Mae couldn't trust this next task to anyone younger. She paired the foursome off and quickly explained a watch schedule, instructing the first pair to stay awake until the moon was at a designated point, then wake the other pair and switch.

"Where are you going?" asked Monica.

"To do some scouting. I'll whistle when I come back. If anyone else comes by, make no noise, even if they call out to you. Stay hidden."

Mae didn't bother giving instructions on what to do if the girls were seized because really, there was no advice to give.

She set out at a light jog, the implant and hope working together to charge up her tired body. This was it. They were almost there. The lights grew bigger and brighter, and Mae soon had a sense of what she was looking at. There were two military outposts, one on each side of the border, Gemmans and Arcadians mirroring each other. It was what she'd expected—and feared. Each side wanted to watch the other, which made sense but meant she had to get through the enemy to get home. She knew the rest of the border was marked with some kind of nasty fencing, barbed wire or electrically charged, maybe both. Whatever it was, it wouldn't be the cakewalk she'd had at Carl's or the salon. Both sides wanted that border up, and both would have sensors going off if anyone tried to cut or cross that fencing. There would also likely be random patrols on both sides. She sized up the situation and made her decision, then hurried back to the sleeping girls.

The second watch had just started, and Mae had them help her wake up the others. The girls were groggy and grumpy and not happy about another trek after so little sleep, but Mae's stern tone soon brought order to the group. "This is it," she told them. "Move quickly and quietly, and soon you'll have all the food and clean clothes you could want."

She shepherded them over the fields, shushing any questions that came along. She kept away from the outpost's borders but knew they were within a range where they might encounter a patrol. Even in the night, the border fence was a formidable sight for the girls, with its wicked spikes and scattered red lights warning of electric shock. Mae settled the girls into a small group near a patch of darkness and ordered them to silence before taking Monica aside.

"Don't move. Say nothing, even if you hear someone approaching—on this side. If you see soldiers on the other side, call to them in a whisper. Tell them you're seeking asylum, that you're kidnapped Gemman citizens and have a chipped Gemman with you that way." Mae pointed to the direction she intended to go. "Do you understand?"

"I-I think so." Monica's eyes were large and fearful in the moonlight, as though she understood just how high the stakes were. "What if soldiers on this side find us?"

"They won't," Mae lied.

She left them and walked along the fence toward the outposts, hoping to run into a Gemman patrol. She was placing a bet that either she or the girls would encounter friendly soldiers, a bet that might very well backfire if she ran into Arcadians first.

Ten minutes into her walk, that fear was realized.

There were two of them, and she saw them a fraction of a second before they saw her. Using her gun as a bludgeoning weapon again, she leapt out with praetorian speed and knocked out one of them before he could attack. The other immediately started firing, forcing Mae to drop to the ground to dodge the barrage. Grabbing hold of his comrade's rifle, she swung out and slammed the gun into the man's legs, forcing him to stumble and briefly stop shooting. She used the lull to spring up and take him down, incapacitating him with a blow to the head as well. It was all done neatly and efficiently—except for the gunfire, which had alerted both sides to her presence.

Mae set off at a hard run, hoping the Gemmans would be faster.

She knew if she got close enough to the outpost, a sensor would pick up her chip and identify her. Otherwise, she'd have to talk her way in. Luck held with her part of the way, and her heart leapt as she saw a group of Gemman soldiers come charging in her direction down the other side of the fence.

"Stop!" she yelled. "Stop, I'm a Gemman citizen!"

Two flashlights and five guns pointed at her. "Put down your weapon," barked one of the soldiers.

Mae immediately complied, slowly raising her hands in the air. "Where's your chip sensor? I'm a citizen, and I have a group of citizens with me, a mile east down the fence."

One of the soldiers, a middle-aged woman bearing a sergeant's rank, stepped forward, her gun still fixed on Mae. "The main sensor's a mile west. The nearest one's a portable one out with another patrol."

"Get them here," exclaimed Mae. "And send someone east. Those are Gemman children. Bring them behind the fence and sort out the details later."

The woman hesitated and then said something into a headset that Mae couldn't make out. Shouts sounded behind her, and she turned, catching sight of approaching flashlights in the hands of individuals who were probably carrying guns and wearing Arcadian uniforms.

"Where's the nearest access point?" demanded Mae. The outposts themselves held the widest points of entry, but smaller doors, only large enough for one person, were scattered all along the border, controlled by both sides for maintenance. Admittedly, that meant someone could walk right over from the other side if they had the proper codes, but they couldn't do it without triggering alarms. Since Mae's cover was already blown, secrecy no longer mattered.

"Come on!" she cried, when no one answered right away. "Your Arcadian counterparts are on their way, and when you find out I am a citizen—*and* that I outrank you, sergeant—you're going to wish you'd made this easier!"

The woman in charge studied Mae a few moments and then glanced at the rapidly approaching figures. Mae wasn't entirely unsympathetic to her plight. There were probably Arcadians constantly trying to jump the border, and Mae knew she looked pretty bedraggled. That being said, her accent had to at least give them pause, as did her demands for a chip reader.

"One click east," the sergeant said.

Mae swore under her breath. She'd passed it leaving the girls—in fact, it might not be that far from the girls at all. "Well, shoot me or keep up then."

She took off down the fence line, the Gemman soldiers keeping pace with her as the Arcadians shouted and grew closer. The sergeant gave a halfhearted order for her to stop, but Mae knew she wouldn't shoot yet, not unless she tried to enter Gemman territory without authorization. Studying the fence, she saw a subtle shift in the pattern of red lights and realized she had indeed passed the door on her earlier trip. She was contemplating overshooting it to retrieve the girls when she saw dark silhouettes approaching and realized they were coming toward *her*. Opposite them on the fence, two Gemman soldiers paced the girls, and Mae saw relief cross the soldiers' features in the erratic light.

"Sergeant," said one. "We found them where you said."

A quick head count assured Mae all her charges were there. "Open the door before the Arcadians get here!" she said.

The sergeant looked the new soldiers over. "Where's your chip reader?"

One of them pulled out a small handheld device and Mae held her hand up as close to the fence as she dared, hoping her chip's signal would be close enough for the scanner to read. Some of the Gemman soldiers turned away and focused their guns on something behind her, which didn't bode well for how close the Arcadians were getting.

"Got it," said the soldier. "She's Gemman, and—sergeant, she's a praetorian!"

The sergeant began entering in the codes on her side that would

335

open the door as her other soldiers began shouting for the Arcadians to stand down. Mae didn't dare look behind but instead began herding the girls toward the small door. The soldier with the scanner looked around uncertainly.

"None of them are chipped."

The sergeant finished the codes, and there was an audible click as the door opened. She met Mae's eyes briefly and said, "Let them in."

The girls entered, and Mae herself stepped through just as a line of Arcadian soldiers arranged themselves on their side and began making their own threats back at the Gemmans. Mae staggered forward several feet and then sank to the ground, not realizing until that moment just how weak and dizzy she was from exertion, lack of food, and the apple tree incident. She didn't worry so much about the altercation behind her. Scuffles and shouting matches probably happened all the time. So long as no one was shot—and she had to imagine they had a lot of practice in self-control—she would be all right until the next batch of red tape. All that mattered now was that she had done it. She'd crossed over.

The girls huddled around her, looking at her with concern. Ava was standing closest, her little face grave in the shadows. "Are you okay, Miss Mae?"

"Yes—yes I am." Mae clasped the girl's hand and tried to manage a smile as she looked into all of the gathered faces. "Welcome to the Republic of United North America."

# CHAPTER 25

# REVELATIONS AND CLAIMS

The Gemman delegation received a lot of fanfare when they returned, and Justin's first few days back in Vancouver were spent in a whirlwind of interviews and other public events. Lucian remained the star, of course, but the press was eager to get ahold of anyone they could, and Justin even found himself getting recognized on the streets occasionally.

In his own household, Cynthia—despite an initial show of emotion at his return—promptly made it clear that she wasn't treating him any differently, "famous celebrity or not." After his week in Arcadia, Justin actually found her abrasive attitude endearing and didn't mind a little bossing around. In fact, after watching the women in Arcadia labor away, he felt guilty at the thought of the work Cynthia put into their home and offered to ease her burden by hiring a cook. This immediately spurred accusations of his not liking her food anymore, and Justin soon learned that there were some battles of liberation best not fought.

He met with Hansen and his friends a few times, ostensibly as a diplomatic gesture to make sure they were adjusting. Secretly, his superiors wanted Justin to check in and make sure the plans to entrap the hackers were still going forward. Lucian had held true to his promise not to waste time, and arrangements for the sting were set for that week. Unbeknownst to the Gemman officials, Justin and Hansen had even more covert discussions about Odin. Justin would've really liked to refer him to Geraki, who had much more experience with this kind of thing, but until the Arcadian drama settled down and Hansen acclimated to society, it was probably best if he wasn't seen associating with someone on a government watch list.

Family life returned to normal, and Justin learned that Tessa had weirdly gotten involved with a youth group supporting Lucian's political party and had also been pretty intently wrapped up in her journalism internship. Rufus was quick to allay any concerns Justin had about Daphne's exploiting Tessa.

"You don't need to worry about the reporter," Rufus explained in the study one day. "I mean, she's slimy like all of them, but I've been around when they're together, and although she does ask Tessa a lot of questions, I think it's more natural habit than anything else. She hasn't tried digging into Tessa's personal life or seemed like she's working that poor-provincial-in-the-big-city angle. I also checked her for surveillance equipment each time she came over. She never got a recorder in. And from what I've gathered, Tessa's cut ties with her anyway."

"Good to know," said Justin, looking Rufus over. "Thank you for watching the situation. And for everything else." He hadn't had much time to talk to Rufus since returning. Mostly the other man stayed out of the way, and both Tessa and Cynthia spoke favorably of him. Best of all, there'd been no incidents or attacks in Justin's absence. Maybe it was coincidence, but he was more than willing to give credit where credit was due.

"Just doing my job." Rufus's expression turned thoughtful. "But on that note . . . well, there's actually something I've been wanting to talk to you about. Actually, I wanted to talk to Praetorian Koskinen, but she hasn't been returning messages."

"She's still preoccupied," said Justin carefully. *Preoccupied in the Arcadian wilderness.* And like that, all the worries and imaginings he'd been trying to push aside since returning came tumbling down on him. He'd tried to distract himself with the press, with his family, with Hansen . . . but there was no getting around it. Mae was still missing, and it was literally keeping him up at night.

"That's too bad," said Rufus after a moment of scrutiny. "Well, then I guess I should give you my notice instead. I really wanted to stay on, but other commitments have come up, and I may have to be gone within the week. I'm sorry for the inconvenience."

Justin dragged his thoughts from Mae. "No, no . . . I mean, yeah, it's too bad. Everyone likes you, but I'm sure Dag can sub in more praetorians. If it's about money—"

Rufus shook his head. "The money's good. I've just got bigger things calling me—no offense."

"None taken," said Justin. "Just let me know when you think you're going."

"Probably in a few more days, but I'll let you know for sure." Rufus turned for the door but then paused. "Maybe Praetorian Koskinen will be back by then."

"Maybe," said Justin, his heart sinking.

On Justin's fifth day back in Vancouver, Lucian showed up unannounced at his door in the afternoon, and that's when Justin knew. It was also the day the Arcadian hackers were being set up, but as monumental as that was, that wouldn't have brought Lucian in person.

"She's back," said Justin.

Lucian's face split into a grin. "She's back."

Justin hurried him inside, giving a brief nod of greeting to his bodyguard. "Come in, and tell me everything."

The bodyguard stayed behind in the living room while Justin brought Lucian to the study with a bottle of brandy and two glasses.

"She's actually been back a few days," Lucian began.

Justin nearly dropped the bottle as he poured. "And you only just now told me?"

"I honestly didn't know. The military's been all over it and didn't let us in on it until today. I guess since I'd already left a statement with them when we came back, they didn't feel the need to check in since her story matched ours—well, mostly matched. I'm sure she was surprised to hear I'd authorized her daring mission. But she's smart. She probably rolled along with it."

"Of course she did." Justin spoke more harshly than he intended, largely to cover up his own spiraling emotions. As it was, he was having to work hard to stop his hands from shaking. "So she really made it in without getting caught? And with the girls?"

Lucian nodded. "All eleven of them, doe-eyed and adorable from what I've heard. They've matched their genes to the registry, and all but two were born from Gemman parents. Doesn't matter, though. No one's going to turn those other two away. Sounds like her niece wasn't the only one smuggled out for convenience either, but that's all for the social workers to sort out."

"As long as you can get one reunited family to gush their gratitude to you in a well-televised way, it'll be a PR job well done," said Justin bitterly.

"That's not the only reason I did this."

Justin knocked back his brandy and noticed Lucian was keeping pace. It was possible the senator had been almost as stressed over all of this as Justin. "I know," Justin admitted. "And I know what a big gamble you took coming out and taking responsibility for this. Thank you. It must've gone a long way in smoothing the path back for her."

"Don't get carried away," said Lucian. "I didn't necessarily do it for you either."

"Ah." Justin paused to pour more brandy. "Right. Finally you've found out how to win your way into her heart or her bed . . . or whatever it is you're after."

Lucian held out his glass for a refill. "Do you really think my motivations are that shallow?"

"I honestly don't know what to think," said Justin. "You've continued chasing her, despite her lack of interest and a million societal reasons going against you. What's your game here? Your most optimistic outcome is a secret one-night fling. That's it. You can't be seen publicly. You can't date her. You can't marry her. Your career won't allow it."

Lucian leaned back, looking far too smug, and rested his feet on Justin's desk. "Have you seen my approval ratings? And that's before all this other stuff breaks. It's going to take a lot to turn the public against me now, and if we bring her into this—actually make it known that she's the one responsible for bravely rescuing a group of orphans—she'll be just as loved. A heritage that she isn't even active in isn't going to matter in the public eye. The Nordics'll be pissed off, maybe. Everyone else'll eat it up."

"I just don't get how you can be that into her," said Justin. "I mean, I do, but you don't really *know* her. Is the blond hair really that appealing?"

"Yes," said Lucian. Then, after a calculated pause: "As is a woman who's a powerful elect."

Justin set his glass down so hard, the brandy sloshed out. "Goddamn it! I knew it. Or I should have. How much do you know?"

"I know that you spend as much time investigating gods as you do their followers. I know about the reports SCI keeps hidden away, the stories of things no one can explain. I know the elect are scrambling—as they should be—to secure their gods' positions."

"Goddamn it," Justin said again. He and Mae had briefly speculated that Lucian might be aware of SCI's secret work but had never pursued the lead. Even before then, Justin should've paid more attention to something Geraki had said: *We're not the only ones who know what's happening. Your human masters know. So do powerful people you don't even suspect.* Justin had been a fool not to guess that someone on the verge of occupying one of the two highest offices in the country would have been tipped off on this.

Justin also realized he was a fool not to have suspected something else. "Who do you serve?" he demanded.

"Looking to join up?" asked Lucian. "He's been very good to me."

"Yes, clearly."

Lucian made a face. "Don't say it like that. I didn't get to where

I am just because of him. In fact, it's because of where I am and what I've achieved that I attracted his attention."

"Yes, because the elect are so powerful and talented and all that other stuff. And you want Mae for your god as well?"

"I'm guessing she's taken," said Lucian. "When we first met, it slapped me in the face that she was one of the elect. Now some god must be helping her hide it. Not that it isn't obvious in other ways. You think any ordinary woman could've pulled off what she did in Arcadia? That's what I'm looking for. The exceptional. You can believe what you want of me, but I plan to do amazing things in this country, and I want a partner who can match that. Read whatever ambition or sordidness you want into that, but I *do* care about her."

Justin stayed silent, mulling over a few things. One was that Lucian had no clue it was Justin who was helping Mae hide what she was, which then brought up another question.

*Does he know I'm one of the elect?* he asked the ravens. *I didn't learn to hide myself until recently.*

*Probably not,* said Horatio. *Even before you made your own protection, having us around obscured your aura to many. He would have had to be pretty adept to see through our glamour.*

*Well, he must be somewhat adept if you never picked up on him being one of the elect,* argued Justin.

*He may have an entity of his own,* said Magnus. *Or he may be using a simple charm. He's risen far in mortal dealings, but my instincts tell me he's still new to the larger game. He's too cocky and arrogant.*

To Lucian, Justin asked, "Is it you who really plans on doing amazing things in this country, or your god? They want followers, Lucian. You have to know that. And dazzling displays in Arcadia and reform back home don't immediately get people to your god's altar."

"Not immediately," agreed Lucian. "And certainly not before I'm consul. But you must have seen enough to know this won't stay under wraps forever. Too many unexplained things are happening, and I have religious-freedom lobbyists knocking on my door every day."

"So you plan on opening up the RUNA's eyes to the divine, when you'll be able to conveniently point people to the worship of *your* god?"

"I have no intention of turning us into Arcadia, if that's what you're getting at," said Lucian. "I want a society where public officials and the average person can worship without stigma. You can have freedom of belief *and* rational thought both, you know."

"Actually," said Justin, "my entire job is built around the principle that you can't, in fact, have those two things together."

Lucian finished his brandy and stood up. "Then lucky for you, you've got a friend with connections when the time comes to find a new job. I'll call you if I hear more about Mae. In the meantime, trust that I really do have good intentions—for her and for the country." He put his hand on the doorknob and glanced back. "And don't make plans tomorrow night. After the Arcadian scandal blows up today, we'll be having an impromptu celebratory dinner."

Justin watched Lucian walk away and soon heard an excited burst of chatter from the living room. Even Justin's own family adored Lucian. The universe was definitely playing unfairly.

*Is it?* asked Horatio. *What's he really done wrong? He wants to advocate for his god and find a way to fit that into your country's current framework.*

*Whose side are you on?* asked Justin.

*You just don't like his designs on Mae,* chastised the raven. *I don't either. But if he's eventually able to create a greater acceptance of the divine in your culture, that'll be good for us too. You may be working for different gods, but don't dismiss the idea that you can work together for a mutual goal. Not all of the elect are at each other's throats. Some are seeking allies too.*

As Lucian had declared, the news broke that night with the story of how three Arcadian spies had been set up and caught, thanks to the hard work of Gemman intelligence and a group of brave Arcadians willing to sell their countrymen out for a chance at living in the Jewel of the World. Lucian, of course, was on hand for countless interviews, describing how they'd known they had to take action when they learned of the conspiracy during their recent visit. A few of the RUNA-supporting Arcadians were dredged up as well and had clearly been coached beforehand as they gave statements about how they were happy to help in the takedown and how grateful they were to Senator Darling for the opportunity. Hansen wasn't among them, but he called Justin the following night as he was getting ready for Lucian's dinner party.

"Are you coming tonight?" asked Hansen, his face eager on the wall of Justin's bedroom screen. "All of us have been invited to celebrate our role in catching Cowlitz's men."

"I'll be there," said Justin, buttoning his tuxedo shirt. "Lucian would never let me live it down if not."

Hansen grinned. "Great. Look, I was going to ask you this there, but with so many people around, I didn't know if I'd get a chance. Now that Cowlitz's group is settled and we've been given refugee status, when can we start having regular worship of Odin?"

Justin was tempted to say "never" but instead replied, "Ah, that's difficult to say. You have to remember that religion is still frowned upon publicly."

"But groups *do* exist," the other man insisted. "Legally."

"Yes, but people in my position don't publicly belong to them. We'd have to meet in secret," Justin explained.

"Then we'll meet in secret."

"It's really not a good idea for you and yours to be seen sneaking around to clandestine meetings. You need to look as though you're embracing model Gemman life. You're still going to be watched for a while."

"You'll give us something, though, right?" Seeing the desperation on Hansen's face made Justin wish this was a voice-only call. "You have to. You're our priest. We need Odin's guidance. He brought us here, and we want to serve him well. You owe it to us. To him."

Again, Justin had to bite back the words that technically, he didn't owe any of them anything. He'd made no vows to Odin, save to learn some of his wisdom. Leading the god's followers was no obligation of Justin's, and he was glad for it. But it wouldn't do to alienate Hansen or let on that Justin's own relationship with the god was tenuous.

"Be patient," Justin said. "We have to wait until the time is right. Odin understands this. Pray in your own way, and he'll accept it."

*Be careful,* said Horatio. *Soon he won't need you. Maybe he'll be a priest in his own right.*

*He's welcome to it,* replied Justin. *Then maybe the pressure'll be off me.*

*Don't you want to experience that power again?* asked Magnus. *That bliss?*

*Too many strings,* said Justin.

*But many rewards,* said Magnus.

As though on cue, the bedroom door pushed open, and Mae stepped through, grinning at Justin's surprise. He stared in shock for several moments and then turned quickly back to Hansen on the screen. "We'll talk later. Just be patient, you'll see. Disconnect call."

Justin took a few steps forward, then paused, uncertain as to what he was going to do. Mae made the decision, closing the distance between them and giving him a hug that left the fragrance of apple blossoms behind when she stepped back.

"You're a little underdressed," he said at last. "But I don't think anyone will judge." And honestly, after a week in those horrible Arcadian clothes, her normal jeans-and-tank-top ensemble was the height of fashion as far as he was concerned.

"For your victory dinner tonight? No, thanks. I had a message from Lucian inviting me, but the last thing I want to do is sit around and expound on our trip to Arcadia. I figured I could at least catch you before you went out." She gestured toward his coat and tie, hanging on a chair. "Go ahead. Don't let me stop you. I just wanted to talk a minute."

Justin continued getting ready, feeling self-conscious with her eyes on him. "I figured you'd have a group of little ones trailing you everywhere—or at least one in particular."

A bit of Mae's good humor faded. "I did. On both counts. We were stuck at the base I crossed over to for a couple of days, and then the Citizens' Ministry got involved and began contacting parents and relatives—of those who wanted to claim their children, at least. Per policy, they had to contact my sister and Ava's father too."

"Ava?"

"My niece." Mae's expression softened as she spoke about the girl. "Imagine my surprise to find out Claudia's plebeian fling was an upstanding young man who went on to become a chemical engineer and marry a primary school teacher. I guess he was just on the Nordic land grant that summer for a temporary job. Even more surprising was finding out he wanted custody of Ava. It defaulted to him technically anyway, but the social worker from the ministry told me I'd have a good case if I chose to petition for custody myself." Mae dropped her eyes and sighed. "I didn't."

Justin abandoned his grooming and sat beside her on the bed. He had a million questions about the details of her escape, but for now, her emotional well-being took precedence. "And how are you feeling about that?"

"Shitty," she said. "But not about her. It was the right thing for Ava, I know it was. They're a stable couple—and believe me, I did every background check I could on them, legal and otherwise—with a house and lots of land for her to play on . . . unfortunately it's in San Francisco. Not convenient for me, but how could I hoard her for my own selfish reasons? And what life would I give her? I travel so much, she'd be with a babysitter half the time. Amata—her new stepmother—is going to take a leave of absence from her job to work on socializing Ava so she can go to school. I never would've thought about anything like that. I figured we'd get back here, Ava would jump into school, and life would be perfect." Mae sighed again. "Letting her go with them was the right call. She liked them, even though she was still a little nervous about all the newness.

She'll be happy, and I can visit her. I just wish I could shake this feeling of . . . I don't know. Failure. I worked for years trying to get her back."

Justin slipped his arm around her. "And you did. You got her out of that nightmare existence, back to where she belongs. Her—and the others, I might add. She's in a good place. What you've done is the furthest thing from failure." He hesitated before asking his next question. "I, uh, don't suppose there's any chance your sister will petition for custody?"

Mae scoffed. "My sister's too busy with lawyers. Her and my mother too, I imagine. It wasn't very hard for the Citizens' Ministry to figure out which girls were taken by force and which were thrown away."

The enormity of what Mae had done, both for her niece and to the rest of her family as a result, struck him, and he drew her into his arms. She sank readily into him, resting her head on his chest. "I can't even imagine what you've had to go through. I don't think I slept the whole time you were lost out there."

She tightened her hold on him. "You had no faith in me?"

"I had the utmost faith," he countered. "But I still worried."

"It was awful sometimes," she admitted. "I saw some terrible things . . . but I saw some incredible things too. I know you've been saying getting involved with the gods is trouble, but after what I've seen, I don't know if I could've done it without help. Some goddess got me through. Her"—Mae lifted her head and met his eyes—"and thinking about you."

She kissed him before he could protest, not that he wanted to protest. Not when he'd dreamed about this for the long days of her absence, not when the kiss was an echo of that parting one in Arcadia. It was filled with that same phantom sweetness he'd had so much trouble understanding . . . but craved nonetheless. In their tangle of complicated interactions over the last few months, he'd often found himself pining for how it had been in Panama, but now he realized that was wrong. That encounter between them had been hot and exciting, yes, but those feelings had only been the warm-up for what he felt now, something richer and deeper that resonated within each of them.

Mae eased back on the bed, bringing him down with her. "See?" she said, as though she could read his thoughts. "You aren't just my easy outlet for implant-driven lust." A mischievous smile played over her face. "Though I'd be lying if I said there wasn't some of that going on too. Still, you're going to have to find another excuse this time. What'll it be?" She paused to trail her lips down his neck. "You don't do second dates? I hold no appeal anymore? I was an idiot to believe those things before, and I won't this time either. You're going to have to come up with something really convincing if you want to get out of this."

"I don't want to," he said, voice ragged. And it was the truth. Her body was pressed to his, her eyes an endless sea of blue and green. He wanted to give in to this power that kept bringing them back together. He wanted to feel her bare flesh against his, to lose himself in her, her and a world where there were no other political and godly complications. Unfortunately, no matter how much he pretended, he wasn't sure such a world existed.

"I don't want to," he repeated. "But—"

"Then no buts," she said. Despite the obvious passion burning through her, there was something canny in her eyes that made him think she'd been bracing for this conversation. "I'm done with games. I know how I feel about you, and nothing's going to change that, no matter how infuriating you are. Blow off dinner tonight and stay here with me. Or if you don't want to do it here, we'll go to my place. We'll stay in bed all night and make love and talk and you can finally get out from under all those secrets that burden you and tell me why you kept pushing me away. And then we'll make love some more."

She kissed him again, momentarily throwing off the response he'd been starting to formulate. He felt like his whole life was balancing on a razor's edge, and the easy thing, the thing he wanted most, was to jump off with her. But no matter how much he tried to ignore it, no matter how much he wanted to forget, the memory of those words spoken in that fateful dream came back to haunt him, as they always did: *You'll know her by a crown of stars and flowers, and then when you take her to your bed and claim her, you will swear your loyalty to me.*

The old panic seized him, and later, he would wonder if he would've felt differently if Hansen hadn't called just before she arrived. Maybe if he hadn't had that reminder fresh on hand, the consequences of swearing loyalty to a god wouldn't have mattered. But Hansen *had* called, and through Justin's haze of desire, an image came to him of a lifetime of service to Odin, leading around a congregation of other Hansens, forced to bring others to the fold and jump at the god's whims.

Mac saw that fear in him when Justin broke away, and she tried to pull him back. "No," she said. "No more lies."

"I'm not going to tell you any lies," he said, struggling to sit up. "I'll tell you the truth—as much as I can, at least."

She sat up with him, her hair tousled and cheeks flushed. That almost broke him, almost brought him back to the bliss of her arms and her lips and the rest of her body. And then those words resounded in his mind once more: *When you take her to your bed and claim her, you will swear your loyalty to me.*

He clasped her hands in his, fearful even of the temptation of that small touch, and met her gaze squarely. "Listen to me. You're right—what I said, the second-date nonsense and all that—were lies. Lies born out of both fear of any kind of real human connection and fear of . . . well, some other things I'll try to get to. But here's the truth. There's no one else for me but you. I knew it in Panama, when I looked at you and the whole world stopped, but I was too foolish to acknowledge it then. I don't think I really, truly accepted it until we were in Arcadia, when I had to come to terms with the possibility of never seeing you again. All those other flings I've had are just ashes in the wind, scattered and forgotten. But you . . . you're the real thing. The fire that keeps burning in my life. You're the one. There's no one else I feel this connected to. And if I could do all those things, stay with you, make love—with the lights on—tell you everything that weighs on me, I would. Believe me, Mae, I would. But—"

"Justin—" She reached for his face, but he pushed her hand away.

"No, listen. As much as I want to—and believe me, I do—there are still forces at work bigger than both of us that don't necessarily have our best interests at heart. You said when you were out there you saw things that made you believe in the goodness of the gods . . . well, I'm still not sure. And I can't explain it, but if you and I are together, if we cross that physical line again, there will be consequences neither of us can change."

"So, what, then? No physical line?" she asked. "Is that what you need?"

For a moment, he considered it. Was it possible . . . a nonphysical romance? Neither of them had a history that suggested they'd be able to pull that off. That wasn't to say he wasn't happy in just her presence. He was, and he didn't want to lose that . . . but he didn't trust himself—or her, for that matter. They'd slip one day, unable to resist, and he'd end up back in her arms and Odin's service.

"I don't know. I don't think so, at least not until I know more," he said at last.

Mae was quiet for several moments. "How can you say these things to me? How can you tell me you want me, that I'm the only one . . . but that we can't be together?"

"I can only imagine how it sounds," he admitted.

"No," she said. "I don't think you can. What else is there? What else aren't you telling me?"

*That you're the woman a god picked out for me, and binding myself to you binds me to him.*

He could've spoken those words, and maybe she would've understood. Except, the thing was, Justin was afraid she *wouldn't* understand, that she would tell him service to a god was worth the price of their happiness. And looking at her now, at that lovely face and eyes filled with affection, Justin wondered if he might end up agreeing with her.

"I can't tell you yet," he said, releasing her hands. "I would if I could. If we could be together, if there were an easy way, I swear it, Mae—I would. But I can't right now. I'm sorry."

"Justin—" The hurt in her voice made his heart ache, but whatever else she might have said was cut off when he heard a sound at the door.

It was mostly closed, but someone pushed it open now, and he heard Rufus say, "Praetorian Koskinen? Are you—oh." The man appeared in the doorway, immediately assessed what was happening, and took a step back. "I'm sorry. I—"

"No." Mae stood up from the bed and ran a hasty hand over her eyes. "It's okay. I was just leaving. Is something wrong?"

Rufus still looked deeply flustered. "No, ma'am. I just wanted to say good-bye. I don't know if Dr. March told you, but I'm leaving, and this is my last night."

"No," said Mae stiffly. "He's told me a lot of things tonight—but not that. Come on. I'll walk you out. He needs to finish getting ready anyway."

Justin thought she'd leave without another glance, but she paused in the doorway and looked back, her heart in her eyes. *One word,* Justin thought. *One word, and she'll come back to me.*

But he didn't say it, and Mae gave a nod of farewell. "Have fun tonight."

And then she was gone.

# CHAPTER 26

# LIGHTS OFF

M ae held it together as she thanked Rufus for his service and urged him to get back in touch should his circumstances change. She even held it together when the March family told her good-bye, resulting in hugs from Cynthia, Tessa, and Quentin and stories of how they'd worried for her as much as Justin on the trip. It wasn't until she was on the train, headed back downtown, that Mae started to lose it.

*Unacceptable,* she told herself, forcing back tears. *I am a soldier. I've fought for my country and risked my life countless times. I won't break down now like some adolescent just because a boy told me no.*

Except, Justin hadn't exactly told her no. That was what had hurt the most. How did someone do that? How could he say that she was the one, that he'd never had that kind of connection with another woman . . . and then turn away? Mae had had men shower her in gushing words for her entire life, praising her beauty and going overboard with all the grandiose things they'd do for her to prove their love. No one had ever put it so simply: *There's no one else for me but you.* And those simple words had struck her with more power than any other elaborate declaration could have—which is why it had hurt so much. She almost wished he'd lied to her again. Almost.

"Praetorian Koskinen?"

A voice called to her in the crowded station as she stepped off the purple line, and it took her a moment to orient herself and find the speaker. When she did, it was no one she'd expected—or really wanted—to see.

"Mr. Devereaux," she said formally, as Geraki approached her. "It's nice to see you again."

"You don't look like you mean that," he said. "Forgive me, but you don't look like you're happy to see anyone just now."

"It's been a complicated night," she said bitterly, nearly laughing at her own understatement.

"Is there any way I may be of assistance?" he asked, in a genteel way that contrasted with the religious-zealot persona she associated with him.

"I don't think anyone can help, but thanks. I need to get home."

He caught her arm, and she almost welcomed the rush of endorphins brought on by a potential threat. The look in his eyes, however, suggested no fight, just more unsolicited advice.

"That's not true," he told her. "The part about no one being able to help you, that is. Sometimes it may seem that way on earth, in human affairs, but there are higher powers able to strengthen and sustain us."

This time, she did laugh, surprised she'd find amusement in something so absurd. "Are you trying to convert me in the middle of a subway station?"

"No need," he said gravely. "From what I hear, you've already taken up quite nicely with a goddess."

"How do you—" A startling, impossible thought hit her. "You . . . you sent me the amber knife."

He sketched her a bow. "I'd say 'guilty as charged,' but I have nothing to feel guilty about. The Lady wanted to connect to you, and I simply helped make it possible."

Mae was stunned. She'd meant what she'd told Justin, that her experience in the wilderness had been life-changing. The goddess had held true to her word, delivering and protecting Mae, and that sense of communion and life had been glorious. Mae wasn't entirely certain how to feel about that now. She'd just been thinking that there might truly be something to serving a goddess like that . . . but now, that image was tainted knowing Geraki was involved.

"You serve her too?" Mae asked.

"No, no," Geraki chuckled. "I serve a different god, but they are allies, and I have great esteem for her. That was how I came to be the messenger."

"I didn't know that," said Mae, feeling slightly relieved. "That they were allies. But I mean, I don't really know much about her yet . . . or anything about your god."

"No?" He genuinely seemed surprised at that. "Our mutual servitor friend has never mentioned my god?"

"Justin? No, why would he?"

Geraki's expression was a mix of exasperation and amusement. "No reason at all, I suppose. Never mind him. If the Lady has brought you any sort of fulfillment at all, then I'm glad."

"She has," said Mae softly. "Though I still don't know what to make of it. Or what I want."

"Then I'll give you some quick advice because I see the blue line pulling up. Find out what you do want from her, and you may find that whatever else is bringing you down doesn't matter so much. My master tells me she's led you true so far. If you let her continue to do so, you may find petty and human affairs are exactly that: petty and human. Good luck."

He started to turn for his train, but this time, she held him back. "Wait—what is her name?"

Geraki hesitated. "Generally the elect must earn their gods' names. Only those engaged in simple worship get them easily." Something in her face must have touched him, because he finally said, "Freya."

"Freya," repeated Mae, the word tasting of power.

"Look to her." Geraki's expression softened a little. "Not to whoever's broken your heart."

He disappeared into the crowd, and Mae stood there a moment before continuing on her way, heading up to street level. She said the goddess's name over and over in her head as she walked home, wondering if Geraki—madman that he was—was right. When the pressures of her home life had reached a breaking point, Mae had found purpose in answering the higher call of the military. Was it possible now, in the midst of romantic turmoil, that there might be something for her she'd never dreamed of in the service of this goddess? It was a startling revelation, especially considering Mae's rocky beginning with the Morrigan.

But Freya felt different, and that bore some serious consideration before Mae could make any hard-and-fast decisions. Besides, when she got home later, Mae couldn't deny that no matter how petty Geraki might have thought human affairs were, the power Justin still held over Mae's heart was a formidable thing. Freya's power in the wilderness had filled Mae with exhilaration . . . but then, so did thinking of Justin now. That was a hard thing to get over.

It was made harder still when he showed up that night.

She almost could've believed her eyes were playing tricks on her when her bedroom screen displayed his image down at her building's front door. He should've been at Lucian's dinner, but there he was, looking up at the camera as he waited for entrance. With his chip, he actually could've come straight to her door, because he was among a handful of people she'd authorized in the building's security system. She wondered if he was afraid of his reception, as though she might not have welcomed him to her door after the way they'd left things.

He needn't have worried. Mae authorized his entry, her heart pounding furiously as she counted the seconds until he made it to her door. Whatever thoughts of higher callings over human affairs Geraki might have inspired vanished. That earlier sense of feeling like a schoolgirl came over her as she took a hasty look in the mirror and tried to smooth her unruly hair. She was nothing special tonight, but it didn't matter. Not anymore. Not if he was coming to her.

She flung open the door when he arrived, and both of them

stood there, momentarily frozen. There was a hunger and tension radiating off him that left her breathless, and Mae suddenly found herself caught in an uncharacteristic state of rambling. "What are you doing here? Why aren't you with Lucian? I thought you said you couldn't—"

"I was wrong."

His voice was low and husky as he slammed the door behind him and pulled her to him. That first kiss was crushing and all-consuming, as though he might lose this chance if he didn't take advantage of it. The tenderness she'd felt back in his room was gone, replaced by an almost primal intensity that spoke to her baser instincts. She let herself get pulled into that animal passion, knowing there'd be time—all the time in the world—later for tenderness.

He swept her into his arms and carried her effortlessly into her bedroom, pausing to shoulder the light switch off before setting her on the bed. The streetlights outside painted them in shadows as they shed their clothing. The foreplay Mae remembered from Panama was gone, abandoned in the urgency of the moment. He went at her almost as desperately and furiously as an implant-driven praetorian might, and although it was a surprise, it wasn't necessarily unpleasant. Mae's own body was so supercharged and flooded with hormones and endorphins that the instant gratification was welcome in some ways, even as his tight grip on her wrists bordered the line of pleasure and pain. All that mattered was that they were finally together, as they should've been long ago.

Along with that fury and intensity came brevity, and when it was over, he rolled off her with a great, content sigh, releasing his hold on her. Some of Mae's initial desire had been met, but she was a long way from being sated. *All night,* she reminded herself. *We have all night to make love and talk and then make love some more....*

She turned to her side, wanting to simply hold him now. His breathing was heavy, his skin damp with perspiration, but she could see little else of him in the patchy darkness. She called to the room's sensors to turn on the lights and then smiled as she met his eyes.

"I'm glad you didn't go tonight," she said, cradling his face in her hands. "I'm glad . . . for a lot of things."

"Me too," he said, trailing a finger down her neck. She shivered at his touch, hoping it would lead to more. The odds seemed good as he traced the line of her cleavage, pausing to examine the charm he'd given her, which she still wore on its plain cord. It had stayed on when the rest of their clothing had been heedlessly flung away. The content look on his face shifted to a frown as he touched the symbol etched on the charm. He opened his mouth to speak, then seemed to think better of it and stayed quiet.

A surreal moment struck Mae, because she'd been almost certain he was about to ask her what the charm was—which made no sense since he'd given it to her. "Surprised I've still got it?" she asked.

He gave no answer and simply drew her hands to his lips, kissing the tops of each of them. That strange sense of something being off spread through her, even though she tried to ignore it and focus on the way his lips felt against her skin, the way the light shone on his dark hair and—

"Why did you turn off the lights?" she asked suddenly.

It was an old joke between them. Mae, never comfortable with even her lovers seeing her vulnerability, tended to have sex in the dark. That was how it had been in Panama, and afterward, he'd warned her that next time, he'd keep the lights on so that he could watch every emotion play across her face in the throes of passion. It had been a threat that had started off terrifying but had become tantalizing the more time had passed, and she'd found herself longing to give all of herself to him, not just her body. In fact, she realized, he'd even alluded to it back in his room earlier tonight: *You're the one. There's no one else I feel this connected to. And if I could do all those things, stay with you, make love—with the lights on—tell you everything that weighs on me, I would. Believe me, Mae, I would.*

"I thought you'd like it better that way," he said now.

Mae felt her breath catch and couldn't make her voice work for several moments as a coldness filled her. "Because I asked for it earlier," she suggested.

"Yes," he said. He started to relax, but she must have given something away in her face, given away that she'd caught him in the lie. He jerked away at the same moment she reached for him.

"Who are you—" she started to say, her words painfully cut off as he backhanded her with a force she wouldn't have thought Justin capable of. He sprang from the bed and tore out of the room naked. The hit threw her off for a few seconds, giving him a slight lead, but then she recovered and took off after him, ripping a robe off the wall as she passed by it.

She made it to the living room in time to hear her front door slam. Without even the slightest hesitation, she gave chase. Whoever he was—*whatever* he was—she had the advantage of her implant. Surely, even with his lead, the burst of life and adrenaline powering her would close the distance. But she heard the lobby's main door close while she was still on the stairs, and when she finally burst outside, he was nowhere in sight. A few pedestrians gave her a curious look as she tightened her robe and peered around, certain he couldn't have gone far. She checked both directions on the street and sidewalk and even looked in the hedges surrounding the building's entrance. Nothing. It was as though he'd vanished into thin air.

*No one can do that,* she thought. But then, no one should have been able to walk into her home wearing Justin's face. She returned to her apartment shaking, both from the implant's letdown and fear of what she couldn't understand. Her mind nonetheless tried one last attempt at rationalization, refusing to admit that she had just been involved—*very* involved—with something beyond normal human abilities. Maybe it had been Justin, confused and high on some drug that had made him forget things he had no business forgetting.

She settled on her couch, wrapping her arms tightly around

herself as she told her living room screen to call him. For a moment, it didn't seem he would answer, and when he finally did, she wished he hadn't.

There was no question where he was, from his tuxedo to the well-dressed people milling behind him to Lucian's voice echoing on a sound system in the background. Justin was at the senate party, where he was supposed to be. He wasn't running naked down her street. He wasn't here. He never had been. Bile rose up in Mae's throat.

"Sorry it took me a minute," he said, pitching his voice over the background noise. "I had to sneak away to answer and—what's wrong?"

The trembling in her body threatened to become a seizure. She could form no words, only shake her head as he asked her three more times what was wrong. After that fourth time, he told her he was coming over and walked out of the party.

He came straight to her apartment door, as the real Justin would have earlier. Mae's state hadn't improved, but as he sat with her on the couch, she managed to finally speak enough to get out a slightly disorganized but otherwise accurate retelling of what had taken place. Partway through, he started to reach for her and then seemed to realize she didn't want to be touched. His hands fell back into his lap, and a storm of emotions played over his face, disbelief and horror and anger and compassion. She knew they must have made a ludicrous sight, him so polished in his tuxedo and her disheveled in the robe. Nonetheless, she tried to use his face and steady eyes as a centering point to calm herself down. Instead, all she achieved was an internal berating that she could've possibly confused anyone else for him.

"I have to go," she said abruptly, when she finished the sordid tale. "I— I have to shower. I have to wash him off me. I can still feel him everywhere. I have to—"

"No, wait," said Justin, grabbing her arm. He immediately let go when she recoiled. "No—don't. Not yet. I know it's a terrible thing to ask, but if you go to a hospital, check in as a rape victim—"

"I wasn't raped!" she exclaimed. But then she faltered. "I mean . . ."

"Call it whatever you want. They can do a DNA check. They can ID whoever this was from the registry. We'll find out who did it."

"And what if the results come back, and they find out it was *you*?"

He winced at that. "I suppose that's very possible, depending on the extent of this . . . I don't know, illusion. Look, we'll say you and I went out tonight, had sex at my place, and that you were attacked walking home. That park around the corner's got a lot of shady spots, and I'm pretty sure there are no cameras. Give some generic plebeian description, say you couldn't see much in the dark, and then just wait for science to do the rest."

"And so I go on record saying I slept with two guys in one night." She stiffened. "*And* that I'm a praetorian who let herself get assaulted. If they believe that, then they'll probably lose all faith in our military."

Justin remained calm, despite how difficult she knew she was being. "Mae, I know this is hard on your pride, but please. This is the fastest way to get answers. We've talked about the War of the Elect, and now it's found you—in a way I don't think either of us could have predicted."

"We don't know that it was an elect," she said.

"Who else could it have been? There's no question someone with considerable power—shape-shifting, illusion, whatever—is responsible, and only the servant of some god could do that. Why this and not an outright attack? I don't know, but the first and best way to get answers is to get a name. Please do this." He started to reach for her again out of habit but remembered and stopped. "I'll go with you. I won't leave you."

*Only the servant of some god.* Mae felt ill, suddenly remembering the words spoken to her by the goddess—by Freya—when she'd brought the apple tree back to life: *This is the kind of power you have in service to me, the power of life and love and fertility. As my priestess, you will bring life where you choose. As my warrior, you will bring death when necessary. You will bring comfort and healing.*

*You will ignite desire. And always, always, I will have my hand upon you, empowering you.*

Was this Freya's idea of empowerment? To be so desired that someone would use magic or their god's favor to deceive her and take her unknowingly? Mae, who'd had countless casual lovers without a second thought, suddenly felt dirty and violated. Her body no longer seemed like her own, and she hated herself for it—and hated Freya for it. Where had the goddess's hand and protection been when that phantom had been in Mae's bed? Was this what it was truly like to be in the service of a god? Where was Geraki's higher calling?

"I'll go," Mae told Justin. "I'll go to the hospital with you."

The story they'd contrived sounded as convoluted as she'd expected, but even Mae could recognize that she was in a shell-shocked state and that went a long way in convincing the intake officer. Equally convincing were the signs of physical assault. In the sterile lights of the hospital, Mae could now see red marks on her wrists that would be bruises tomorrow. It again made her feel foolish for not suspecting something sooner. Why would Justin, who had played her body with such skill in Panama, have resorted to such crude and fumbling tactics? She'd written it off to the heat of the moment, believing he was so wild for her that he couldn't control himself. In reality, she was the one without enough self-control to stop and consider that maybe everything wasn't actually falling into place like she'd dreamed.

After her exam, the staff offered to discharge her, but she and Justin wanted to wait there to get the results as soon as possible. Matching one DNA sample against the entire registry was a time-consuming process. It had taken over twenty-four hours for the refugee girls, though in criminal matters like this one, law enforcement could expedite things. It was still almost two in the morning when the results came back, and when they did, the doctor who delivered them was clearly astonished

"I'm sorry," he told her. "There was no match in the registry."

"What do you mean there was no match?" demanded Justin.

361

"Every living Gemman is in the registry! Was there something wrong with the sample? Didn't it run long enough?"

The doctor shook his head. "No, everything was done properly. It just seems your assailant wasn't a Gemman citizen."

"The registry keeps DNA samples of people here on visas," insisted Justin. "Check those."

"We did," said the doctor. "But not all those on visas are logged. And it's possible it could've been a fugitive, someone not legally in the country, as rare as that is."

Justin, who'd been so calm throughout all of this, had finally reached his breaking point. "You made a mistake! Run the damn test again, and find the son of a bitch who—"

"No," said Mae, standing up and taking his arm. "There's no need. Thank you."

"If you want," said the doctor, "we can do a peripheral test and attempt to find any close genetic relatives, but that takes more time and gets more difficult to—"

"No," repeated Mae. "We're done. Let's go."

She practically had to drag Justin out to keep him from going back. "Mae, there's a mistake," he reiterated, once they were standing outside the hospital's entrance.

"Is there?" she asked. "Justin, think. Whoever did that to me had the ability to change their fucking appearance! Do you think they'd then carelessly let themselves be ID'd by a hospital's genetic test? There's no telling how far their god's power extends." Another thought occurred to her, one that nearly made her sway on her feet. "That, or there was no match to a human in the registry . . . because he wasn't human."

"They do a standard DNA map," Justin said, calming down again. "If he wasn't human, it would show."

Mae wasn't sure of that, and it only increased that sickening feeling of violation. But Justin did agree with her that whatever god had done this had apparently helped cover up his or her servant's tracks. Justin nobly vowed that they'd still get answers, no matter the cost, but Mae felt disillusioned and doubtful.

"I don't know," she said. "I just want a shower . . . but I . . . I don't want to go back there. Back to my place."

"Well," said Justin, "that I *can* fix."

They took the purple line out to his place, where they found the rest of his household asleep, save for one of the rotating praetorians keeping watch that night. It was someone from a different cohort, a friend of Dag's, and his presence reminded Mae of her own weakness tonight. She sent the guy home, telling him she was taking over the watch and that he should go find a Saturday night party. He accepted gladly.

Justin gave her full access to the bathroom adjacent to his bedroom, which had a shower nearly twice the size of hers. She stayed in it for almost forty minutes, scalding and scrubbing every part of her body. When she emerged into the steaming bathroom, she found he'd quietly slipped in his best shot at a change of clothes for her: a plain men's cotton T-shirt and drawstring pajama pants. She changed into them and stepped out to the bedroom, finding him reading in bed in a similar ensemble. Rather than feel amused at the match, however, she felt a small pang in her heart. He usually preferred sleeping in boxers, and she had a feeling the extra clothing was a kindness on his part, in case seeing him half-naked freaked her out. The sad part was, it wasn't a bad assumption. She knew this was the real Justin, but the memories of the earlier phantom were hard to shake.

But she surprised both of them by slipping into bed with him. She'd been afraid of his touch all night, but now, she suddenly found herself in need of warm, human contact. She rested her head on his chest, and after several moments, he tentatively placed an arm over her back. They lay like that for a long time until Justin finally broke the silence.

"I'm sorry."

"For what?"

He swallowed. "This is my fault. If I'd been brave enough earlier, if I hadn't turned you away, if I'd stayed with you instead of going to the party—"

"Justin," she interrupted, "this is in no way your fault. Not in the least."

"I've all but served this god in every way already. I should've taken the plunge and made it official. I could've at least finally gotten something I wanted that way." Justin smoothed the hair away from her face, again using great caution and gentleness. "That's what it was, you know. The cost for being able to have you is becoming his priest and swearing my loyalty to him. But I don't care anymore. It's worth it for you, Mae."

His words struck her profoundly, especially after her earlier revelation and disgust with Freya. "No," Mae said at last. "I don't think it is. You were right about everything—about how they mess up your life and how there's always a cost. You were right to keep away and not bind yourself. I understand that now and am glad you did what you did—or rather, didn't do. Keeping yourself free of them is what matters."

"Right now," said Justin, his voice cracking slightly, "*you* are the only thing that matters, Mae." He lightly brushed his lips over her brow, and she tipped her head back, offering him her lips. He hesitated and then accepted, kissing her with the precision and emotion that had so been missing with his doppelgänger. He kept the kiss short and sweet, which was exactly right. It was all Mae was capable of right now, and he knew that because he knew her.

And as he fell asleep next to her, Mae knew that even if she had been ready to jump into sex again, she wouldn't have. She couldn't, not knowing what she knew. The last piece of his erratic history fell into place, and she truly was glad he hadn't given in and bound himself to that god's service. She had had living proof tonight of the chaos and destruction the gods brought to mortal lives. The goddess who'd promised her such glory hadn't been able to protect her. There was no higher calling to be found in divine service. Mae knew that now and worried that Justin possibly didn't. She didn't want him enslaved to a god because of her. It was better for both of them to be free of divine entanglements, but that was easier said than done.

After an hour mulling it over, however, Mae thought she might have a solution. She slipped out of his arms, careful not to wake him, and left the bed. He'd left the lights on for her, and she stood at his doorway for a few seconds, memorizing his features in this rare moment of peace before turning the lights off. Once outside his house, she used her ego to call the praetorian scheduled to take over in the morning. She convinced him to come over now and then made a second call for a hired car. It was too late and too complicated to navigate public transportation to where she needed to go. As she waited, she tipped her head back and gazed at the sky, as lightning played across dark clouds ushering in a summer storm. The backup praetorian showed up just as her ride did, and she let him inside before heading out.

By the time the car dropped her off at her destination far outside of town, a full downpour was in effect, soaking her when she sprinted from the car to the massive house she sought. A surprised butler let her in, leaving her to drip in the foyer. At first, he refused to do anything for her, but after identifying herself and insisting on the urgency of the matter, she finally convinced him to wake the man they both answered to.

General Gan came down the spiral staircase ten minutes later, wearing a quilted velvet robe and the exhausted expression of one woken unexpectedly in the middle of the night. His eyebrows rose as he looked her over in her soaked state, and she didn't need his next words to know he was thinking of the night she'd walked through the rain to enlist with him.

"Praetorian," he said congenially. "You really need to start carrying an umbrella."

Mae straightened and greeted him with a rigid salute, mustering as much dignity now in soaked men's pajamas as she had in a pink party dress. "General," she returned, "I apologize for the late hour . . . but I've come to ask a favor."

CHAPTER 27

# WORD CHOICE

Justin wasn't surprised to find Mae gone when he woke. She didn't need to sleep, and he wasn't self-centered enough to believe that his own charms were great enough to keep her lying by his side all night.

*She's in the kitchen,* said Horatio. It was the first he'd spoken in a while. The ravens had been unusually quiet throughout the recent drama, which Justin found surprising. Yesterday's events had certainly seemed like they'd provide plenty of material for commentary.

But concern for the ravens vanished from his mind as he left his room and strode down the hallway. He was still deeply upset about what had happened to Mae, still felt deeply guilty for what he saw as his role in it. At the same time, he felt resigned and filled with hope. The barriers between him and her were finally down, and no matter what it took, he was resolved to track down the bastard who'd—

Justin, and his thoughts, came to a screeching halt as he rounded the corner and entered the kitchen. Mae was there, as Horatio had said . . .

. . . and she was in uniform.

In all their time together, Justin had never seen her in praetorian black, and he was startled by the effect. Once, when she'd been temporarily banned from wearing the uniform, she'd spoken of the power it imparted. He could see it now. There was something about the uniform, with its mandarin collar and form-fitting black material, that seemed to wrap her in shadows, excellently conveying the fear and regality the praetorians strove for. She stood up straight against the wall, arms crossed, with her hair wound neatly back into a French braid. There was a fierceness to her beauty, and he decided then that she couldn't have looked any more like a Valkyrie had she been in armor and a winged helmet.

"I feel underdressed," he joked, heading for the coffeepot.

Tessa, sitting with Cynthia and Quentin at the table, blurted out, "Mae's leaving."

For a moment, he assumed she meant leaving for the day, but an assessment of the family's somber faces set an alarm off in him that something wasn't right. "Going where?" he asked, forcefully keeping his tone light.

"I've been reassigned," Mae said. She was doing that thing she excelled at, so perfectly keeping any emotions and other contextual clues from her face and voice . . . which was, in itself, a warning sign. "I'm leaving within the hour. I can't give the exact location, but I'll be joining some other praetorians in the borderlands."

"After what just happened in Arcadia? There's no way they'd move you to active duty! Go talk to Gan. He'll fix this."

"I *did* talk to Gan," she explained. "That's how this happened."

He stared at her in disbelief, as the truth of what she wasn't explicitly saying hit him. "Then go talk to him again!" Justin exclaimed. "Make it un-happen. This is a fool's errand, born out of a hasty emotional response and not letting yourself properly recover!" He regretted his words as soon as he said them, seeing lines of anger begin to crack her calm façade.

"Fool's errand?" she asked. "This is an important job our country's asking me to do! *Ordering* me to do. It's not something I can just go ask to get out of!"

"You should've never asked to get into it!"

"Enough!" Cynthia abruptly stood up and shot meaningful looks at a wide-eyed Tessa and Quentin. "If you're going to continue this conversation, then do it outside."

"Gladly," snapped Justin. He gestured grandly toward the front door. "After you."

Mae stalked off without a word, and he turned to follow. As he did, Cynthia grabbed his hand.

"Justin," she hissed, "if she really is being deployed somewhere, then there's a chance you might never see her again. Think very, very carefully about what you're about to say."

He jerked his hand back. "I know what I'm doing."

Outside, he found Mae waiting in the front yard and the world misty from last night's rain. "What the hell happened?" he demanded. "Where did this come from?"

"Where do you think?" she returned, struggling to get her calm back. "I realized last night that I can't stay here, so I went to Gan directly to override Internal Security's request to keep me assigned to you."

"You think running away is going to change what happened? That toting a big gun around will somehow heal you?"

"I'm not 'running away.' I told you, I'm serving my country as they need me to."

"They don't need you specifically," he countered. "They need bodies to send to the border to fight for them. Get Gan to pull you back."

Mae's face filled with outrage. "Why do you think it's that easy to pull me back? And why do you think so little of my job? Didn't you pay attention to the way they live in Arcadia? All these privileges and freedoms you enjoy here are because of the military— because of those bodies out there fighting for you!"

"I think very highly of your job," he insisted. "It's the rest of your motives I question."

"I can't stay attached to IS forever. That's not the kind of work I enlisted for."

His attempts at self-control unraveled. "You enlisted to be killed? If you really wanted to get out of IS, then why aren't you being assigned with the rest of your cohort here in Vancouver? Why aren't you doing monument duty with Val and Dag? Why are you going out to active combat in the borderlands? Why do you *want* to go out to active combat in the borderlands?"

He wasn't the only one who snapped. "To get away from you!" she cried. "To get away from all of this—but especially you."

Justin stood there frozen, as immobile as if he'd been knocked to the ground. "I see," he said finally. "So, I guess that part about how nothing was going to change how you feel about me was kind of an exaggeration."

"No," she said, fists clenched at her sides. "It wasn't. And neither was the part about you being infuriating. But there's no way I'm going to let you do something stupid because of me. I won't let you commit yourself to that god—"

"That's my choice," he interrupted.

"Not if it's contingent on being involved with me," she shot back. "I won't let you do that. I'm pulling myself out of the equation. I'm freeing you from that god, and I'm freeing myself too. I'm done with this game, with godly affairs. I shouldn't have dabbled in the first place. If I hadn't, then last night—" Mae faltered and then found her resolve again. "Well, last night might not have happened."

She looked so strong and beautiful out there, his Valkyrie in black, but the waver in her voice pierced his heart and told him the truth. Last night's attack had had colossal effects. But how could it not have? Sexual assault wasn't something one easily recovered from under so-called normal circumstances. Muddling it all up with this supernatural war . . . well, it was no wonder she wanted to leave.

"Do you think it won't follow you to the battlefield?" he asked. "Do you think the gods won't follow you there?"

"I'm sure they have better places to be," she said.

"They followed us to Arcadia, Mae! They're everywhere. They'll go wherever you go. There's no escaping what we're involved in."

Her face hardened. "I can't believe that. I refuse to give in to them, and you should too. If you know what's good for you, you'll resign from your job and . . . I don't know. Go back to teaching. Go back to anything, anything that's not this."

"This is what I've got, and I'm willing to face it on my terms, to serve him if it means having you in my life to—"

"No," she exclaimed. He'd started to reach for her, and she pulled back. "No. Don't. Please. Not for me."

"Mae, I know what happened last night was hard—"

Her eyes widened. "Hard? *Hard?* You have no idea! No idea what it feels like to live with the aftermath of something like that—"

"Then let me help you!" he cried. "Let *me* help you heal from this, not some dangerous decision that you made on a moment's notice. Together we'll find out who did it—"

"Justin." Her voice was low again, though the emotion written on her face showed how upset she still was. "This decision is made. I'm leaving."

*Look at her,* said Magnus, speaking up at last. *You say you know her so well, so look at her. She's telling the truth. She's leaving, and you can't stop her. Your best bet at salvaging this situation is telling her you understand and that you support her and that you'll be here waiting for her. If you have any sense left at all, you might even tell her you love her.*

*If she had any sense,* Justin informed the raven, *she wouldn't leave me.*

And with those words, Justin had enough self-awareness to realize that was a huge part of the problem here: She was leaving him. Oh, there was no question he was upset about the rest. He was upset that she was leaving without properly letting herself recover, that she was leaving without any further effort at finding her assailant. And, yes, he was absolutely upset at her willingly walking into another life-threatening situation. Waiting for her while she'd escaped Arcadia had been hard enough. He couldn't imagine another stretch of endless days not knowing if she was dead or alive.

But it was that personal sting, that after a life of women who'd meant nothing, he'd found one who meant everything—and she was leaving him. It didn't matter that she wasn't leaving him personally, exactly. This was the result of forces beyond their control, but the result was the same. She would be gone, and he would be back to being surrounded by others who made him feel alone. It hurt in a way he wasn't prepared for, and he knew lashing out at her was a selfish reaction to that pain. He knew also that Magnus and even Cynthia were right: If Mae was leaving, then he needed to part on the best terms possible.

But that pain and the inability to deal with it were too great, and he found himself blurting out, "This is a mistake. You're making a mistake."

Her face started to fall, but she quickly recovered and took on her ice princess persona. Too late, it occurred to him that maybe she was hurting too and that she was waiting for him to say all those things he should've said.

"I'm sorry you feel that way," she said coldly. "Here. I've got a couple of parting gifts for you." She produced the amber knife from her boot and handed it to him. "Give this to Geraki."

Justin took it more out of surprise than anything else. "Geraki?"

"He's the one who sent it. Tell him I have no use for gods who can't deliver what they promise." From her belt, she produced a golden neck torc with dragons on the ends. "This is for you . . . or whatever you want to do with it."

Justin took it in confusion. "What is it?"

"The eagle staff," she said. "Or it was. When I touched it, it transformed into this."

He was still upset, still heartbroken . . . but those words made his jaw drop. "When did you get this?"

"I made a side trip after rescuing the girls. The staff changed shape when I touched it." She spoke casually, like robbing a country's religious leader really had been just a side trip.

"You . . . you touched it?" Justin remembered the ravens saying only the strongest of faith could do so. "And . . . it changed shape?"

"That's what I just said," she snapped. A hired car slowed down in front of the house, and Mae turned toward it. "That's for me. I'll see you around."

"Mae . . ."

Justin wanted to say more but found the words stuck on his tongue. Lucian had claimed Justin could talk anyone into anything, but he was at a loss here. He didn't even know if he had the power to get her to forgive him. She disappeared into the car, and he stood there forlornly on the wet lawn, knife in one hand and torc in the other, watching until she vanished down the street. When he could finally muster the initiative to move, it was to look down and examine the knife.

*Before you ask,* said Horatio, *no, we didn't know Geraki gave it to her.*

*Is it Freya's?* asked Justin, thinking back to the revelation that had begun to emerge in Arcadia.

Magnus answered. *Most likely. Geraki wouldn't have given it if it wasn't at the behest of an ally, and the fact that the torc didn't change shape when you touched it means it's sacred to the same pantheon you serve. Freya best fits the description of the goddess Mae has been working with.*

Was *working with,* corrected Justin. *She's done with that now.*

Mae's words replayed through his mind as he slowly walked back into the house: *I refuse to give in to them, and you should too. If you know what's good for you, you'll resign from your job and . . . I don't know. Go back to teaching. Go back to anything, anything that's not this.*

Maybe she was right. A surge of anger welled up in him, anger for the hurt he was feeling and at the role the gods were playing in messing up their lives. But *was* it entirely the gods' fault? Really, when Justin looked at it, things had fallen apart because of one person, the man who'd worn his face to take advantage of Mae. Thinking about that, it became easier and easier for Justin to channel the pain of Mae's loss into hatred and a desire for revenge against the mysterious assailant.

He ignored Cynthia's attempts at conversation and stormed to his room, slamming the door behind him. *Okay,* he told the ravens. *Get your master on the line. If he wants me, he can have me. Mae's pulled herself out as a bargaining chip, but it doesn't matter. I want* to find whoever did this to her. If Odin can help me do that, I'll swear my undying loyalty to him and act as his priest.

The declaration lifted a huge weight from Justin's shoulders, and he expected any number of reactions from the ravens. Joy. Disbelief. Smugness. What he got instead was almost a sense of . . . discomfort.

*Ah. That won't be necessary,* said Magnus.

*We've, um, been meaning to talk to you about this, but things got so hectic last night that we figured we should wait to tell you,* added Horatio.

*Tell me what?*

There were a few moments of silence, as though each raven were daring the other to speak.

*It's done,* said Magnus at last. *You are bound to our god. You fulfilled the terms of the deal already.*

*What are you on?* demanded Justin. *I did no such thing! I know that deal word for word. I have to take Mae to my bed and claim her before swearing to Odin, and in case you haven't been paying attention to my screwed-up love life, I've gone out of my way to avoid that scenario.*

*And yet,* said Magnus, *you enacted it last night.*

Justin was indignant. *Really? Did you see something I missed?*

*Only if you missed the part where Mae was in your bed, and you poured your heart out to her, claiming her as the only one in the world for you,* explained Horatio.

*That wasn't sex!* protested Justin.

*Who said it had to be?* asked Horatio. *You've been going on about how "claiming" someone in bed is such an archaic way to talk about sex, but really,* you're *the only one who's been hung up on that term There are many ways to interpret those words, and you fulfilled them in a very literal way last night by claiming her as your soul mate.*

*I know I never used that term,* Justin said, still unable to believe what was happening.

*No, but that's not what matters. What matters is that you can claim someone in a number of ways, and really, declaring that they're the one, that there's no other for you . . . well,* said Horatio, *call me a romantic, but that's a much more profound way to claim someone as your own than through sex.*

*Odin never clarified the meaning!* Justin protested. *It's a trick. A trick based on one word.*

*You never asked for clarification,* said Magnus. *And you played a similar trick on Odin when you dodged the deal the first time you made love to her.*

*First and apparently only time now,* said Justin. *This isn't fair.*

*Fair?* Magnus had no sympathy. *He let you out of the deal fairly because you had the power of words on your side. This time, the words and meanings played you. Accept it gracefully. This is binding. You've fallen into the deal and must now serve him.*

*I get nothing! I don't get Mae. I don't get the power to find her assailant.*

*Nothing?* asked Horatio. *You get to serve our god! You have the honor of being his first and greatest priest in your country, and this torc Mae gave to you in anger will only aid your quest. I'd hardly say that's nothing. And Odin may still help you find her attacker.*

*But no guarantees,* said Justin morosely. He set the torc on his bedside table and felt nothing as he stared at it. A great and powerful artifact meant nothing without Mae.

*No,* agreed Magnus. *The time for bargains is over. You've led him a merry chase with your ability to wheel and deal and make the most of twisting words. It's a trait our god possesses in abundance and is what he admires in you. Now is the time to serve and fulfill your promise.*

The truth of the ravens' words settled in Justin's gut, just as it had when another word trap had landed him into learning Odin's runes and lore. Justin had recognized his inability to bargain then, just as he'd known he had the power to escape after sleeping with

Mae before. But now? Now he could feel Odin's chains settling upon him. Intentional or not, Justin had claimed Mae with his heart, if not his body, and now he was bound to the god as a result.

*I wish you wouldn't look at it as a punishment,* fretted Horatio, sounding legitimately upset. *Odin truly is a great and generous god who cares about you. You will find joy and meaning in his service.*

*The only thing that brought me joy and meaning is on her way to a war zone,* Justin retorted. *But rest easy, I'll stand by my word and serve. In fact, I think I'll start celebrating my new vocation right now.*

Eight hours later, he was still drinking.

It hadn't been continuous, of course. That was largely because he'd passed out in the afternoon after overdoing it in the first part of the day. As evening rolled around, he found himself in a far better position to pace himself, simply keeping a steady supply of drinks coming that maintained his buzzed state but protected him from being sick or (hopefully) getting alcohol poisoning. He'd made his way to an upscale bar downtown, finding the atmosphere much more welcoming than the one at home, after Cynthia had thrown him out for "turning to self-destructive behavior as a way to feel better about screwing up."

She was wrong, though, because none of this self-destructive behavior was making him feel better about anything.

"Is this seat taken?"

The voice surprised him, largely because Justin had gone out of his way to avoid any female interaction so far this evening. It wasn't that he couldn't—after all, there were no commitments between Mae and him—but the thought of wooing female company for the night seemed like a lot of work for not very much reward. Besides, he knew enough to know when he was charming drunk and when he was just drunk drunk. He was definitely the latter, and while that still didn't rule out his chances with women, it didn't necessarily help them either.

When he saw the speaker, though, he silently cursed his inebriated state. Daphne Lang sat down beside him.

"I have nothing to say to you," he said, wondering how quickly he could sober up. No time was ever a good time to be cornered by a reporter, but when you weren't in full possession of your wits, it was probably the worst time. "And you should be ashamed of yourself for following me."

"Relax," she said, waving over the bartender. "This is a happy coincidence. I live around the corner and come here all the time. I admit, however, I was planning on speaking to you at some point."

"The usual?" asked the bartender, earning a smile and a nod from her.

"It doesn't matter," said Justin when they were alone again. "Word has it Tessa's done with you, and I'm not selling her out to give you some crap human-interest story. Go scavenge somewhere else."

"Do you really think I'd do that to her?" asked Daphne sweetly.

"I don't believe it's a coincidence that you just happened to be looking for an intern and then conveniently stumbled on my sweet provincial girl." His hands itched to pick up his glass once more, but he again remembered he needed restraint around her.

"It's not a coincidence," Daphne agreed. The bartender brought her drink, and she swiped her ego to pay. "I was already doing a lot of research when that intern posting so happily popped up. But she wasn't the one I was looking into."

Justin's bourbon-addled brain made the connection a few beats later than he would have under normal circumstances. "Shit."

Daphne looked momentarily surprised at his reaction. "Oh," she said after a moment. "You think I'm talking about you?"

"Well, you're talking to me," he said, hoping he didn't show how relieved he felt. Admittedly, he was puzzled as to who she meant. "Figured maybe you were after a story about how a servitor expenses high bar bills."

She smiled and paused to drink. Whatever expensive lipstick she used left no mark behind on her glass. "Maybe that can be my backup story. Don't take it personally, but I'm afraid my real target was your friend the illustrious senator, Lucian Darling."

Justin's wariness immediately returned, but he laughed to cover it up. "You and every other reporter looking for dirt on him. Hang on . . . are you telling me you got involved with Tessa because of her very tenuous connection to him through me?"

Daphne shrugged. "I had to take what I could get. Someone like me doesn't get in to see someone like him that easily."

"So you used a poor provincial girl trying to better herself. And now that she's not working out, you're hoping I'll get you that interview." It was a comfort to know Lucian was the target, not Justin, but anyone who'd track down a one-off connection like Tessa and then try to use her still wasn't to be trusted.

"Well, that would be nice, but no, I've actually come to you with a business arrangement . . . one that might further both of our careers." Daphne leaned closer, and Justin recognized the look of someone who thought she was going in for the kill. "What would you say if I told you that your friend and his political party were knee-deep in a secret religion—a religion that sees him as the divinely chosen leader for this country?"

Justin made sure his smile didn't so much as twitch. "I'd say show me the proof."

Daphne looked mildly chagrined. "I'm afraid that's a little easier said than done . . . although I have it on *very* good authority from a source even you might believe. And one you might actually help me to convince to come forward with her story. Though we'd still need more to go on."

"Considering you just used 'might' twice in the same breath, I'd say *you* still need more to go on. There's no 'we' here."

"But there could be." She crossed her legs, making her skirt ride up. "Imagine what this could do for you. Your whole job is about uncovering dangerous religious undercurrents in our society . . . imagine finding them in the highest tiers of our government! You don't think there'd be career rewards waiting for you if you revealed that our future consul thinks gods are returning to the world and that he's a divinely chosen person called an elect?"

Justin's heart nearly stopped. "A what?"

Daphne turned smug, thinking she'd one-upped him. "See, there's all kinds of things I know. That's just one of them I'm kindly giving you the courtesy of learning about before I go public with this."

*She knows about the elect,* Justin thought frantically. *Or thinks she does. How could she know that?*

*Obviously from whatever sketchy sources she's drawn from,* said Horatio.

*She doesn't have proof,* Justin told the ravens. *Otherwise, she would've already exposed Lucian.*

*Do you care?* Horatio asked.

Justin considered for a moment. *Yes. Putting aside the fact that he is my friend, exposing him exposes the elect and the game being played. SCI doesn't want that. I don't want that. The time isn't right.*

*Will it ever be?* asked Magnus curiously.

*I don't know,* Justin admitted. *But her selling out Lucian could ruin what we're trying to do for Odin. Worse, it could eventually come back and expose me.*

Justin took a deep breath and tried to summon that outgoing, magnetic persona that could allegedly talk people into anything. He leaned toward her. "You're lying. You're not going public without me. You don't have the evidence to or else you already would have. What you probably have is enough evidence to make yourself look even more ridiculous than you already do on North Prime and sink your career even further. Sure, sensational stuff like this always leaks out—especially during election season—and it'll make a little noise. But do you seriously, *seriously* believe anyone's going to see you as a legitimate journalist with a story about gods returning to the world? That Lucian Darling is part of it? Fuck. Have you seen his ratings lately after Arcadia? That man is untouchable. There are people who want to take him down, sure, so you'll get your five minutes . . . and be rolled in with all the other bottom-feeders trying to dredge up equally scandalous stories about mistresses and discretionary spending." Justin settled back in his chair and even felt brazen enough to sip the bourbon. "Unless you've got a signed statement from him confessing to all of these theories of yours, you've got nothing."

Daphne stayed silent and wasn't nearly as good at hiding her feelings as he was. Indecision played over her as she considered her next move. He'd gotten to her, that much was obvious. She might balk at all his slights against her network, but she knew she and North Prime didn't hold much credibility. What he'd told her hadn't been entirely fabricated either. A story like this would gather attention on the edges of the news but make little progress beyond that without more proof. People like him had been doing their jobs too long for the population to easily get on board with the idea that supernatural powers were returning to the RUNA. That being said, he still needed to find out what she actually knew. It was time for his master play, now that he'd made her doubt herself.

"I'll tell you what, Daphne," said Justin, deciding to act before she could. "I like you. I want to help you."

"How very kind," she said dryly.

"I'm going to give you the chance to tell me whatever crackpot theories you've got and see if they could really hold water with SCI backing or not. I'm guessing not. But if you play your cards right, maybe I'll hook you up with a story that actually *will* make your career."

"Really?" she asked. "You just happen to have a career-making story in your pocket that you've been waiting to share with some lucky journalist?"

"Actually, my guess is that Lucian's people are lining up lucky journalists from one of those news channels you so covet. But I'll make it so that you're the one his people line up to break the story."

Her eyes lit up at Lucian's name, but she was still wary, suspecting some trap. "What kind of story?"

Justin glanced around. "I can't tell you here, but let's put it this way. We weren't just uncovering Arcadian spies intent on bringing down our way of life. There's another story that's going to emerge from our trip, one that's going to—if possible—make Lucian even more goddamn popular and is full of the human interest and melodrama you love. Only, unlike your usual drivel, this is the kind of stuff that'll make top headlines and launch you into the career you've been wanting."

"And you have the power to give me this story?" She was intrigued but still not sold.

"Maybe. We'll see how things go."

Justin didn't actually know for sure that he could get Daphne exclusive rights to the story about the Gemman girls liberated from Arcadia, but he had a feeling that once he talked to Lucian, the senator would be more than willing to use an independent journalist if it meant keeping other more clandestine affairs off in the shadows.

"Then sit back, and I'll tell you what I know." She was playing it cool, but her body language told him she really wasn't confident in her story's credibility. That was a good sign for him and for Lucian.

"No," he said. No way was he going to invite a discussion of the elect in public. "Not here." Triumphant, he stood up and gestured toward the door. "Let's go talk about this somewhere quieter. You said you lived nearby?"

She stayed seated and looked him over from head to toe. "You know, I've looked into you too. You don't think I know what it means when you invite yourself over to a woman's place?"

"I think it means I'm offering you the opportunity of a lifetime," he said cheerfully. "And a great chance for your career too. As for how it all unfolds . . . well, that'll depend on you, Miss Lang. Are you coming or not?"

She hesitated a moment more before standing up and joining him. "I'm coming."

# CHAPTER 28

# GODS WHO DELIVER

Mae had thought she'd feel at home, once she was back in uniform and on assignment with other praetorians. Three months ago, she would have. She would've fallen in line with this group—a mix from the Maize and Azure cohorts—without a second thought, easily slipping into the roles given to them by their country. But even though she sat comfortably and made casual conversation with them in the base's mess hall, she couldn't shake the sense of "otherness" she now felt in their presence. She'd seen too many things and done too many things, things that went beyond even these supersoldiers' experience. She envied them in some ways. They still had the simplicity of their belief that even in their dangerous assignments, their superiors still had everything under control and were making the correct decisions. Mae no longer believed that.

*This is Justin's fault*, she thought.

Immediately, she knew that was unfair. In the past, she'd been able to lay any number of grievances at his feet, but not this new worldview of hers. Having her eyes opened to the insidious forces lurking beneath the surface of her reality was the result of many factors, some of which had been in play since the time of her birth. Like her, he was simply trying to stay afloat in these treacherous waters. He'd even tried to help her, but she'd thrown it back in his face.

No . . . now she was being unfair to herself. She'd tried to help *him*. She'd come here to remove that temptation from him so that he could be free of divine entrapment. If she was gone, that god—whoever he was—could no longer use her as a bargaining chip against Justin. She wished Justin could've seen it that way, but the pain in his face had suggested otherwise. It hadn't helped matters that what she'd seen in him had pretty much been a mirror of what she felt inside of her.

*He'll get over me,* she thought. *He has to. He's probably picking up someone in a bar as I sit here. He's never been serious about anyone. Why should I think I'm special? Hopefully he'll stick to women who have no involvement in the supernatural.*

But as she thought about that last night, the things he'd said to her, the protective way he'd held her in his sleep . . . Mae knew she was being unfair to him yet again. That made her own healing process that much harder. Far easier to believe that he didn't care. And Mae had no interest in seeking quick distraction in the arms of another—though she'd had plénty of opportunities. A few guys had already made flirty passes at her, in that way praetorians had between active assignments. She'd rebuffed them all politely—despite her internal fear and revulsion—wanting to keep things friendly with her new comrades but unable to imagine herself opening her body up to anyone any time soon. That encounter with the phantom Justin had scarred her deeply, leaving a taint on her that she couldn't shake.

"Going to Mexico soon, praetorian?"

An officer in the gray and maroon of the regular military sat down beside her at the table, which she hadn't even realized had emptied of the other praetorians she'd eaten with. She'd been so lost in her own thoughts that time had slipped by. She'd been unable to muster much of an appetite, and an uncharacteristic headache was now coming on. She rubbed the back of her head, waiting for the implant to dull the pain.

"Yes, sir." The man's uniform identified him as a major, putting them roughly at the same rank. Technically, he might have been a little higher, but the praetorians were in a separate branch of the military and different ranking system. "I came in with a group from Vancouver. We're waiting for another bunch to join us before heading out. Are you going?"

"You might see me there." He crossed his long legs and leaned back in the chair, striking a remarkably casual pose for someone of his rank, even if he was off duty. "It's certainly my kind of place. All sorts of chaos there. Did they give you any of the background? That it's an area Arcadian settlers took to a while ago? Unfortunately for them, it's full of oil, which even the RUNA can't entirely shake its need for. So off to war we go. It'll be grand, I'm sure."

Mae looked him over uneasily. If they weren't actually in the middle of a base, she might've thought he was someone dressing up in costume. "Are you sure? We were told this is an area that wants to become a Gemman protectorate but keeps getting threatened by Arcadians and other local dissidents."

He gave her an exaggerated wink with hazel eyes that bordered on yellow. "Yes, of course they told you that. That's a much nicer story. Much easier to believe you're fighting against nasty insurgents instead of innocent settlers who just want to be left alone— even if they *are* Arcadians. I understand you're not the biggest fan of their culture, and I can't really blame you there. A place like that has no appreciation for a girl of your talents."

"Who are you?" she asked, a chill running through her. Her involvement in Arcadia was highly classified. No one of his rank should have known. Gan had granted her this reassignment, but now she wondered if he'd done it with strings. Had he sent someone to spy on her?

"A great fan of yours, Praetorian Koskinen," he said softly. He leaned toward her and smiled. Aside from the unusual eyes, the rest of his features were uniformly plebeian, and his long face, though handsome, had an odd quality that made it difficult for her to pin an age on him. Thirties, maybe? "A very, very great fan. I thought you and I might never meet, but fate unfolds in a way that even the gods can't predict."

Mae stiffened. "You're one of the elect."

"Please," he scoffed. "Don't belittle me. I've said nothing but nice things to you."

"Then what are you?" she demanded, her thoughts spinning, despite the pain of her growing headache. Was this some entity like Justin's ravens?

"Someone in need of a Valkyrie, and I'd like you to be mine. I've always wanted one, and as I said, I'm a great fan of yours. I think the two of us would get on beautifully, and I'd do much better things for you than Freya ever could."

Mae almost laughed. "You talk like you're a—" She stopped, unable to say the word.

He tilted his head. "Yes? Do go on."

"That's impossible," she said, looking around uneasily. Surely, *surely* if she were having a conversation with a god in the middle of a cafeteria, someone else would notice. But all those gathered, soldiers and civilians alike, moved about their business as though Mae and her companion didn't exist.

"I'm surprised 'impossible' is even in your vocabulary anymore," he told her in a chastising tone. "I am what I am and have gone to the trouble of a personal appearance to ask you into my service."

"If you know so much," she said, "then you know I'm done with gods and their affairs."

"I know you're done with gods who can't protect their own. With gods who don't deliver." He trailed his fingertips along the edge of her jawline, and she found herself powerless to pull away. "No Valkyrie of mine would be forced to leave her lover behind. No Valkyrie of mine would be victimized by another of the elect."

Mae's breath caught. "Do you know who it was?" Then the question that had really been eating at her: "Do you know what it was? Was it one of the elect?"

"Most certainly. I mean, I wasn't there, and no, I don't know who, but the powers involved are consistent with an elect. What else do you think it would be?"

"I don't know," she admitted. "I was just afraid it . . . it wasn't human."

He chuckled and dropped his hand. "Well, don't be afraid then. Not of that, at least. Lesser entities—spirits, demons—have no romantic interest in your kind. And gods . . . well, let's just say we wouldn't have to go to nearly that much effort. No, my dear, your mysterious assailant was all too human, and I will help you find him."

"I told you, I'm done with gods."

"And I told you, you're done with loser gods, gods who leave their servants vulnerable and play mind games. Here I am, talking to you directly, making my offer in plain terms. No games. No cryptic visions."

"But there are strings," she said. "There are always strings. You offer to help me, but what do you want in return? What does it mean to be your Valkyrie? A lifetime of slavery?"

He shook his head. "Hardly. That would be boring for both of us. I don't have the attention span for a lifetime of commitment. I simply need someone to conduct my earthly matters for the time being, and all I'd ask is that you do so until the time I help you find your attacker."

"Oh, is that all? Somehow I doubt you'd be motivated enough to help me very much if finding that guy frees me."

"Not true," he declared. "I'm very interested to know who did that—or more specifically, who he serves. I need to know the players and what they're capable of if I'm going to win this game. And as I said, I'm a different kind of god. I'm straightforward. If I deliver for you, I can't help but think you'll want to keep working with me—of your own free will. And frankly, that would delight me more than any clever bargain locking you into a lifetime of servitude."

Mae studied him for several moments and could hardly believe what she was considering. "No. *No.* I left to get away from all that supernatural business!"

He tapped the center of her collarbone. "Then why are you

wearing that charm under your uniform? You might want to get away from it all, but deep inside, you know it's still going to go wherever you go. And you're right. So join the winning side. Help me regain my place, and help me find your attacker so that we can make him suffer excruciatingly for what he did to you. And don't pretend, Maj Erja, that you aren't interested in revenge. I've seen the joy you take in punishing those who harm others. You shed no tears for that salon owner in Arcadia. I can only imagine the need you have to get back at someone who specifically targeted *you*."

It infuriated Mae because he was right. She had told Justin she wanted to let everything go, even the pursuit of her assailant . . . but deep inside, a spark burned within her that yearned to find the phantom and make him pay for the pain he'd caused her. And now, this stranger—this *god*—claimed he could be the means to do it, if she aligned herself with him. Justin had told her once that there was always a cost for working with the gods . . . and yet, he'd also told her she couldn't escape them. If that was true, was it time she stopped letting nebulous gods control her? Was it time to place her energies into someone who really could make things happen?

"Something wrong with your hands, praetorian?"

Mae had fallen into silence as her thoughts swirled, rubbing her hands together unconsciously. There'd been a pins-and-needles sensation in them, like they were falling asleep, and she dropped them in her lap as she looked the stranger squarely in his yellow eyes. "You say you're a 'different kind of god.' You say you're straightforward. If that's true, then tell me your name . . . or do I have to earn it like all the other elect do?"

"Not all," he said. "I meant what I said and stand by it. My name is Loki." He held out his hand. "It's very nice to meet you, Mae Koskinen."

# THE GHOST

I t was starting to rain when the man wearing Rufus Callaway's face arrived in Seattle. He thought he'd left the rain behind in Vancouver, but apparently it had followed him here. Or maybe it had started here. He didn't know, and he didn't care. His mood was too good, and as he began walking from the train station, he knew it would take more than a little wet hair and clothing to bring him down.

Admittedly, things hadn't gone quite as he'd planned. It had been his own vanity, he supposed. He'd been careless in what he'd said around Mae, not realizing the depth of her relationship with March. If not for that slip, he might well still have been in her bed this morning, languishing in the afterglow of a night full of planned pleasures. And he *had* had a lot planned. That brief, frantic fumbling had barely sated his needs, though it had certainly proved his dominance. His blood still burned at the memory of the way she'd felt underneath him, completely under his control. She might have balked against submission in her daily life, but he'd seen the way she'd looked at him after he'd taken her, those luminous eyes filled with adoration. Love, even.

But could he say she'd really been looking at him? After all, it wasn't *his* name she'd called out in the heat of passion.

That reality brought a dark edge to his thoughts, but by the time he reached his destination, completely soaked, he'd recovered. It didn't matter who Mae thought she did or didn't love now. When all was revealed, she would come around and recognize who she truly belonged with.

"You're late."

The woman standing at the door crossed her arms over her chest and fixed him with a glare. Her name was Donna, and he knew she was intently jealous that Tezcatlipoca hadn't given her the blessing of skin-changing.

"I had things to do," he said mildly, resting his hand on the scanner she held. With people always coming and going in different guises, only the chip reader could speak the truth of who was who—for most of them, at least. The chip he bore now wasn't the one he'd been given as a child, but that one wouldn't let him move with such freedom in the RUNA, seeing as he was supposed to be dead.

"Things to do for two weeks?" Donna asked pointedly.

"I received authorization," he reminded her. "If it was good enough for our master, then it's good enough for you."

It had been a happy coincidence, that bodyguard job popping up when he was between assignments. Of course, it would've been happier still if it had happened at a time when Mae was in the country. Nonetheless, he'd been able to learn what he needed about her in his brief stint as Rufus Callaway, and the ending of his personal mission . . . well, that had been an unexpected bonus. He truly had been coming to say good-bye when he'd overheard the last bit of her conversation with March and discovered the opportunity her unrequited desire provided.

"How long are you going to wear that face?" Donna asked.

"As long as I choose," the man snapped back, stepping past her. The young woman really was getting uppity these days. He'd have to say something to the others. It was one thing to be ambitious and covet future powers, but Donna also needed to learn patience and respect—just as they all had.

Nonetheless, as soon as he stepped past her into the building's foyer, he headed straight for the mirror that hung just inside. It was blackened and warped after having been consecrated in fire and smoke to Tezcatlipoca, but that marred surface held a power that was of immense use to the god's servants in their transformations. Distorted, Rufus Callaway's image looked back at the man one last time as he summoned a prayer and drew on the power of skin-changing.

An uncomfortable crawling feeling ran over his body, one he never got used to. Then came the sensation of being stretched and kneaded, as though he were dough in some capable baker's hands. But once it was all over, the stocky, weathered face was gone from the mirror. A younger face looked back, one with black hair and eyes born of pure Mediterranean heritage, paired with a taller and more muscled body. His clothes hadn't changed and now stretched oddly with the new fit, but he didn't care.

Being a ghost was certainly useful, and he'd long since learned to enjoy the privileges and movement his anonymity allowed him. But no matter how many times he performed the shape-shifting magic, no matter how many different guises he went through, it was always a relief to return to his own face and body. It felt comfortable . . . like coming home. That, and Porfirio Aldaya just liked the way he looked.

He gave his reflection in the darkened mirror one last, fond glance before he turned around and headed deeper inside the building, off to see what his master had planned for him next.

# AGE OF X GLOSSARY

**Age of Decline**—Official name for the fifty years between Mephistopheles and the discovery of its vaccine.

**Age of Renewal**—Official name for the period of time including the discovery of the Mephistopheles vaccine and the rapid rebuilding of Gemman society that followed.

**Age of X**—Tongue-in-cheek political term for the RUNA's next age, its "unknown age" to come.

**annexed lands**—New territory recently conquered by the RUNA, usually undergoing unrest as they adopt Gemman policies and uniform culture.

**Arcadia**—Post-Decline country formed by part of the southern and southeastern former United States. It possesses moderate technology and a religion-centric government. There's a lot of tension between it and the RUNA, because of both current border disputes and Arcadia's feeling as though it was abandoned after the Decline.

**Cain**—A hereditary set of genetic defects created by Mephistopheles. It often involves damaged skin and hair, poor fertility, and asthma. It usually only shows up in those without mixed genetic backgrounds, like the patricians or those from the provinces.

**castal**—Slang term for someone who belongs to a caste.

**caste**—Slang term for a patrician group, those who clung to their ethnic heritage and were exempted from genetic mandates after the Decline because of financial contributions to the early government. Patricians identify with a particular culture (Irish, Egyptian, etc.) and select for features associated with that culture. Many patricians still live off that early wealth and have established aristocratic mini-societies in special regions allocated to them, called land grants.

**Church of Humanity**—A "secular religion." The only religion officially endorsed by the government. Although it has temples and priests, there is no deity involved. It is meant to encourage decent, humanitarian ways of living, which are synced up with the RUNA's laws and philosophies.

**consul**—One of two leaders of the RUNA's senate. Consuls are elected from currently serving senators by other senators. A very powerful position.

**contraceptive implants**—Mandatory devices all Gemman women get upon reaching puberty and are required to keep until they're twenty years old.

**Decline**—Name for the years immediately following Mephistopheles's devastation.

**Division of Sect and Cult Investigation**—The subdepartment within Internal Security that the servitors work out of. Sometimes called SCI.

**Eastern Alliance**—Called EA. The RUNA's sister country, formed from parts of the former China and Russia. It shares many genetic policies with the RUNA, including population swapping, but has a looser stance on religion. It nearly matches the RUNA in technology and order. Its primary language is Mandarin, followed secondarily by Russian.

**ego**—A small handheld device that functions much like a smartphone and then some. It controls communications and is synced to the media stream, as well as the owner's identity chip. Unless a special code is entered, egos will not function if they're too far away from the owner's chip.

**Gemman**—The term for citizens of the RUNA. It comes from the country's motto, *Gemma Mundi*, which means "Jewel of the World."

**genetic mandates**—A set of laws that the RUNA employed to create a diverse population resistant to Mephistopheles. Part of this included forcibly swapping parts of the population with others from the EA. For much of the RUNA's history, citizens were not allowed to reproduce with those who wouldn't produce genetically diverse offspring. Later, the law was amended to allow freedom of reproduction but with monetary penalties for those who didn't reproduce optimally. In the current-day RUNA, there are no penalties, but those who still seek genetically diverse mates receive stipends from the government.

**genetic resistance**—A numeric score, from one to ten, that identifies how resistant an individual is to Mephistopheles and Cain. The more mixed the person's background is, the higher his or her score tends to be. Most plebeians now have a score of eight to ten. Patricians average around five.

**identity chip**—A small chip in the left hand of each Gemman citizen. The chip is keyed to the person's DNA and an entry in the National Registry, which contains all of his or her basic information. Chip readers scattered throughout the country regulate who enters secure areas and also help locate criminals and outsiders.

**Internal Security**—The ministry within the RUNA that handles threats and security inside the country's borders. The Division of Sect and Cult Investigation, which the servitors work out of, is part of it.

**land grants**—Exclusive regions of the country where patrician groups are allowed to live. Most are in the middle of the country. Although the land grants have a caste's cultural slant, Gemman loyalty is still strongly enforced, and borders are kept open to Gemman officials.

**media stream**—The RUNA's equivalent of the Internet, containing access to the country's data, resources, and entertainment channels (there is no separate television service). The media stream is a public resource, accessible to all citizens through egos and home screens. Called "the stream" for short.

**Mephistopheles**—Common name for a virus released into the world in the early twenty-first century that killed half of the earth's population. Those of diverse genetic backgrounds have greater resistance to it and the hereditary disease it created, Cain. A vaccine created in the RUNA fifty years after the virus's release has mostly wiped it out.

**National Registry**—Database of all Gemman citizens, containing their basic and genetic information. Identity chips are synced to the registry, and all citizens must have names of Greek or Latin origin.

**patrician**—Term for a member of a group that clung to its ethnic heritage and was exempted from genetic mandates after the Decline because of financial contributions to the early government. Patricians identify with a particular culture (Irish, Egyptian, etc.) and select for features associated with that culture. Many patricians still live off that early wealth and have established aristocratic mini-societies on special regions allocated to them, called land grants. "Castal" is a slang term for a patrician used by the rest of the country.

**plebeian**—Term for most of the RUNA's population, those created from its genetic mixing programs. Most plebeians have dark hair and eyes, with tanned skin.

**population limits**—Gemman women are only allowed to have two children before being sterilized unless they can provide proof that they have the financial and social stability to care for more. Those qualifying may have up to four children total, with no exceptions.

**praetorian**—One of the RUNA's "supersoldiers." Praetorians have a small positive-feedback implant in their arms that will increase whatever neurotransmitter is being actively produced in the body. For example, when adrenaline is naturally produced in a fight, the implant will increase the body's production, enhancing the praetorian's abilities. Praetorians are divided into color-coded cohorts and serve for eighteen years, from age twenty-two to forty.

**primary schooling**—Elementary school in the RUNA.

**provinces**—The generic term used by Gemmans for any part of the world that isn't the RUNA or EA. It isn't an official designation in those regions, which range from semiorganized countries to completely unregulated areas.

**Republic of United North America**—Commonly called the RUNA. A country formed from Canada and parts of the former United States during the Decline. It is the most stable and technologically advanced country in the world. Its primary language is English, followed secondarily by Spanish. Its official colors are maroon and dark purple.

**RUNA**—Pronounced "roo-na." See *Republic of United North America.*

**secondary schooling**—Collective term for middle school and high school in the RUNA.

**servitor**—From the Latin *"servitor veritatis,"* or "servant of the truth." Employees of Internal Security who license and investigate religious groups. Although much of the job is paperwork and interviews, some situations become volatile, and servitors have quick access to law enforcement and military resources. Their subdepartment is the Division of Sect and Cult Investigation.

**stream**—See *media stream.*

**tertiary schooling**—A required two-year degree that all Gemman citizens must complete, starting when they're eighteen. Unlike primary and secondary education, which is fairly standardized, tertiary education is more specialized to the person's interests, in the hopes of encouraging continuation with a four-year college degree. Those starting college by a certain age have their education paid for by the government.

# He just wanted a decent book to read ...

Not too much to ask, is it? It was in 1935 when Allen Lane, Managing
Director of Bodley Head Publishers, stood on a platform at Exeter railway
station looking for something good to read on his journey back to London.
His choice was limited to popular magazines and poor-quality paperbacks –
the same choice faced every day by the vast majority of readers, few of
whom could afford hardbacks. Lane's disappointment and subsequent anger
at the range of books generally available led him to found a company – and
change the world.

*'We believed in the existence in this country of a vast reading public for intelligent
books at a low price, and staked everything on it'*
**Sir Allen Lane, 1902–1970, founder of Penguin Books**

The quality paperback had arrived – and not just in bookshops. Lane was
adamant that his Penguins should appear in chain stores and tobacconists,
and should cost no more than a packet of cigarettes.

Reading habits (and cigarette prices) have changed since 1935, but
Penguin still believes in publishing the best books for everybody to
enjoy. We still believe that good design costs no more than bad design,
and we still believe that quality books published passionately and responsibly
make the world a better place.

So wherever you see the little bird – whether it's on a piece of
prize-winning literary fiction or a celebrity autobiography, political tour
de force or historical masterpiece, a serial-killer thriller, reference book,
world classic or a piece of pure escapism – you can bet that it represents
the very best that the genre has to offer.

## Whatever you like to read – trust Penguin.

read more
www.penguin.co.uk